THE PACT

by

Jonas Saul

PUBLISHED BY:

Imagine Press Inc.

Ebook ISBN: 978-1-927404-46-1

Paperback ISBN: 978-1-998047-40-6

Hardcover ISBN: 978-1-998047-41-3

The Pact

The Decoy (Thirty-Three)
The Disappearance (Thirty-Four)
The Whole Truth (Thirty-Five)
Alex (Thirty-Six)
Parkman (Thirty-Seven)
Darwin (Thirty-Eight)
Aaron (Thirty-Nine)
Remains To Be Seen (Forty)

The Jake Wood Novels

The Immortal Gene (Book One)
The Immortal Target (Book Two)

Standalone Novels

'Til Death Do Us Part
The Drowning
The Woman in the Woods
The Threat
The Specter
The Mafia Trilogy
A Murder in Time
Frequency of the Dead

Co-Authored Novels

Collision Course (Written with Gary Ponzo)
There Will Be Blood (Written with Rania Stone)
The Soulless (Written with Rania Stone)

Short Story Collections

Twisted Fate (Tales of Horror)

Twists of Fate (Tales of Hope)

Chapter 1

Vivian Roberts, now dead for twenty-five years, left behind a prophetic note in a time capsule that was meant for her sister's eyes only. While alive, Vivian had talked to the dead. Now dead herself, she talked with the living.

The sun was setting over the ocean as the taxi pulled up out front of Sarah Roberts's parents' home in Santa Rosa. She paid the driver and exited the vehicle. Her shoulders hitched as she let out a sigh. What could Vivian have known twenty-five years ago? Did it have anything to do with Sarah's boyfriend, Aaron? How could she have known about him so long ago?

After the taxi pulled away from the curb, Sarah looked both ways, hoping Aaron hadn't listened to her and come anyway. But the street was quiet, empty. Sarah's father had contacted her in Las Vegas and urged her to return home as soon as possible to deal with the time capsule Vivian had left behind.

According to Caleb, Sarah's father, she was to trust no one. He instructed her to not speak of the time capsule and to exclude Aaron.

"It's the only way," Caleb had said.

He'd said it was too dangerous to repeat Vivian's message over the phone. But why? Who would be listening? And if someone was, how would Vivian have known that twenty-five years ago?

There were too many unanswered questions.

Sarah missed Aaron. After her recent ordeal with the Enzo Cartel and then an insane woman attempting to bomb the Sands Convention Center in Las Vegas, she needed Aaron with her. She wanted his comfort, his touch, but most of all, she needed his presence. But he was gone, back to Toronto.

Was Vivian's letter that important?

Sarah had spent years saving the lives of others to the detriment of herself, her life, and those around her. Wounds could be counted by the scars littering her body. What couldn't be counted were the emotional wounds. Like when she told Aaron to fly home to Toronto so she could travel to Santa Rosa on her own without much of a reason. He was supposed to just trust her. He said he understood. As much as he tried to hide it, the underlying tone in his voice said otherwise.

The two of them had recently made a pact based on trust. One that would take them to a new level in their relationship as they moved forward. To break that pact with Aaron not one hour after making it left an empty feeling in her gut. For the two days since she felt a loss so profound, it was as if Aaron had slipped away from her emotionally.

So when Sarah's father told her to tell no one and come to Santa Rosa alone—especially leave Aaron out of it—she had broken her pact with her boyfriend.

They'd said goodbye at the Las Vegas airport as he boarded a flight to Toronto. Two hours after that, she boarded a flight that took her to Los Angeles and then to Santa Rosa.

Alone on the sidewalk in front of her parents' house, Sarah summoned the courage to knock on their door, the will to read the letter left by her long-dead sister, and the determination to fulfill whatever the letter asked of her.

As life passed her by, it was growing more and more apparent that it was Aaron who kept her grounded, kept her moving forward. His love for her, and her love for him, grew stronger daily, year by year.

A thought occurred to her as she hesitated on the sidewalk. The internal conflict, the nagging feeling that she hurt Aaron unintentionally by coming to Santa Rosa, led to a realization. She wanted to be with him, not just now, but forever. She wanted marriage, kids, and family life. Sarah wanted a family. Aaron would be a wonderful husband and an even better father.

Contrary to that thought, she wondered if she should bring children into this cruel world. As a mother, would she still live so recklessly? Or would her days with Vivian be over?

None of those questions would be answered if she continued treating Aaron like she did. A man could only take so much.

Steeling herself, Sarah started for the house, determined to read the note, deal with whatever Vivian had left for her, then get back to Aaron. Evidently, there was a lot more to discuss about their future than a pact regarding their commitment to trust.

The front door opened before Sarah knocked. Her father, eyes glossy and rimmed red, stepped outside the house and engulfed Sarah in his arms.

"So glad you're here," he said, his voice muffled by their hug.

"Me too, Dad."

He pulled away, grabbed her shoulders, and drew back to look at her.

"You've lost weight," he said. "You eating enough?"

"Yes, I'm eating enough. Can we go inside?"

"Of course." Caleb stepped aside and gestured for her to enter before him.

Not much had changed since she'd been here last. Furniture was the same. The TV was on mute in the corner, actors engaging in a soundless spat. A large table along the left side of the living room was new. A puzzle lay half done, the remaining pieces scattered around the uncompleted area.

A fleeting glimpse of her past sent a chill up her back. Homework, her bedroom a mess, depression. The TV was always on mute as her father read the newspaper in his chair. The blackouts and strange notes appearing. She recalled pulling her hair out, piece by piece. Trichotillomania, they'd called it. Once she met Mary Bennett, that all changed. Sarah had accurately interpreted the note from her dead sister after a blackout and saved Mary from a planned kidnapping.

The beginnings of Sarah's purpose-driven life.

Coming home left her feeling slightly awkward. Out there, she was the adult, the one who had it all together. The snarky girl could hear her dead sister in her head. Back home, she was just little Sarah again with her mom and dad.

"Mom's doing a puzzle?" Sarah asked.

"We're doing it together," Caleb said. "It's something new we decided to spend time on." He shrugged as he moved past her. "I was thinking of building model airplanes again as I used to when I was a teenager. It was your mother's idea that we would try puzzles first." He walked over to it. "Come here. Take a look. It's a picture of the Vatican."

Sarah kicked off her shoes and walked over to stand beside her father. The puzzle's box cover showed a gorgeous photo of the Vatican with all its many columns. The half-done image on the table in front of her didn't bear a likeness quite yet.

"A ways to go," Sarah said, feeling the elephant in the room.

They both knew why she was there, but her father hadn't mentioned the time capsule yet.

"It's two thousand pieces." He laughed. "Yeah, a ways to go. Come on, I'll get you a glass of wine. You must be tired."

"No drink. Unless you're making tea." Sarah followed him toward the kitchen. "Where's Mom?"

"She's coming. When we saw the taxi pull up, I went for the door. Your mom headed into the spare room to prepare the time capsule stuff for you." He looked back over his shoulder as they stepped into the kitchen. "You sure I can't fix you a drink? You may need it when you see what Vivian left for you."

Sarah narrowed her eyes and frowned. "I'm fine. Earl Grey or a glass of water. Then show me what Vivian left for me, and then I'll sleep. I went through Hell in Vegas."

"We heard a little about it. Parkman called."

She looked up, surprised. "Is he here? In Santa Rosa?"

Sarah sat at the kitchen table while her father flicked the switch on the kettle. On the corner of the table, a small red light blinked on the phone. Someone in the house was using the phone.

"I'm sure he'll be around soon. Your mom said she'd call him." Caleb grabbed a mug from the cupboard.

Seconds later, the red light on the phone blinked out. Then footsteps came up the hall. She turned as her mother entered the kitchen behind her.

"Mom," Sarah said as she bounded from the table and hugged her. When she pulled away, she looked for Vivian's message. "Your hands are empty. Dad said you were getting something for me."

"It's all ready." She exchanged a glance with her husband. The kettle grew louder in the small kitchen. "I left it in the other room." Amelia faced Sarah. "I think it best you examine everything on your own. Vivian's message was for you and you alone. We went too far when we read the first page." Her mother shrugged. "Vivian was my daughter, too."

"I don't blame you." She made a tsk sound. "How dangerous could information be anyway?"

Amelia moved to the kitchen table. Sarah studied her mother's face a moment longer. Worry lines creased her brow.

"I'll go look at it now," Sarah said.

Amelia bobbed her head once toward the hallway. "Go. We'll have your tea ready when you come out. We'll talk then."

Down the corridor to the guest bedroom, she hesitated at the open door. The bed was made. On the white blanket, laid out in a neat and orderly fashion, was the time capsule with its bounty spread out beside it. Vivian had chosen a small tube for the twenty-five-year-old message, similar to the kind that held posters when they were shipped in the mail.

Before reading a single word on the handwritten pages, Sarah examined the tube. A note on the outside asked the reader to keep it sealed until spring 2016. It didn't say for Sarah's eyes only. There were no warnings to restrict anyone from reading the contents held inside.

She set the tube down and picked up the first page.

This message is for my sister Sarah ...

A shudder ran through Sarah's shoulders as she read her sister's handwriting from twenty-five years ago. In the cursive, Sarah saw familiar lines and arches that resembled her own writing. A tear leaped to her eyes when she thought of the sister she never got to have in life. A sister to play with, do makeup, and talk about boys. That era was over, but she would've loved to have had Vivian be a part of that.

Sarah read on, noting important details and memorizing a few facts. Near the middle of the second page, she understood why Aaron couldn't be made aware of what was on these pages.

It foretold his death.

A chill rippled through her as she got to the meat of the message.

Vivian wrote of her intention to enter into a pact with Sarah. Without the pact, their communication was cut off. A pact could break that silence between them forever. Vivian added a side note questioning the kind of communication they had. In her prophecy, it wasn't revealed how the sisters would be talking in the future.

"Don't we have a pact already?" Sarah asked the empty room. "Why do I have to do this?" Her voice cracked. "It doesn't make sense, Vivian."

Could this note still be accurate? Could the living Vivian have predicted events about to happen that well over two decades ago?

Did any of it matter? Why couldn't Vivian just talk to Sarah like she always did? Guide her through the next few weeks.

"Vivian?" Sarah asked. "Just tell me where to go, what to do. You're in my head now. We're closer than we've ever been." She waited for an answer, but none came. "Vivian? Are you there?"

Sarah reread the part about their communication being severed, at least until they made a pact.

"Vivian? You're gone?"

After no response, Sarah continued reading. Vivian wrote that she had been offered a glimpse of Sarah's blueprint. In it, she saw Sarah die.

She had also seen a man in Sarah's life—Aaron—whose blueprint ended roughly the same time. Vivian's theory of life was called the blueprint. A person's life, struggles, their family, their triumphs were all written down by that person before their incarnation on Earth. Coming to Earth is a form of evolving our souls, making us better entities as we live out our blueprint. The pain, the struggle we encounter along the way, is there to teach us humility, love, and understanding. Life was sometimes overwhelming, but we never wrote more than we could handle.

Vivian had caught a glimpse of the man's name in Sarah's life, calling him Aarow instead of Aaron. The only way for the sisters' relationship to remain the way it was for years to come was for Sarah to enter into a pact with Vivian. But her sister wasn't given the information twenty-five years ago on how to do that. And she wasn't able to tell Sarah now as communication had ceased.

Sarah closed her eyes and focused. She waited for Vivian to enter her consciousness, but she didn't. Sarah spent time with Aaron in Vegas for the last two days. Vivian had been strangely quiet, but Sarah hadn't paid particular attention to it as she wanted to spend quality time with Aaron without distractions.

Vivian, Sarah whispered in her mind. *Talk to me.*

Silence. Nothing.

"Damn it."

Sarah read the end of the note. Aarow—Aaron—was to be murdered in Toronto. Sarah had just let him fly home the other day. Had she stuck to the pact they had made in the hotel not two days before, he would be in Santa Rosa with her, reading the letter, and not in Toronto about to be killed.

"No, no, no," she moaned, rolling her head back and forth. "It's not possible." She dropped the pages on the bed beside her and looked up at the ceiling. "After all I've done, Vivian, you can't do this to me." Sarah dropped her head and let the tears flow. She missed Aaron and felt remorse for how she'd treated him in Vegas. She felt bad for being here alone after agreeing to be absolutely honest with him.

She could have kept him from going to Toronto.

She snatched up the letter and tried memorizing the parts that might make sense later.

Vivian said the clock would murder Aarow.

How will time kill him?

She also said to protect a Dane. If the blonde Danish dies, that could spell trouble. Don't let the blonde Danish die.

Blonde Danish?

Sarah surmised Vivian was talking about a blonde woman from Denmark. At least, she hoped that was right.

There was a man named Oaf and his son. But Vivian admitted in her note that she might be missing a letter in Oaf's name.

Who would call their son Oaf?

PAIN was behind everything, Vivian wrote. Stop PAIN, and everyone lives, but boys will continue to be violated.

Goosebumps rose on Sarah's forearms. This part of Vivian's letter didn't make sense. Boys violated? Stop PAIN? Was there a religious meaning in there somewhere? Sarah recalled her time in Los Angeles, where someone was killing Catholic priests for their transgressions. Is that what this was about?

In the end, it was the foretelling of Sarah's death that shook her. She had spent several years receiving messages from Vivian. Nothing shocked her. It had been a long time since Vivian was so vague. Recently, with her sister directly in her head, everything was quite clear. The letter in Sarah's hand reminded her of the automatic writing stage of their messages. Clues, hints, and riddles.

Sarah would never forget the clue for a kidnapping that read North Face. The girl about to be kidnapped walked right by Sarah, wearing a North Face jacket, and Sarah missed it, thinking she was supposed to *face north* to see the kidnapping. It almost cost Sarah her life.

As now, the message was spotty and riddled. And it portended the end of Sarah's life.

Sarah flipped the pages over. Another paragraph was written on the back of the second page. Vivian said that she had taken it upon herself to write letters. Those letters were in the time capsule. They were not to be opened by anyone except by the person whose name was on the envelope, and whoever found the time capsule had the responsibility to properly stamp and mail the letters. Sarah's life depended on those letters getting through.

She looked inside the capsule tube. The letters were gone.

The last paragraph said goodbye.

Tomorrow, Mom and I are going shopping, Vivian wrote. *At the mall, I've been instructed to run away from her. If I lose Mom, I can stop a man named Stew Art. I think his first name is Almond, but I'm not sure.*

Armond Stuart.

The man who kidnapped, raped, and murdered Vivian all those years ago after she went missing. Armond was dead after Sarah hunted him through the United States and Europe.

Sarah read on,

I'm told this is the only way for you to stay alive. If you do, I'm also informed that we, as sisters, will create a bond that'll stop dozens, if not hundreds, of bad people from hurting others in the future. It's the right thing to do, Sarah. So I have decided to lose Mom tomorrow at the mall. Please tell her it was not her fault. This is my choice. I want to do this. I don't want to live in a world with so much pain. Especially if I can do something about that. I'm left with no choice. So I say goodbye, Sarah, and I pray you live through this so we can do what my teacher from the other side has done for me.

Enter into a pact with me, Sarah. If not, we will be reunited very shortly, and our work on your plane will be over.

I love you, little Sarah.

The tears came in torrents. Why did the world's problems fall to this family? Why did she have to lose her sister?

Breathing through her open mouth, her nose clogged as her sinuses filled from crying, Sarah reread the end of the note, the page gripped tight in her palm.

The guest room door opened. Her father stepped in, a glass of whiskey in his hand.

"Sarah," he said softly. "I turned off the kettle. Thought you'd want something stronger." He handed her the whiskey. She took it and drank it back in one gulp, then gasped. "Don't worry about a thing. Your mother and I have thought about this for the last few days, and we have a plan. We think it'll work."

Sarah rolled the handwritten pages and stuffed them into the tube, missing the tip of the opening a couple of times because her eyes were too blurry with tears.

In a daze, she allowed herself to be led to the kitchen. Parkman sat on the living room couch with his arms crossed.

"Oh, Parkman," Sarah managed.

Parkman pushed off the couch and got to his feet. "Sarah," he whispered. They embraced. "We'll find a way through this."

"I'm afraid it won't be that easy this time." She pulled away from him, grabbed the bottle from the coffee table, and refilled her whiskey glass. "Vivian has abandoned me up here." She tapped the side of her head, then drank the whiskey back. "Vivian's gone, Parkman."

"Not yet, she isn't. I got one of the letters she wrote."
Her father put a hand on her shoulder. "So did we."

Chapter 2

THE CLOCK BIT THE end of the granola bar off and chewed methodically. The interior of the building across the street was dark. Not a single light glowed from within. It had remained dark since the last person locked up for the night and left the premises.

The Clock studied the buildings on either side. They were also closed for the evening. This would be an easy job. In and out. Just after midnight. No one was around except for the odd car passing by. But what could the occupants of a passing vehicle see once The Clock was inside the building?

Alarms wouldn't be a problem. There was nothing of considerable value inside. If they had an alarm system at all, it would be a cheap ADT system—without cell backup. People who ran businesses like the one across the street rarely paid the exorbitant extra cost for cell backup.

He swallowed, then bit into the granola bar again. The

time to go was precisely 12:15 a.m. That was the time he had structured this operation for. Inside the building for ten minutes. Then out. Back in his hotel by one in the morning. Five hours later, he would rise at six and do his hour routine of yoga and stretching, then shower, have breakfast, and return to this location. He would watch the curtain fall over the business across the street. His client would want a picture of the damage, the carnage. His client would want the deaths caught on camera.

His approach to killing was why people hired him. As a hunter would shoot a giraffe and pose with it, The Clock killed humans and posed with them. Well, sort of. He didn't do selfies. After forty-two confirmed kills as a private military contractor, it wouldn't help his business any if he posed with the evidence.

After the final bite of the granola bar, he neatly folded the wrapper, tucked it into his pocket, and checked the time.

12:14 a.m.

He adjusted the straps on the backpack, checked that his Glock 42 was safely stowed, and studied the street around him. In the alleyway he hid in, two large garbage bins sat to his left. The shadows cast by the buildings meant he could stand beside the garbage bin completely undetected by anyone who happened to glance his way. As long as he remained immobile, someone could walk right by his position and see nothing. Learning the art of not moving, remaining rigidly in one spot, was something trained into him for years as a sniper in Afghanistan.

As a Danish-born sniper with the U.S. Navy Seals, he logged more kills—170—than most of the men they sent over. The record of 173 goes to an unnamed British Royal

Marine, but he knew he'd beaten that record by a dozen kills or more. Definitely more than Navy Seal Chris Kyle, and they made a movie about him.

Whether he was too lethal or the fact that he was from a small island in Denmark, the American government kept his records sealed. No one knew his true identity, and no one ever would. He had gotten too good, too precise, too detailed. When they told him to retire, he protested. To murder, to hunt humans, was all he ever wanted to do, and to have it sanctioned by the government, *and* get paid for it, was glorious.

The officer who informed him he had no choice but to go home died slowly. No one told him what to do unless they were paying him.

He disappeared that day. Changed his face and his passport—one of many—and now worked his way toward creating a legend that would rival The Jackal, a notorious assassin from the seventies and eighties.

He achieved several nicknames during his time in Afghanistan. The Clock was the one he liked the most and the one he still used today.

Time was important to him. Kills happened on time. People lived and died on The Clock. Everything was about time and managing it properly. The time a bullet took from the barrel to the forehead. The time allotted for a job to be completed could affect the job.

Time was also a killer as it worked its machinations on everyone daily. Even he, The Clock, would be a victim to time. Eventually, his hands wouldn't hold the Glock just so, his eyes wouldn't acquire the target accurately, and time would kill him.

But not yet. All in good time.

He smiled to himself as he glanced at his watch.

It was time.

With one last look up and down the street, The Clock pushed off the wall and started toward the building. At the front, he headed south until he got to the end of the building and moved into the shadows to his left. At the rear of the building, he quickly located the back door.

Beside the door, he located the phone box attached to the building's brick wall. From his Kydex sheath, he withdrew his partially serrated SOG Seal Team knife with its seven-inch blade and severed the phone lines. Unless the building's alarm system had a cell backup, no one would be notified of the break-in until morning.

Even if the authorities were called, he would be in and out before anyone got there.

He retrieved the lock pick set from his inner breast pocket and counted the ten seconds he allowed himself to gain access to the building. On the eighth second, the lock clicked open.

The Clock pushed the door inward, then stepped inside the back room of the karate dojo. The smell of the gym hit him first. Rubber mats combined with sweat. They worked hard here. The back room was tidy and clean.

From the backpack slung over his shoulder, he removed the small bombs with timers attached. As he placed them throughout the dojo, setting the timers as he went for ten in the morning, he watched the clock and listened for the sound of approaching vehicles. They often had the registered key holder attend the premises if he tripped an alarm. The police didn't always respond. A key holder he could handle and still get the job done.

Ten devices were secured in vents and in two separate places behind floorboards in less than six minutes. Without a bomb-sniffing dog, there was no way they would get every device in time. He left two small bombs in his backpack for later use.

He checked his watch.

Time to go.

The Clock slipped out the back door, closed it, and made sure it locked securely. The only evidence of his presence was the cut telephone wires. By the time the karate teachers arrived in the morning and the first class began at 9:30 a.m. as advertised on the front door, no one would pay much attention to a phone line being down. He was pretty sure Bell Canada or Rogers or whomever Aaron Stevens had servicing the phone at his Shotokan dojo wouldn't have a worker out first thing in the morning. And even if they did, that employee would die in the blast along with the first class of karate students.

The same class that Aaron taught every morning.

The Clock had watched Aaron from the airport when he landed from Las Vegas. The Clock had called the dojo and inquired about tomorrow's class. A man identified as Daniel told him that Aaron was teaching that class as he was back in town.

The Clock had brought lunch with him as he followed Aaron from the airport to the dojo, where Aaron did an hour of administrative duties, collected his mail, and went home.

If anything, The Clock was precise. The client wanted the dojo destroyed. The client wanted Aaron killed along with it. The Clock didn't ask why. It was none of his business. All he concerned himself with was doing the job right.

And getting paid.

A hundred thousand dollars for a simple pyro job. Not bad. The only downside was he would miss seeing the agony on the face of his kill. The aftermath, the charred bodies, sure, but he'd miss the life fleeing the eyes of his victims.

That was the hard part. In a way, he was being cheated because the client wanted an explosion.

He walked around the outside of the building, crossed the quiet street, and walked the two blocks to his rental car.

This was the client's deal, the client's money. He was paying for an explosion, so he got an explosion.

But The Clock was already looking forward to the next job.

It was with the same client. He was to pick up a girl at a hotel in Mississauga. Hold her for a week in the hotel, then kill her. Those were the simple instructions from the client. An easy job. Again, no details on why. Just a paycheck. And this client was efficient. It seemed like he knew everything. The client knew the flight number and time Aaron Stevens would arrive at the Toronto Airport. He knew where Aaron would be, when Aaron would be at the dojo, and where the girl was supposed to be.

The Clock liked working with this particular client. His tasks and their particulars were transmitted to his iPhone, and money was transferred to his off-shore account.

He checked his watch.

On-time to the minute.

He started the rental and drove away, wondering how much sleep he would get before waking for his morning exercises. There was simply too much excitement in his life at the moment.

Chapter 3

ANTON OLAFSON STEPPED OUT of the Folketing, the Danish Parliament, and bounded down the stairs, raising his briefcase above his head to shield himself from the rain. He trotted through the Christiansborg parking lot, reserved for members of parliament until he located his car near the back. Meandering through the tightly-knit cars from the Traffic Committee to the Radical Center Party, around and through several puddles, Olafson was happy to get to his car without a soaker. He fumbled with the keys, opened the door, and dropped into the front seat, shaking rainwater off his briefcase before setting it on the passenger seat.

After slamming the door, he took a moment to catch his breath. The rain pounded the roof, staccato music only the criminally insane or lunatic campers could enjoy. He hated the rain and everything to do with it. Anton often asked his parents why he was given the unfortunate luck of being born in Denmark and not Greece, where the sun shone over ten months of the year.

After starting the Tesla, he connected his phone to the car's Bluetooth and tried calling his daughter's cell number again. Her voicemail picked up.

Clara hadn't answered her phone all day. She had joined him on the ride to Copenhagen yesterday, then headed to a friend's place on the other side of the city, claiming she'd be back this afternoon. The last contact he'd had with her was yesterday around lunch. She'd texted him a picture of a heart and a smile. Her way of telling her father she loved him.

With her not answering her phone and not leaving the friend's address, Anton had no way of contacting her. He'd left meetings early today to head home. Maybe she was already at home waiting for him. At twenty-three years of age, Clara still lived with him, and he wouldn't have it any other way. He made plenty of money. It was hard for today's youth to find good-paying jobs where they could live independently.

The new position at work had kept Anton busy over the past six months, but he planned to take a long summer break. He would make up for lost time with Clara then. Maybe they'd go to Fanø Island and rent a summer cottage on one of Fanø's huge beaches.

The car's interior warmed enough that his fingers weren't so cold. He probed his ears to get at the rain water and winced when he bumped the new black helix ear piercing. He had wanted an industrial piercing but felt his Danish government colleagues would frown on it. A rook or an anti-helix piercing was on the list, but Anton ended up with one helix on his right ear for now. As an openly gay man in government, he monitored how far he pushed his superiors. One never knows when one will reach their limits.

Marriage hadn't worked. As much as he tried to be a heterosexual man, he and Clara's mother didn't see eye to eye. They divorced when Clara was eighteen, and a year later, Clara's mother died of an aneurysm. It was so sudden neither he nor Clara had made it to her bedside before she died.

Maybe that was why Clara still lived at home. She wanted to remain close to her one remaining parent.

He tried Clara's cell number and got the recording again. He flicked on the wipers and started out of the parking lot, the pit in his stomach getting heavier.

Where was she? Why wasn't she answering? This was so unlike her. He avoided thoughts of what could have happened to her. They were baseless and a waste of time. Refusing to consider the worst, he still worried for her. What if something did happen to her? What if she was hurt somewhere or worse? He was her sole protector. He should have done a better job.

"Where are you, Clara?" he asked aloud in the empty car. He glanced at his expression in the mirror and looked away to watch the road.

To access the E20, he changed lanes and headed out of the city. Work brought him to Copenhagen only a few times a month now, being able to do many of his parliamentary duties from his home in Skanderborg and his office in Aarhus, the second largest city in Denmark. It was at least a three-hour drive from Copenhagen back to his house in Skanderborg. Three long hours to ponder where his daughter was.

Yesterday morning when they drove to Copenhagen together, Clara had told him she would take the train back to Skanderborg later that night. The trains in Denmark were efficient. Clara could take the train from Copenhagen and get off right in Skanderborg, then walk ten minutes to their house on the water by Skanderborg Lake. She was probably there now, reading in the living room by the fire as this spring hadn't brought warm weather. Only rain. Too much rain.

Anton rationalized that his daughter's cell phone battery must've died. Nothing else made sense. Denmark was a safe country. They were rated the happiest people on Earth. What could go wrong?

Yet the pit in his stomach grew with each passing kilometer. No one had answered the house phone either. He was sure Clara wasn't home and that something had happened to her. The nagging feeling scared him to the marrow.

Denmark did have its fair share of problems. Anton Olafson was the director of the Danish National Cyber Crime Center (NC3), which had only been established a couple of years ago. Olafson was transferred to NC3 six months ago to liaison with the Danish Data Protection Agency (DDPA) on a case where a hacker had published stolen information from the Danish Land Registry. Because the hacker made the stolen information public, the cybercrime unit deemed it a breach of intellectual property, which broke Danish data protection laws.

As a director, Olafson's job was to keep the agencies working together to reach a common ground—which they did. The hacker, known only as PAIN, was shut down. His IP addresses—several hundred of them from around the world

—had been monitored closely to ascertain they were his, and then their access was severed from Danish government servers.

After receiving praise from several government parties at different levels, Anton Olafson was appointed to a full-time position with the NC3 as director and placed in the Aarhus office, which worked wonderfully for him as he lived in Skanderborg, a twenty-minute drive from Aarhus.

He tightened his grip on the steering wheel, rotating his hands around the thin wheel.

Where could she be?

He shook his head and rubbed his face. Everything would be okay. Clara was an adult. What could possibly happen?

Olafson turned the heat down and slowed the wipers as the rain had abated south of the city. He would stop for coffee soon, then relax on the road for the last couple of hours. He would hear from Clara tonight, or he would call the authorities. What would any other parent do?

In the middle of a lane change, his cell phone rang. He punched the answer button on the dash.

"Hello? Clara?"

Someone breathed into the phone.

"Hello?" Anton checked his mirrors and signaled to pull off the highway. He slowed the Tesla quickly on the shoulder and turned on his four-way flashers.

"Hello?" he asked again, an anxious, sinking feeling coming over him as he thought this call would be about his daughter. "Who is this?"

"Who I am is not important." The voice was metallic. It reminded Anton of the kind in horror movies where the stranger covers the mouthpiece with an electronic device to mask his voice. "Why I'm calling is of the utmost importance, though."

Anton checked his rearview mirror out of habit. He glanced to the right and stared at a row of large white turbines in a field, their arms spinning slowly with the wind, waiting for the caller to tell him why he called.

"Clara Olafson, your daughter, is with me."

Anton jerked at the mention of his daughter's name. He blinked, stared at nothing for a brief moment, then gasped.

"Where is she?" he asked.

"With me. Fulfill one condition, and then she's yours again."

"What?" he nearly screeched. "What are you talking about?"

"Come on, Mr. Olafson. How many children have you hurt?"

The question startled him. No one knew what he did in his private time. No one knew who he really was. There was no way Clara knew anything. The guy was fishing. That's all this was, a fishing expedition.

"Who are you?" Anton asked again.

Ignoring the question, the caller said, "Your private dealer in using young flesh, Damien, is finished. Call his number. Email him. Or read about it in tomorrow's paper. You have to find someone else who deals in your specific kind of fantasies."

"You're mad," he shouted, barely recognizing the pitch his voice had taken on. "This is ludicrous."

"For Clara's life, do one thing."

He swallowed, then spun in the driver's seat and watched

cars race by. How much did the caller know? How much could he know? Damien arrested? Impossible.

"If you touch one hair on Clara's head—" he started.

"Temper, temper, Mr. Olafson. Be careful. Do not threaten me." There was a clicking sound on the line. For a brief second, Anton thought the caller had hung up. "Check your email. I will wait."

Anton grabbed his phone and hit the email icon. Four messages. Two from colleagues at NC3 and one from a friend. The fourth was a strange email address made up of numbers and letters. He tapped on the email, and a picture began to download.

It was Clara. She was at an airport.

"There are two pictures," the caller said. "One picture is from yesterday when Clara departed Copenhagen Airport. The other is today as she landed at Toronto's Airport."

Anton scrolled down and saw a sign behind Clara's head that said welcome to Toronto. He turned off the hands-free option and put the phone to his ear so hard he winced at the pain.

"What have you done?" he breathed into the phone, anger rising, crowding out the fear and worry.

"She is with me in Canada. She is mine until you do one thing for me. I'll give you a week. Do this, or you will never see Clara alive again."

"And I will hunt you down and kill you myself," he shouted into the phone. "I'll fucking kill you." Furious anger seethed out through his teeth as he tried to cope with what was happening.

"Threats only make me want to hurt Clara more. Like you've hurt so many of Damien's underage boys. Don't threaten me, Mr. Olafson. Just do as I say, and all this goes away. Clara will be safe for another week."

A large rig passed the Tesla, shaking it, the name BILKA on the back of the trailer in big block letters. Anton watched it moving away until BILKA was barely legible.

"What happens in a week?" Anton asked, using every ounce of will to remain calm.

"If you do as I ask, Clara is free to leave. She can fly home to you if she wishes."

"*If* she wishes?"

"The choice will be hers and hers alone. Don't make me tell her who you really are."

"What am I supposed to do?"

"To make things right, I need you to murder a random girl."

Anton heard the words but didn't put them together.

"What? How does murder make anything right?" Even though the caller couldn't see him, Anton shook his head. "There's no way I would kill anyone."

"Like you've killed those little boys you take to your hotel room?"

"I never kill them," he screamed into the phone. "We talk. That's it."

"You kill their hopes, their dreams. You kill them on the inside."

Anton wiped the tears from his eyes. This call had turned into a nightmare.

"What's this about? Are you recording this call? Just tell me where Clara is."

"One week, Mr. Olafson. A girl. Video it. A small mirror under her nose will be all I need as proof. A stranger's life for

Clara's. Your daughter's life is truly in your hands, Mr. Olafson."

The line clicked, then died.

Anton pulled the phone from his ear and stared at it like he held a chunk of contaminated plastic in his hand.

He moaned as the conversation ran through his head.

"Clara ..."

He couldn't drive. The vibration in his hands scared him. His eyes were glazed over. He could only hunch over and gasp until the panic attack ebbed.

What was he going to do? He would never kill an innocent girl. He wasn't a murderer. Sure, he had a little fun occasionally, but the little whores didn't mind. Damien assured him the boys he hired were into it. Anton never hurt anybody. And he would never *kill* anybody.

Unless this was a trap, he was untouchable with the Damien business. Money transfers were from ghost accounts with false names. Damien helped him set things up so no one could ever trace it back to an NC3 man. Even NC3 couldn't track their transactions.

So that's what this was. Damien got himself arrested, and now someone was trying to get Anton on murder charges because they knew Anton was untouchable.

But whoever they were, they had Clara unless the pictures sent to his phone were doctored. But if they were, why wasn't Clara answering her cell phone? And how did Clara get to Toronto? The time since she last texted him fit with a sixteen-to-twenty-hour flight to Canada. But why? Who was in Canada? How was she drawn there?

He turned off his flashers, dropped the Tesla in gear, and kicked up dirt as he slammed the accelerator to get back on the highway. In moments, he was traveling thirty kilometers over the speed limit. He needed to get home. He needed to see if Clara had left any clues for him. Maybe he could access her computer. Maybe she'd left her iPad behind.

Or perhaps she'd left a note for him.

He could only wish.

Worst case, he would check flights and airlines and see if his daughter's passport was used recently. He had colleagues in high places that could help.

He'd get to the bottom of this immediately.

Anton Olafson screamed in frustration behind the wheel of the Tesla as the comfortable world he had enjoyed for decades crumbled.

Wherever the pieces fell, he would be ruined unless he found Clara.

It slowly dawned on Anton that this could be the beginning of the end of his life.

Chapter 4

Sarah plopped down on the couch. "You guys got letters, too?"

"They were addressed to us," Caleb said as he sat in the easy chair across from her. He raised his right eyebrow. "Accurately too. It would be hard to believe that if I didn't open the time capsule myself. And even harder to believe if I didn't know what you're capable of."

Sarah looked at Parkman. "What about Aaron? Has anyone told him what Vivian said? We have to save his life."

Parkman nodded. "He got a letter. It's taken care of."

"I have to call him. Warn him. Vivian said something about him dying because of time. It didn't make much sense."

Parkman shook his head. "Leave it. It's all handled."

She glanced at her mother, then back to her dad. "Okay, then. Will someone tell me what these letters say? I'm at a loss here."

Parkman shook his head. "Can't. Not this time. We have to trust Vivian."

"What?" She nearly leaped off the couch. "Trust Vivian? Isn't that what I've been doing for the past decade?"

"Sarah," her mother whispered, her tone almost condescending. Her mother got a pass, well, because she was her mother.

Parkman crossed his legs and leaned back on the couch, his hands clasped together. His attempt at nonchalance wasn't selling her. He was itching to spill the beans but knew he wasn't supposed to. And he didn't have his trademark toothpick sticking out of his mouth. That told her something.

"It'll alter the future, Sarah," Parkman said. "We can't tell you more than what was on those pages in the other room. Everything is flipped upside down. We hear Vivian now, through her letters, not you."

"Alter the future?" she gasped. "Isn't that what I've been doing all this time?" Sarah nearly screeched. "Altering the future because of something Vivian told me *about* the future?"

"This is not like that. This is different. Others are involved. It's for your own safety."

Sarah slapped the couch open-palmed in frustration. "Why is this so maddening?" She took in a deep breath. "Don't we need to talk about it? Read what Vivian was trying to tell you guys? Work it all out together?"

"In time, Sarah," her father said. "In time. For now, you need rest. Then tomorrow, you need to go to Toronto and, after that, Denmark. I've already bought your plane tickets."

"You what?" Now she did screech.

"My letter from Vivian told me what plane, what time to book it for, and where to send you. Vivian instructed me that this was the only way. I need you to trust us. Trust Vivian."

Sarah stared off into space for a moment. Details began to slip away from her. Trust Vivian? She had based her life on that. Trusting her dead sister had become the only way to stay alive. But now she was being asked to trust a girl who lived twenty-five years ago. A girl who sent letters to people Sarah knew. Parkman wasn't in Sarah's life until Sarah was twenty-two years old. How could Vivian have known to send him a letter? How could Vivian have known about Aaron?

The answer to all her questions was obvious, but for some reason, she seemed unable to handle it. Vivian had been psychic in her own way, as Sarah was now. But the dynamic had changed. The rules were different. Others were involved in the prophecy, and Sarah had lost the voice in her head.

She knew she would go forward carefully. There was no other way. This wasn't about her. It never was. This was about the lives of others, keeping them alive, and doing what she could to stop violence and crime.

Vivian had said in her letter to Sarah that everyone would live if she stopped the pain. But even then, the boys would continue to be violated.

What the hell could that mean?

Everyone had stayed quiet for the last minute, allowing her time to think, to absorb things. They waited for her to say something, letting her put her thoughts together.

She studied her parents' faces briefly, then asked, "Have you talked directly to Aaron?"

Caleb said, "No. I overnighted his letter to him."

"Why? I mean, it's fine, but why? Was there an added

note from Vivian? Is there anything you can tell me?"

Caleb exchanged a glance with Amelia, then met Sarah's eyes.

"We know how you feel about him. Whatever was in that envelope, we're confident he'll respond in the right way. But the letter was for him. Not us. Not Parkman. And not you."

"Did you read it?"

Caleb shook his head. "No. We did exactly as Vivian directed. You have to remember something, Sarah. We're talking about Vivian here. The notes and the letters brought up memories for us. We recalled the odd things she did when she was alive. When we opened the time capsule and read the letter to you, which I admit we shouldn't have done, it brought back a lot of the things she used to do. When we saw, in her own handwriting, that she chose to leave your mother at the mall that fateful day, we went through a series of emotions."

"That must've been hard," Sarah admitted.

"It was," Amelia said. "I've lived with the guilt ever since that day."

"I'm sorry." Sarah wanted to go to her mother and hold her. Amelia sat hunched up, her shoulders curled over the top of her chest, bottom lip quivering.

"Vivian unselfishly did it for others, for strangers," her father continued. "She gave up not just a piece of herself or some time. She gave up her life. A chance to grow up, to grow old. To get married. It really hit us hard when we read everything." The dark circles under Caleb's eyes led to tears as his eyes glazed over. "We can't lose you, too. That's why we called you right away and couriered that letter to Aaron, or Aarow, as Vivian called him. She was bad with names. In

Parkman's letter, she separated his name to say Park Man. Vivian must've thought the message was for a man who managed or took care of the local park."

Parkman laughed quietly for a brief moment. The tension in the room eased. It gave her father a chance to wipe his eyes.

"Excuse me," Amelia said as she got up.

They watched her head to the guest bathroom.

"When's my flight, Dad?"

"Tomorrow morning at eight." He grabbed a couple of papers on the table to his left. "It's all right here. In Toronto at five-thirty after a quick layover." He handed her the itinerary. "Then off to Denmark. You're to land in Copenhagen, transfer planes and fly to a small city called Billund. There you're to find transportation to a city called Skanderborg. That's all I was told. I did my part. Now you have to do yours and get on those planes."

She took the rest of the papers from him. "Any idea why I'm to fly to Skanderborg?"

Caleb shook his head. "None. Sorry."

"Parkman? Anything from you on this?"

"Nothing." He shook his head, too, truth in his eyes.

She gathered the sheets and folded them, taking note of the time. It was almost ten in the evening. She would want to shower and get to the guest room within the hour.

"I need one more shot of whiskey before bed."

Caleb got the bottle and filled her glass.

"I can't figure out the part about Vivian's pact with me. Isn't that what we already have?"

"I tried to figure it out as well but couldn't." Caleb set the whiskey bottle back on the table. "And how is Aaron to be murdered by time? And how can pain be behind everything?"

Something clicked for Sarah. It occurred to her that they were looking at it all wrong. She jumped up from the couch, nearly spilling her whiskey.

"I think I've got something."

"Got what?" Parkman asked.

Sarah ran for the guest room, passing her mother on the way. Once she'd gathered the letter from Vivian, she went back out to the living room.

Amelia sat beside her husband, looking refreshed.

Sarah scanned the letter, rereading the parts she had misunderstood earlier.

"Sarah, you have us all in knots here," her mother said. "What have you figured out?"

She looked up from the letter. "They are names. People's names or nicknames. The clock will murder Aaron. Vivian means someone known as The Clock. A nickname. Someone known for being on time." Sarah scanned the letter. "Pain is behind everything, Vivian says here." She looked up. "Whoever Pain is, another nickname, he's the one causing the problem. Find Pain. End this."

Parkman sat forward on the couch. He was nodding. "That makes a lot of sense. Any idea who Oaf and son is yet? Or the Danish blonde?"

"No, but something tells me I'll find out soon enough. I'm going to Toronto, right? As soon as we figure out who Pain and The Clock are, it'll lead us to figure out the rest." She drank back the rest of the whiskey. "Now, I need a computer, and I need sleep. I need to see if someone named Pain or The Clock are known in Toronto. Especially The

Clock. If I'm right, then he's the bastard that wants to kill Aaron."

Parkman jumped up. "I'll help."

Caleb held up a hand. "Sarah."

She turned to him.

"Whatever you do, don't die on us. The letter foretold it. But just don't."

Sarah hugged him. Then she hugged her mother tight, holding on a little longer.

"Nothing will happen to me. I won't die. Vivian has had my back all this time. And even now, when she's not in my head, she wrote letters to keep me alive. It'll all work out." She kissed her mother's cheek. "Don't worry."

When she got to the guest room and powered up her mother's MacBook Pro, a shiver ran through her. She wasn't so sure she would make it this time. How could she do this without Vivian in her head? The only way she'd stayed alive in the past was by having Vivian in her head.

And now she wasn't.

Chapter 5

The Clock got up at six in the morning on the dot. He rose on an elbow to reach for the cell phone on the end table.

No message from the client.

He laid back down, closed his eyes, counted to ten in his head, then lifted off the bed and positioned himself on the yoga mat he had prepared before sleeping. The time between the sleeping body to the waking body was a transition of consciousness. The former Navy Seal learned years ago in a boot camp that it took him ten seconds to go from one to the other.

After a forty-minute yoga routine that released toxins, awakened the body's muscles, and prepared him for his daily tasks, The Clock was ready. In the hotel restaurant, he ate a light breakfast of oats and berries mixed in yogurt and drank their rancid coffee—espresso beans only for him. Hotels weren't as health-conscious as he or the Italians were. He checked out with plenty of time to witness the dojo's destruction at ten.

Downtown Toronto had plenty of small parking lots. He chose one on Shuter Street, a few blocks from Yonge Street, and began walking to Aaron's dojo. At just after nine in the morning, downtown Toronto was already bustling. His planned explosion would cause havoc and initially be blamed on a terrorist group. In fact, he had a colleague waiting to place an anonymous phone call after the explosion claiming a breakaway Taliban group was responsible. The young Justin Trudeau had pulled Canada's military from their Syrian campaign, but Canadians still had to pay a price. The caller would announce new targets in Ottawa, Montreal, and Vancouver, but it was all a bluff.

The sun warmed The Clock's face as he smiled at the thought. He waded through the stream of businessmen and women hurrying along the sidewalk to their stressful jobs and nondescript cubicles in office towers. They were completely oblivious to the Danish-born, American-looking Navy Seal sniper who was about to scare the shit out of them with his bombs and subsequent terror message.

Maybe he would walk right by Aaron. Wouldn't that be a hoot? Meet the man who was set to die. If he did, he'd shake his hand, look him in the eye, and talk to him about his line of work.

An idea formed slowly.

Why couldn't he toy with his prey? Cats toyed with mice before eating them. The Clock could play with Aaron before he murdered him.

He hurried his pace. The Clock had to be on time.

A few minutes after nine-thirty, he turned the corner to

Aaron's dojo and headed up the street. At the front door, he slowed, pretending to study the pamphlets and brochures pasted to the outer window describing the various classes a new martial arts student could take.

The door opened. A bell chimed.

"Beautiful day," a man said.

The Clock turned. Their eyes locked.

Aaron Stevens. His intended target.

"Yes," The Clock said. "Quite."

He had spent years in his youth focusing on his accent, making sure it sounded more American than the Danish accent he had when he was a young boy. On a few words with the letter V, the Danish in him still crept in. If he was to say vampire, it came out, wampire. In order to fix that, he spent considerable time speaking the V to himself and avoiding the use of that letter in public when he could.

"Interested in a class?" Aaron asked.

"You caught me." The Clock shot his hands out to the sides. "Red-handed."

They exchanged a polite laugh. In that laugh, The Clock saw something strange in Aaron's eyes. Did he know The Clock? Had Aaron located one of the hidden bombs? There was no way he could've located them all. Or was he being overly suspicious, and Aaron was just having a bad day?

"Come on in," Aaron said. "Let's talk about what you're looking for. Maybe we have something that'll fit your needs."

The Clock looked at his watch. "I think I've got time." It was 9:42 a.m. "I have a meeting just after ten up the street." He met Aaron's eyes and studied his face for any sign of recognition. "It won't hurt to talk for ten minutes or so."

Aaron held the door open.
The Clock entered the dojo.

Chapter 6

ANTON OLAFSON MADE IT home without another phone call interrupting his drive to Skanderborg. He turned onto his street—Sølystvej—and drove down it slowly as the sun set.

Could he consider the call a prank? He didn't think so. Did the authorities call him? The ones handling Damien's case, in an attempt to get him to reveal his guilt, his crimes on tape? He didn't think that was it either.

Wishful thinking made him believe his daughter would be home waiting for him and that this was all a nightmare.

He drove past the Skanderborg rowing club. The lake, Skanderborg Sø, was calm this evening. Usually, an afternoon wind whipped it into a frenzy. He drove slowly past the Johnsen's house, then came upon his own, two houses down from the rowing club.

No lights were on. The house seemed dark, lonely.

He eased the Tesla into the driveway and turned it off.

Almost afraid to leave the car, Anton waited, staring at the house, his mind racing with what-ifs.

What if they were waiting for him inside the house? What if the police were on their way to arrest him because Damien opened his mouth? What if Clara was dead? What if, what if, what if?

He snatched his phone from the charger and got out of the car. His briefcase could wait. Entering the house empty-handed made him feel better. What if someone lurked behind a door, waiting to surprise him? He needed his hands free to defend himself.

Anton closed the Tesla's door gently and started for the house. The grass needed mowing. Weeds needed pulling. The paint chipped away on the frame of the front window. He wondered why he would notice such things now.

He unlocked the front door and swung it open. Before entering, he leaned inside and flicked the light switch.

The front hall lights came to life. At least the electricity still worked. Whoever was after him, whoever claimed to have kidnapped his Clara, they hadn't invaded his home or cut the power. Not as far as he could tell yet.

Once he was inside, he closed the front door quietly. In the three-hour drive from Copenhagen, his running shoes hadn't completely dried. With each step, they offered up a moist squishing sound. He'd only made it two steps inside the house when he stopped and listened. His heart raced in his chest, making him glad for all the time he rode his bike. At his age, exercise was necessary. Otherwise, he would become a round blob of fat, and his heart, which seemed determined to break a world-beating record in his chest at the moment, would disapprove. Even the increased pulse pounding in his ears was louder than the silence of the house.

Even though he was convinced no one had violated his home's sanctity, Anton remained in stealth mode, moving from room to room, only stopping momentarily in Clara's room. Once he cleared the house, retrieved his briefcase from the car, and secured the front door, he poured himself a glass of wine and headed down the hall to Clara's room.

He stared at her bed, the rumpled sheets, the untidy desk, the cluttered dresser. He wasn't too hard on her now as he was the only parent. Perform well in school. Aim for a well-paying job. Work in the government somewhere, just like her dad. Give back to the people. Do something. But don't slouch around, get piercings—like your dad—or get tattoos. What worked for Anton did not always work for Clara.

Their biggest issue had been fashion. He knew fashion. He dressed better than ninety-five percent of all government employees, and he knew it.

But try to tell a teenage girl that, or the budding woman Clara became, and she went into hysterics. Even though they resolved to let her choose her own clothes, he still advised her. Much to her chagrin, Clara listened to his advice several times over the past year or two. In her early twenties, their relationship had become more of an adult-to-adult understanding. He had actively stopped advising and stopped trying to teach her things. She had responded by being more responsible, more grown up. Mutual respect had formed between them as well as a higher level of trust.

The drive to Copenhagen yesterday morning had been wonderful. They had bonded as father and daughter and even listened to each other's music. On the road yesterday, he played her his Harry Connick Jr. album, and she played the

Danish group Nik and Jay and then the new Danish phenom Lukas Graham. He had to admit; he liked Lukas Graham a hell of a lot more than he expected.

But now Clara was gone. According to the caller, she was kidnapped and going to die unless he killed a random girl and proved it on video.

There was no guarantee that Clara would be set free. If the caller was to be believed, she was in Toronto, Canada, a world away, with a six-hour time difference.

Anton drank a little wine from his goblet, still standing at Clara's bedroom door, surveying her room. He set the glass on her desk and began looking through her notebooks.

He couldn't believe she would fly to Canada without telling him a thing. They trusted each other. They were solid together. Unless the caller—or Damien—had told Clara who her father really was. If she knew what he did on a weekly basis in Aarhus, he had no doubt she would flee Denmark, and Canada was one of the best nations to start fresh. He'd heard people say that Denmark was a smaller version of Canada.

Clara's notebooks spoke volumes of her hobbies, her interests, and a guy she was thinking of dating. Nothing in both of the ringed pads of paper talked of a trip to Canada. Where did she get the money? Did the caller supply the money? Did the caller persuade Clara to fly to Canada just to walk into a trap? But why? What was the personal gain? It seemed a little too elaborate.

She had to have been lured to Canada. Who could kidnap someone in Denmark and successfully transport them that far?

So many questions without any answers. He had no idea

who called, why his daughter was in Canada, or what would happen next. Anton couldn't think of a single enemy who would come after him in such a way.

The one thing he knew was that he was no murderer. That left him a week to solve this mystery and save his daughter. A week? Is that all his daughter was worth?

He slammed the notepad down on the desk as he tried to control his emotions. In one large gulp, he drank half of the glass of wine.

A search for her iPad or computer turned up empty. He saw Clara with her cell phone yesterday, so he didn't expect to find that in her room, either.

Without a single thread of evidence to go on, he drank the rest of his wine in Clara's bedroom. He thought about her demeanor on the ride to Copenhagen yesterday. Nothing whatsoever seemed amiss. Not unless being happier than usual was a crime.

That led him to believe this wasn't about him. Clara did not know about his weekly visits to Aarhus. She couldn't know. If she knew the truth about him, she wouldn't have acted as jubilant in the car. But why so happy? Was it the promise of a new life that drew her? Had she met someone online?

That made the most sense. The man who called with his proposal knew things about Anton that no one else did. If that was possible, then it wasn't a stretch that the caller knew things about Clara. Things that would endear her to him. He could sell her on the kind of man he was by appealing to her interests and tastes. In other words, the caller lured his daughter away from him to use as bait to get Anton to do what he was asked to do.

It all came back to the question of why? Who gains?

The irony of a Danish National Cyber Crime Center Director being hacked and coerced into performing crimes was not lost on him. He spent all his time hunting hackers. If that were the case, then the caller would've hacked Anton's personal computer.

He jumped up from Clara's desk and ran to his home office. Seated behind his desk, he fired up his iMac. As usual, it didn't take long. The normal picture was still there. He opened his files and found them all there and accounted for.

Then he clicked to access his personal folder, the password-protected one with the images Damien sent him before he made the trip to the Aarhus hotel each week. Anton took his own photos as well. Sometimes he revisited his appointments throughout the week by scanning those photos.

The password window opened. He typed it in and clicked enter.

Password denied.

He frowned, rubbed his chin, thought about which of his several passwords he had used, then tried again.

Password denied.

His stomach dropped. His hands shook. He would have to take a hammer to his computer if he couldn't access that file. If Damien had been arrested in Aarhus, and if he gave up his client list in some deal for a lenient sentence, the authorities would be barging in Anton's door within days, if not hours.

He needed to access and delete that personal file or destroy the computer.

One more try with an old password didn't work. Nothing worked. He had been locked out of his personal file.

Something he thought was impossible. Although he shouldn't have. With all the hackers out there, the best, the elite, could easily see everything on his hard drive.

The familiar email notification sounded, and a rectangular bar slipped into the upper right corner of his screen, announcing he had just received a new email.

It seemed like the room grew darker as he brought the mouse down and clicked on his mail icon.

The message came from pain@legacypainpact.com.

Against his better judgment, Anton clicked to open the message.

Anton Olafson,

You have tried three times to access your personal folder. Why? There is nothing there for you anymore. I have all the photos and all the proof. I have changed the passwords on your computer. Do you know why? Because I am untouchable. I do this because I can. I do this because I enjoy it. I do this because I love playing God.

Stop wasting time trying to cover your tracks and begin thinking about murder. You have just over six days left to do as I wish, or Clara will decide to never come home again. Ever.

I'm watching. From every computer, from every street corner. I'm watching. Log on to this computer when you are ready to provide me with evidence of your deed. Make it real. Clara is counting on you to pull through for her. We all are.

Yours Truly,

Pain.

Anton sat back in his office chair, gasping for air, a hand on his chest. He read the last part without breathing, then gulped air like he was eating it. He clenched his clammy hands and tried to compose himself. He stared at the screen without seeing it, dazed by what he had read, breath still bursting in and out of his mouth.

The cursor on the screen moved.

He moaned and leaned back farther, tipping the chair. The cursor headed to the delete button.

Someone's on my computer right now! The thought screamed inside his head.

He lunged forward to grab the mouse, but it was no use. Whoever had taken over his screen—commandeered by remote screen-sharing—had full control.

The email got deleted.

The icon closed his email window. Then clicked on his personal file.

The password was entered from somewhere else, each letter or digit represented by an asterisk.

The file opened in front of him. Each and every picture of him with underage boys as he defiled them.

Even though he was sure he had blanched, heat rose to his face, and his hands numbed.

Am I having a heart attack?

The hacker scrolled through the pictures, stopping on the most explicit ones. He enlarged one, zoomed in, then took a screenshot. Anton's face was quite clear in the photo. So was the young boy's face.

Damien had assured him none of the boys were under the age of fifteen, but Anton remembered this particular boy. Anton could've sworn he was younger than that but didn't debate it at the time.

And now the image filled his screen.

While someone else, somewhere in the world, stared at

it, too.

He was ruined. As good as dead. He would never survive in prison.

The options were to lose Clara forever and go to jail for sleeping with underage prostitutes or kill a random woman and go to jail for murder. Those were his only two options because whoever had hacked into his home computer was good, better than good.

He was ruined.

His computer shut down remotely.

The room darkened as the screen clicked off.

Anton wept as he decided he would rather kill a random girl, someone who lived on the streets than lose Clara.

He just hoped it would stop there.

But somehow, he doubted it.

Chapter 7

AARON MOVED BEHIND A desk and produced a brochure. The Clock took it from him, his smile widening.

"I'm Aaron Stevens." Aaron held out his hand. "This is my dojo. And you are?"

The Clock thrust out his hand and gave Aaron his real name. There was no harm in that, as Aaron had less than twelve minutes to live.

"I'm Ansgar Holm."

"Ansgar? Interesting name. Is that Finnish?"

"Danish. My last name, Holm, is derived from Old Norse, meaning small island. My parents lived on the Island of Fanø before I was born."

"So you're Danish, living in Canada."

Ansgar eyed him for a brief moment, wondering if Aaron knew more than he should.

"Danish background," he said, his tone deeper.

"American now, spending time in Canada."

"Enough time to be interested in a class?" Aaron asked, his smile widening in return.

"That's about it," Ansgar said.

Aaron is on to me. I can feel it.

"We've got plenty of classes," Aaron said. "Ones to suit all levels, from beginners to avid street fighters to simple self-defense courses."

Aaron went on for another minute detailing what one would benefit from joining his dojo. He seemed like a nice enough man. When meeting his kills before termination, Ansgar often wondered what that person did to warrant the hit. What could Aaron have done to make the client angry enough to not only want him dead but to also blow up his business?

"Can I take this?" Ansgar held up the brochure. There were less than eight minutes left until the bombs he had planted the previous evening decided to make their presence known.

"Of course." Aaron stepped around the desk and stood in front of Ansgar. One-on-one, without martial art training, Ansgar was sure he could take Aaron in a fight. Although that was contingent on how good Aaron was. If he was Jet Li good, then maybe not. But as a Navy Seal, Ansgar had done serious hand-to-hand combat and was quite confident in his skill.

"How long are you in Canada?" Aaron asked.

"Six-month contract," Ansgar lied. "Plenty of time to work something out."

A door opened along the side wall. The sound of students training increased in volume momentarily as a young man with a gym bag slung over his shoulder stepped into the main office. Skinny and small in stature, the man slipped past Ansgar, waved at Aaron, and opened the door to the street.

"Nice training in there today, Alex," Aaron said.

"Thanks."

Ansgar watched Alex lope by until he was past the windows.

Ansgar checked his watch.

9:55 a.m.

Aaron's got five minutes to live.

"Well, I must be going. Thanks for this." He held up the brochure and backed toward the door.

"We're here if you decide to come back and sign up." Aaron moved behind the desk and dropped in his seat.

"Will do."

Ansgar stepped outside, where he waited until the door closed.

9:56 a.m.

Four minutes to fireworks. He wanted to be across the street and up a city block before his little friends did their deed.

One last turn to wave at Aaron, and then Ansgar started up the street. At the corner, he crossed with the light. While doing so, he glanced over his shoulder. No one had exited the dojo. It would blow in two minutes, killing everyone inside. Unfortunate for the students. How were they to know Aaron had pissed off someone important? Someone with money. Someone who could remain anonymous and murder so easily.

Ansgar assessed his distance to be enough, but to avoid a random piece of shrapnel, he moved down another ten feet and leaned against a building's column. If anything flew his way, it would make contact with the column first.

9:59 a.m.

No one had left the building.

Ansgar watched a Toronto taxi drive by. A woman in a business skirt hustled down the sidewalk toward the dojo.

"Don't walk so fast, my pretty," he mumbled to himself.

She made the street light where he had just crossed moments before and had to stop for the red light.

It was funny how fate worked. Fate was a fickle bitch at best. One day soon, that woman will realize that a red light saved her life.

He checked his watch.

Ten seconds left.

He closed his eyes and counted them down in his head. On the third to last second, Ansgar opened his eyes and peered down at the entrance to the dojo.

The red light changed on the street, and the woman began walking.

The front window of the dojo lit up like the sun for a brief moment, then the front window and door blew out. The briefest of moments later, another concussion shot bricks and chunks of wood across the street.

Then the dojo was obliterated upward and outward.

Ansgar leaned back behind the post to protect himself from unwanted pieces of building entering his flesh. Someone was screaming. Car alarms blared somewhere. His ears rang from the initial explosion, but he could still hear most of the aftermath.

From where he stood behind the column, the sound of flames licking the remains of the dojo was loud.

He leaned out to get a better look. The dojo was a self-contained building with no rooms above it. Each building on either side sustained minor damage to its façade.

Ansgar was happy with this result. He wasn't a crazed lunatic. He had been hired to destroy the dojo and do it with Aaron Stevens inside, so that's what he did. Blowing up random buildings wasn't part of who he was. The people inside Aaron's dojo were collateral damage. It happened in his business.

The woman who had stopped at the red light was on the sidewalk, holding her leg. Blood oozed out of a wound. She screamed for help.

A siren wailed in the distance.

The Clock was done. The contract had been completed.

Ansgar Holm grinned to himself and walked away from the carnage. He pulled out his cell phone and texted the number for the client.

Our mutual friend has left the building. The building is no more.

At the street light three blocks up, he turned back as fire trucks arrived on the scene.

Movement caught his eye.

That guy who had walked out when Ansgar had been talking to Aaron—the name Alex popped into his mind—slipped into a café four doors down.

Ansgar was sure Alex had been staring right at him.

Ansgar trotted back to the café's door, ripped it open, and jumped inside.

Several customers stood by the front window, watching the carnage down the street, their coffees forgotten on three different tables.

A woman with a white apron strapped to her waist addressed Ansgar.

"Did you see that?" she asked, then frowned. "Hey, are you okay, mister?"

He nodded.

"I'm sorry. Can I get you a coffee or maybe something stronger?"

She seemed like a genuinely nice woman. Pretty smile. Nametag read, Lisa Brown.

"Did a man slip in here less than twenty seconds ago?" he asked.

Lisa frowned again. He studied her eyes. All the tells were in the eyes. Lisa's eyes didn't avert. She simply looked at him, dumbfounded at the silly question.

"I was watching out the window," Lisa said. "Didn't see anyone. Just that." She pointed at the razed dojo.

Ansgar checked toward the back of the café. It was empty. Everyone was at the front window.

"I'll just use your washroom," he said.

He started for the back without waiting for a response. At the door to the bathroom, he turned left and entered the back room of the café.

Empty.

He ran through and pushed the back office door open.

Empty.

Could he be wrong? Did Alex enter the business next door?

When he spun around to leave through the back door, it sat ajar.

He smashed it open with his shoulder and jumped outside, his hand hovering over the holstered weapon in his waistband.

The back alleyway was empty.

It appeared that young Alex might prove to be a problem.

Whoever the hell he was.

Chapter 8

AN HOUR INTO THE second flight, after changing planes at LAX, Sarah rested her head back and closed her eyes. A light meal had been served. She'd had one glass of wine which calmed her enough to rest.

The anticipation of landing in Toronto, clearing customs, and getting downtown from the airport as soon as possible meant she wouldn't get to Aaron for over five more hours. What did his letter from Vivian say? Did Vivian warn him in time to save his life? Did the letter even get to him in time?

Maybe that was why he was to die. The timing was off, and the letter misses him.

She exhaled in an elongated sigh. Why did she send him home from Vegas? They had a pact. They agreed to keep nothing from the other one going forward. Their pact was one of full disclosure.

When her father called and told her to come home to

Santa Rosa and tell no one, she did that. And now a man nicknamed The Clock—at least that's what she thought Vivian's note meant—was set to murder Aaron in Toronto, exactly where Sarah had sent him.

Aaron's death would be on her head. She couldn't take that kind of guilt. She refused to. When she called his number from the airport, she got voicemail.

Sarah rubbed the back of her neck as the plane bounced slightly in turbulence, wishing it to fly faster. Several hairs brushed her fingers. She clasped them, rolled them in a circle, then eased outward. Pulling didn't have the same calming feel it did when she was eighteen. It used to release her internal tension, but now it seemed to annoy her.

She let go and fidgeted with the hem of her shirt as she ground her teeth.

What would she do without Aaron? She had to believe Vivian's letter to Aaron would steer him clear of danger. That was it, wasn't it? Vivian had something blocking her from direct contact with Sarah. Whatever was blocking her was revealed to the living Vivian all those years ago. And as always, Sarah's sister prepared for that event by writing letters to people Sarah hadn't even met yet.

How could she know those letters would reach the right people in time? How could she know those people would do what was asked of them? What about the time capsule? How did Vivian know that her parents would wait the full twenty-five years or open it a few months early?

There were too many variables. Too many things could go wrong when everything had to go exactly right, so the people involved remained on the surface instead of under the ground.

Her hands opened, then clenched into fists.

And why Denmark? What the hell was happening there that had anything to do with her or Aaron? Skanderborg?

What the fuck?

No one heard her except herself. Vivian was absent.

The plane bumped again. She turned to her seatmate. The row had three seats, the middle one empty. An older man with graying hair, a nice suit, and shiny cufflinks sat in the aisle seat, scanning his iPad.

He must have detected her staring because he looked up.

"Hey," she said.

"Hi." He smiled. A George Clooney smile. It offered warmth and understanding. "Bit bumpy, eh?"

A Canadian.

"Yeah. Not so bad, though."

She had the luxury of not fearing what other people feared. For Vivian to tell their father what flight to place Sarah on meant this flight would make it to Toronto as well as the subsequent flights to Denmark. Unless, of course, Sarah was supposed to endure another plane crash like when she landed in Amsterdam just a few months ago.

"My name's Glenn." He extended a hand. "They call me Splinter. I'm a jazz player. Horns."

"Sarah." She shook his hand, hoping he didn't care about her clammy palm. "They just call me crazy," she added. "I like jazz. But the horns I'm familiar with are the ones on top of people's heads."

He offered her a warm grin. "Like those bastards in Toronto."

A rush of warmth came to her face as she leaned closer. "What bastards?"

"You haven't heard what happened in Toronto this morning?" Glenn held up his iPad. "It's all over the news."

Sarah gawked at the picture. A building had been destroyed. Two Toronto firefighters were in the photo, black hoses behind them, streams of water shooting out in front of them. In the scene, part of a yellow rope had cordoned off the area. Every ounce of her being knew this had to be related to her or Aaron, but she refused to believe it at first glance.

"What happened?" she asked, maintaining a modicum of control over her voice.

Glenn leaned back in his chair and looked down at his iPad.

"Terrorists are claiming responsibility. Some breakaway sect of the Taliban." He faced her, eyebrows raised. "Can you believe that? In Toronto?"

"What did they do?" She swallowed. "I mean, what building did they blow up? A government one? A newspaper?"

"A gym." He slapped his armrest and stared straight ahead as if in thought. "Why a gym? How is that strategic in any way? Can you believe that?" He seemed to have a habit of asking her if she believed things. Glenn added, "They interviewed a witness, too."

A gym? Where people work out? Or train? Like a dojo?

Glenn kept talking. "Apparently, it was a martial arts place. Some guy who remained anonymous said he was a student there. Barely escaped with his life. Left minutes before the explosion."

Sarah struggled to breathe.

Martial arts place.

It couldn't be. Downtown Toronto. Martial arts. Aaron's

dojo was downtown.

Turbulence shook the plane. Sarah's stomach roiled.

Glenn was still talking. "The owner was inside. An entire class was doing a routine when it went sky high at precisely ten in the morning." Glenn shook his head. "So sad. They interviewed a woman who had been crossing the street." He held up the iPad to show the picture of the woman. "Interviewed her on a stretcher. She caught a leg wound from flying debris. Saved by a red light, she claimed. I just can't believe this is happening in Toronto. Just as our prime minister pulls all our resources out of Syria, then this."

Sarah had a hard time focusing. Her mouth had gone dry. She broke into a cold sweat. She needed to know but couldn't ask if they'd offered any names in the news.

Glenn continued talking about it, head down, staring at his iPad. She couldn't shut him up even if she wanted to.

"Some guy named Aaron Stevens ran the gym. The student who made it out in time named him, along with several others, as being inside the building when it blew. Police have not confirmed names other than to say that several bodies were among the smoldering debris." Glenn shook his head back and forth, a finger at his lips now. "So sad."

The plane bumped after hitting a rough patch of turbulence. The seatbelt light came on. An announcement followed that people were to remain in their seats until the captain turned off the seatbelt light.

Sarah jumped from her seat, pushed past Glenn's legs, and ran up the aisle for the toilet. Nausea had crept up fast. She was suddenly very weak and needed to vomit.

Aaron was dead.

They all confirmed it on the news without contacting the next of kin first. After all he had done in his short life, the disrespect was a travesty.

It was her fault. Aaron died because of Sarah. How could she live with that? The weight was too much to bear.

She wrenched open the bathroom door, slipped inside, and slammed it shut behind her.

Before she vomited the second time, a flight attendant knocked on the door.

"You have to return to your seat, ma'am."

The truth, the reality that Aaron was dead and Vivian did nothing to stop her from sending him to Toronto when she was in Vegas, and still in her head, made her vomit again. How could Vivian be so cruel after all they had done together? How could she be sure Aaron would receive a *letter* from her in time? Was this Vivian's way of freeing up Sarah's time? To have her all to herself?

The flight attendant knocked again.

Sarah ignored her and slouched on the tiny floor of the lavatory. She lowered her head into her crossed arms and waited for the shivering and the pain to stop.

It didn't.

Chapter 9

ANTON OLAFSON WOKE WITH a splitting headache. The images from his computer screen rose to his consciousness. The nightmare crept back in, and with it came a weight pushing down on him. A weight of his own doing. And undoing.

He rolled off the bed and sat on the edge. Six days left. Then what? The hacker would expose him? And what if he really did kill a random girl, then what? Who's to say the hacker wouldn't expose him anyway?

How would he keep Clara safe? That had to be the question. The right thing to do was whatever got Clara to safety. Once she was safe, he would deal with the aftermath.

According to the hacker, the only way to get Clara back was to commit murder and offer the hacker proof.

He decided that if killing a random girl meant Clara could come home, he would do it. Anton would spend a decade or two in jail for what he had already done to those boys. It would matter little to add to his arrest record if that meant Clara could come home.

Clara's safety had to be his focus.

Emboldened by his decision, he showered, dressed, and headed for his home office. No messages from Clara. He called work and booked a week off. There were plenty of sick days to accommodate him.

After a breakfast of rugbrød with cheese and jam and a small wienerbrød, Anton headed out for a walk. It was time to scout areas of Skanderborg for a random girl to kill.

Refusing to turn on his computer for fear of it being taken over in front of him, he left all electronics at home. Today was a scouting day. He would deal with the hacker tonight.

The sun warmed his back as he walked toward the center of Skanderborg. The smell of Kvickly's bakery wafted out to him as he walked by the store. People were headed to work. Others were shopping. Mothers pushed strollers and left some outside stores as they browsed inside. Life went on in small-town Denmark while Anton searched for someone to kill in order to save his daughter's life.

By the time he crossed Asylgade Street and started past the Løvbjerg grocery store, he turned around and headed back the way he had come.

This was ridiculous. There was no way he could grab a human being off the street and murder them. The thought angered him. To be in such a position was maddening. Damned if he did, damned if he didn't.

To him, Clara's life meant more than any stranger's life. That was an easy deduction. But who would he kill? And in that final moment, just as he was about to do the deed, would he be able to go through with it? If not, criminal charges of kidnapping, or even attempted murder, could be leveled against him.

It had to be all the way or nothing. Get Clara free and turn himself in. The police would probably be waiting for him when he got home anyway. What was to stop Damien from talking?

He passed an old neighbor. Gunter smiled and waved. Anton waved back but kept his head down. He passed the Bog & Idé store. Books and Ideas. A large orange sign in their window announced they were having a "Slut Spurt." Even though it translated to "Final Sale" in English, many foreigners snickered at the choice of words.

At the Kvickly again, instead of heading home, he turned left and followed Banegårdsvej, which led to the train station. The internal conflict and frustration with the situation he found himself in didn't allow him to go home yet. There was nothing to do there but brood alone. Clara was gone. The house was silent, empty, with only the computer to keep him company, and he didn't want to turn the damn thing on.

Uninterrupted all the way up Banegårdsvej, he made it to the train station, where he entered the 7-11 convenience store attached to the station and bought a coffee. The clerk was friendly, but Anton wasn't in the mood. Even with a nice car like the Tesla, he still rode the train to Aarhus frequently. People recognized him here. He was a friendly face.

An idea began to form. In one respect, people familiar with him here were a good thing. When a girl went missing from the train station, no one would suspect him. He worked for the government. He used the trains often.

He stepped outside the 7-11 and stood out in the sun on

the platform, sipping his coffee. He would do it right here. A girl coming home from Aarhus. A girl traveling to Skanderborg from Copenhagen. Traveling by herself.

Anton would come each day, buy a ticket, and wait for the train. He would do it at least twice a day until he saw the right opportunity, the right girl. Then he would pounce. In order to do that, he would need a few things first. Chloroform. A rental car. He could never use his own. He would follow his victim into the downstairs tunnel walkway under Jernbanevej, the 445. As she exited the walkway, Anton would jump on her, wrestle her to the ground, and apply chloroform.

Once she was packed in his rental car trunk, he could easily drive her to his home, enter the garage, and in privacy, take her to the spare room where everything would be prepared for her to die.

Save Clara. That was how he needed to look at this. Save Clara at all costs.

His new mantra: Save Clara.

He had to forget about himself and his life. Everything he did had to be for his daughter. He had ruined his life. Taking those pictures of his trysts in Aarhus was for him and him alone. When aroused, he could use those pics to remember his time with his conquests. But those pictures would be his downfall now.

Inside the small train station, Anton sat in a small room to the side where people ate pastries and drank coffee. He remained there long enough to drink the rest of his coffee and only stopped when the last few sips were cold. He watched people come and go. Three trains stopped and left at that time. He saw young girls, older women, people traveling alone, couples, and several groups of teens laughing and joking with each other, each with a cell phone in hand. Not a care in the world other than their homework load.

What he didn't see was someone as alone as he was. Someone with a similar level of torment and anguish. Denmark was often quoted as being the happiest country on Earth, but Anton wasn't feeling much of it at the moment.

In fact, depression settled over him. And this depression was the kind only murder could solve.

He got up from the bench after an hour and headed home, confident that he would kill a lonely girl within two to three days to save his daughter.

For Clara, he would kill a dozen if tasked to do so.

She was all he had left in the world, and he wouldn't let her go quietly.

"Save Clara," he whispered. "Save Clara."

Chapter 10

ANSGAR HOLM, AKA THE Clock, kept what he knew about the man named Alex to himself. The client didn't need to know about Alex, the student who followed him up the street after the dojo blew up. As far as The Clock was concerned, no one needed to know about Alex. It was an error. A minor mistake that led to nothing. Alex would die, and the error would be resolved.

The media reported a witness—one of Aaron's students—who got out minutes before the bomb exploded. This witness wanted to remain anonymous. That could be for a plethora of reasons. One, in particular, was to remain anonymous to The Clock. Alex didn't want Ansgar to learn his name. If Alex truly believed Ansgar razed the dojo, he was staying mum about it with the authorities, or the police were keeping it from the media.

Ansgar turned on his blinker and turned into the Travel

Inn Airport Hotel by the Toronto Airport. Clara Olafson had checked in yesterday after flying in from Denmark. The client had tasked Ansgar to keep her company in her room. Keep her quiet, feed her. Don't let her leave. Then escort her out of the room five days later and discard the body.

After parking, Ansgar reread the text from the client. The subject must be responsive and available for a phone call for the entire five days.

Not a problem.

He collected his backpack and started for the hotel's front desk.

The client was thoughtful. It was one of the reasons Ansgar enjoyed working with this particular client. He had arranged two rooms side by side on the tenth floor. At the end of the hall, room 1032, was Clara's. Across the hall, room 1034, was his. They were reserved for the week. Prepaid and arranged in Ansgar's alias.

As far as the client understood, Clara was in her room at that moment, waiting for a man to show up and drive her to meet a prospective boyfriend. Although that would not be happening. Clara wasn't going anywhere, and there was no boyfriend, just a fake account on a dating website.

Several people milled around the hotel lobby, but no one was in line to check-in. A family of four sat by their suitcases, staring at a TV suspended from the wall as a newscaster relayed the day's notable events. The sound trickled out of the TV, barely noticeable.

Ansgar walked up to the check-in counter and placed his Canadian driver's license and credit card in the name of Peter Ford on the desk.

"Checkin' in," he said. When he was Peter, an entirely

different image emerged from his character. He was chipper, seemed permanently elated about something, and smiled wide at everybody. Nothing you would expect from an ex-Navy Seal hitman.

"Name, sir?" the clerk asked.

"Ford, Peter Ford." He gestured at the computer. "You probably have me in the system." He clucked his tongue. "Ford. Like in Rob Ford. Ex-mayor. Rest his soul."

The clerk—Karen by the nametag—squinted at the screen at the mention of Rob Ford. She used her finger to follow something, then stopped.

"Here it is. Got it. You're in room 1034."

"Oh, how perfect." He offered her a wide grin. "Is that facing the airport?" he asked, knowing full well it was.

Karen smiled back, probably relieved they weren't talking about Rob Ford anymore. "It does," she said. "Now, if I could just get your credit card—"

"Go ahead." Ansgar pushed the card toward her. "Your tag says Karen, but the last name is scratched off." He squinted and leaned in. "It looks like Karen Dove." He stood up straight. "I have to ask." He reared back in glee. "Is your last name Dove?"

Color rose to her cheeks at his odd attempt at merriment. She tilted her head sideways, eyebrows raised, an embarrassed smile on her lips.

"It is."

"Well, I'll be," he said. He clapped his hands together once. "I just love doves."

She handed him back his credit card and a paper to sign. All business.

"I put a preauthorization on your card for the room." She

moved back to her computer screen and typed something. "Will you be parking a car with us?"

"Yes, ma'am. I have a rental out back."

"There's a ten-dollar-a-day parking fee."

"That's no problem. Just add it to my bill."

As she placed a room key card on the counter, the TV in the lobby rose in volume. The family of four waiting with luggage for a ride to the airport had turned up the TV. The screen was filled with firemen in their gear as the anchor spoke of terrorism on the streets of Toronto. The father of the family shook his head slowly, a worried look on the mother's face.

"Here's your ID and your room key, sir." Karen Dove moved everything across the top of the counter toward him. "Is there anything else you'll be needing?"

"Dinner and wine sent up to the room would be great." He offered her a final grin that could not be contained. One fueled by how perfect he was. To kill as easily as he did. To blow buildings up and have everyone running around panicking as they thought a terrorist had done it was hilarious. He danced from one foot to the other.

"The restaurant is just down the hall, and they do room service."

"Thank you so much. I think I'll get settled in the room and then call down." He pocketed his ID, grabbed the backpack off the floor, and shouldered it, then started for the elevators. "Enjoy your evening," he called over his shoulder.

"You too, Mr. Ford," Karen shouted back.

Once the elevator doors closed, his face fell. Ansgar was back. Sure, Peter Ford was a happy-go-lucky kind of guy, but he could only act that way in snippets.

On the tenth floor, he entered his room. After several minutes of setting things up for Clara Olafson, he pocketed the twist ties, the ball gag, and the pepper spray, then stepped back into the hallway.

It was time to meet his victim.

Clara Olafson. Apprehend her. Contain her. Keep her alive. Then dispose of the body. Five days in the hotel. Room service. Do what he wanted with the woman. Any damage, physical or mental, meant nothing to the client. The more, the better, in fact. Just make sure she was available for a phone call throughout the five days—if one was needed.

Ansgar Holm could do that. And he would enjoy it. He was a man, after all. He only hoped Clara was hot. It would be all that much more fun.

The tenth-floor corridor was empty. He left his door open a smidgen.

After listening to Clara's door for a moment, he heard nothing.

He knocked.

Something rustled behind her door. Footsteps approached. Darkness filled the peephole as Clara checked him out. He stood back, his hands empty and visible, so she would see him smiling and warm.

A click sounded, and the door opened.

"Can I help you?" Clara asked.

She was stunning. A gorgeous woman. Barely twenty, extremely pretty. Bright white teeth, a luscious smile. Long blonde hair flowing down over one shoulder. The thought of ruining and killing a woman this smoking hot bothered him for one second. The delay it took him to respond.

"A man interested in you sent me. I'm the driver. He told

me to tell you the password."

A bashful, almost immature smile crossed her lips as she looked toward the carpeted floor.

"Which is?" she asked. "The password, I mean."

"Plenty of Fish."

Clara nodded. She opened the door wider.

"Come on in. I'm almost ready."

Like the vampire who needed an invite to cross the threshold, Ansgar stepped inside at Clara's request, knowing tonight would be a long night of fun for both of them.

Whether Clara was a willing partner or not, she was about to have her world rocked in so many ways.

At least for five more days.

Murder was such a sweet ending. No witness to testify against him in a rape and aggravated sexual assault trial, and then nobody to offer evidence against him in a murder trial.

Just a missing girl. One who traveled alone. And opened her door to strangers with a fucked up password.

Stupid girl.

Such a stupid girl.

In a world filled with them.

Chapter 11

After much coaxing, Sarah exited the lavatory a half hour after the seatbelt light had been turned off. Perturbed that Sarah had not listened to them, the flight attendants let her go with a warning after talking to her seatmate, Glenn. He explained in her absence that Sarah had blanched and ran for the bathroom after hearing the news coming out of Toronto.

Sarah was too weak and tired to argue with them. In her defense, she didn't speak a word as she offered them a thousand-yard stare while breathing through her open mouth. A pleasant attendant led her to her seat and got her belted back in. Sarah remained there for the rest of the flight. Nothing else mattered. Turbulence meant nothing. The crying baby two seats back didn't penetrate her consciousness. Nothing got in.

Abandoned by Vivian. Aaron dead. Was this what she had been working toward for the past decade? Was pain her legacy? As much as she had learned to trust her sister, how was it possible that Aaron could be gone? Sarah couldn't believe it. Refused to believe it. She would demand to see the body or what was left of it.

Glenn tried to talk to her. He left her alone after she didn't acknowledge him. Attendants brought drinks and snacks around, but Sarah waved them away.

If the news was to be believed, and she had no reason to not believe it, then her boyfriend was gone. She would stay in Toronto for the funeral. There would be no subsequent Denmark trip. Once Aaron was buried, she would want to spend time with Daniel, Alex, and Benjamin. They, too, would be in mourning. Her life as a gallivanting vigilante would come to a close. Vivian was gone anyway. What was the use?

She hadn't brought luggage. No bag of clothes. Just her passport and a small carry-on bag with essentials. She would have to buy something black to wear.

The thought of shopping for Aaron's funeral made the realization surface. He was dead. His dojo was gone. It was truly over. How could she ever love again? Be with a man? Only Aaron understood her.

The notion she avoided was that Aaron should've been with her in Santa Rosa. She should've never sent him home. The bomb would've gone off, and others would've died.

But at least Aaron would still be alive.

Selfish? Sure it was.

How often do I think of myself? How often do I put myself first?

She lowered her head into her hands and wept. She tried to keep it quiet, personal, to herself, but she was sure Glenn could tell.

An emptiness opened inside her core. A loss so enormously large and intense encompassed her. It covered her in a heavy emotional tar, weighing down her limbs. Everything seemed difficult, even breathing. How could she move forward? How could she get up and off the plane when it landed?

Time heals all wounds, but this wasn't just a wound. This was a limb hacked off. This was a decapitation, a paralysis. Nothing healed this grief. Nothing.

Her shoulders quaked with repressed sobs as she held her head in her hands. There had always been the chance that someone close to her would die. She almost lost her parents a while back to a sick woman. She had almost lost Parkman several times. Dolan Ryan and Esmerelda were gone. Good people, killed by lunatics. When it came to her life, Sarah had Vivian and only Vivian.

Aaron.

All she could do was find out who was responsible and destroy them. If it were the Taliban, then she would go underground and kill each and every Taliban she could. A flight to Kabul. Access to weapons. Then hunt the terrorists. Maybe pretend to join them. Claim a belief in Islam. Anything to get inside their private group. Then murder as many as possible to avenge Aaron's death as well as all the innocents those kinds of groups killed yearly.

In the end, it would be a good thing. Maybe that's what Aaron's death represented. Maybe that was why Vivian let it happen.

Or perhaps Sarah didn't need Vivian anymore. What was left to deal with if she was incommunicado and Aaron was dead?

The captain announced that he was starting his descent. The plane dropped slowly. Her stomach hardened, weighted down in grief. She wiped her runny nose, then brushed her hand on her jeans. No matter how many times she swallowed, there was a lump in her throat.

Aaron.

Fifteen minutes later, the plane touched down on Toronto soil and taxied to the terminal. She stared out the window while her fellow passengers prepared to deplane.

"I'm sorry," Glenn whispered as he rose from his seat.

Sarah nodded for his benefit. She'd lost Aaron. The people responsible would die. In the meantime, she wouldn't be rude on purpose. She would try to be nice to people. At times it would be hard, but she could try.

The thick line of travelers began to disembark. Sarah waited until the aisle was relatively empty, then got her carry-on from the overhead bin.

Near the door, the flight attendant who accompanied her to her seat after the half-hour in the lavatory offered an awkward smile. Sarah smiled back, averted her eyes, and entered the ramp toward customs.

After a twenty-minute line, she cleared customs, walked by the luggage claim carousel, and headed for the exit that led into the main terminal.

A glimpse of her face in a side mirror revealed red-rimmed, bloodshot eyes, sunken cheeks, and signs of depression. She hated depression. Fought to get out of it in her teenage years and succeeded. Never again. Grieving was natural. It would take its course, then be done.

She walked past the roped-off area and the throng of

excited people waiting for loved ones to come out, knowing that the grief of losing Aaron would never subside. Even time couldn't heal such a deep wound.

People converged everywhere. She sidestepped a woman holding a baby, waited while a group of five wheeled their luggage by, skirted around them, and was stopped by two large men in suits holding placards with names like Smith and Whistler on them.

If the crowd didn't thin fast, she would go insane. People checked her out. The swollen, puffy red eyes. The running nose. She wanted to hide and cry for days. She wanted to be alone. Even the draw to pull her hair returned, and everything was wrong with the world again.

Aaron.

Someone bumped her from behind. She jerked sideways and elbowed a man who had his back to her.

Without offering an apology, she kept meandering through the crowd. Controlling her ire, she saw an end to the multitude of humans conglomerating in one spot, leaving an egress available.

Another person bumped her from behind. She almost spun around to push them back but hopped by an overweight woman, then turned toward an opening and jumped through.

Hands landed on her shoulders. They clamped down and forced her to turn around. Just as Aaron taught her in those long grueling hours of self-defense training, she allowed the hands to spin her, giving her momentum.

Fist clenched at the end of the turn, she raised it and swung. Something blocked her fist. He was fast. Too fast.

She dropped her center of gravity, snapped out another punch, had it blocked, too, then lunged forward with her shoulder.

The person spun sideways and yelled her name.

Sarah lost her balance in the lunge as she hit nothing. After two extra steps, she collected herself and stood to her full height. When she faced the person assaulting her, the strength in her knees caved, and she almost dropped to the polished tile floor of the Toronto airport.

"Daniel," she moaned and rushed into his arms. No wonder she couldn't land a punch. Daniel was one of Aaron's best teachers at the dojo.

He hugged her hard. "It's okay, Sarah."

She cried in his embrace.

"No, Sarah," he added. "You don't understand."

Her shoulders shook with the tears.

"Sarah," he whispered. "Stop crying. It's okay."

She jerked away from him. "Aaron's dead, Daniel. How is that okay?"

Daniel scanned the crowd.

"What?" Sarah asked. "Who are you looking for?" She was thoroughly confused.

He studied her face.

Sarah put her hands on her hips. "You gonna talk?"

"Come with me." Daniel offered a hand. "We need to discuss things."

"We can talk right fucking here," Sarah said, her voice coming out louder than she wanted.

Daniel glared at her. He leaned closer and spoke through gritted teeth, his jaw hardened. "Keep it down. Draw no attention to yourself. Come with me. Now."

His voice was so stern, so commanding, Sarah listened to him. She owed him that. Daniel was Aaron's friend long before he met Sarah.

Daniel led her along a corridor that angled to the right. After passing several sliding doors that opened to the outside, he led her through one. Sarah followed, eyes roving, constantly alert.

Once outside, the noise of traffic and a gathering of a strong afternoon wind would drown out any kind of conversation for casual listeners.

"What is it?" she asked. "Why the cloak and dagger?"

Daniel reached for her hand. She placed hers on her hips.

"It's about Aaron," he said.

"I know. I heard about it on the plane. The dojo's gone, too."

Unable to contain them, tears streamed out of her eyes again.

Daniel shook his head and took another look around.

"Only the dojo is gone. Insurance will cover that."

She frowned and sniffled. "What?"

"Aaron's alive. Everyone's alive. Sarah, I came to get you to tell you before you heard about it on the news. But it looks like I'm too late."

"Aaron's alive?" she whispered in a daze, her mind racing through a thousand calculations. The fear of raising her hopes only to have them dashed quelled her belief.

Daniel nodded. "He's here. Waiting for you in the car. Come on. We have a girl to save, too."

Sarah lost most of what he said as she stumbled and caught herself on a concrete beam to her left.

Aaron's alive.

She gathered her composure, adjusted her shirt, and faced Daniel.

"What's this about a girl?" she asked.

Chapter 12

BEN WILSON SAT AT his filthy computer terminal, eating a Mars bar. He stared at the screen, chewing methodically and loudly. Anton Olafson, the Danish asshole who played with boys, hadn't turned his computer on in almost two days. Ben's patience was already thin and didn't need to be tested. He knew its limitations.

"Quite well," he whispered to himself, then popped the last of the Mars bar into his mouth.

Ben had Anton's cell phone tracking turned on. The cell phone was in Anton's house. Whatever Olafson was up to, he was staying off the grid. That could be good or bad. Staying off the grid limited what Ben saw. But it also meant Anton was plotting the kill.

Ben swallowed the remainder of the chocolate bar. Open-mouthed, he gawked at the computer as a reminder popped up.

Jessica's birthday was today.

He moaned. "Beam me out of here," he said to his computer.

She would probably come knocking on his door, bearing gifts for him like she did every year. That was one of the things he hated about Jessica. It was supposed to be her birthday. People bought gifts for her, not the other way around. And they weren't going steady anymore anyway. He broke up with her over three months ago, but she continued to come over on Tuesdays to go to some stupid vegan café.

He checked the calendar. It was Tuesday.

"Ohhh, shit, bugs and bingo." He sighed and dropped his forehead to his desk, tapping it twice. Then stopped because it hurt. "I'm doomed."

Drool oozed from his open mouth. He sucked it back up and typed like a fiend on his computer.

Ten seconds later, he activated the virus planted in Anton's computer. If Anton didn't want to use his home computer, then Ben Wilson—aka PAIN—wouldn't let him. Ever.

Anton's cell phone was all Ben needed to track and deal with Anton. The man could even record the kill event on the cell phone. It would instantly download to Ben's external terabyte hard drive, and he would have what he wanted.

Ben had chosen the acronym PAIN, Passive Aggressive internet Nomad, after spending his entire life being called a nerd, which in the nerd world meant Never Ending Radical Dude. Acronyms were so cool that he used them often. His company name was Imagine, which stood for Ideas Manifested As Great Ideas, Notions, Etc.

With Imagine, Ben would be the first gamer to create a

live web experience with real footage. A kind of gamer slash movie thing. It had taken time to set up. No one would ever be able to trace it back to him, but it had all the elements of the best games like World of Warcraft, StarCraft, and Diablo 2.

"Even if they track me, I'll be dead by then."

Ben's game would have the hot girls, the murder and mayhem, the intrigue, and the wonder. Everything Peter Jackson did for the *Lord of the Rings*, but better. Ben's game would be similar to World of Warcraft, played online for a fee. That was one of the reasons behind stealing Anton's personal files and making him murder a random girl. Once Ben had that footage, it would be the murder mystery part of the game. He needed explosions and got that with the dojo downtown in his city. Not seven blocks from his home on Shuter Street, his personal private military contractor, The Clock, blew up Aaron's dojo with Aaron in it.

Nothing could be more deserving for Ben because Aaron Stevens had once taught Ben's stepdad martial arts. John Ashcroft was once a married man. After Aaron beat John, he was never the same. Aaron went to court over that, but John being the better man, had all the charges dropped against Aaron. After the ordeal, John lost his first wife and daughter and ended up with Ben's mother. John treated Ben like a man. But now John was gone. Before the stepson Ben Wilson died, he needed to make sure Aaron Stevens paid with his life, and he'd done that. John Ashcroft deserved that, at least. Even though what Aaron did to John changed him, Aaron never paid his debt, and Ben was the debt collector on John's behalf.

Ben knew the moment and time when he would die, and

that day was coming soon. Ben would be dead when his company released the online game LEGACY: PAIN PACT. Once the game went live, no one would be able to contain the exposure. Covering his tracks now while adding live footage and add-ons for the game was utterly genius. He loved his own brilliance. He loved playing God.

He had always been told he had an IQ greater than his body weight.

Making ordinary people perform *extra*ordinary tasks was something people had been doing to each other for centuries. The Romans did it. The Greeks raised Olympians. Today, the government sent ordinary men to fight wars that funded a war machine and made others rich while touting the veteran as a war hero. And why not?

Depravity equaled revenue.

People equaled shit.

All he was doing was riding the shit wave in and cashing out at the end of the day.

"Shit wave," he mumbled. "I like that."

Ben emulated the government. He wanted to make people like Anton Olafson—a criminal who should spend decades behind bars for what he had done to preteen boys— kill others and get caught doing it so Anton would never be released from prison. In the end, Anton got what he deserved, and Ben got the game of a lifetime just before he died. Later, Anton could blab all he wanted that he was coerced, but no one would believe him. There would be no evidence to prove someone else made him do it. In fact, there would be plenty of evidence for the police to go through when Ben forwarded Anton's private file to the Danish authorities. And with Anton's daughter dead in Toronto, Anton's life would be over.

Ben snapped his fingers as an idea slammed into him.

"A girl that resembled Clara. That would make sense. A life for a life. Bingo."

Ben typed on the keyboard as he set up the next stage in Anton's game. As soon as Anton looked at his phone, he would see the new instructions.

All of Ben's forays into Anton's electronics were hidden. Any electronic doors he opened, he closed, and his presence disappeared as his digital fingerprint vanished.

There had been others before Anton. He had one woman film herself having sex with ten different men until he released her from the PAIN PACT. She returned to her husband, who she had been cheating on before Ben's involvement, and received a package in the mail a month later in her husband's name. All the proof he needed to secure a solid divorce. Maybe next time, she would think about her actions and not cheat on the man she committed to.

Another man Ben terrorized with his PAIN PACT before Anton was an American living in Vancouver. A tax evader. Ben had found him by mistake. He'd been searching through the files of a private security company in Vancouver when the man's name appeared in a file on a missing person's case. Ben checked the man's personal files, hacked his computer, and noticed glaring financial discrepancies. Ben found over two hundred thousand dollars in unclaimed income in an hour's work. He was pretty sure he had figured out why the man's relative was missing, as the relative had also stumbled upon this financial discrepancy.

Since his computer-designed game centered on human depravity, Ben needed someone to maim and kill domesticated pets. The guy in Vancouver took it one step further and left clumps of soft dog food throughout a busy dog park. The food was laced with poison and killed over a dozen animals in one day. Overzealous, the American living in Vancouver did this several times before getting caught, more than Ben had asked of him, and even tried to blame it on some computer guy that was blackmailing him. As expected, no one listened to his plea, and Ben got all the footage he needed.

During the process, Ben felt nothing. He never had. When his mother, Margaret Wilson, died of cancer, he felt nothing other than the loss of not having his lunches made for him anymore. Her demise turned out to be a good thing. Ben was her only son, so Margaret bequeathed everything she owned to him. The paid-off house. The money in the bank. Everything. All his. At least until he died of pancreatic cancer.

Oh, what joy. What bliss.

He opened another Mars bar and bit the tip-off. One more week of depravity and his game would be ready to launch. People would pay for the privilege of playing LEGACY: PAIN PACT. They would perform computer tasks to level up. At each level, the game worsened with more bloodshed and more action, just like any Call of Duty game, except Ben's game would be like watching a TV. The murders would be real. The killing would be intense, the explosions not faked. A snuff game.

A camera across the street from Aaron's dojo had recorded the explosion. Ben had hacked into the camera's feed minutes before ten in the morning, recorded what he needed, then severed the feed and removed all evidence of ever being in their system.

And to think he'd started as a lowly hacker, checking out people's photos in search of lewd activity to get off on. What he found was depravity at every turn. For the most part, more than half the people he hacked had something in their computer system that would be deemed illegal by today's laws.

He concluded that since most people were criminals, he would make them pay for their bad deeds by performing something for him while recording it. That recording would be their downfall, Ben's windfall. Amassing a compilation of strangers' recordings meant nothing unless he could put them to use, hence the realistic gaming experience idea. In the meantime, he enjoyed orchestrating people's lives from his chair, surrounded by five computers.

"Because I love playing God," he whispered.

The Mars bar dwindled fast. He washed it down with a Coke, then tossed the wrapper on the floor. Jessica used to clean for him, but he stopped letting her after they broke up. She was too emo for him. Too gothic.

Once she was dead, the last person alive to see him would be her brother, Homicide Detective Shawn Bryant. A noob. Shawn was the man who had teased him and called him names when they were in school years ago. Names like dweeb, dork, twerp, dolt, geek, and nerd. Soon the big detective would see the vengeance a nerd got. Soon the dweeb would rise and crush the noobs and everyone they love.

Killing Jessy would bring the homicide division of the Toronto police. They would summon Detective Bryant. And Ben would get his revenge and end his life simultaneously because he refused to be killed slowly by pancreatic cancer. Not like his mother did. That was no way to die, all withered up in pain and moaning for pills.

He jumped when someone knocked on the door downstairs.

Grocery delivery? Today?

He checked the date again and bounced his knee up and down.

"Right, it's Tuesday."

Jessica's birthday. It had to be her.

He flicked on the camera at the front door and stared down at Jessica's pitch-black hair.

"Bingo."

She waved with one hand, a large bag swinging from the other. He leaned into the microphone.

"Go away," he said.

Her smile widened in the camera. He watched as she set the bag down on his front step and proceeded to open it.

He was going to have to let her in. People would see her, notice what she was doing, and he wanted the least amount of attention to the property as possible. Shuter Street was right in the heart of downtown Toronto. People walked by constantly.

"Go away," he whined into the mic a second time.

She raised something for him to see. It looked like a *Star Wars* R2D2 lunch bag.

"Shit wave, she brought me presents. It's her shit birthday. Dammit."

Jessica set the R2D2 down and brought something else up to the camera. It was a Mine Craft foam sword. No way he could refuse her entry now.

"Come on in," he said into the mic.

She inserted her key. On camera, she grabbed the bag and stepped inside. The house, mostly hollow, echoed her entrance from downstairs. He heard the door shut, the deadbolt click into place.

There was no way he could shut everything down before she entered his office, which used to be his mother's master bedroom. It was large enough to house his extensive computer station. On the other side of the room, a sixty-inch TV was mounted on the wall and connected to a PS4, the internet, and a new Apple TV. This was basically the only room he used in the house, except, of course, the attached bathroom, but he only used that when he had to. Without Jessica in his life anymore, he showered less than once a week.

One button shut down all his monitors, leaving the computers on to continue tracking.

He started for the door, already conscious of his smell. What did it matter? Jessica wasn't his girlfriend anymore. He could do what he wanted and shower when he wanted.

"Why is she here anyway?" he whispered to himself.

"Because it's my birthday," she said from the other side of the bedroom door.

He started, having not heard her come up the stairs. Damn, she was fast.

A quick swipe through his greasy combed-over hair did nothing. It fell back in place, tickling his forehead. After adjusting his T-shirt, he saw the yellowish food stains and wondered how long he'd worn the same clothes. It had been over a week since his last shower, and he had hotdogs that day. With mustard.

Shit wave, I haven't changed in a week.

The Anton business had riled him up. Manipulating Clara Olafson to come to Toronto under false pretenses had been a challenge. He had been so smooth he thought she was falling in love with his online persona.

She wasn't feeling the love now, he thought. *Unless The Clock was giving her a licking that kept on ticking.*

He barked out a laugh and stepped from the master bedroom to meet Jessica in the hallway. Just as before, she honored the rule that no one ever entered his office. Ever.

Smart girl.

Although it wouldn't save her life.

He despised her now for what her brother had put him through. If only she knew that Shawn and Ben had history. If she did, it would probably save her life because she would never come back.

They'd had sex a few times, but Jessy was awkward and shy. Claimed to have issues with someone seeing her body. They had to disrobe in the dark. Ben was a visual person. He wanted to see her, feel her.

But then, nothing worked right with Jessy. Even breaking up with her didn't work. She was just fucked that way.

"I see your emotions on your sleeve," he said.

It was his way of talking about her going emo. She didn't mind discussing it when he was kind and gentle.

The usual Jessica was overjoyed and jubilant, an absolute contrast to her appearance. The black hair, nail polish, and boots made one believe she was Goth. But Jessy hated Goth. She claimed she'd rather be emo than Goth.

"I'm not okay, Ben," Jessy said, tilting her head sideways. The small mouth and large blinking eyes almost made her appear ready for a stint in an asylum. "But you know me. I smile and laugh through it all."

She was one of those people that spoke with a contained laugh in their voice, like she was always on the verge of busting a gut.

"I know, Jessy. You're a happy girl. I can tell by looking at you." He gestured at the bag. "What's in there?"

"Gifts for my birthday."

"For you?"

"No, for you, silly."

She yanked out the R2D2 lunch bag. When would he ever use a lunch bag? It was cool but useless. Then came the Mine Craft foam sword. This one he liked. At the bottom of the bag was a World of Warcraft giant Foam hammer.

"Love the hammer," he said, already thinking about the toys and gimmicks people would make from his game.

Jessica giggled, then covered her mouth like she always did. As if letting out a small laugh was akin to farting. He suddenly wanted to ask her why she was the way she was. Who hurt her? Who raped her? Who stunted her growth?

As suddenly as the questions popped into his mind, he chased them away. Those questions had been asked before, and they made her withdraw into herself.

It'll all be over soon, lovely.

He would kill Jessica. He would need to do it soon. It was the only way to draw out her brother. Then little Ben Wilson, the *nerd* who suffered abuse for years from the high and mighty homicide detective, could force Shawn Bryant to use his weapon on him. Death by cop. How fitting. Ben even had the toy gun that resembled a nickel-plated magnum that he would aim at Detective Bryant tucked away and ready for use when the time was right.

Jessy stepped back and studied him.

"Like what you see?" he asked.

That smile never left her small mouth. "Ben, you're such a dork."

"Always." He placed a hand on the wall and leaned into it. "What's up?"

The conversation was always inane with Jessy. It led nowhere and ended up somewhere.

"It's my birthday." She giggled, covering her mouth.

"I know. And?"

"Wanna do something?"

"Like what?"

She waved a finger back and forth in front of her. "I don't know. You decide."

"I'm busy."

"It's my birthday." She started bouncing on her feet.

Next, she'll lose the smile. Then pout.

He had to get rid of her. What if Anton's cell left the house? What if The Clock sent him a message? He needed to be on point with so much happening.

"Let's celebrate another time," he said.

She pouted.

Shit wave at a bingo. Such a predictable bitch.

"How about the vegan café?" he asked. Anton had five days left to kill a girl. Then Clara would die. By then, he could wrap up most of what he was doing and be ready to die. "We'll go next week. Next Tuesday? Seal it."

He placed a hand out, palm facing up.

The pout disappeared, and a smile as wide as her hips flashed across her face.

"Consider it sealed." Jessy slapped his palm.

That had always been their personal handshake.

Jessica was twenty-eight years old, two years younger than Ben, but it was easy to forget her age when she was around. She acted like she was still in grade nine. Whoever fucked her up did a really good job.

He would've wanted to meet the uncle or the father that destroyed the girl on the inside. He'd bring that person a gift on Ben's birthday in Jessy's honor. A long serrated blade is to be inserted into the rectum. Maybe the man who ruined Jessy was her wonderful brother, Detective Bryant. If so, then Ben would be doing her a favor when he ruined Bryant's life.

He *had* to kill Jessy, but that didn't minimize the seriousness of what she had gone through, the pain she carried inside her.

"You gonna go now?" he asked. "Gotta get back to work."

Her hair shook out of place when she nodded. With a quick skip and a hop, she turned to head back down the stairs. He followed her. He had to piss.

At the front door, she stopped.

To reassure her, he said, "I'll shower and change before we go out on Tuesday."

"Seal it." Her hand shot out.

He slapped it.

"Bye."

Jessy slipped out his front door. He closed and locked it, then leaned on it.

"Poor Jessy, only a week to live. It won't be messy, but you have to give."

He let out a small giggle and covered his mouth to mimic

her.

He deepened his voice and tried to emulate an actor whose name he couldn't remember. "Your giggling days are numbered, little lady."

After a moment, he pushed off the door and headed to the toilet.

He had PAIN PACT business to play with Anton Olafson. And he wanted to check in with The Clock to see if he was keeping time with Clara.

The giggling and snickering at his own joke didn't stop until he closed his mouth to chew on another Mars bar while he urinated.

People had always feared or envied him. That was why they hated him in school, which fueled the idea of doing what he was doing now.

It reminded him of his favorite movie from years ago, *Evil Speak*. Stanley Coopersmith, played by a young Clint Howard, was Ben's hero. As a social outcast, Stanley found a way to summon demons using his computer. His tormentors paid the ultimate price.

It was time for people to fear Ben for something he had *actually* done instead of fearing him because of a perception.

Minutes later, back upstairs in the master bedroom, Ben typed on his keyboard like he was the Employee of the Month at Lucifer's company, where the pain was served electronically to over a billion daily.

And he smiled while doing it.

Then ate more Mars bars.

"Shit wave, I forgot to get my house key back from her. Dammit."

Chapter 13

Sarah had been strong for so many people over the years, but when it came to herself, her life, and the people close to her, strength became dependent upon their needing her. Becoming nauseous and vomiting because she thought Aaron was dead denoted a weakness she rarely felt. She realized that she loved Aaron so much that the thought of losing him made her physically sick.

Whatever the case may be, she was grounded again. Eyes dry, sinuses clear, breathing fine, no longer crying, and ready for answers.

In the parking garage of the Toronto airport, Daniel led her toward a rented minivan that sat in the back corner by itself. Only the front windshield wasn't tinted. Inside the front seat, Alex's white face stared out at them as they approached.

"Is Benjamin here?" she asked.

"No," Daniel said. "He's waiting in the hotel restaurant."

"Good. One less person to witness what's about to happen."

Daniel slowed and turned to her. "What's going to happen?" he asked.

"Aaron's about to be killed for making me think he was dead."

Daniel raised a hand in the air. "Now, hold on, Sarah. Wait until you hear the whole story."

"You can tell me later. This is between Aaron and me."

She pushed past Daniel and strode to the van.

"Sarah," Daniel moaned behind her. "Be nice."

"Fuck nice."

She reached the van and tried the door. It was locked.

When she smacked the window beside Alex, he didn't flinch.

"Open this door." She smacked the window again. "Now."

"Sarah." Aaron's voice came from the back of the van.

His tone weakened her resolve. She wanted to punch him and hug him at the same time.

"Sarah," Aaron called. "You gonna play nice?"

"Open the damn door. Take your chances."

Overwhelmed at hearing his voice, *knowing* now that he didn't die, killed a lot of the anger at being duped. He had to have a good reason. It probably had everything to do with the letter Vivian sent him. If so, how could she be angry with him because he didn't tell her he would fake his death beforehand? She didn't tell him everything when she left the Vegas hotel and headed to Santa Rosa.

Tit for tat.

But fuck it. I'm still pissed.

The sliding door on the side of the van clicked and slid open.

She jumped sideways, grabbed Aaron's collar as he leaned from the van, and yanked him out the rest of the way.

They embraced. After a moment of smelling him, touching him, she pulled away and punched him several times before he grabbed her flailing wrists and pulled her back into him. She knew he allowed those punches. He was too good. If he didn't want to be punched, every lunge would be blocked.

They held each other for another moment longer.

"Aaron, I thought you were dead," she said into his collar.

"I know, Sarah. But I'm not."

"Why?" she asked, her words muffled by his shirt's collar. "How?"

"I got a letter from Vivian. Explained everything."

She pulled away and gazed at his face. "What, everything?"

"Get in. I'll tell you on the way."

"Where are we going?"

Daniel walked around them and hopped in the van.

"To save a girl who has been kidnapped. Clara Olafson."

"Olafson?" Sarah mumbled under her breath. "Olafson?" Sarah stared at the concrete floor of the parking garage while she tried to remember what Vivian had said in her letter to her. "Oaf and his son." She met Aaron's eyes. "Vivian told me Oaf and a son. She might have a letter wrong or something. But it's Olafson?"

He nodded. "Clara needs us. I don't want to be late.

Hurry."

Emotionally numbed by the sequence of events, the sense of a cloud circling her head, Sarah climbed into the van. She touched Alex's shoulder as a greeting and sat beside Aaron. Daniel was already in the driver's seat.

He fired up the van and started away.

"I called when you were at your parents' house. There was no time to tell you our plan. Rationally, no one thought you'd hear the news on the plane."

She held his hand and remembered her mother on the phone while her dad made her a cup of tea. The tea she didn't drink. Sarah had thought her mother had called Parkman.

"It's not like you didn't think I was dead over and over in the past few years. I guess you got one back on me."

"That wasn't the intention." His face drooped, and he looked at her with puppy-dog eyes. "I'd never intentionally hurt you, Sarah."

Daniel slowed to pay for parking at the ticket booth. He slipped a ticket into the machine, and the gate lifted.

"No money?" Sarah asked.

"Already paid. You pay on your way to the vehicle. Then you have a certain amount of time to leave the parkade."

"I didn't see you pay. You were with me."

"Alex did it when he saw us coming."

But she didn't see that either—although seeing Alex when he didn't want to be seen was almost impossible.

"Tell me what's going on," Sarah said. "Vivian's not talking to me right now until I enter into a pact with her. So these letters are supposed to be her substitute. Fill me in. I'm feeling quite lost."

She turned to Aaron, still coping with the fact that he

wasn't dead. She had gone through a lot to save his life when he was kidnapped by the Enzo Cartel in Mexico. She couldn't save his missing finger, the one they delivered to her in Greece, but after getting him out alive and herself, losing him to a terrorist bombing in Toronto had been unbearable. That pressure on her shoulders was already lifting.

Aaron twisted in his seat toward her. "Vivian's letter told me that The Clock would destroy the dojo. She said it would be at ten in the morning exactly. So we canceled all the classes. The four of us waited at the dojo."

"Waited for what?" Sarah asked. "To be blown up?"

Aaron shook his head. "Someone slipped in the night before and planted the bombs. We detected the phone lines cut in the morning, which severed our alarm system. Since we can trust Vivian—"

"Big risk," Sarah cut in. "Maybe we can trust her now, but this letter was written twenty-five years ago. Basically, you trusted an old document's accuracy with your life."

He looked out the windshield momentarily as if he was collecting his thoughts.

"We trusted her," he said. "And we decided to do it together." His eyes found hers again. "Because pyros love to watch the explosion or visit the scene of the crime afterward, our plan was this. We would wait inside the dojo until a minute to ten, waiting, watching the outside for loitering strangers. Then we'd vacate out the back and watch the people gawking at the fire afterward, taking pictures. Our goal was to put a face to The Clock."

"Did it work?"

"Better than we thought. The bomber himself, The Clock, entered the front of the dojo and picked up a brochure.

He talked to me about classes. Alex opened the back door and made it seem like he was a student leaving a class. Daniel and Benjamin made a lot of noise as if they were teaching a class while Benjamin took a photo of the man talking to me. Our guest left a few minutes before ten, and we bolted out the back."

"So, where is this guy now?"

"With Clara Olafson."

"What?" Sarah tried to wrap her head around what he was telling her. "He blew up the dojo, then kidnapped a girl?" Bits and pieces of Vivian's letter came back to her. Something about protecting the blonde Danish girl.

"As far as we can tell, that sums it up."

"Why?" she asked, letting his hand go so she could raise hers to her neck to brush at an itch.

"That's what we're going to find out."

"Did you learn anything else?"

"His name. He's Ansgar Holm. From a small island in Denmark called Fanø."

Denmark? How come everything's pointing at Denmark?

Sarah lifted her right eyebrow and cocked her head to the side. "I'm at a loss for words." She swallowed. "How did you get his name and where he's from? I'm assuming he didn't just come right out and say it."

"He did." Aaron's face lit up. "Just like that."

"You're shitting me."

"Nope. Since we were going to die anyway, he probably felt it safe to say whatever he pleased. Darwin Kostas helped us with the rest once he received the picture and the name."

"What? Did Darwin get a letter from Vivian, too?"

Aaron shrugged. "Don't know about that. But we learned

a lot about the ex-Navy Seal sniper who wanted to kill me. He was nicknamed The Clock because of his precision in Afghanistan. His confirmed kills are classified, but some speculate he has the highest number of confirmed kills on record."

"Great. A fucking war hero is out to kill you, and he's kidnapping girls, too. Who's behind it all? Or is this Ansgar working on his own?"

"He's a merc. A hired killer. Some call him a PMC, which stands for—"

"I know," Sarah cut in. "Private military contractor. When we take this Clara Olafson from him, I'll ask him who he works for. I want to be the one to ruin his day."

"Be my guest. Just keep in mind this guy has seen combat. He's a hardened war hero. Confrontation and interrogation are what guys like this eat for breakfast. It'll take a lot to break him if we even can."

"He'll break. Everyone has something, some weaknesses. He'll break." She looked out the window as Daniel slowed the van and turned. "Where are we headed?"

"The Travel Inn Airport hotel."

Sarah turned back to him. "Vivian had that much detail in her letter?"

"No, this is Darwin's gem. He did a little friendly hacking and learned several aliases Ansgar travels under. Peter Ford has checked in to the Travel Inn. He's on the tenth floor in the room across from Clara's."

"What's the plan?" Sarah asked without wasting a second. Ansgar tried to kill Aaron. His dojo was gone, something insurance would cover. But attempted murder? And now Ansgar was after a woman named Clara?

Aaron shrugged. "Don't really have a plan."

Dark clouds hovered over the hotel as Daniel pulled in, maneuvered around an airport shuttle van, and found a parking spot on the second floor of the parking garage. Aaron donned a baseball hat.

"I've got to remain dead until this is over so we can learn why Ansgar came after me. Also, when you're talking to Vivian next, thank her for me. It's incredible that she saw all this happening that long ago."

Sarah cast her eyes downward, then watched as Daniel and Alex got out.

"I'm not talking to Vivian at the moment," she whispered loud enough for only Aaron to hear her this time.

"What?" Aaron asked as his breath hitched in his throat. "Wait, you said something about that earlier. Why not?"

"She's gone." Sarah lifted her eyes and stared into Aaron's. "Until this is over, I fear she's gone forever. There's not even a residual feeling of her presence in my head. The truth is Vivian saw our connection severed all those years ago. Hence the letters. Without the letters." She choked back a sob. "I can't bear the thought."

"Yeah, I'd be dead right now." Aaron swallowed. "I don't like that thought either."

Daniel stuck his head back in from the front. "You guys coming?"

Aaron waved him away.

"We good?" Aaron asked.

"Yeah. We're good." Sarah punched him in the arm. "Just don't die on me, or I'll kill you."

"Sarah?"

"Yeah?"

"I'd be dead if I died."

"Don't care. I'd kill you anyways. Now let's go hurt this Ansgar guy."

She moved for the door but stopped when Aaron pulled her back.

"We can't hurt Ansgar too bad," Aaron said.

"Why not? That makes no sense to me."

"He's the only lead to whoever's behind all this. We need him to tell us who's pulling the strings."

"We can hurt him first. Then talk."

Aaron shook his head.

"I'm sure he'll be more inclined to talk when his legs are broken." She shrugged. "Don't you think?"

Aaron crossed his arms.

"Then what are we doing here?" Sarah asked. "You said it yourself; this guy is an ex-Navy Seal. Tough as they come. The only way to ask a guy like this a question is to hurt him. Bad."

"We figure whoever he's working for keeps in touch with him. Instead of hurting him, why not take Clara and then tail Ansgar?"

Now it was Sarah's turn to shake her head. "Never work. If he's half the professional I think he is, the only way to get answers is to hurt him."

Daniel nodded when Aaron looked at him. Then Alex did. In the distance, a rumble sounded in the sky. A storm was coming, and judging by the wind, it was coming in fast.

"You guys just gonna go up and knock on his door?" Sarah asked.

They looked at each other, then nodded.

"Once he opens his door," Daniel said. "We'll do our

thing and get Clara out of there."

"Okay, not good." She wagged a finger back and forth. "Don't do that. Keep in mind the kind of guy we're dealing with. He's armed. Locked in a hotel room with a victim. Also, extremely well-trained. C'mon, I've got an idea."

They climbed out of the van, and Daniel locked it. Assembled in a huddle, Sarah gave them her thoughts on how to get Clara away from Ansgar Holm and how to hurt Holm in the process.

When she was done talking, the clouds opened up and released a torrent of heavy rain. The parking garage offered them cover, but they'd have to sprint through the downpour to get to the hotel.

The day only got darker.

Chapter 14

Ansgar Holm stood by the hotel room window and stared at the heavy rain as it fell urgently. He loved the way the rain made him feel. After years as a sniper, Ansgar embraced the rain, let it cool him, cleanse him. Or maybe it was his Danish blood. Denmark received its fair share of rain every year. Regardless of the reason, he stared at it, mesmerized, as Clara slept at his feet.

She had been a good girl since he'd had her in the hotel room. Only a small amount of whimpering, accompanied by soft sobbing and sniffles. He could handle that. A woman crying didn't bother him. Moaning loudly behind her ball gag, kicking things, or just plain making too much noise would bother him. Clara had forsaken that kind of attitude for rewards like food and drink and bathroom privileges. That was their deal. Only one week. Be good and live. Be good and enjoy her time with him. Be loud, act out, or try to

119

escape, and he wouldn't be so nice. There were ways to change her as a woman for the rest of her short life. She would never get the horrors of the hotel room out of her head if she disobeyed him. And before he took her life, he would take her like a man should take a woman. But that could wait. Take her too early, and she could become a fighter.

The Glock was in his waistband at the small of his back. The two bombs he didn't use on Aaron's dojo were secure in the hotel room's safe. Clara was at his feet, waiting for the order to kill her to be texted to him. Then what? He pondered his next move, the next city. When he was done with Clara, where would he go? The client had no other tasks in the near future. Ansgar had money. Maybe it was time to relax and travel for pleasure instead of traveling around the globe to kill.

Clara stirred in her sleep. He glanced her way and watched her facial expressions. Her ankles and wrists were bound with white plastic cuffs. A ball gag filled her mouth. Short of squirming around the room, she couldn't do much to escape. The ball gag only came out to feed her. Every bathroom break was done together. It didn't matter what she had to do in there; he joined her. The risk of her breaking glass and cutting herself loose or killing herself was too great. He would even bathe her when the time came each day.

Clara didn't seem to mind the toilet arrangement as long as he wasn't too invasive. And he wasn't. A true gentleman. But that wouldn't last. It had to for now, as Clara might be required to speak on the phone in a proof-of-life phone call. Violating a woman before a proof-of-life call didn't always work out well.

Her eyes fluttered, then opened. She looked around furtively as if coming out of a dream and just then realized where she was.

"You're awake?" Ansgar whispered. "Thirsty?"

She looked up at him and recoiled, then her face softened. Understanding dawned there, recognition of her situation. She nodded slightly.

He brought a water bottle over and leaned down beside her, the gun in the back of his pants digging into his flesh. He ignored the irritation and eased the ball gag out of Clara's mouth. After letting it drop below her chin, he uncapped the water and placed it against her lower lip. She swallowed twice, then gagged, coughed, and pulled away.

"Take it easy," he whispered. "There's lots of water."

Clara rested her head back on the carpet and watched him. He capped the bottle and tried to put the ball gag back in place.

"Wait," she muttered.

He paused, the gag still in his hand, one eyebrow raised in a question.

"Were you the one I talked to online?" She swallowed. "Did you lure me here?"

He shook his head. "Not me. I was hired to keep you company for a week."

He lifted the gag. She turned her face away, an expression of fear filling her eyes as they widened.

"Wait," she moaned. "Please."

"What?"

"Can we talk?"

"We're not here to talk."

He grabbed the side of her face to force it back up to jam

the gag in.

"Please," she begged. "Just tell me what's happening. Why are you doing this—?"

It was easy work gagging her again. She moaned under the gag, her bloodshot eyes watering.

"I do this for money." He rose to his feet and stared down at her, the pressure from the weapon easing off the small of his back. "Nothing more. Just a paycheck."

Back at the hotel window, he stared at the rain as it eased off a bit. "Just a paycheck," he repeated.

Clara moaned and squirmed on the floor.

Ansgar's cell phone dinged.

The screen lit up with the client's message. He needed a picture. Something current. Something with her bound.

"That'll be easy."

Ansgar grabbed the newspaper that was left at his door that morning and held the date of the paper close to the camera with Clara squirming on the floor in the background. He took several pics, then sent them on his burner phone to the client.

Moments later, the client thanked him.

"Pics sent. More money in the bank. Easy job."

Clara squirmed when he went to stare out the window again. He could do this in his sleep. Sitting still for hundreds of hours as a sniper had prepared him for jobs like this. He had to be right in his mind to take this on. He had to be right with himself. The time spent alone was enormous, the time spent thinking, deducing the life of the target. What had they done to warrant a death sentence someone else was willing to pay for? When it came to those fuckers in Afghanistan, he knew it was the religious fundamentalists who had ruined

Islam for everyone because the Koran was quiet and peaceful as a rule. But when it came to non-religious hits, he always wondered why.

With Clara, it was different somehow. Being young and pretty, with her whole life ahead of her, made him doubly curious why she had to be held for a week, then executed. What could she possibly have done to deserve this?

Ansgar headed over to the minibar and poured himself a glass of wine. The bottle was almost empty from earlier, so he topped his glass up to the rim. He would watch the rain and, in the distance, the Toronto airport, then take a nap. It would be a long week. A time to offer reflection. A time to imagine and plan his next move, his next country.

Back at the window, the instant his wine glass touched his lips, someone knocked.

Then came a muffled female voice. "Housekeeping."

Clara swung her head toward the sound and moaned loudly.

"Not today," Ansgar shouted as he stepped closer to Clara.

The woman on the other side of the door tried the handle.

"Housekeeping," she called again as if she hadn't heard him.

"I said, not today," he shouted.

Clara wouldn't be quiet. She thrashed on the floor between the wall and the bed, moaning quite loud now. He had to shut her up.

The door clicked like it was being opened.

"What the fuck?" he muttered.

Ansgar set his wine on the bedside table and dove over the bed to Clara's side. With his shoes still on, he lifted his foot and kicked her in the side of the head hard enough for any Striker to appreciate.

Clara quieted instantly; the fight knocked out of her.

The door clicked behind him.

He spun around. It was still closed.

Without a second to lose, he hopped off the bed and rushed to the hotel room door.

Someone was going to lose their job today.

"Or I'll just fucking kill you along with Clara," he whispered as he grabbed the door handle and tore it open.

Chapter 15

In the hotel lobby, Benjamin was nowhere in sight. Soaked through from the rain, Sarah headed for the hotel restaurant while Daniel and Alex fanned out to search the common areas. Aaron went up to check the room they had rented for the week, which kept him less visible to members of the public as he was supposed to be dead. They agreed to meet back in the lobby in five minutes.

Sarah found Benjamin in the hotel restaurant nursing a coffee. He'd strategically taken a table that gave him visual access to the lobby.

"Sarah," he said as she approached his seat. "So good to see you."

They embraced. "Sorry, I'm soaked. We had to run through the rain from the parking garage, but now we're heading up to Clara's room."

"I've watched the elevators all day. I haven't seen either

Clara or Ansgar. They haven't come down."

Sarah pushed his coffee away, took him by the hand, and led him to the lobby, where she filled Benjamin in on their plan to get Clara away from Ansgar. She shivered twice as her wet clothes lay like a coating of ice on her skin. She would change into a maid's uniform soon anyway, providing they found one without too much trouble.

Alex and Daniel showed up moments later. Aaron came off the elevator and joined them.

It was time to go for Clara.

Sarah left the group and started down the corridor toward the restaurant until she came upon the maid's room. She entered and scanned the shelves looking for anything resembling a uniform. The shelves were loaded with towels, bedsheets, paper coffee cups, creamers, little packages that held stir sticks and coffee mate, and many other items that the maids filled rooms with, but no uniforms.

She moved deeper and lifted towels and a laundry bag out of the way to see what was behind them.

Nothing to wear. Nothing resembling clothes anywhere.

The door opened, startling her.

"Can I help you?" a woman asked.

Sarah righted herself and faced the woman. A fully uniformed hotel maid, a nametag on her chest. How convenient. On the other hand, Sarah couldn't take this woman's uniform. Not if they would stay in the hotel for a few days.

"I'm soaked through," Sarah said. She lifted the edges of her shirt, looked down, then back up, a sheepish grin on her face. "Just wondered if I could get an extra towel for the room."

At first, the maid didn't look like she believed her. The expression on her face was one of distrust. She grabbed two towels and held them out to Sarah.

"Here's two towels. There's nothing over there," she added, referring to how far inside the room Sarah had gone.

Sarah looked down at the floor, trying her best to appear self-conscious. "I'm sorry." She met the maid's unwavering eyes. "Just wanted to get new bedsheets as well. Had an issue last night. Kinda didn't want to bring it to anyone's attention." She scrunched up her face and looked away. "It's embarrassing."

Like a cloud lifted off the woman's face, she smiled, and the suspicious gaze turned to one of warmth.

"It's okay. Here, let me help you."

The maid moved into the room, close enough for Sarah to see her name on the tag over her breast pocket. Pam Prall.

"Thanks, Pam," Sarah said, relief in her voice. "I really appreciate it."

Pam handed her a clean white sheet.

"Is that all you need?" Pam asked. "I can have more brought up to your room."

"No, this is perfect." Sarah stepped around her. "Thanks."

"What room number are you in so I can write it down on our inventory sheet here?"

Pam grabbed a clipboard and held a pen over the paper attached to the board.

Without knowing the number of the room Aaron had gotten at the hotel, she had to make one up on the spot.

"Room 1025."

Pam frowned, then wrote the number down on her

clipboard.

Sarah backed out of the room and started for the elevators. When she knocked on Ansgar's room, she would have to go dressed as she was, but at least she carried bedsheets and two towels. It would look somewhat authentic with the explanation that her uniform got wrecked in the rain.

She waited for the elevator, the details going through her head with less importance the more she thought of them. The only important thing she needed to focus on was getting access to Ansgar's room.

She got on the elevator, pushed the number ten, and mentally prepared herself for what she was about to find. Hopefully, Clara was still alive and in good condition. With four men like Aaron and his dojo teachers, Ansgar—ex-Navy Seal or not—was in for a world of hurt if he had damaged Clara in any way.

On the tenth floor, she exited the elevator and read the signs for which way to go. Ansgar's room was to her right. Heading down the length of the hall, she felt alone but knew at least three of the four men she was here with watched her. Aaron and Alex were in the stairwell beside Ansgar's door, and Daniel was at the other end of the hall. Benjamin hid farther back, still not fully recovered from a bullet wound courtesy of the Enzo Cartel. Even though Aaron had lost a finger to that cartel, he wasn't letting that stop him from participating in this operation.

As she stopped in front of Ansgar's door, Sarah leaned closer and listened to the room beyond. Silence. She leaned closer still. Nothing.

The stairwell door opened a crack. Reinforcements were close. Their plan was solid. Things could go wrong, but they were ready.

Sarah knocked. "Housekeeping."

A man's voice offered a muffled reply.

Sarah scanned the hallway, hoping no one opened their room doors, and stepped out to see her.

She knocked again. "Housekeeping."

Then she tried the door to make Ansgar think she would walk in.

"I said, not today," he shouted.

Sarah was sure she heard someone moan from the other side of the door.

She pulled on the handle, harder this time.

A muffled male voice said three words that could have been, "What the fuck?"

She was getting to him. A loud thump, like someone jumped and landed on the floor hard, resonated from the room.

She played with the handle some more, hoping it drove him insane.

Then someone moved toward the door. As he stomped toward her on the other side of the door, Sarah couldn't make out what he was saying. She stepped back and prepared herself.

The stairwell door behind her vibrated as Aaron and Alex got ready.

Ansgar's room door clicked as the lock disengaged, then it was yanked back to reveal a large man who looked part bodybuilder, part UFC fighter. The man's neck was thick, a vein pulsing by his collarbone. In a tight T-shirt, his thick chest, broad shoulders, and meat hooks for arms, almost made her stumble back out of reach.

"New towels and sheets for your room, sir."

Sarah moved toward him. Ansgar's meaty hand clamped down on Sarah's shoulder as he leaned out and looked down the length of the hallway. When he righted himself, the door to the stairwell behind her ripped open.

What they didn't account for was how strong Ansgar was. One second, Sarah was in the hotel hallway, and the next, Ansgar's hand tightened on her shoulder and yanked her inside his room. He slammed the door closed with his body, engaging the lock at the same moment Aaron and Alex smashed into the door.

Sarah had stayed on her feet. She took the entire room in with one quick look. Clara's feet stuck out from behind the bed by the room's outer wall. White ties were wrapped around her wrists and ankles. She wasn't moving. A redness, like a bruise starting, formed on her cheek.

Sarah pivoted back to face Ansgar.

She was too late.

Something careened off her jaw. The impact was so hard and fast that she lifted off her feet, dropped the bed sheet and towels, and flew onto the queen bed. Before she could turn over and get off the bed, Ansgar was on her. A fierce thunder of pounding smashed into the hotel room door as Aaron and Alex tried unsuccessfully to come through it.

Ansgar was fast. Too fast. Sarah flailed at him as he grabbed her arms in a vice grip, crossed them over her chest, and leaned his body weight down onto her. She spat at his face and bucked under him, but he remained in a place like a large boulder, his weight enough to subdue her.

"You're not housekeeping," he breathed out through a tight jaw.

She bucked again, harder.

He tightened his grip to the point where her wrists felt like they'd snap like brittle twigs with another ounce of pressure.

"Who the fuck are you?" he asked, an inch from her face.

"I'm the one," she breathed deep, his weight making it hard to fight and talk, "who is going to," she forced breath in again, "break your nose."

She jerked her head up, her forehead smashing into the bridge of Ansgar's nose with a sickening crunch. His hands released her instantly as he reached for his face. He had made a mistake by getting too close to her. With her pinned down, Ansgar had felt safe.

He sat up, his weight still wedging her into the bed. Blood poured from his nose, dropped over his lips, and continued down and off his chin. She couldn't get out from under him, though. He had to weigh in at two hundred and twenty pounds. She thrashed left and right, but he stayed on like he rode a bronco at a local rodeo.

Frantic that he would rain fists down on her in the helpless position she found herself in, she looked to the bedside table for a weapon. Her jaw, where she had been sucker punched, felt twice its normal size.

The pounding on the hotel room door hadn't abated. Sarah needed this to end before a hotel guest called the authorities.

A full glass of red wine sat on the bedside table.

Sarah grabbed it, turned back to Ansgar as he let go of his nose and balled up a fist, and thrust only the liquid at him, keeping the glass to use as a weapon.

His arm dropped to block the glass of wine, which

stopped her hand suddenly, spilling the contents all over herself. Red wine covered her already wet chest and face. It got into her hair, her mouth, her eyes, and up her nose.

Sarah gasped, coughed, and braced for a fist, but it didn't come.

The fire alarm sounded throughout the building.

Ansgar twisted on top of her and stared at the door.

"Fuck!" he roared.

She wiped her eyes, waited for a breath, then bucked again. This time she raised him up and forward, so he'd fall on top of her. As he rose over her, his hands flew forward to break his fall, blood descending from his broken nose, mixing with the red wine stains. She lunged under his body, clamped onto his crotch with her right hand, and squeezed.

The fire alarm drowned out most of his high-pitched scream, but not all of it.

Manic to get her to release her grip, he flailed with his arms, hitting her several times without disengaging her hand. She shouted back as she tightened her hand on him.

In a desperate move, he rolled sideways, his weight taking him to the left over the edge of the bed. Even if she could have followed him that way, her hand would've released his package.

The second he was off her and on the floor beside Clara, Sarah rolled the other way, hit the floor standing, and bolted for the door. She needed to let Aaron in. She needed help.

With each step, she dreaded Ansgar's weight landing on her back or the sound of a gun firing behind her.

But then she was at the door. She ripped it open, and Aaron almost fell into the room, followed by Alex and Daniel.

She pointed behind the bed. All three men rushed over. Aaron looked back at her and gave a short jerk of his head. She could only imagine what he was thinking with all the red wine and Ansgar's blood covering her upper body.

Ansgar had disappeared.

She put her back to the wall and scanned the room before pointing under the bed. Aaron dropped. Alex dropped. The bed sheets were flung aside. Aaron popped back up. He jerked his head.

Movement by the bathroom door caught her eye. A blur of motion filled her vision the second she went to turn that way.

Ansgar grabbed Sarah around the neck and lifted her up against the wall. Aaron shouted something, but Sarah missed it because of the pressure building in her head and the fire alarm blaring from only a few feet away now.

Ansgar's eyes widened at the sight of Aaron. Recognition flashed across his face. He understood now. Aaron wasn't dead.

People ran up the hallway. Ansgar saw Alex, and his face changed to one of extreme anger.

Someone stuck their head in the room.

"Is everyone okay?" a woman shouted, loud enough to be heard over the alarm.

Ansgar let Sarah go, spun around the doorframe, and disappeared.

Aaron leaped over the bed and ran for the door. The woman who had stepped inside a moment before jumped sideways to let him pass.

Sarah collapsed to the floor, massaging her throat, trying to get breath through the small tube that had been clamped shut a moment before.

Alex and Daniel were doing something with Clara. Sarah got back to her feet, stars blinking in her peripheral vision, and addressed the woman at the door.

Pam Prall.

Shit.

She tried to smile.

"Accident?" Pam asked, loud enough to be heard. She took in the room, the red wine stains all over the bed. Then looked Sarah up and down. "I think you need more than sheets."

The fire alarm clicked off, leaving them in a deafening silence.

Alex and Daniel helped Clara to her feet, then walked the dazed woman toward the door. Clara seemed half asleep, her eyes opening, then closing.

"Too much to drink last night," Daniel said quietly to Pam. "We got her."

"Wait," Pam said.

They stopped. Pam stepped closer, trying to address Clara.

"What's her name?"

"Clara Olafson," Sarah said, happy nothing in her jaw was broken. Saying Clara's name didn't hurt, even as her adrenaline waned.

"Clara?" Pam said.

"Yeah," Clara mumbled.

"You okay?"

Clara nodded.

Pam stepped back and out of the way. "I just didn't think this was her room."

"It isn't," Sarah said, her voice cracking. "This is Peter Ford's room. He invited everyone for drinks. Clara had too many." She offered Pam an embarrassed smile for Clara's sake. "We'll help her back to our room for coffee. Send Peter the bill for the red wine-stained sheets."

Sarah started down the hall, Daniel and Alex guiding Clara with them.

They had failed miserably. It had been a dumb idea. They got Clara out safely, but they had planned to rush the door when Ansgar opened it like a home invasion. But he was faster than they had expected. Faster, stronger, and more brutal.

Sarah was lucky to leave that room without broken bones, teeth, or worse.

Benjamin opened their hotel room door as they neared it. He stepped out to help. At the door, Sarah paused to look at the length of the hall, but Aaron was nowhere in sight. He had chased Ansgar down the stairs. How far did they get? Were they fighting somewhere in the building? Did Aaron need help?

If Aaron lost Ansgar, where would they pick him up again? They didn't even get a chance to go through Ansgar's things in his room. What scared her was that Aaron wasn't armed, and when Ansgar ran from the room, she saw the bulge of his weapon in the back of his pants.

Everything just got fucked up, and Sarah needed a change of clothes, too. Her T-shirt and jeans were stained with blood and red wine.

"This day just keeps getting better," she muttered under her breath, her throat dry.

Once inside their room, she closed the door. Not half a

minute later, someone knocked.

Sarah checked the peephole, saw it was Aaron, and opened the door.

"I lost him," Aaron said, trying to catch his breath. "Followed the blood trail for a few floors but lost him. I'm sorry. He's gone."

"We fucked up," Sarah said as she closed the door and dropped into Aaron's arms.

"Big time," Aaron added.

"Not totally," Alex said as he stood over Clara, who was sprawled out on the bed.

Alex held up a cell phone. "Ansgar's," he said.

Chapter 16

ANTON OLAFSON HADN'T SLEPT much in the past two days. Wandering the streets of his hometown had proven fruitless. People recognized him and knew where he lived. Trying to find a random girl to kill was a waste of time. His resolve dwindled as he realized he wasn't sure he could go through with it.

He rubbed his face and sat on the edge of his bed. Today he planned a trip to Aarhus on the train. Performing a random kill in Aarhus, the second largest city in Denmark, which was only a fifteen-minute train ride away, was the best idea he had come up with—if he was still going to do it.

In and out. Hit Aarhus, find a back street by the open water or the canal, use his phone to film the life leaving the woman, then send the video to the man calling himself PAIN and fulfill his pact with the man.

Would he get Clara back? Would he get caught? Did it

matter to him one way or the other if he got caught? His life was over without Clara.

His cell phone dinged.

He hadn't turned his computer on in days, not wanting to see what PAIN would do next. The computer age had created so many criminals because of what anyone could do with a computer. Along with that, though, computers caught criminals. Just like him. He should never have kept those images on his hard drive.

His cell phone dinged again.

Anton moaned and got off the bed. He walked by the phone, turned on the coffee maker, tapped the button to boot his computer up, and headed to the bathroom. Whatever PAIN wanted, if that were him texting, he would see it on the big screen. Today was the third day of the PAIN PACT, and Anton planned a long walk through Aarhus with his cell phone. He would do this for Clara. He would do this deed and do everything he could to avoid capture. People died all the time, and it wasn't Clara's time to go.

Five minutes later, coffee in hand, he was back at his computer. He sat down to a blank screen. When he tapped the keyboard, nothing happened. After checking the cords to ensure it was plugged in, he tried the ON button again. Nothing.

"What the hell?" he whispered.

The cell phone dinged beside him.

He set his coffee down and grabbed the phone. Four messages from PAIN. All the same, coming in every few minutes.

"Lonely, asshole?" Anton whispered. "Need attention?"

Anton opened the message.

Your computer is dead. I've killed it. Your PAIN PACT has changed. The girl must look like your daughter. Absolute must. Blond. Tall. Fit. Strong. I'm sure that won't be hard to find in Scandinavia.

Anton's hand vibrated the cell phone as he read the message, his thoughts going to what he would do to the man sending the messages if he could get to him. Tracing someone like PAIN was near impossible. There would be rerouters, VPNs, and remailers.

Anton once tracked a man who had broken into a set of servers and made a virtual network between the servers. Then he connected them and placed his actual computer behind the server computers, using them as a shield to hide behind.

Another hacker had located a free WiFi access point, modified his Mac address, and booted his computer from a "live CD" running only RAM. Had he not changed his Mac address, the access point would have enabled Anton to locate him because access points record the "probe request" when acquiring the WiFi. But Anton and his crew nailed the guy because he was known to the café he'd been using. It would have been smarter for the guy to go to a different café daily, or at least when he wanted to hack someone.

There was almost no way to completely hide an IP address online since the IP protocol requires it to be online, but guys like PAIN use remailers for their email. They use a VPN and then go into a TOR to avoid IP address tracking. The best hackers never use a Windows-based program because of all the holes in Windows, and they're constantly moving around. They often use Linux.

To catch this guy electronically, he would need more time than Clara had left. The hacker going by the name PAIN would probably see it coming, too.

All Anton could do was decide whether or not he would comply with the PAIN PACT. At this point, he was still willing to move forward. Providing he had assurances Clara was okay.

He typed a message back to PAIN asking for something to prove Clara was fine.

After a minute's wait while he sat and let his coffee cool on the desk beside him, a message came through. A picture of Clara. He opened the photo and used his fingers to zoom in.

She lay on her back on a carpeted floor in what looked like a hotel room. Her hands and ankles were bound, a ball gag in her mouth. The look on her face, in her eyes, seemed authentic. She was afraid. Her ashen, pallid looks told him everything. The tendons standing out on her neck, the tight lips, tight shoulders. They were holding her, but they hadn't hurt her.

Seeing Clara in that state convinced him this wasn't a setup. Clara didn't pose for this photo. A kidnapper took it— Anton's blackmailer.

Anton decided at that moment, when he stared at the picture of his daughter bound and gagged, that he would kill a random girl. One that looked like his daughter. He would do it within a few days to secure Clara's release, and he hoped the hacker wouldn't reveal Anton's pictures of his indiscretions, but he felt that was unlikely.

Everything Anton had done came with a price. A price he was willing to pay. But Clara was too high a price. He couldn't allow Clara, his only daughter, to pay the price for him.

He texted PAIN back. He told him that everything was a

go and that he expected him to keep his word and release Clara when Anton forwarded the video of the murder.

The response took four minutes.

PAIN maintained that his terms were to be unquestioned and honored. All he wanted was random murder. Just one girl. One video. Then the nightmare would be over, and Clara would return home.

Just one murder.

Anton shot up from his desk. He grabbed his coffee cup and tried to take a sip, but it spilled down his chin and onto his chest.

With a shout of exasperation, he tossed the full cup across the room, where it smashed into pieces against the wall, the coffee making a splatter mark upward toward the ceiling.

It made him think of the blood.

The blood on his hands.

Chapter 17

It wasn't just Ansgar's nose that was broken. His pride was broken. His ego shattered after being bested by a crazy woman. His connection to the client had been severed. He had to obtain a burner phone as soon as possible to reach out and let the client know he was still in the game. Or find a way to get his own phone back.

He had checked his gun, too. When he flew off the bed, it had jammed into his back. A cursory glance revealed everything was fine with it.

Before contacting the client, he needed a hospital to set his nose. The pain made his eyes constantly water while he breathed through his mouth. A highly noticeable characteristic, too, which made him less able to stay undetected in public.

He hailed a taxi on Airport Road, half a kilometer from the hotel, and told the driver to take him to the nearest hospital. When the driver asked him what happened, Ansgar explained it away as an accident.

Aaron Stevens was supposed to be dead. How could that be explained away? Aaron had to know that Ansgar was the bomber. That's how he figured out where Ansgar was. He'd had that student follow him. Aaron had stood in his dojo and talked to Ansgar like any other customer.

Aaron had played Ansgar and then came looking for him. Correction: Aaron came for the girl. And he brought friends. But how could Aaron have known about him? How did he know about Clara?

Ansgar stared out the taxi's window as the driver raced along the highway toward a hospital in Etobicoke, pondering the various ways that Aaron could know as much as he did, and all he could come up with was the client had lied to Ansgar. It was the only plausible solution. The client was playing both of them. Give Ansgar a job, then tell Aaron what was happening. To what end, though? Why would the client do that? Payment had been made to Ansgar. The money was transferred on schedule. He had done everything the client asked of him without fail and on time. So why send Aaron?

Unless the client wanted out of the rest of the plan. If so, then cancel the deal, and Ansgar would walk away. He would leave Clara in the room and leave Canada. As a PMC, the client would know how Ansgar dealt with the job details changing. He wouldn't care as long as the payment was still made.

To send an amateur martial arts gym owner after him to rescue the girl infuriated Ansgar. The client would need a believable explanation, or he would be dealt a consequence.

But before all that, Ansgar would head back to the hotel once his nose was set. He needed to hurt Aaron. He needed Clara back so he could hurt her—ruin her—until the client explained what was going on.

The only leverage he had was in that hotel. If Aaron were still there when he returned, he would ask the right questions. Then he would kill him. Aaron had to die just as the client had asked of him when he blew up the dojo.

After that, he would explain the new rules to the client. Rule number one was Clara would need to die, too, because the job was over. The client ended the job when he tried to fuck Ansgar over. The payment would be made in full, or Ansgar would have to come after the client as well. He already knew who the client was and where the asshole lived in Toronto. Ansgar never worked for someone he knew nothing about.

As the taxi pulled into the hospital parking lot, Ansgar understood that he had been played for a fool by a group of punks.

Each one would die when he was done with Aaron and those with him. Especially that fucking girl who squeezed his nut sack. Before she died by his hand, he would take vise grips and squeeze her crotch until she bled to see how she liked it.

The taxi stopped. Ansgar paid the driver, got out, and headed into the hospital, eager to get this over with and back to the hotel.

He had too many people to kill and too little time to do it.

Chapter 18

BEN WILSON WOKE WITH a start. He jerked upright on his desk chair and bumped his knees against the edge of his desk. Rubbing his right knee where it hurt the most, he tapped buttons to wake his computer screens up as they'd gone to sleep, too.

Anton Olafson was right where he wanted him. The anticipation of a random Danish girl being killed on camera would be great footage for his game. Like a virgin on her wedding night, Ben anticipated the video Anton would send through within a day or two with bated breath.

Ben unwrapped the end of a Mars bar and bit into it. There were some days that was all he did. Eat Mars bars, sit at his desk, fall asleep in his chair, and manipulate lives like a god.

At first, it was small stuff. Hacking Facebook accounts and screwing with the few friends he had. Then it got more serious when he hacked his mother's bank account and transferred large sums of money to his own personal account. Before her death, she had no idea what he'd been up to. Hacking the account, and transferring money, was something of his forte now. That was how he paid contractors like that ex-Navy Seal guy, Ansgar Holm.

Ben had always been money-centered. Even in high school, a few of his quirky friends got together with him and started a group called S.I.S.T., which stood for Students Invested Stocks Traded. The acronym sounded like the word *cyst*, which was exactly what they were going for.

He had loved acronyms as far back as he could remember and used them as often as possible. Like his online moniker, PAIN. It was much easier to approach the subjects who had to do things for him with a PAIN PACT than it was to say the Passive Aggressive internet Nomad wants to enter into a Performance, Action, Commitment Transaction with you. People responded better to PAIN PACT.

He brought up the local news on the smaller screen to the left and browsed what the *Toronto Sun* newspaper said about the terrorist bombing of the martial arts dojo in Toronto. It took him a second to find anything on it as the police response at a nearby hotel took all the coverage. The fire department had been called to the hotel, but it was a false alarm.

He checked the name of the hotel. It was the same one Ansgar was keeping Clara in.

"Shit wave," he whispered.

His fingers danced over the keyboard as he checked several websites for more information. Contacting Ansgar directly would be a mistake if the authorities had his phone.

When he couldn't learn anything new, he tried to hack into the hotel's computers but was stopped. Then he tried the cameras on the street but saw only police cars in front of the hotel.

He had to reach out. He had to see if Ansgar still had Clara. If they got arrested, that would put him in an awkward position. The last message Ansgar had sent to him was a picture of Clara bound and gagged on the hotel room floor.

Ben typed, *Are you still secure?*

Then he waited.

One minute passed. Then another. With each passing second, his stomach got heavier, and he felt he might have had too many Mars bars.

An image popped up to signify Ansgar was typing.

Ben released pent-up air and leaned forward, waiting to see what Ansgar said, his hands held in small fists.

Secure. Waiting for further instructions.

Ben typed back. *What about a heavy presence at the hotel?*

Pranksters. Nothing to do with us.

Ben lowered his head and breathed through his mouth for a moment. When he looked up, Ansgar had typed another message.

Too risky to stay here. Moving her. Will contact with new location soon.

"What?" Ben said out loud. "That's not the deal."

He typed furiously.

Stay put if the authorities are not there for you.

He waited. Five maddening minutes later came the reply.

You're not calling the shots anymore.

Ben froze in his chair. After a moment, he wheeled it

back and got to his feet, his legs shaking with adrenaline. The pain in his back was minimal today.

"What has happened?" he said. "Shit wave, this isn't right. No one ever talks to me like that. Never."

He jumped back onto his chair and typed quickly, his fingers dancing over the keyboard. The man wouldn't know what hit him when he was done with Ansgar. Ben Wilson was basically off the map. He could do anything he wanted to people like Ansgar Holm without fear of retribution. Ansgar could never find him. No one could.

When he was done typing, he reread the message.

Then he hit send.

Ansgar would think twice before defying the man who controlled the fate of other men from behind a desk. They would all die for him, for his legacy game. Then he would have his retribution. After what the NC3 Director Anton Olafson did to him, he, too, would pay the ultimate price.

And with what Ansgar was trying to do, he, too, would pay.

In the end, Ben Wilson was a god simply collecting debts.

Debts owed the Devil.

Chapter 19

SARAH SAT ON THE edge of the hotel bed, holding Clara's hand to comfort her. Clara leaned her back against the wall, her body scrunched up as if trying to stay as far away from the four men in the room as possible. Aaron paced the floor by the window. Alex sat in the chair, tapping at Ansgar's cell phone. Daniel and Benjamin stood on either side of the hotel room door, taking turns looking out the peephole.

Sarah tapped the top of Clara's hand.

"I assure you, everything's okay now," Sarah said softly. "No one will get to you. Soon, this will all be over, and you can return to Denmark."

Clara gave her a short, jerking nod of her head. The girl was frightened, and it didn't help that Sarah sat before her, covered in Ansgar's blood and in a red-wine-stained shirt. She had to change her clothes as soon as she could. Leaving the hotel was out of the question looking like this.

The time on the bedside alarm clock warned her that she had just over three hours until her flight to Copenhagen began boarding. That left one hour in the room before she had to get to the airport to clear security.

Aaron stopped pacing. He looked like he was thinking about something.

"We can't stay here," Aaron said.

"Agreed," Sarah added.

"Can you tell me what's happening?" Clara asked loud enough for Sarah to hear. "Who are you people?"

Clara spoke English with an accent. Not a harsh one, but enough to sound Scandinavian.

Sarah smiled warmly and softened her eyes. "We're your friends." She adjusted herself on the bed to look directly at Clara. "Tell us more about yourself. Why are you in Canada? How did you end up in that room with that man?"

Clara glanced past Sarah to look at Aaron, then back at Sarah. "It was a mistake."

"How so?"

"I was playing months ago on my computer. Bored. And I joined a website that I shouldn't have."

Sarah resisted the urge to look at Aaron but heard him moving. After a moment, he stopped moving, probably because he took a seat.

"What website, Clara?" Sarah kept her voice soft and gentle.

Clara's cheeks darkened with color. She looked away from Sarah.

"Plenty of Fish," she mumbled. "I met a guy. He was into everything I was. Even quoted Shakespeare. When he suggested we meet, I agreed. He paid for the whole trip to

Canada." Clara shrugged. "What was the worst? I got to see Canada for free." She regained some of her composure and tilted her head to look at Sarah. "So I came a few days ago."

Sarah pointed at the door. "I think the worst was what just happened." She let go of Clara's hand and got to her feet. "What can you tell us about the guy you met online? Do you have an address? Where were you supposed to meet?"

"We were to meet in this hotel. I was to take a room that he'd set up for me. He hired a driver to pick me up. When he knocked, the password was the name of the website Plenty of Fish. When that man said the name, I thought he was the driver." She wiped her right eye. "I've made a terrible mess of things."

"It's okay, Clara. You're safe now. None of the men here will let anything happen to you."

"I don't understand why you're here," Clara said. "No one knew I was in Canada. I didn't even tell my dad."

Sarah and Aaron exchanged glances, then Sarah stared at the window momentarily, thinking about how best to answer Clara.

"Things are all connected," Sarah said. "Sometimes, it's just fate that we met up."

"How do you mean fate?" Clara asked.

Sarah faced her. "You know that building that blew up in Toronto?"

Clara nodded.

"That was his." Sarah pointed at Aaron. "These three guys are his teachers. They were supposed to die in that explosion. Someone wanted to murder them. We traced it to the man who had kidnapped you, and we came to make things right. Our plan didn't work how we wanted, but we got you out. Now we wait for a few days and see what comes next."

"But how did you know he was here?" Clara asked.

"Aaron met him before he tried to blow the place up. A friend of ours did a little research and came up with an alias. We tracked that man to this hotel. Benjamin rented this room and waited for us to get here." Sarah extended her arms, palms up. "And here we are."

Clara seemed to like that explanation.

Sarah walked over to Aaron, then looked down at Alex. She eyed Daniel and Benjamin by the door. "Guys, I have little time. I need clothes. Then you need to leave this hotel. There's one across the street. Or try one farther away. But you need to lay low until I get back from Denmark."

"Denmark?" Clara said from behind her. "Why are you going there?"

Sarah put her hands on her hips when she looked back at Clara. "What is your father's name?"

"Anton."

"Do you have a brother?"

Clara shook her head. "No, and my mother died years ago."

"Okay, I'm going to ask you a horrible question, but I need the truth. Are you okay with that?"

Clara nodded.

"Do you know anything about boys being molested?"

Clara didn't look surprised by the question. She just blinked, seemed to think about it for a moment, then shook her head.

"I know nothing of that stuff except what I've read in the news over the years."

Most of what Vivian wrote in the time capsule was coming together. Oaf and his son were Olafson, Clara's last name. Her father was Anton Olafson. Aaron's death had been averted. They discovered The Clock was Ansgar Holm, and he was holding the Danish girl, the *blonde* Danish girl. Vivian said, *protect the Danish girl*, and that was what they would do.

Sarah still had to figure out what Vivian meant when she said Pain was behind everything and how Vivian said that if they were to stop Pain, then everyone would live. Her sister had added that even then, boys would continue to be molested.

A thought hit her. "Clara? What city did you live in in Denmark?"

"Skanderborg."

The name felt like a punch to the gut. That was exactly where Vivian had instructed Sarah to go. Skanderborg. What the hell was in Skanderborg that was so important? Could Pain be there? If the person behind all this lured Clara to Toronto, why did Sarah have to go to Denmark? Maybe he was luring her away from Skanderborg. Ansgar holding her here kept her away. Or maybe she was grabbing at straws.

Aaron touched her shoulder and gently turned her around. "You have to get ready. You're running out of time."

Sarah touched his hand, then rested her cheek on his shoulder.

"I know. But I don't want to leave you. It wasn't that long ago that I thought you were dead."

"It's Vivian. Look what she has done in the last twenty-four hours. There's no way I'd be alive today if it weren't for her. I understand Vivian saw your death, too."

Sarah lifted her head and stared into his eyes. "I'm not going anywhere. I can't do this. Why is Vivian not talking to me? Why is she talking to everyone else but me?"

"I don't know. But you have to do what she says to stay alive. That's what I'd go with."

After a moment, Sarah nodded. "You're right."

"Who's Vivian?" Clara asked.

"Aaron can tell you about Vivian after I leave."

The phone in Alex's hand buzzed. He looked down at it, then held it up for Sarah and Aaron to read it.

Are you still secure?

"How do we respond to that?" Aaron asked.

"That's Ansgar's boss," Sarah said. "He's the one behind all this. He may even be the guy we're looking for."

"What should I type back?" Alex asked.

Sarah stared at the ceiling for a moment. "Whoever it is might see something on the news about emergency services responding to this hotel. That might be the reason he's asking if everything's secure."

"We need to locate this guy," Aaron added.

"Agreed." Sarah punched her open palm. "Antagonize him. Tell him we're secure and waiting for further instructions. Maybe we'll be able to set up a meeting."

Alex typed. They waited for a response. The phone dinged.

"It says, 'What about heavy presence at the hotel'?" Alex read.

Sarah stepped closer to Alex. "Type back. 'Pranksters. Nothing to do with us.'"

Alex typed. They waited again. After a few seconds, Sarah moved closer to Alex's chair again.

"Add this. 'Too risky to stay here. Moving her. Will contact with new location soon.'"

Alex nodded and typed. The phone buzzed a response. He handed it to Sarah.

She read it out loud. "Stay put if the authorities are not there for you."

Then she typed, *You're not calling the shots anymore*, but hovered over the send button.

"Does this work, Aaron?" She showed him the message.

"If you're riling him up, it works. But to what end?"

"We have to get him out from behind this number on a phone. In the meantime, when I leave for the airport, give this number and everything else you have to Darwin and Rosina. Let's see if they can trace anything. You guys stay with Clara until this is over, and stay in touch with me. As soon as I get to Skanderborg, I'll find out what this is all about and then come home. Three, four days max. Cool?"

Aaron nodded. Then each martial arts teacher nodded as she turned to look at them.

She hit send on the last message.

"Why are you going to Skanderborg?" Clara asked. "Does it have anything to do with my father?"

"Not sure," Sarah said as she handed the phone to Aaron. "I just know I have to."

"But why?"

Sarah smiled. "Too long a story to explain right now. Aaron will fill you in while I'm away."

"I'd like to go home. Maybe I can just come with you."

Sarah shook her head. "I'm sorry. Until this is over, I need you to stay with these men. They'll protect you. Think of them as bodyguards for now."

Clara shrank back from Sarah as if trying to become part of the wall.

"So I'm still being held against my will, just without the restraints?"

Sarah frowned and moved closer to the bed. "No, you're not. You're being kept safe while someone named Pain is out to hurt you. That man, Ansgar Holm, is a military contractor hired to kidnap you. Staying with these guys," she gestured toward the men, "keeps you safe. Sending you back out there makes you a target."

Sarah couldn't tell if what she was saying was getting through to Clara. It was obvious the girl just wanted it all to be over.

An internal conflict raged within Sarah. Vivian was gone. No longer directing her with information and answers. Since Vivian had always been there, an emptiness was left in her wake. The loneliness of not having her sister in her head and having to leave Aaron for the next few days ate at her heart like a cold, wet towel in her stomach.

"I don't want to leave," she said to Aaron. "It's not right."

He cocked his head sideways. "Come on, Sarah. You, of all people, know Vivian. You have to go. I accept that. Why can't you?"

"You're right, but I still don't want to leave. Whether I have to or want to—there's a big difference."

"Who is Vivian?" Clara asked again.

"They'll tell you after. I'm out of time." Sarah moved toward the door. "Aaron, where can I get a change of clothes? I can't go to the airport dressed like this."

"You can't leave the hotel room dressed like that. What's

your size? I'll go buy something and come back."

"I've got clothes," Clara said from the corner. "Take some of mine. We look like we're about the same size."

Sarah looked Clara up and down, then at Aaron. "She's right. That's perfect. Someone take Clara to her room. Get me clothes."

Clara got up off the bed and headed to the door. Aaron came over and eased it open. He glanced down the hall, then shut the door.

"There are a few hotel employees by Clara's door, still working in Ansgar's room."

"Authorities?" Sarah asked.

He shook his head. "Didn't see any."

"Okay. Go." She touched Clara's arm. "You're allowed to enter your own hotel room, but remember, if anyone asks, you were at a party. You drank too much. Aaron's a friend. Got it."

Clara nodded her understanding.

"We'll be right back," Aaron said as he slipped out the door.

Sarah stared out the tenth-floor window for the five minutes they were gone. The rain subsided while she shook with nerves. Why leave Aaron now? Why fly all the way around the world to a small town in Denmark? For what?

Vivian had always proven herself hard to like, hard to get used to. This was one of those times.

"They're back," Benjamin said.

The door clicked. Aaron and Clara slipped into the room. A small pile of clothes dangled over Clara's arm. Aaron held her suitcase.

"Thought she might as well vacate that room," he said.

"We're leaving this hotel at sundown."

Sarah took the proffered clothes and headed into the bathroom. After trying on several pieces, she stopped to examine the look.

"There," Sarah said to her image in the mirror, wearing a white shirt with a flower on the left shoulder. "I look Danish now."

When Sarah stepped from the bathroom, Clara let out a small laugh. It was good to hear her giggle.

"You look like me now," Clara said. "My dad bought that shirt for me two weeks ago. He liked the flower."

Aaron and Alex smiled and nodded at her.

"We could be twins," Sarah said as she walked to the door and looked through the peephole.

Sarah grabbed her small wallet and passport, took Clara's hands, and stared into her eyes.

"Clara, listen to me. I don't know what's happening, but I'll find out when I get to Denmark. You have to promise me something."

Clara licked her lips, then nodded. "Go ahead."

"You have to promise me you'll stay with my friends. Do what they tell you to. Go where they tell you to. When I get back, everything should be over. Will you do that?"

"I don't know what's going on either," Clara said. "I came here to meet a man I fell in love with and got tied up in a hotel room. Sarah, I'm scared, and I want to go home." She cleared her throat and swallowed. "I saw what you did for me in that room. You took a great risk to save me from that man. For that, I will listen to you, even though I don't know you. I will listen to you because that man is still out there somewhere, and he scares me."

Relief swept through her. This is what Vivian asked of them. Protect the Danish girl. It would be good to do that without a fight from the Danish girl.

"Good. These guys will stop at nothing to keep you safe. You have my word."

Clara leaned in close, and Sarah took the opportunity to hug her. After a moment, they stepped back.

"Is there anything I should know about Skanderborg before I go? Biker gangs? Muslim extremists? Anything?"

Clara smiled and shook her head, hair flying.

"No, there's nothing dangerous in Skanderborg. It's a small town. I love my little city. It's right on Skanderborg Lake. So beautiful. You'll love it."

"What about your father? Is he there?"

Her expression turned serious. "Are you going to see my dad?"

Sarah shrugged. "I have no idea. I'm just supposed to go."

It was Clara's turn to frown. "You're going to Skanderborg, and you have no idea why?"

"That's about it."

Clara licked her lips again. "Sarah, that seems strange. Or do you just not want to tell me?"

"I assure you, if I didn't want to tell you, I would tell you it was none of your business. As I said earlier, it's a long story. Aaron will fill you in."

Sarah reached for the door.

"Sarah, can you check in on my father?" Clara added, her tone softer.

Was Clara on to something? Was this about Anton Olafson? If it was, why have Clara come to Toronto?

"Where would I find him?" Sarah asked.

"Just down from the train station. Two houses away from the rowing club by the lake. Here, give me the hotel pad of paper there and a pen. I'll write the street name and draw a little diagram."

Daniel grabbed the pad and gave it to Clara. After a minute of doodling, she handed it to Sarah. It was easy to see the train station, the road leading away, and how to walk to the rowing club. A large X was drawn over the house two away from the rowing club.

"How do you pronounce that street name?" Sarah asked.

Clara said, "Sølystvej. The sound of the O with the line through it stays in your throat. Like you swallow the sound."

"Okay." Sarah glanced up from the paper. "Not sure I'll learn Danish on this trip."

"You won't have to. Everyone speaks English in Denmark. Only a few of the older generation don't. You won't have a problem."

Sarah took a deep breath, then grabbed the door knob.

"Wait," Aaron said, his voice like the crack of a whip.

He moved behind her. They embraced long and hard.

"Take care of yourself," he whispered.

"You too, fucker."

They kissed. He let her go, and she opened the door, then closed it and turned back to him.

"I can't go."

"Why not?" Aaron asked.

"I thought I'd lost you forever. And now I have to fly to Europe for who knows how long. It's just wrong somehow."

"Sarah, you, of all people, understand. We have to listen to what Vivian wrote for us. There's no other way. I'd be dead right now if I didn't."

She eased back into his embrace. The others in the room looked away.

"She saw my death, though. How am I supposed to live with that?" a soft chuckle escaped her when she thought of what she'd just said.

"You just have to," Aaron said.

She leaned away, lowered her head, and looked up at him with a half-smile.

"What?" she asked. "You trying to get rid of me?"

"Stupid." He yanked her close. "Never."

She wanted to stay, be held by him, and let the worries of the world fall on someone else's shoulders. What also troubled her was how soft she was getting. She wasn't the same girl from the days of fighting madmen in the crypts of Italy and Hungary with Parkman. This wasn't the same girl who fought Gert and won all those years ago. Who managed to live through Rod Howley and his successor from the Sophia Project. No, this new Sarah was in love and wanted kids and wanted to be married. Maybe even have a nice home one day, an average job.

One day ...

"You're right," she whispered for only Aaron to hear. "I need to do this."

Allowing herself to pull away, to have Aaron's hands release her, made it final. She wouldn't hug him again, or she wouldn't let go.

Leave now or never leave.

She pulled the door open.

"Wait," Alex said.

Aaron's hand shot over her shoulder and closed the door.

"What?" Sarah asked, her impatience for herself coming through in her voice. It would mean nothing to Alex as he didn't seem to care what people said or how they said it. Alex was only interested in actions.

"Here." Alex handed over Ansgar's cell phone. "The guy on the other end texted back. This was his last message."

Sarah read it to herself, then handed it to Aaron.

"Not very smart of him to threaten a man like Ansgar."

Aaron shook his head as he read the message, then handed the phone back to Alex.

"Whoever he is, he doesn't think Ansgar can get to him. Stupid if you ask me."

"It worked, though. We got him riled up."

Aaron nodded.

"Just stay together. Stay safe. I'll be back in a few days, and we'll deal with Ansgar. Then it's over."

Aaron winked at her. "Then it's over," he repeated.

Sarah opened the door before she had time to think about it. She edged into the corridor, saw it was empty, then started down the hall toward the elevator without looking back. She had to get on that plane, or she would return to the hotel and not make it to Denmark.

The mystery that Vivian started with the letters was almost unraveled, and Sarah resolved to see it to the end.

Even if it killed her.

And if it did, she would kick Vivian's ass.

Chapter 20

The hospital took longer than he thought. The emergency room at the hospital was full when he arrived, but after complaining of difficulty breathing, they took him ahead of others who weren't injured as badly.

Now, with small white bandage strips on either side of his swollen nose and a thicker one crossing the bridge, Ansgar caught a taxi at the hospital's main entrance and returned to the hotel. The sun left behind a purple sky as it dipped over the horizon.

The intruders could have the police waiting for him. Aaron, Alex, the girl who attacked him, and whoever else they had with them could be waiting to finish their fight. Ansgar chose not to enter the hotel. He would wait outside like he used to as a sniper in Afghanistan years before. Eventually, one of them would exit the hotel, and he would dispatch them.

For a man like him, with his experience, it was a joke that the girl got the better of him. She would pay for that.

The cell phone would be a problem. The client would attempt to make contact, and Ansgar wouldn't be there. Unless the room had been searched, the cell phone would be in evidence, and the client would be placed in jeopardy.

This did not bode well for future contracts.

All that was left for him to do was stack up the bodies.

Ansgar would wait out front of the hotel. He would watch for the gang that interrupted his time with Clara. If none came out, he would be Peter Ford, enter the hotel, and attempt to access his room.

Aaron and his team were there for revenge. They brought a girl with them to gain access to the room. A girl fighter. She was good with her hands, displaying little fear. Aaron had a good team. Ansgar would give him that. And Ansgar would break that team apart one by one. Then maybe he could continue his job for the client. This would go down as a minor setback.

When he got to the girl who broke his nose, he would offer her a minor setback as well. A broken kneecap would work. A severed spine. Two dislocated shoulders. One eye poked out. A few missing teeth. And, of course, a broken nose. That girl would never walk again, never eat right again, and have difficulty breathing through a tube for the rest of her short life when he was done with her.

That was the thing about Ansgar. He didn't discriminate. He took jobs whether the target was a woman or a man. He even took a job to kill a rich guy's ten-year-old son once so the ex-wife couldn't have him in a divorce battle. In the animal kingdom, predators didn't stop to evaluate age prior to a kill, and neither did Ansgar. In both instances, the kill put food on the table.

The taxi pulled into the parking lot of the hotel.

"Here's good," Ansgar said.

He tossed two twenties over the seat and got out. The cab pulled away, leaving him in the large parking lot, staring up at the hotel.

An Air Canada flight flew overhead as it prepared to land at the Toronto airport. Ansgar followed it until his eyes stopped on the tenth floor of the hotel, where he studied the window to his room. It was dark. That was a good sign. If the authorities had taken over the room, a forensics team would be scouring it into the night.

Ansgar eased backward until he stood between two towering parking lot lamps in the darkness. Keeping to the less-lit areas, he weaved his way toward the back of the parking lot and found a spot in the grass to sit where he had a good view of the hotel's front doors. Anyone coming and going would use those doors.

The side of the building to his left had one exit door. A fence lined the back of the property. If Aaron's team used that door to leave the hotel, they would have to hop the fence or walk into view.

Wherever they were, he would see them.

Then they would tell him how they found him and how they knew about the bombs. They would be happy to explain everything. Ansgar could be quite coercive.

Then he would kill them.

All of them.

Especially the girl.

That fucking girl.

He touched the gun in the small of his back.

The Clock sat back and waited for his kills to come to him.

In time.

Chapter 21

Anton Olafson got off the train in Aarhus and walked out into the late afternoon sun. It didn't warm his skin. It did nothing to make him feel better.

Find someone that looks like Clara. Kill someone that looks like Clara.

What if he found a random girl, killed her, and then PAIN didn't accept it? Would he have to kill again?

Why do it in the first place? Why was PAIN making him kill someone randomly? For his jollies? Was this something PAIN wanted to do himself but couldn't? Was he some kind of demented voyeur?

Anton followed the crowd surging across the street toward Aarhus's walking streets. He would hunt for a girl who walked alone. He would follow her and wait for an opportunity to catch her in a private area, away from curious eyes.

This evening, Denmark was celebrating Midsummer, the Burning of the Witch. All over Denmark, a fabricated witch would be placed atop a pile of twigs and shrubbery and then lit afire. Even though it was meant to remember the Lutherans who were persecuted during the 16th- and 17th-century religious wars, it had become something of an unintentional attack on women. Anton couldn't think of a better day to murder a lost soul on the streets of Aarhus.

He had his cell phone in case PAIN tried to reach him. He had it to film the murder as well. Then he would appeal for Clara's safe return and the destruction of the files that PAIN had hacked. Everything could still work out as long as he did his job.

After walking a few blocks along the shopping streets, he came to Salling, a large department store. Salling offered everything from cosmetics to clothing, groceries, and alcohol. Once inside, he rode the escalator to the lower level and headed to the liquor section near the back. They offered samples of their whiskeys for a prospective buyer, and today Anton needed a couple of shots of something hard.

The attendant, Bjorn, helped him with a taste of three different whiskeys before Anton explained that he would search out his wife and return to purchase the bitterer brand.

Lightheaded, he rode the escalator up to the second floor, then stood in line at the bakery to grab a pecan pastry before heading out onto the evening streets in search of someone that resembled his daughter.

He didn't feel like himself. How could he have gone so far as to walk the streets of the city he worked in, looking for a stranger to murder? It seemed impossible, yet he was prepared to do it.

He had made mistakes in his life. He would pay for them. That's what justified this action. One kill. One payment. Clara set free. Life could go on. Worst case scenario, he would be jailed for the rest of his life for his crimes, but at least his daughter would be free.

The pecan pastry sated his small appetite as he headed toward the canal that ran perpendicular under the walking street. After an hour of watching pretty blonde girls, most of them with somebody else, he sat at one of the cafés along the canal and bought a cappuccino.

His phone had no messages. The hacker was silent. There were four days left in the PAIN PACT. That wasn't enough time to do anything else but stay on course, and Anton intended to do just that. Although finding the right girl at the right time and in a quiet area posed a problem. Maybe he needed to stay in less busy areas. Perhaps he was going about this the wrong way.

The cappuccino tasted great but cost a fortune. The café charged more for the convenience of being near the picturesque canal.

The sun was mostly gone for another day. Anton paid the bill and headed back toward the train, dejected. His shoulders slouched, he walked along with the myriad of people heading this way and that, enjoying their lives, taking in the sights, oblivious to his mission.

A group of seven, four of them blonde girls in their late teens, walked up ahead of him. He listened to their banter about school and friends. At a safe distance, he listened while they discussed one particular person and how crazy that person was for wearing that stupid shirt to class. As the group passed the new Starbucks, three of them split away and said their goodbyes. Two of the blonde girls that looked the closest to Clara continued trudging along toward the train station with their other two companions. At the last street crossing, the foursome split up. Three entered the train station, and one blonde girl headed left toward the Aarhus harbor.

Anton followed the girl. He stayed far enough back to not be noticed but close enough to keep her in sight. He asked himself if he could really do it. How would he do it? With his hands around her throat? With the knife, he had brought with him?

He chastised himself for not bringing the small vial of pepper spray he had at home. Pepper spray would incapacitate the victim enough for him to make the proper amount of lunges with the knife. He wasn't a fighter and didn't want to encounter too much resistance from his chosen kill.

The girl turned left on a street, checked over her shoulder, and then crossed the street.

Did she see me?

He slowed his pace but kept her close. A sudden realization flashed into his mind.

I can't do this.

He couldn't harm the girl. She had a family waiting for her. A mother, a father. How could he end her life while people waited at home? What kind of monster could do that? Was he so selfish that he would murder someone else's daughter so that his daughter could live?

He stopped walking. How could the hacker ask this of him?

Before taking his eyes off the girl, he watched as she

dropped down a small set of stairs and entered a gaming store.

His prey was gone. Just like that. And with her, his hopes of getting Clara back alive.

But he had to do it. He just had to.

Maybe he could catch the train back to Skanderborg in time for the Burning of the Witch ceremony. It would be dark. Hundreds of people would be milling around, talking, and eating snacks from a local vendor.

There would be targets. They would be close to home.

Why didn't he think of it before? They always burned the witch on the grass by the lake, just down from the library. It was a perfect place to drag an unconscious teen into the bushes and do the deed. He could be home and chatting with a neighbor before anyone found a body. Linking it to him would be virtually impossible with that kind of alibi.

Anton headed back toward the train station. He needed to be on the next train to get back in time to scope out the area and talk with the Skanderborg locals. There had to be a girl who looked just like Clara at the event.

Two blocks from the train station, he checked his watch. The train to Skanderborg would be leaving in four minutes.

He bumped into a young couple as he sprinted for the station.

He even ran through the red light as he crossed the street in front of the station.

A girl named fate waited for him in Skanderborg, and he intended to meet her. He had bad news for her.

He had to do it. There could be no turning back, no second thoughts.

But he would stop and pick up his pepper spray canister

at the house first.

Then he would do what was required of him.

For Clara. Always for Clara.

Save Clara.

Chapter 22

Aaron waited until past two in the morning before rousing Clara, Benjamin, and Daniel. Alex had stayed awake to mind the door. As far as they could tell, Ansgar had not returned to his room. Every time the elevator doors opened, the people exiting had gone to a different room. Twice the elevator disgorged a waiter bringing food to someone two rooms down.

Their room offered a small coffeemaker. Aaron had prepared the water and set it to make two cups for whoever wanted it as he woke them up.

Aaron stood by the overhead light by the door.

"C'mon, guys," he said. "We need to get up and get alert. I want everyone out of this room within half an hour." He checked the peephole. The corridor was empty. "We'll be secure in a new room within the hour. We can all get some sleep then."

Benjamin was the first to get to the coffee. Once he poured himself a cup, he poured another for Daniel.

Clara had the bed to herself. She leaned up on one elbow, still fully clothed, and rubbed sleep out of her eyes.

"What time is it?" she asked.

"Just after two in the morning."

"Why are we up so early?"

"To move to another hotel."

"Okay."

She kicked her legs over the edge of the bed and stood up.

"I call the toilet," she said, disappearing inside the washroom.

"Did you hear from Sarah?" Daniel asked.

"We know she made the plane here in Toronto. The next stop is Amsterdam, where there's a three-hour layover. After that, she flies to Copenhagen and then to Billund. I'm sure she'll contact us when she lands in Amsterdam to let us know she made it safe."

"Any idea when that is?" Daniel asked. He held the steaming coffee to his lips, eyes closed.

Aaron checked his watch. "About four more hours. She lands in Amsterdam our time just after six in the morning. She should be in Billund by ten at night. Either she'll get a hotel or a ride to Skanderborg, which will get her to her final destination by—"

"Eleven, maybe twelve," Clara broke in as she stepped from the bathroom. "Billund's about an hour's drive to Skanderborg. Nice drive, really."

"Thanks," Aaron said. "Coffee?"

She shook her head.

"Good, because there's none left."

"Tea?"

"In the next room. That okay?"

Clara cocked her head to the side and yawned. When her mouth closed, she blinked heavily, then said, "Sure. It's okay."

Aaron was grateful for how well she had adjusted to spending the night in a hotel room with four men she had just met yesterday. It probably had a lot to do with how Sarah was around them, not to mention how Sarah was the one who took on Ansgar singlehandedly to get Clara away from him.

"Finish the coffees, guys. Gather our things. We leave in ten."

Murmured acknowledgments circled the room as Aaron moved to the window to watch the parking lot below. It had been over an hour since the last of the large passenger jets stopped landing and taking off at the airport on the other side of the highway.

The streets were empty, with only the random car passing by. It was quiet outside, three hours before the sun rose on another day.

He turned from the window and saw Alex at the peephole in the door.

"We cool?" he asked.

Alex looked over his shoulder and nodded, then returned to the door.

Five minutes later, with Clara's things packed and the men ready, Aaron's cell phone chimed.

"Sarah?" Daniel asked.

Aaron grabbed it and thumbed the screen. A message from Parkman.

Everyone safe?

Aaron typed back that they were.

Good. Is Sarah off?

Aaron told him that she was.

Send my love to everyone. I'm doing what Vivian's letter told me to do. Don't understand it, but following it to a tee.

Aaron knew better than to ask what Parkman's task was. He just typed *Good Luck* and turned off his phone.

"Parkman's doing his thing. We need to do ours." He wrapped his hand around the doorknob. "Everyone ready?"

The three men and one woman standing in a semi-circle around him nodded.

"Let's roll."

Aaron opened the door, and as a group, they left the safety of their hotel room.

Chapter 23

PARKMAN HAD LANDED IN Denmark the day before and was still fighting jet lag. The small café in the library in the center of Skanderborg had very good coffee but at a steep price. He wasn't used to Danish prices.

His business as a licensed private investigator hadn't gotten off its feet yet. A few clients had come and gone. With Sarah in his life, he just didn't have the time. This trip to Denmark had cost him a large chunk of his savings, something he would have to find a way to recoup in the coming years by keeping a job.

For now, he was comfortable, having saved and invested his income from the police department all those years ago. In time, he would need a source of income if he intended to continue flying around the world for Sarah.

He sipped his coffee and watched the people around him mingle and chat. Tonight was Denmark's midsummer celebration. He was here just as Vivian had asked him to be. He knew Sarah had also been instructed to come to Denmark, but he had no idea where she was or why she was there.

What was important was doing what Vivian instructed to the best of his ability based on what her letter said. Or based on what he interpreted her letter was meant to say.

The letter had been labeled Park Man. His address was simply stated as Santa Rosa. No street number, no name. Unlike the other letters, which had addresses.

Parkman had to admit that that scared him a little. If Vivian didn't see much for his life, his future, was he on a death mission?

Inside the envelope, all it told him to do was take a break. Go to Copenhagen, Denmark. Stay one night. Enjoy the sights and the food. Then rent a car and drive to Skanderborg for the Midsummer event. Stay one or two nights. Be a tourist. Eat out, sleep in. Then fly home. That was what Sarah needed. Vivian said she couldn't see more.

On the bottom of the page where Vivian wrote her message to Parkman, she added a couple of lines saying she regretted his role. Maybe it was something about him being a cop. Maybe she wasn't allowed to see what he needed to do because it would change too much in the future.

Whatever the reason, Vivian implored him to take vacation time, then go back home.

Vivian's trepidation and hesitant tone in the letter scared him to the core. Even though Vivian's letter to Sarah told her to come to this very city, and the letter to Caleb, Sarah's father, told him to arrange the flights, Vivian declared Parkman's role as unclear.

"Great," he had said to Caleb. "I finally get to talk to

Vivian like Sarah does, I finally get a premonition, and all it says is take a vacation. What am I supposed to do with that?"

Caleb had patted his shoulder and made him another cup of tea.

"Do exactly as the letter states. You have no idea why my daughter saw your presence in Skanderborg as important. But what is important is that she saw you in Skanderborg. So go. Figure it out. But go."

Parkman glanced down at the letter in his hand that night, an hour after Sarah had gone to bed in the guest room, a couple of shots of whiskey under her belt.

"I'll go. I just don't like not knowing what I'm walking into."

"Isn't that the way it always is?" Caleb asked from the other side of the kitchen.

"No, it's not. Vivian's always there in Sarah's head when I'm working with Sarah. Now she isn't. Sarah said it herself. Vivian has abandoned her. We're all walking into this blind. Unless these vague letters are meant as our guide into the fray. If so, then we're all in trouble."

Parkman drank from his cup again, thinking back to that night. What he wouldn't do to learn what this was all about. And the thought of missing a cue, screwing something up, and learning later that Sarah was hurt or, worse, killed would destroy him. She was supposed to be in town later that night. He was already there, and other than himself, only Sarah's parents knew about his presence in Skanderborg.

Whatever the reason, it had to be for Sarah, but how was he supposed to find her?

The coffee cup was almost empty. He drew the last bit into his open mouth, set the napkin inside the cup, and got up from his chair. Outside the café's windows, people gathered around a five-foot stack of twigs and prepared to burn what looked like a Halloween witch attached to a thick branch on top of the twigs.

Parkman fumbled with a toothpick, tossed it into the corner of his mouth, nodded at the girl behind the café's counter, and left through the side door. He descended the concrete stairs moving toward the water. At the bottom, he turned to the right and joined the Danes as they gathered around, beer and hotdogs in hand, to watch the burning.

Maybe Sarah was already here. Once they hooked up, he would have more clarity as to why a young girl wrote him a letter almost twenty-five years ago.

If it weren't for Sarah, he wouldn't be here. No one would perform the tasks Vivian set out for them if they didn't know Sarah. Without Sarah, the letters would have been disregarded and seen as the rantings of a schizophrenic, or worse.

He meandered through the crowds until he reached one of the vendors, where he bought a beer. It was supposed to be his holiday, so he would drink, be merry, and enjoy what the Danes had to offer before he flew home.

He considered that maybe having him over here was to avoid his untimely death back home. If Vivian saw him killed in Santa Rosa this week, maybe she just sent him to Skanderborg because that's where Sarah was going.

He slipped the toothpick to the other side of his mouth, drank some of the beer, and moved to the edge of the crowd as someone fired up the brush under the Halloween witch. Surveying as many people as he could, careful not to miss anything out of place or weird, he concluded the Danes were a happy bunch after all.

As he drank more of his beer, he kept an eye on everyone, looking for furtive movements and people who didn't belong or were acting out of place. Everywhere he looked, people were talking and laughing, playing Frisbee, tossing a ball back and forth, and talking to each other. One group of teens played a small radio a bit too loud, but it didn't seem to bother anyone else. Probably because the songs they played were from Lukas Graham's new album. With Lukas Graham doing so well abroad, Parkman could see why the Danes loved him.

Out on the lake, several small boats had anchored close to shore to watch the enormous bonfire. Parkman idly wondered if people had brought marshmallows.

An hour and two beers later, the sun had dropped, and the fire was losing some of its power. People began dispersing, moving toward the parking area by the library, others heading up to the street to walk home.

Parkman had taken a spot on the grass on the side of a small hill where he had watched everyone, taking it all in. He hadn't seen Sarah, and as far as he was concerned, nothing looked out of place.

"Is this a waste of time?" he whispered under his breath.

When he got to his feet, he stumbled a moment, wondering how the beer could have that much effect on him.

Since the event was winding down, he might grab one more beer before the vendor closed up, then nurse it back to his hotel. Just like in Vegas, walking down the street with open alcohol wasn't a problem in Denmark. Doing it made him feel like a rebel because he had toed the line so much his entire life.

Beer in hand, he moved toward the library and leaned against the outer wall to watch the stragglers as they left the event. Five more minutes and he would retire to his hotel. No sign of Sarah and nothing amiss left Parkman in a bored state.

The teens with the small radio were dispersing. He counted eleven in total. Seven guys, four girls. Most of them moved toward the parking lot. Two girls started his way. When they passed him immersed in a Danish conversation, none of what they said made sense. The Danish language was a mystery to him. He had nailed the word for thank you—tak—but that was it.

The girls disappeared at the base of the stairs. They turned behind the building to walk the length of the shore by the lake. Two more people went that way, a man and a woman. Then a tall man in a thick coat, hands in his pockets, followed them.

Parkman didn't like the man in the thick coat. Something about the expression on his face. He seemed angry or simply distraught. But at what? The Burning of the Witch had been a success. And that coat looked too thick for the temperature.

Parkman drank the rest of his third beer and headed for a garbage bin ten feet away, thinking about the man in the thick coat. Why such a thick coat for a warm evening? Wouldn't the Danes be used to the cool June evening? It wasn't that cold. He let the beer glass drop into the receptacle and then fished out a toothpick. The second he popped it in his mouth, he dropped it. A small yip sounded from his left, startling him. It was so soft he wasn't sure he heard it right.

Then a woman screamed from around the corner.

The shrill volume raised goosebumps on his arms and

charged him into a full run for the stairs.

At the bottom of the stairs, as the girl continued to scream from somewhere behind the building, Parkman ran around where the two girls had gone not one minute before him.

It was the way the man in the thick coat had gone.

Chapter 24

ANTON OLAFSON HAD CAUGHT the train on time in Aarhus and made it home to collect his pepper spray. Then, wearing a jacket too heavy for the warm evening, he headed out toward the Burning of the Witch by Skanderborg Lake. He got there just as the crowd of people headed home.

"Fuck," he muttered under his breath. "Too late."

It seemed like fate had chosen to work against him. He walked Skanderborg the first day, looking for a target. Then the busy center of Aarhus. And now, under the cover of night, where hundreds of people would be milling around watching the flames of the witch rise, drinking and relaxing, targets would be aplenty. But hardly anyone remained. It wasn't even that late. About a dozen people stayed close to the dying flames. Scattered on the lawn beside the library, there couldn't be more than twenty people left, mostly adults.

A group of teens stood by the library steps laughing and

talking. He homed in on them, the pepper spray in his right hand, concealed inside the jacket pocket.

Two girls broke away from the group and headed for the shoreline. They were walking toward the path that led up to his house and the rowing club.

Anton couldn't believe his luck.

Even as his feet started moving in their direction, he wondered if he could do it. Could he actually take a girl's life?

The two girls disappeared around the corner of the building. They would be out of sight for approximately one minute, by his estimate. Out in the open like this, he couldn't run. That would draw attention to himself. Everyone knew him in this small city.

Another couple turned the corner where Anton saw the girls go and walked out of sight. Whether he could do it or not would depend on that couple. Would they interfere? Would they be a problem? He wasn't worried that the girls were walking together. He only needed to kill one of them on camera. Both of them could be pepper sprayed until they were blinded. He'd kill one and take off. The deed would be done. Clara would be set free.

If that couple were too close, he would have to wait.

As he passed the library and turned the corner, he hurried down the path by the shoreline. Immediately he realized that fate was, in fact, on his side. The couple had come back there to kiss and feel each other up. The man held the woman by the library's back wall, his mouth digging into hers, his hands roaming under her shirt.

Up ahead on the path, the two blonde girls walked slowly, holding hands. Anton sped up and closed the distance quickly. Fifteen meters behind them, the girl on the left detected his presence. She glanced back at him and smiled.

They were two houses away from reaching the empty parking lot of the Kvickly grocery store.

Anton withdrew the pepper spray and started to walk around the girls. They slowed to allow him passage as the path was slightly overgrown on either side.

"Tusinde tak," he said. *A thousand thanks.*

As fast as a viper, Anton latched onto the nearest girl's wrist and yanked her toward him while bringing the pepper spray around. He unleashed a torrent of spray as the girl's friend released a small scream of shock. The first girl struggled and fell backward into the grass.

Anton turned his attention to the other girl. She stepped back. His left hand latched onto her belt and yanked her toward him as she screamed so loud his ears rang.

This was bad. Very bad. He couldn't allow them to attract so much attention. He pressed the red button on the tiny canister in his hand, firing a volley of the toxic substance into the second girl's face, covering her eyes and nose.

The scream died as fast as it began. The blonde dropped back into the tall grass, writhing around, gasping for a breath.

Someone was running nearby. The first girl had crawled away and was about to fall into the lake. She must have deduced that the water would help clear the mess on her face.

More people clomped the dirt path toward them in the dark.

The second girl was moaning and crawling away blind, chunks of spittle dropping from her mouth.

He had failed. All he did was spray two innocent girls. He couldn't murder one of them in the time he had left. With the lack of experience of regularly murdering people, he didn't have his phone out to record the event. He hadn't jumped on the girl to restrain her and choke the life out of her. It would take mere minutes to end her life, but curious strangers were closer now. There was simply no time left.

Anton turned from the carnage he had caused and ran for the Kvickly parking lot. He had screwed up. They were going to catch him. If they did, it was all over, and Clara was as good as dead.

He didn't stop running until he was cowering in his backyard, where he hid in thick bushes and waited for that knock on the front door. The one when the police arrived after talking to the two young girls he had hurt.

At one point, he thought he heard someone walking by the bushes he hid in, but he couldn't be sure. If someone did, they were extra quiet.

Maybe the girls hadn't seen him clearly enough. Maybe they couldn't identify him. It was dark back on the path by the water. His large jacket had covered his identity, but it would give him away if they saw it. Still hiding in the bushes at the back of his house hours later, Anton discarded the jacket, then placed the pepper spray canister in his back pocket. He placed the jacket in the garbage bin beside his house.

The second he set the bin's lid back in place, he heard the soft rapping of someone at his front door.

They were here. The authorities had found him.

Clara's dead.

He leaned against the house so he didn't fall over.

The knocking came again. He checked the time on his phone. It was just past midnight. Visitors at this hour were unlikely. It had to be the police.

Hiding from them would be impossible. He wasn't that kind of person. He had no idea what it took to stay hidden under their radar, a fugitive of the law. He would never make it on the run.

Decision made, he pushed off the side of the house and walked unsteadily toward the front, mentally preparing for the worst.

The knocking had only come twice. As he rounded the corner, he did not see a police car. In fact, there was no car at all.

Standing there, like an angel sent directly to his house, was a girl looking down at a piece of paper. A blonde girl that didn't just look like Clara; she could be Clara's twin. She was even wearing Clara's clothes.

He knew it because he bought that white top with the flower on the left shoulder two weeks ago. Those pants had to be Clara's as well.

Fate looked down on him with fondness.

He eased the pepper spray canister out of his back pocket and stepped away from the side of the building.

It was time to finally kill a random, stupid girl.

Then he would get his daughter back.

Fate smiled.

Save Clara.

Anton clenched his teeth and ran at the girl who stood out in front of his house wearing his daughter's clothes. A rush of anger fueled his charging feet.

He hit her as she was just looking up from the piece of paper in her hands, knocking her off her feet.

She smacked into the concrete so hard that a gush of air

escaped her lips. She moaned a word that sounded like his name, but he wasn't there to chat with her.

Anton emptied the canister of pepper spray into her face.

192

Chapter 25

AARON LED THE WAY off the elevator into the lobby of the hotel. Alex stayed close behind him. Then Clara, and finally Daniel and Benjamin took up the rear. Aaron led at an average pace, watching the windows and the front doors straight ahead.

At the front desk, Aaron dropped the room keys on the counter and stopped. The clerk stepped out from the back, his salt and pepper hair ruffled and bloodshot eyes. Aaron guessed he had been napping in the back.

Aaron told him the room numbers they were vacating, then turned back where they had come and started for the side exit.

"Sir?" the man behind the desk said.

Aaron stopped and tilted his head sideways, eyebrows raised questioningly. The rest stayed by the hallway wall, keeping Clara concealed.

"The side doors are locked at this hour. You have to use the front door." He gestured toward the front, a pen in his hand.

Aaron glanced back to check with Alex, who nodded. They were good to go. The men were aware of the danger and prepared to walk through the front door.

At the window, Aaron stopped and studied the parking lot for movement. Alex joined him at the window.

"Nothing," Aaron whispered. "You?"

Alex shook his head. Aaron saw it in the reflection from the glass.

He stepped around Alex, which activated the double sliding doors, then moved outside. Without realizing he had been holding his breath, he let it out, tried to remain calm, then moved toward Carlingview Drive to the left. The four of them behind him stayed close.

On Dixon Road, a few cars raced by on the wet pavement. The rain had stopped, but it left a chill in the air.

Aaron stopped to let them all gather around.

"Okay, I propose we hit these lights at Dixon, cross, and go into any of those hotels on the left. We'll grab two rooms on the same floor. Deal?"

Heads nodded in response.

"Do you think that guy's watching us?" Clara asked. Her voice cracked from a shiver. He hadn't noticed how much the cool temperature was bothering her.

"I think Sarah broke his nose. He's probably in a hospital. If he comes back here, it'll be tomorrow. Maybe whoever was behind this shit is sending someone else. We're just taking precautions."

"When we check in at another hotel, won't the people

looking for us be able to find us that way?" she asked.

"That's why we're going to have two rooms. One will be empty. If they go to that room first, we'll know."

"What if they come to the room we're in first?"

"We'll be waiting."

Clara shrugged. "Doesn't sound like a good plan."

Aaron moved closer to Clara. Debating this out in the open was a waste of time. "Look, whoever's behind this wants me dead. These guys, too." He gestured at his friends. "But they kidnapped you. If they wanted you dead, you wouldn't be here right now. Going to another hotel gives us a layer of secrecy. If they find us, then fine. We'll deal with it and figure out what's going on. But remember, they don't want you dead so they won't shoot first. There's nothing short of an elite SWAT team that could get the jump on us four."

Clara nodded. "Sarah said you'd take care of me until she got back. I'll go with that and not question how you're doing it."

That surprised him. He rarely heard people talk in such a blunt manner, although he preferred it. That's why he loved Sarah. She spoke her mind. He had a higher level of respect for people like that.

Aaron adjusted his shirt, tucked it in at the back, turned around slowly, and started along the sidewalk. The footfalls behind him were loud enough to know they were all staying close.

A small two-door car pulled up to the red light at Dixon and Carlingview. Seconds later, the light changed. As the vehicle accelerated, it backfired, making Aaron duck at the sound.

"Whoa, that was loud for such a small car."

Someone moaned behind him. He spun around, crouching into a defensive posture. Benjamin held his right leg and bounced on the other one.

"What happened?" Aaron asked.

Alex and Daniel had crouched low, holding Clara down.

The car backfired again. This time Benjamin dropped to the pavement.

It wasn't a car backfiring.

Someone was shooting at them.

"Get down," he shouted. "Gunfire."

Alex and Daniel shielded Clara with their bodies as Aaron rolled to Benjamin. Clara tried to say something, but Daniel shushed her. Alex's head shot up like a periscope, searching the immediate area.

"You okay?" Aaron asked Benjamin. "Where are you hit?"

Benjamin's face was tight with worry, his jaw clenched. Through his clenched teeth, he yelled, "Why am I always the one who gets shot?"

"You're the ugliest," Aaron replied, touching Benjamin's leg where the pants were torn in the shape of a small hole. He ran his hand over the leg wound, finding only one bloody area.

"Gee," Benjamin gasped. "Thanks, camp counselor. You sure"—he breathed in deeply when Aaron touched close to the wound—"know how to make a guy feel special."

"The bullet went in and made a clean exit. Doesn't look like it hit anything vital. Assuming you don't get shot again, you'll be okay."

"The camp counselor is a doctor now."

Gunfire erupted somewhere in the dark to their left. All of them dropped flat on the sidewalk. Daniel stayed over Clara's back to keep her vital organs insulated with his body. Alex had slunk away and was running bent at the waist around a car fifteen feet from them. They had to get off the sidewalk. They were sitting targets in the open like this.

Aaron spun on his stomach at the sound of a heavy engine revving, the wetness on the ground from the rain earlier soaking through to his skin. A Park 'N Fly van turned the corner up ahead.

"Everyone. Stay down," Aaron ordered. "I'll have you out of here in less than a minute."

He got into a crouched position, waited for the Park 'N Fly van to come closer, then jumped up and dodged out in front of it, waving his arms frantically. The instant the driver saw him, he hit the brakes and jerked the vehicle to a stop. Aaron ran around the front of the vehicle to use it as a shield from the shooter.

The airport van's doors opened.

"You damn fool," the driver shouted. "I coulda run you clean over."

Aaron hopped on. "Someone shot my friend." He pointed at the group of three still lying flat on the sidewalk. "We can't wait for an ambulance. We need you to take us—"

"The hell I won't." The driver was looking out his window. He turned back to Aaron. "Get off my truck," he shouted. "I want nothing to do with the likes—"

The glass to the left of the driver shattered. The driver's head bobbed once as blood and brain matter splattered onto the inside of the windshield. Aaron jerked back and almost fell off the vehicle. If he hadn't been holding the railing bar on his right, he would've landed on his back in the street.

The truck slid forward as the driver's foot came off the gas pedal. Without time to think, he reacted by grabbing the driver and yanking him down and out of his seat. The dead weight fell to the left. Frantic to stop the Park 'N Fly van from rolling, Aaron hopped into the driver's seat and slammed his foot on the brake. The truck stopped one foot shy of the curb.

The hole in the glass was right beside his head. Risking a bullet in the face, he lowered his mouth to the opening.

"Get in the van," he shouted. "Stay low."

Then he jerked his head back and bent over to make himself less of a target. His wet shirt clung to him, a coldness causing him to shiver once.

Carlingview was dead at this hour. Not a single car passed them as Clara climbed up and around the dead driver on the floor. A small gasp escaped her lips before she jumped around the body.

"Stay on the floor," Aaron said.

Daniel came on next, holding Benjamin up with an arm around his shoulders. The second their feet left the pavement, Aaron took his foot off the brake and dropped it on the accelerator.

More glass shattered as another bullet entered the van to Aaron's left. The bullet exited the van through the windshield, where a large hole formed, cracks wending away from the hole.

"Holy shit," Aaron yelled as the van picked up speed.

Heart racing, covered in a dull sheen of sweat and rainwater, Aaron sat up and placed both hands on the wheel when they were more than a block away. Unless there was more than one gunman, or they had a car and were about to give chase, the immediate danger had ended.

Over his shoulder, he saw Clara curled up in a ball on the van's floor. Daniel held Benjamin, his face white in the darkened van, blood oozing out of his pant leg.

Something knocked on the back door.

Aaron checked his mirror, ready to slam on the brake or the accelerator, depending on what was needed.

Alex clung to the outside of the van. Aaron turned the corner a block away and slowed to a stop. A moment later, Alex hopped on the van.

"Find him?" Aaron asked.

Alex shook his head.

"Fuck."

He turned back in his seat and performed a U-turn, aiming the van at the hotel, then pulled to the side of the road and stopped.

"Daniel, park at the hospital. Carry Benjamin inside. Explain the shooting in front of the hotel. We had just checked out, and someone shot at us. They killed this man. The police will come. That gives me a half-hour head start."

No one replied. Benjamin groaned at the pain in his leg, and Clara sobbed.

"I'm going back," Aaron said. "I can't let Ansgar get away. We'll always wonder when he'll just show up if I don't deal with him now."

"That takes me out of this fight," Daniel said. "Cops'll keep me for a day or two. You sure about this? Gunshot wounds come with questions."

"They'll keep Clara, too. She'll be safer with the police. Don't leave her side. And Clara, if the cops let you go, wait for Daniel."

Clara nodded quickly. With part of the driver's head missing, his body slumped at her feet. She seemed cowed into doing anything Aaron said without question.

He bounded down the steps and hit the pavement running. Behind him, the Park 'N Fly van did another U-turn and started away in the other direction.

Another set of feet ran close.

He knew it was Alex. Silent Alex. Sneaky Alex.

There was no way Alex would ever let Aaron face an armed hitman on his own. Aaron knew Alex would take a bullet before he ever let Aaron get hurt.

That's just who Alex was, and he loved him for it.

Aaron ran toward the hotel with Alex at his side, prepared to kill a hitman with his bare hands.

Chapter 26

Ansgar Holm watched them as they exited the front of the hotel. They were stupid. Why not use a side door? Why not have a taxi meet them at the front? He'd kill the cab driver and then fill the car with lead, but they had to be smart to avoid him, and they weren't. They were just stupid kids.

They must think he was at the hospital to deal with his nose. Or completely out of commission after what that fucking girl did to him.

He allowed himself a smile as he breathed through his mouth. Their night was about to end abruptly.

Fifteen cars away, near the edge of the grass that lined the parking lot's perimeter, Ansgar—The Clock—had waited, and now the waiting was over. He flexed his legs with slow, measured squats, then twisted on the spot to ease his back.

When the group stopped to talk by the street, Ansgar raised his Glock in front of him and watched the group through the reflex sights. The reflex sights allowed him to watch them with both eyes open. All he had to do was superimpose the red-dot reticle over the target and fire. Providing he had proper trigger manipulation and the sight had been adjusted accurately, it would result in a hit on his intended target. Since he'd adjusted the sights himself, there was no doubt of its accuracy.

The group started walking as one, Aaron leading the way.

Ansgar acquired his target. Aaron's chest would be perfect. Blow the man's heart out with one bullet. His weapon steady, arms resting on the trunk of a car, Ansgar squeezed the trigger as a vehicle pulled away from the street lights to his right.

Aaron hesitated on the sidewalk. Then he spun around. He didn't fall, though. And his chest was still intact.

Ansgar had missed his target.

"What the fuck?" Ansgar said under his breath, his voice nasally.

Aaron's friend had dropped out of sight. Another man tended to him.

Ansgar brought the Glock up to bear, aimed the red dot on Aaron's face, and fired again.

The entire group dropped out of sight.

"Shit."

Bent over, he scurried three cars closer. A quick check of the sights showed they needed adjustment. It had to have been knocked in some way when he was fighting with that girl in the hotel room. He remembered landing on the Glock, the weapon digging into his back, but he didn't think to check it.

Worried the group would scramble back into the hotel

and disappear from sight, Ansgar ran five cars closer. He racked a round into the chamber, slammed his arms onto the trunk of a Buick, and took aim at whatever was moving.

An airport van was driving by. Aaron ran out in front of it, waving for the driver to stop.

What the hell is he doing?

Ansgar aimed the Glock skyward and watched from seven parking spaces away. When Aaron came back into sight, he would die.

He watched Aaron talk to the driver through the van's side window. The driver looked at something on the ground beside the van—out of Ansgar's sight line—and looked back at Aaron.

Ansgar knew what Aaron was doing. The van driver had glanced at Aaron's group, where they hid from his Glock. Aaron was getting them a ride out of the area.

Without using the red dot as an aiming reference, The Clock aimed his weapon at the driver's head with all the experience of an expert sniper in his past and fired with confidence. As expected, the driver slouched in his seat.

Ansgar raised the weapon skyward and waited.

What are you going to do now, Aaron?

From where he hid, it was easy to see Aaron drag the driver out of the seat. Aaron's group ran around the van before Ansgar even knew they were on the move. There were simply too many cars between them for him to see when they crawled away.

Then the group was in the van and out of sight.

He dropped the Glock into position and fired at Aaron's head in the driver's seat. At that second, the van pulled away, and the bullet went wild. Only the familiar tinkle of glass shattering let Ansgar know he had hit something.

A moment later, the van disappeared from view. An odd sound accompanied its departure. The soft rapping of feet pounded the pavement. He tried to see what had made that noise but couldn't. The flutter of a shadow ran along the far sidewalk, but that was nothing more than his eyes playing tricks on him.

He slipped the Glock away and covered it with his bulky shirt. The night was silent as he stood to his full height. A quick scan of the hotel rooms looming over him revealed dark windows. Only two had their lights on at this early hour, but no one was standing in their windows.

"Hello?" someone called.

Ansgar turned to the voice, his hand reaching for the Glock. The hotel clerk had come out on the front steps and was looking right at him.

"Did you see that?" the clerk shouted.

"Yeah," Ansgar said, then winced as shouting flared the pain in his nose.

"I'm calling the police," the clerk said as he turned to reenter the hotel.

"Wait."

The clerk turned back. Ansgar headed toward him.

"What was that all about?" Ansgar asked. "Did they have guns?"

The clerk's head bobbed frantically, his eyes wide.

"They were part of the trouble earlier on the tenth floor. They tried to check out in the middle of the night. I saw what they did. I saw the whole thing."

Ansgar was getting closer. Twenty feet separated them.

"What did you see?" he asked, then took a deep breath,

the pain making his eyes water.

"They hid themselves over there." He pointed. "Then waved that Park 'N Fly van over. That guy went on and shot the driver. He dragged the body out of the seat and then called for his friends to join him. I saw the whole thing. They're murderers."

Ansgar removed his hand from the butt of the Glock. "That's what I saw, too. It scared me so much, I hid behind those cars back there until they drove away."

Ansgar started up the steps to the lobby. He stopped beside the clerk.

"I don't blame you," the clerk said. "I would've hid, too. Now I'm going to call the police and tell them the names of the people who were in that room. They'll find them. Not many people driving an airport van around at this hour." The clerk stopped talking while he studied Ansgar's nose and the tiny bandages around it. "Were you the one who was attacked and chased out of his room earlier today?"

Ansgar tried to smile. He held out his hand. "Name's Peter Ford." They shook hands. Ansgar shrugged. "I don't know if they wanted to rob me or just beat me up." He pointed at his nose. "But they did a good job. Spilled my wine, too. I have to be honest when I say that I might try another hotel in the future."

"I'm so sorry about that. We'll fix it. I'll talk to the manager myself in the morning."

The clerk jerked away and hustled through the doors as they slid open. After he disappeared inside the hotel lobby, Ansgar stared out into the night, looking across the roofs of the cars where the moon reflected back. He breathed in deeply through his mouth. Contemplation over, he turned around and entered the hotel. He needed to overhear the phone call to the police to mentally record all the names the clerk had for the hotel room Aaron had been in.

A moment ago, he had almost killed the clerk. Now the clerk was an ally after seeing his own version of the incident. Ansgar would have to leave the clerk alive. The police would hear that Aaron was a fugitive. For Ansgar, people were either allies or victims. Those were the only two categories he slotted people into.

Aaron would be found and killed within hours. If not, it wouldn't be more than a day. Then he would retake Clara Olafson. Or he would kill her. It didn't matter to him anymore. All that mattered was how this job ended.

It would end on his terms now that he was emotionally invested.

After all, anger was an emotion.

He clenched his fists as he listened to the clerk's version of the sordid tale to the 911 dispatcher.

Chapter 27

PARKMAN RAN ALONG THE path by the lake's edge in semi-darkness as the sun dropped behind the horizon. The screaming had only been brief, but the moaning and gasping for breaths led him forward until he came upon the two girls. One of them was rolling in the thick grass, wheezing in and out while she wiped at her face. The other girl was in a foot of water to his right, dumping her face in the lake, then coming back up gasping.

The smell of pepper spray grew in intensity the closer he got to them. Both girls were fully clothed. The one on the ground still had a tiny purse on her. This wasn't an attempted robbery or a sexual assault. It looked like the guy had just walked up and sprayed the girls in the face for no apparent reason.

"Det gør ondt," the girl in the grass said.

Parkman knelt beside her.

"Do you speak English?" he asked.

"Yes," she said. The word came out in a wheeze.

"Was it the man with the thick jacket?"

She nodded.

"Which way did he go?"

"Toward Kvickly," she said. "I cannot see. I heard him run that way."

"Did you recognize him?"

The girl shook her head.

More people were coming along the path now.

"Okay, these people will help you. I'm going to find this man. I'll be right back."

Parkman got to his feet as two other men came up. He told them he got a good description of the man who did this and that he was going after him. One man pulled out a cell phone and called for help as Parkman left them with the girls.

He followed the path to the back of the Kvickly parking lot, then ran toward the street. Checking both ways, he saw nothing. The man in the thick coat was gone.

He ran back through the parking lot of the Kvickly and jumped down onto the path by the water. To his right, half a dozen people milled around the girls. The one in the lake was being helped out of the water now.

To his left, the path vanished in the darkness. He started that way. At the edge of the building, where the parking lot lights lost ground, and the dark grabbed a foothold, he slowed down and eased up to the building, waiting for a few breaths until his eyes adjusted.

This had to have something to do with Sarah. Why else was he in Skanderborg hours before Sarah was meant to arrive? He was directed to be here by Sarah's sister, no less.

This attack had to be attached somehow to the purpose. The man with the thick coat was the connection. But where did he go? He could have gotten anywhere in the time it took Parkman to reach the girls, pause to talk to them, then continue past the grocery store.

He started along the beaten-down path, going slow to avoid tripping over an errant branch and ending up sprawled in the lake. The water lapped the shore softly to his right, darkened houses to his left. He steered closer to the water to get around a thicket of bushes. After passing several houses, he found a small dock where several boats were moored. The building to his left had a barely legible sign. The Skanderborg Rowing Club. He left the path and walked around to the front of the building, where he stopped and listened. Other than the sound of a distant vehicle, the evening was silent. He waited for a full minute, eyes closed, ears open. A distant rumbling moved closer. The train was entering the station up on the hill. As far as he was concerned, the man in the thick coat could already be at the train station.

Parkman headed back to the path and wended his way by the Kvickly until he returned to where the girls had been attacked. Half a dozen people lingered around the girls using water bottles to flush the remainder of the toxic substance from the girl's faces. People spoke Danish to one another, which kept Parkman out of the conversation.

It was late. The man in the thick coat had gotten away, and there was nothing else he could do. He wasn't here in an official capacity. It was time to leave them to their own law enforcement. He could stay and offer a description of the man, but he didn't want to. He wanted to find the man before the authorities did. The man in the coat was the connection to Sarah, to why Vivian sent them to Skanderborg. From what he discovered online, Skanderborg is a relatively crime-free city. To be that close to an attack on two teenagers meant he was in the right place at the right time.

He only hoped he didn't screw up whatever he was here for. If he was supposed to nab the man in the thick coat and didn't, then he had already screwed up.

Screw-ups cost lives.

And Sarah was on the way to Skanderborg.

He walked away from the crowd on the path and headed back toward Kvickly.

Determined to locate the man in the thick coat, Parkman decided to walk the area, street by street, until he found him or until the sun rose in the morning.

Chapter 28

AARON AND ALEX SLOWED as they neared the front of the hotel. Near the corner of the building, before stepping out into the open, Aaron heard men talking, then silence. He stopped and listened.

"Alex," he whispered. "Head around the other side?" He gestured behind Alex. "We'll meet at the front."

Alex nodded and took off sprinting.

Aaron waited a few moments, thoughts of Benjamin's wound fueling his anger. Ansgar would end up in the hospital when they were through with him. Aaron's teachers had saved his life once before. Years ago, a man abducted him and flew him to Greece, where he shot Aaron. If it weren't for his three teachers, Aaron would be dead. He owed them his life, yet they risked their lives for him and Sarah every time he turned around.

After a couple of deep breaths, he stepped out of hiding

and went to the front of the hotel. He surveyed the cars in the parking lot for any sign of movement. The chances Ansgar was still out there, ready to shoot him, were slim. Once the airport van pulled away, Ansgar would've come out of hiding, hence the reason for doubling back.

He stopped at the edge of the window and glanced inside the lobby. The clerk was behind the counter, a phone to his ear. Ansgar was walking away from the counter toward the elevators.

Was he going to his room?

A movement drew Aaron's eye to the other side of the lobby windows about twenty feet away. Alex had made it around the building and was seeing what he was seeing.

When he looked back inside, Ansgar slipped onto an elevator.

Aaron pushed away from the wall and ran for the front door. Alex got there first, prompting the front door to slide open. They stomped inside and headed for the elevator. Aaron needed to see the floor it stopped on.

The clerk saw him and jumped back.

"He's here," the clerk shouted into the phone. Then he ducked below the counter. "The man I told you about is in my lobby. He returned. Tell them to hurry."

Aaron exchanged a glance with Alex, then they were past the main desk and standing at the elevators as the one Ansgar took stopped on the tenth floor.

"Got a plan?" Aaron asked.

"Enlist the clerk's help. The empty room above or below Ansgar's. I'll get in from the balcony while you knock on the door."

"Why do I have to knock?" Aaron asked, pretending to

be offended. "He could open the door and shoot me while you're playing with the lock on the balcony's sliding door."

"You're more afraid of heights than I am."

Alex walked away and headed back to the clerk. Aaron followed. He was off the phone now but had broken out in a sweat, his face glistening. A nervous smile seemed pasted on his face as he stepped back to the wall behind the main desk, bumping it.

"Is room 1134 or 934 available?" Alex asked.

The clerk nodded but didn't move.

"Did you hear the gunfire outside ten minutes ago?" Aaron asked, taking on a serious tone. They couldn't afford to waste time and have Ansgar walk off the elevators behind them while they were dicking around with the clerk.

The man nodded. "Yes," he said, firm and steady despite appearing quite nervous.

"Then answer his question," Aaron added. "Is room 1134 or 934 empty?"

The clerk leaned forward, touched the closest computer's keyboard, then looked up.

"1134 is empty."

Aaron set his hand on the counter, palm up, then gestured with his fingers.

"Give me a key to 1134. I'll return it within fifteen minutes."

The clerk looked from Alex to Aaron, then back to Alex.

"C'mon, man," he said, adding irritation and anger to his voice. "Key."

The clerk jolted and pushed away from the wall, grabbed a keycard, typed something in on a small keyboard, and ran the card through a reader.

"This gonna work when we get up there?" Aaron asked, holding the card up in the air.

The clerk nodded profusely. "Yes, yes, sir."

He tapped Alex's shoulder, and they ran for the elevator. Once inside and ascending to the eleventh floor, he handed the keycard to Alex.

"What was his problem? He seemed extra nervous. We were the ones being shot at, not him. He should've been nervous when the shooter was standing in the lobby with him, for fuck's sake."

Alex nodded once in reply.

The doors opened on the eleventh floor, where Alex disembarked without a word.

The doors closed, and Aaron rode it down one floor. Hands up, standing in a defensive posture, he stood to the side as the door opened on the tenth floor.

The hall in front of the door was empty. He held the door open and peeked out toward Ansgar's door.

Empty.

Both ways.

Aaron got off the elevator and let the door close.

This was stupid. At any point, Ansgar could open his room door, raise his weapon and empty it into Aaron. There was no defense against a bullet. He wasn't wearing Kevlar and had no weapon except his hands.

He did have Alex, though.

Whether it was rage that brought him to this volatile place or not, he had to move forward because Alex would be in Ansgar's room in minutes, and Aaron was still standing by the elevators.

Hoping they both would make it out alive, he started

toward Ansgar's room, fists clenched.

Chapter 29

SARAH ENJOYED THE UNEVENTFUL flight to Copenhagen. Regardless of what was happening to her and Aaron and everyone else involved, she had been able to catch up on much-needed sleep during the flight. In Copenhagen for a long layover, she had a few drinks in the bar, then boarded her flight to Billund.

Just under an hour later, she landed in Billund and deplaned, walking right by the luggage carousel as she traveled so light she didn't even have a bag. A passport, a small wallet with ID, bank cards, a little cash, and her cell phone were all she needed for the few days she'd be in Denmark. Sarah was used to buying a new piece of underwear or socks, discarding the old, and boarding the next flight home. Carrying luggage, even small carry-on bags, weighed her down. This was her preferred way to travel unless she was going on a vacation.

On the way to Skanderborg, she bought a small flask of whiskey from inside the terminal. Once there, she would sleep like a baby in whatever hotel was the closest. The booze helped her deal with the loss of Vivian and the ache that missing Aaron had created in her core.

How had she let anyone get that far inside her soul? Her lifestyle didn't allow her to be tied down, to love like this, yet she fell so hard over the last year that she wasn't even aware of it until she broke their pact back in the Vegas hotel. Then she thought Aaron had died because of it. The realization that he was gone only to be returned to her made her want to grab him and hold on tight so he couldn't go anywhere.

But she couldn't. Vivian called. They needed to complete this job, whatever this job was. And even if she did it right, little boys would continue to be molested.

What the hell does that mean, sis?

Still no response. Not even a whiff of her presence.

Outside the terminal in Billund, she got a few quotes from taxis and went with the best deal. A one-hour ride to Skanderborg. Halfway there, she finished the flask of whiskey. Headlights coming toward them seemed to jog left and right. She closed and opened her eyes. The shaking car upset her stomach. She closed her eyes, slipped lower in the seat, and rested her hands on her stomach.

The car came to a stop.

She snapped awake and sat up. She grabbed the seat on either side to steady the dizziness.

A red light. The driver met her eyes in the rearview.

"Almost there, ma'am," he said. "Two more city blocks."

Sarah nodded, then regretted it. She lowered back in the seat and waited until the driver pulled into the train station in

Skanderborg before she sat up again.

He reminded her of the amount they had agreed upon. She fished the new currency out—Danish Kroner—and paid him.

"Tak," she said, learning the word for *thank you* in Danish while in Copenhagen.

"Selv tak," the driver said as she exited the vehicle.

She turned back, holding onto the open door.

"What's that mean?" she asked, feeling the effects of the alcohol more as she bent down to look at the driver. This was a serious mission to Denmark, and she'd drank more than she should have. She knew that now. Nothing a good night's sleep wouldn't fix, though.

"Basically, it means *you're welcome*. But it's interpreted as thanks back to you."

"Okay, well then, selv tak."

Sarah shut the cab's back door and turned too fast. She shuffled her feet to regain balance and surveyed the city lights in the dark.

What the hell did she need to deal with in Skanderborg? How were they tied to what was happening so far away in Toronto? The only person she could come up with was Clara's dad. But that didn't make any sense. How would people be molested if they fixed everything? Nothing made sense, and it wouldn't become clear while she was this drunk. She needed a hotel. Then sleep. In that order. Then find Anton Olafson and see if he could understand what was going on.

It was late, and the streets were virtually empty. She turned in a full circle and didn't see a single building that resembled a hotel. No Best Western or Holiday Inn near the train station in Skanderborg.

She frowned and looked down at the ground.

"Why didn't I have him drive me to a hotel?" she asked herself out loud.

A taxi came up to the street light about fifty yards away. She started toward it, waving her arms. On the green, the cab turned and disappeared toward what looked like the center of town.

At the light, Sarah waited until the walk sign came on, then crossed the street. She decided she would walk until she saw a hotel or sobered up. She would walk an hour or two, and if nothing happened, she would call information and ask them for help.

Did Denmark use information like they did in the States? Was their emergency phone number 911 like the States?

As she walked, she pulled out her phone and Googled these questions. It turned out that 911 was actually 112. The website said she had to dial 112 in Denmark for emergencies.

"112?" she said to herself. "That seems like an odd number." She shrugged as she walked. "No big deal."

She brought up the maps feature on her phone. A blue dot revealed her location. Another dot revealed where Anton Olafson's house was. She had typed his address in while on the flight to Copenhagen.

"Shit, he's close."

Maybe he would be a kind gentleman and let her sleep the night at his place before they figured out what was happening in the morning.

A car sped up behind her. She turned to see who would drive so crazy. The red and blue lights on top of the police car were blinding. After another minute, two more police cars raced by as she walked on the sidewalk.

Something big was happening in small-town Skanderborg, but it had nothing to do with her. She was a block from Anton's house now and figured that was the best place to go.

The maps application instructed her to turn left and head down a small road past the rowing club.

Clara had said something about a rowing club being two houses away from hers.

She passed the rowing club a minute later and slowed, checking the map. Once she stood out in front of Anton's house, she put away her phone and studied the front. All the lights were off. It didn't look like anyone was home.

"Shit. There goes my good night's sleep."

To be sure, she headed up the front walkway and knocked on the door. She waited, then knocked again.

Nothing. Not even a hint of movement inside the house, like footfalls on the stairs.

She trudged out to the road and stood in the center of the small street under the light of a small lamp, where she pulled out the piece of paper Clara had written on back in the Toronto hotel. She stared at the drawing of the house where Clara had placed a large X, two down from the rowing club. This was the house, no doubt about it. Anton Olafson's house was right in front of her, but Clara's dad wasn't home.

Sarah wavered on her feet. Even though she'd slept on her way to Copenhagen, she needed more. The whiskey and wine from earlier made it hard to stay upright.

A rush of movement close by caught her attention, but she didn't see what it was before it smashed into her. Then she was airborne. The ground came hard and fast, knocking the wind out of her lungs.

She struggled to breathe. The name Olafson came out in a gasp, unintelligible. The man who bumped into her shot his arm out and sprayed something on her face.

Her hands shot to her face as she was blinded and couldn't breathe properly. Panicked, Sarah struggled to catch a breath through the toxic spray. As the man dragged her along the ground, she vomited from the alcohol and feared being unable to breathe.

The bile in her throat did nothing to open her airways.

In fact, all it did was make it even harder to breathe.

Blinded by the spray, Sarah hacked and wheezed until she passed out for lack of oxygen.

Chapter 30

ANTON DRAGGED THE BARELY breathing girl off the road and through the front door of his house. In under two minutes, he had her bound in the spare bedroom. He debated gagging her, but since she couldn't breathe too well, he decided against it. He couldn't have her dying on him until he was ready to kill her. For a brief moment, it didn't sound like she was breathing.

He moved closer to listen.

Nothing.

He closed his eyes and held his breath as he leaned down to her nose, where he detected the faint rasp of air forcing its way along her nasal passages, mostly via her open mouth.

After checking the bungee cord wrapped around the girl's wrists and ankles, Anton bolted back outside and scanned the windows of his neighbor's homes. Lights were out in the houses on either side of his. No one walked the street at this late hour near his property. Therefore, no one saw a damn thing. He was in the clear. And he had a blonde girl that looked exactly like Clara subdued in his home.

It couldn't get any better than that.

Compelled to smile, Anton slapped his hands together, blew out air, and stared up at the starry sky. Tonight he would secure Clara's future, and in doing so, he would save himself from personal damnation.

He plodded back to the front door and stepped inside. Once the front door was shut, he locked it and used the window beside the door to peer outside. The street was dark and still empty. He waited, staring at shadows, gazing back and forth, but no one came out of the dark to point their finger at him. No one came and knocked on his door. Witnesses to his spraying and abduction of the girl in the other room were nonexistent.

She was a gift from the heavens. She was perfect.

He leaned against the doorframe and stared down at her, frowning. Why was this girl standing in front of his house? Who was she, and why was she dressed in Clara's clothes?

Could the hacker have sent her? Was that what this was? The hacker needed this girl killed, so he orchestrated an elaborate plot to have Anton kill her? If so, it was a risky plot. Anton could've killed a random girl the first day. Or he could've done it in Aarhus. The hacker changed the details halfway through the week, too. Locate and murder a girl that resembled Clara, he'd said. But why, and did it really matter? Anton believed the hacker would hurt Clara, and wasn't that all he needed to move forward?

He pulled out his cell phone and texted the hacker.

I've got a subject. Want to watch live?

He waited, but no response was forthcoming. After a minute, Anton checked the girl's breathing again and then headed for the kitchen. He would make a cup of tea and wait for the girl to wake up or the hacker to respond.

If the girl woke up, he would grill her on who she was and why she wore his daughter's clothes.

If the hacker responded and wanted the deed completed, he would murder the stupid girl where she lay.

As long as he received assurances that Clara would be safe, he would do anything and everything needed to guarantee that safety.

What parent wouldn't?

Once the kettle was warming and the tea bag was in his cup, he slipped into the bathroom for a piss. Midstream, mind wandering, a loud banging resonated throughout the house.

His urine was cut off as he ducked like someone attacked him with a sledgehammer.

He fumbled with his pants and ran out to the kitchen, where he flicked off the kettle to kill the noise it was making.

The banging came again.

Someone was at the door. The clock on the microwave said it was just nearing one in the morning.

This had to be the police. They would want to talk about the two girls he attacked on the path by the library. It could ruin him. If the girl in the other room woke when the door was open, he would spend the rest of the night in a holding cell.

A few spots of piss clung to his legs. He rubbed the pants on his thighs to dispel that cool feeling, then started for the front door.

The last thing he needed was the police banging on his

door at this late hour and waking the girl in the spare bedroom. Nor did he want his neighbors to see the police presence at his door.

He would talk them away and contact a lawyer. He could fight an assault charge by claiming he thought he was being attacked in the dark. He could apologize and make reparations to the families of the young girls. In essence, Anton was confident he could make it all go away.

The knocking came again, louder this time.

He ran for the door, his stomach churning at the thought of losing Clara.

At any point, if he fucked this up, Clara would be dead, and he wouldn't let a stupid cop stop him from saving Clara's life.

Even if that meant he had to kill the cop, too.

Chapter 31

Street by street, winding his way through neighborhood after neighborhood, Parkman had passed only five people at that time of night. The streets of Skanderborg were relatively empty now that the Burning of the Witch was over. No one resembled the man in the thick coat.

Parkman hadn't seen Sarah either. Frustrated that he was missing something, he stopped by the train station to check their arrival schedule. Not another train until three in the morning and then at five.

Directionless, which sucked for him as the private investigator of the bunch, he grabbed his cell phone and dialed long distance to Caleb's house in Santa Rosa while chewing on a toothpick.

It was answered on the first ring.

"Caleb, it's Parkman."

"Good news or bad?" Caleb asked.

"No news."

There was a pause on the other end of the line. Parkman lumbered toward the street light in front of the train station.

"What's happening?" Caleb asked. "You're in Skanderborg, right?"

Parkman spit the toothpick out. "Yeah. I still don't know why, though."

"Has to be Sarah related. Aaron called yesterday to update me after Sarah left Toronto. One sec." The phone pulled away. Parkman detected the punching of keys on a keyboard. "Here it is. I just brought up the flight to Billund. Sarah landed hours ago." Caleb's mouth moved closer to the phone. "That's an hour's drive to where you are. That means she is most likely in Skanderborg and has been for hours."

Parkman made it to the light, turning in a full circle as if Sarah was close enough to see. It angered him to know she was somewhere in the same small town, and he had no idea where.

"I haven't seen her. I'm at the train station. It's just after twelve-thirty in the morning here, and I've got nothing, Caleb. Could use some help."

"Here, I'll text you an address."

"Whose?"

"A man named Anton Olafson. He's Clara's father. I got it from Aaron. They have Clara safe and secure in Toronto. When Sarah headed for Skanderborg, as far as I was led to believe, she was supposed to go to Anton's"—Parkman's phone dinged as a message was received—"house to talk to him about his daughter. Maybe the man's address will help."

"I got the message," Parkman said. Then a thought occurred to him as he started across the road at the green light. "Hey, Caleb. Is there a chance you have a picture of Anton Olafson?"

"Sure, I have it somewhere. I looked his name up after Aaron gave it to me. I wanted to see if he was a police captain or a warden of a prison or some shit that would make Sarah's life difficult. Turns out he works for the Danish National Cyber Crime Center out of Aarhus."

Parkman continued walking toward the center of town, anxious to get the picture so he would know what Anton looked like when he saw him. If Sarah was supposed to check this guy out, maybe that was where she was now.

"Here it is," Caleb said. "I'll text it to you in a minute. Anything else happening?"

"Nothing, really. They burned a witch here tonight."

"What?" Caleb gasped. "They did what?"

"Look it up when you have a moment. Too much to explain now, and I don't have the full story. Some kind of celebration to mark something in European history. Anyway, after the burning, I chased a guy who pepper-sprayed two girls. Other than that, nothing doing in Skanderborg."

There was a pause again.

"Caleb?" Parkman said.

"Yeah. I'm here. Just don't like it."

"Like what?"

"Sarah's there. Vivian sent her. You're there for a reason. Just worried something'll go wrong. I hope this witch-burning thing isn't some kind of cosmic foreshadowing."

"I know. Sarah's not a witch, though."

"It's just, Sarah's all we have, and she's always off fighting someone. When she has Vivian in her head, we feel pretty good about it. But it's all upside down right now.

These messages Vivian wrote are twenty-five years old." He coughed, then cleared his throat. "Parkman, you'd think having kids would be easier."

"Is it ever easy?" Parkman asked.

In the background, Amelia called out Caleb's name.

"Look, Parkman. I have to go. I'm at the end of the phone line if you need anything. Just call."

"Yeah. All I need is the picture of Anton. I should be good for the night after that."

"Sending it as soon as we hang up."

"Be strong, Caleb. This'll all be over soon."

"I will. Gotta run."

Parkman clicked off and checked the address Caleb had sent him. He fed it into his maps application and assessed the distance from where he was. Anton's house was a ten-minute walk away.

He zoomed in on the location for a better look at the area. The house was on the water. Two houses down from the rowing club. On the path that led from the library. He had been on that path earlier tonight, walking right behind Anton's house.

He pulled the pack of toothpicks from his back pocket and almost dropped them. Once one was in the corner of his mouth, he slipped the pack away and started off.

After a few blocks, he turned down a street to his left, following the phone's directions. When he hadn't received the picture of Anton from Caleb, he texted him asking for it as he was coming up to Anton's house in a few minutes.

On the access to Anton's street, Parkman slowed and took it all in. When the rowing club was to his left, his cell phone dinged.

He opened his messages and downloaded the picture of Anton Olafson that Caleb had snatched off the internet.

The second it loaded and lit up Parkman's cell phone screen, he knew who it was.

Anton Olafson was the man in the thick coat. He was the man Parkman had chased and was looking for the past few hours. And now he knew how Anton had escaped. The man lived on the path he had used to get away.

Parkman strode the last twenty feet and stopped in front of Anton's house. A light flickered somewhere inside the house. He took a deep breath and detected the residual scent of pepper spray.

He dropped to his knees in the dark to move closer to the heart of the smell. The flashlight application on his iPhone lit up the side of the street. Near the shoulder of the road, he found a piece of paper from a Toronto hotel pad. On it was a diagram of the area with a large X marking Olafson's house.

Clara must've drawn this for Sarah to guide her to the house. Since the paper was no longer in Sarah's possession, she had to be inside Anton's house.

He got to his feet and put his phone away. He studied the house, flipping the toothpick from side to side. Without wasting another moment, Parkman marched toward the front door and banged on it hard. After a moment, he spit the toothpick out and banged on the door again.

If Anton Olafson had attacked those girls in public earlier tonight, what would he do to Sarah privately?

If Anton had done anything to Sarah, he would not just break a few bones. He would break the man in half. The man would eat with a straw for months and not speak right again until Parkman had Sarah home and safe.

Parkman was in Skanderborg for Sarah. It would be his fault if anything happened to her. It was his fault because the man with the thick coat had been in spitting distance of Parkman earlier this evening, and he had let him get away.

If anything happened to Sarah, how could he live with himself?

He banged on the door again.

Even harder this time.

Chapter 32

AARON APPROACHED THE CLOSED hotel room door tentatively, making sure to give Alex enough time to get into position as much as staying cautious to not be surprised by Ansgar. The Clock could've simply entered his room, did a fast search of what was left behind, then stepped out just as Aaron went to knock.

The problem with the hotel hallway was the lack of escape routes, as all the other room's doors were locked. The only exits were the stairwells at either end of the hall—one beside Ansgar's door—and the elevator.

Aaron was fast, though. If he detected the lock disengaging, he could turn and race the length of the hall in seconds. He couldn't outrun a bullet, but he could certainly try not to have to deal with one.

At the edge of Ansgar's door, he leaned in closer and listened. The room beyond the door was silent. He waited a moment longer but heard nothing.

Could Ansgar have already left and headed back downstairs? If so, the clerk would tell him about Aaron and Alex and that they took a key for the room above Ansgar's.

He had wasted enough time. Alex would have already gained access to the room above Ansgar's and would be dropping down to the balcony by now. Aaron had moved slowly, cautiously, but Alex wouldn't have been slowed down on the eleventh floor.

Aaron stretched his arms, did one squat to wake muscles up, took a deep breath, and knocked on Ansgar's door. It unnerved him that he didn't have a weapon. If Ansgar opened the door with a gun, things could get dicey fast. Aaron believed Ansgar wouldn't shoot first. He would want to know where they'd stashed Clara. At least, that's what Aaron was banking on.

When the door remained shut, he knocked again.

On the third knock, Aaron was sure Ansgar wasn't in the room. A shadow hadn't clouded the door's peephole the entire time.

He placed an ear to the door's surface and stopped breathing to listen.

Nothing.

A lock clicked.

Aaron jumped back from the door and almost bumped into the door of the room behind him, which had been Clara's room. He didn't bump into it because it had opened.

The second he gained his balance, a firm object bumped into the back of his skull at the top of his vertebrae.

"A Glock 17," Ansgar said behind him, "can do significant damage at this close range." Ansgar's voice was all nasal. "I wouldn't budge. Not so much as a whiff of breath. If a tiny hair on your head moves the wrong way, I'll get to see just how much damage a Glock 17 can do."

A pounding in his ears increased as he eased air in and out through his mouth. He had been foiled. Ansgar must have figured he'd be followed and had sequestered himself in Clara's room, waiting for Aaron to come knocking.

"Move slow," Ansgar ordered. "Start toward my room across the hall. Do anything I don't like, and I will end your life. The sound suppressor on my Glock works expertly. Now move."

Aaron willed his right foot forward, then his left. If he dodged fast enough to the right and raised a foot backward into Ansgar's crotch, he might have a chance. Maybe an elbow to the face. Without disarming Ansgar, The Clock, the ex-Navy Seal sniper, Aaron wasn't sure he'd survive any attempt to attack him.

Another step. Then another. The gun didn't go off. Aaron was now inside Ansgar's room as the door was unlocked.

"Move toward the bed."

Ansgar jammed the tip of the weapon into Aaron, nudging him forward. He scanned the room for Alex as he walked slowly toward the bed.

The gun wasn't against his flesh anymore. Ansgar had pulled away from him. The sound of the door closing behind him told him why. The lock clicked home. They were alone in Ansgar's room.

"Turn around," Ansgar said.

Aaron did, slowly, keeping his hands away from his sides in a non-threatening manner. Really, he just wanted his hands up and ready to do something when needed.

"How's your friend?" Ansgar asked, a wry smile pasted on his lips.

Aaron ground his teeth and glared at the man standing across from him. Ansgar shrugged, then moved toward the chair in the corner. He sat on the arm of the chair, the gun resting on his leg. It was a taunt. An are-you-faster-than-my-gun tease. At this point, Aaron wasn't interested in testing it.

"Where's the other friend?" Ansgar asked. "The smaller one."

Aaron didn't respond.

"Why didn't you just drive away? You could've regrouped. Thought about a better plan than coming up here unarmed. Pretty stupid of you, wasn't it?"

After another moment, Ansgar got up and approached Aaron. The Glock was level and aimed at Aaron's stomach.

"You're supposed to be dead," Ansgar said. "How did you know I had planted the bombs at your dojo? And knowing that, why didn't you do something when I talked to you that morning about joining the classes?"

Ansgar seemed to study Aaron's face, looking at his chin, then his forehead. He placed the weapon up under Aaron's chin.

"You can answer my questions," Ansgar said. "I won't bite. Not yet, anyway."

Aaron studied the bandages on Ansgar's face. The damage Sarah did in such a short time was eye candy to Aaron. He let a smile play across his lips.

Ansgar raised the gun and placed it against Aaron's forehead.

"Look up at the gun. I have something to tell you."

Aaron stared at Ansgar's face.

"I said," Ansgar jammed the gun forward, knocking Aaron's head back, "look up at the gun."

Aaron complied with Ansgar's request. The second his eyes landed on the Glock, a lightning bolt of pain shot through his abdomen, and he crumpled to the floor.

When he looked up, the man had kneed Aaron in the crotch. Aaron rolled into a tight ball and moaned. The unique pain of being hit between the legs rippled through his body while Ansgar laughed.

"Big tough guy on the floor," he said in a baby voice. "Whatcha gonna do, widdle baby?"

Ropes landed on Aaron's chest.

"Tie yourself up. Start with the ankles. I'll do the wrists."

The pain hadn't even begun to subside when Ansgar kicked him in the back.

Aaron arched like a landed fish on the floor of a boat, then curled back into a ball.

"I said, tie yourself up," Ansgar roared.

Aaron eased out of the ball he'd formed and tried to straighten his body. His eyes had watered, and the room was a blur, but he still caught the movement behind the curtain. Ansgar had his back to the room's small balcony.

The curtains whooshed up as if a soft breeze ruffled them, then Alex suddenly appeared behind Ansgar.

Aaron wiped his eyes and got into the best defensive position he could on his back.

"I told you to tie yourself—" Ansgar stopped talking. He must have detected the change in the room because he spun around, bringing the Glock up to pistol whip whoever was behind him.

Alex easily ducked out of the way of Ansgar's swipe,

jumped sideways, pushed off the wall to gain height, and landed on Ansgar's back. Ansgar was a large man, muscular and thick compared to the lithe Alex. But Alex knew pressure points and how to cripple a man with his fingertips, no matter what the man weighed or how much he could bench press.

The second Alex had landed on Ansgar, the man rushed back toward the wall. Alex seemed to have a grip on the man's neck, but whatever he was going for was too little too late. Ansgar grunted, and his left side slanted downward as he smashed into the wall. Alex was sandwiched momentarily between the large man and the wall.

Powerless to help, Aaron watched as Ansgar snapped his head back, barely missing Alex's face. Then Ansgar rammed elbow after elbow into Alex's abdomen as he held him pinned against the wall by sheer force.

As fast as it started, it was over. Ansgar jumped away from the wall. Alex crumpled to the floor, rolled sideways, and hopped behind the curtain again.

Other than grunts, they fought without a word.

The intense pain flared in his crotch as Aaron tried to get to his feet.

Ansgar tracked Alex with the Glock in his hand that was aimed at the curtain.

Aaron leaned against the bed, halfway to a full standing position. A pffft sounded from the Glock as a bullet exited the silencer. The curtains kicked up where the bullet hit.

Ansgar shot at the curtains again.

From his side of the room, Aaron saw Alex jump onto the small balcony of the tenth-floor hotel room. There was no escape for Alex.

Aaron made another feeble attempt to get to his feet. He

lunged for Ansgar to stop the madness but was batted away by the man's forearm as he moved left and looked out at the balcony.

Ansgar raised his gun and aimed it at Alex.

In the time it took to blink, Alex flipped upside down and disappeared over the balcony railing.

Ansgar stomped onto the balcony and looked down. He returned a moment later.

"Looks like your friend didn't have wings after all." Ansgar shrugged. "Oops. So much for your guardian angel."

Chapter 33

ANTON OLAFSON REACHED THE small window by the door and stopped when he saw who had knocked.

It wasn't the police. It was a man, and he was alone.

"Yes?" Anton moaned through the locked door. "What cause would you have to knock on my door and wake me at this horrid hour?"

The man jolted at the sound, then leaned down to the window and tried to peer inside, but the clouded glass around the front door made that impossible. Anton was shrouded in darkness on the inside, yet there was enough light for him to see the man on the stoop.

"Open up," the man said. "Police."

"Bullshit," Anton shouted. "A Danish cop with an American accent. Fuck off. Go bug one of my neighbors."

Anton slipped back behind the front wall so his silhouette wouldn't show through the clouded glass. He waited for some indication that the man would leave but heard nothing.

"I know it was you," the man said. "Open the door. Talk to me or talk to the police."

Anton didn't respond. Maybe the man would think he had gone back to bed.

"You walked past me before you sprayed those two girls with pepper spray. Your name is Anton Olafson."

He gasped and covered his mouth with a hand. Who was this man, and how did he know so much? Anton almost said something but decided not to. He chanced a look at the guest room door to make sure the girl hadn't untied herself.

"Anton, open the door. Your daughter is safe. But she won't be for long."

My daughter?

How did this man know about Clara?

He chanced a peek around the corner of the wall. The man stood outside the door, unmoving.

Did the hacker send him? Had he been following him? To what end? Anton had the girl in the other room. He was prepared to murder her tonight for Clara's freedom. Did he have to perform this horrendous deed, or was it over?

"Why won't my daughter be safe for long?" Anton asked before he could stop himself.

"If you hurt a single hair on the girl you have in your house, Clara will never make it home. I personally guarantee that. Now open the door so we can discuss this."

His stomach dropped. Sweat slipped down his spine. The hacker gave him instructions to protect Clara. He was following those instructions. Now a strange man was at his door telling him the opposite. Was he the correct one? Should the girl in the other room be let go? If so, what was Anton basing that on? The hacker saw the photos on his computer. The hacker knew about Damien's arrest and Anton's indiscretions in Aarhus. The hacker lured Clara from Denmark without his knowledge. As far as Anton was concerned, he would stick to the plan that he and the hacker had worked out. Whoever this man was and what he knew meant little to Anton. Let him spew his bullshit. When he stepped away from the stoop, Anton would carry on with what he set out to do.

He wiped his hand on his pants, then ran one through his thinning hair. He stopped his hand near the back of his head and scrunched up a batch of hair, pulling until the pain soothed him. His eyes glazed over.

What had he gotten himself into? There was no escaping this. A part of him knew that from the beginning. He had gone forward anyway. For Clara. Everything was for Clara.

Save Clara.

"Open the door, Anton," the man said as he knocked again. "I know you have Sarah. Is she unconscious? Is she still alive?"

Anton slipped down the wall until he was sitting on the floor. He would listen until the man left. Once he departed, Anton would film the murder of the girl, with or without the hacker, on a live feed. If he didn't do it soon, he would lose the nerve.

"I know she's not conscious," the stranger said. "If she were, you wouldn't've answered the door. She would have."

He drew his legs up and rested his head on his forearms. The man was silent for a few moments. Anton waited for more.

He knocked again, this time lighter.

"I will return with the police. I hope you're hearing me, Anton. I know you have Sarah Roberts in there; she would never go quietly. For your sake, I hope she's just sleeping." The sound of boots on the front steps resonated through the door. "I'll be back with the authorities."

Sarah Roberts?

Had he heard that name before? Did he know the girl?

What did it matter who she was? Her life was over. A trade. Sarah's life for Clara's life.

Anton rose from the floor, slapped his hands together to brush them off, and shrugged.

"Sarah Roberts, whoever you are, will be dead in under five minutes." The thought of saving his daughter with this one act made him feel heroic. "I thank you for your service to my family."

Anton Olafson went to get his cell phone to record the murder and a small mirror. He was going to give the hacker all the proof he needed.

The consequences would come later.

He would deal with them then.

Save Clara.

Chapter 34

ANSGAR HOLM SLIPPED HIS Glock into the back of his pants and strode over to Aaron. These stupid kids thought they would get the jump on him, a man with a long service record. A body-building, hand-to-hand combat veteran that now hired out his services as a private military contractor.

The pathetic face of their leader, Aaron, looked up at him with something akin to poison in his eyes.

Ansgar pulled his foot back and kicked Aaron in the side of the face, knocking the kid's head into the bedpost. Aaron's head bounced once off the carpet, and his eyes fluttered, then shut. He moaned something, then tried to open his eyes again. A faint trickle of blood oozed from his mouth.

Ansgar was sick of playing these schoolyard games. He needed answers before he left the hotel for good. With the gunfire earlier and the dead kid on the ground who had just jumped from the tenth-floor balcony, the authorities would be roaming the area soon because the clerk downstairs had called them about the airport van.

In the corner by the bathroom door, Ansgar grabbed the clothes iron and added water to it. He plugged it in and waited, watching Aaron as he tried to get up off the floor.

The man was missing a finger. The loss looked recent the way the ragged stump appeared.

"How'd you lose the finger?" Ansgar asked.

"A dead man thought he could use it to buy something." Aaron rolled onto his back and sat up, using the bed to rest his back against.

"A dead man did that?"

"No, stupid. He died because he did it."

"Is that a warning? Are you telling me I'll be dead for what I'm doing to you?" Ansgar glanced at the iron. "Or what I'm going to do to you?"

Aaron moaned when he touched the cheek that had swollen. He wiped the blood from his chin.

"I'm not part of the equation," Aaron said. "You're dead regardless of what has happened or will happen. It has nothing to do with me."

Ansgar barked out a laugh. "You're quite the asshole. Threatening me when I hold the cards." He clucked his tongue. "This'll all be over soon, and I will go on to another job. When I do, I will think back to you and smile. At least you had balls. Can't say that for many of the people I kill."

He unplugged the iron, pulled out the Glock, and walked over to stand in front of Aaron. With his foot, he drew the side chair closer and sat. The Glock never wavering, he set the iron on the carpet and kicked his shoes off. Then he removed one of his black dress socks and balled it up.

"Where's the girl I had in my possession?" Ansgar asked, balled sock in one hand, Glock in the other.

Aaron shrugged.

"Where's my cell phone?" Ansgar asked.

Aaron tilted his head toward the balcony. "He had it last."

Ansgar didn't like Aaron's smart attitude. When he finished him off, he would burn the attitude out of him.

He glanced at the iron, then back to Aaron.

"How did you find me here in this hotel?"

Aaron met his gaze. In his eyes, Ansgar saw defiance mixed with a tinge of hatred.

"How did you know I was going to kill you at the dojo? Since you knew, why didn't you try to stop me?"

"Fuck your mother," Aaron said. "I fucked her and wouldn't do it again. She's an ugly, dirty skank."

Ansgar jammed the balled sock into Aaron's mouth, forcing it in as Aaron squirmed under the pressure by placing the Glock at Aaron's neck.

"I will shoot you in the throat," Ansgar whispered.

Then the sock popped into Aaron's mouth, forcing his jaw to its limits.

With his free hand, he grabbed the iron and raised it over Aaron's right forearm. It had cooled some since it was plugged in, but it was definitely hot enough to burn flesh.

Their eyes locked. Ansgar was reminded of a Taliban sympathizer he'd tortured in an underground hideout using a metal rod heated in a fire. That man's eyes looked like Aaron's. He knew the pain was coming, and he knew it would be a lot of pain. What was most important was he knew that he was powerless to stop it.

Ansgar pressed the iron onto Aaron's flesh and leaned into it as Aaron screeched with pain behind the balled-up sock.

The acrid smell of hair and burning flesh stunk up the hotel room. He pulled the iron off, and Aaron slumped onto the carpet, writhing with the pain.

Outside, the sound of police sirens wailed in the distance.

Aaron had to be convinced to give him the answers he needed faster. Once Aaron was dead, he would hunt Aaron's teachers from the dojo. They had seen his face. They knew who he was. He would retrieve that Danish girl and kill them all. He was on a mission. The amount of fuck ups were too high. It was time to clean up the mess and move on.

He lowered the iron and seared the flesh of Aaron's other arm to the wonderful sound of Aaron's muffled screams.

The man would talk. Ansgar would burn the answers out of him.

Or he would die a silent idiot.

Either way, it mattered little to Ansgar. The torture was the reward. He loved someone else's pain. There was great enjoyment in wading through the levels of pain in others.

Combat taught him that.

Chapter 35

Anton Olafson was ready. The hacker had not responded to his text so that the live feed wouldn't happen. He would record the event and send the hacker the video.

His cell phone battery was at fifty-three percent. Plenty of juice to film the few minutes he would need to kill the girl. He had a couple of small mirrors but chose to go with the circular pocket mirror he had found in Clara's bedroom.

He collected everything and started for the guest room with plans to do it right there on the floor. The body would be easy to hide for the first few days. Before it began to smell too much, he would discard it in the lake in the middle of the night, weighing it down with the bags of gravel he had in the garage.

If he could ask for one small reprieve, it would be that the girl—Sarah Roberts—still be passed out when he started.

But that wasn't going to happen.

When he stepped into the guest room, her eyes followed him. He didn't look at her. He shut the door to block any noise and set the small mirror on the bedside table.

The girl was tied up so tight that no amount of struggle would release her wrists or ankles. Immediately after the man left his front door, he jammed a large white sock into Sarah's mouth to stop her from screaming if she woke up while he wasn't in the room. He didn't fear her throwing up and dying on him. That would actually be a blessing as it would avoid an up-close-and-personal murder.

She was his completely. Lucky for her, he was not too attracted to fully developed women in their twenties, or he would have had a small adventure on her before she retired from this life. He liked flat-chested, small, skinny males; this woman was the opposite. Tall, standard attractive blonde with an average-sized chest was too common for Anton.

But none of that mattered. What mattered was how he was going to end her life. He needed it done quickly to get the body into hiding before that man returned with the authorities.

Sarah moaned behind the sock, her eyes pleading. He cared little for what she had to say. In fact, communicating with her would only make what he had to do over the next few minutes that much harder.

He had debated with himself how he was going to do it. Whether or not he would blindfold her, use his hands to cover her mouth and nose, or stab her to death. In the end, he chose to use a pillow. Since she was bound so securely, a pillow over the face for at least two minutes would be all he needed. No bruising, no blood, no pleading eyes watching him.

He placed the cell phone on the floor up against the wall and pushed record. Once he saw the timer counting, he ensured the girl's face was visible on the screen.

Her eyes were on him the entire time. He felt them stabbing into his back and was sure those intense eyes would haunt him for years to come. He had even come to terms with spending the rest of his life in prison for what he was about to do. After what he had been doing to underage boys for years, prison was his final destination. But with this one act, he would do that knowing Clara was free. Did he trust the hacker? Not really, but he had no other choice. The hacker had Clara, and this was what he asked of him. So he would do it.

He stepped over the girl.

"Sarah Roberts," he said for the sake of the camera. "This is my one act that begs your forgiveness in the face of what I must do for my daughter."

Sarah moaned again as if she was attempting to communicate something.

He pulled the pillow off the bed and grasped it on either side.

Her eyes widened. She stared at the camera, then up at him.

"I'm so sorry," he whispered.

Before she could squirm sideways or flip over entirely, Anton dropped down on her and secured her bound body under his weight. He felt like he was fighting an epileptic experiencing a seizure.

He lowered the pillow onto her face and pressed the edges around her ears, holding the pillow and her body as securely as possible.

Sarah fought him like a wild boar, bucking and kicking. Riding a bull in a rodeo while attempting to stay upright flashed through his mind. This girl was strong. He hadn't anticipated the violence in her subdued figure.

It couldn't last, though, not without a supply of oxygen. As long as he maintained the pillow over her nose and mouth, the fight would wane quickly.

Anton redoubled his efforts after thirty seconds, panting and sweating into his eyes. He blinked the sweat away and let his own grunts of exertion seep out of his mouth.

Somewhere in the house, there was a loud banging. Someone shouted.

That fucking man was back. He came back too fast. If only he'd waited another couple of minutes.

Anton leaned in over the pillow and forced its edges to touch the hardwood floor on either side of Sarah's face, completely wrapping her face in it. The fight in her had already diminished to less than twenty percent of what it was.

The banging again. Anton would not open the door until they had a search warrant. He would refuse entry until he could deal with the body. Even though he resigned himself to prison for the rest of his life, he still wanted to do what he could to avoid it if possible.

The banging on the front door stopped.

The girl's body slowed. It twitched once. Then stopped, her bound hands easing off his stomach where they had been pushing upward uselessly.

Anton held the pillow firm, his body sprawled across the girl's body. He waited for more knocking from the man, for more fighting from the girl, but neither came.

The camera was still recording. In the small window of

the phone, he didn't recognize the man he had become. Political meetings in Copenhagen, joining the NC3, taking Clara to dinner to celebrate. None of that was Anton Olafson anymore. He was a murderer now. A cold-blooded killer.

He eased off the girl slowly, ready to leap back on her if her calm was a ruse.

He saw something he had never seen before when he lifted the pillow from her face.

The open stare of the dead.

"Sarah Roberts," he whispered. "I now declare you," he paused to ensure the camera picked up the word, "dead."

He snatched the phone up off the floor and grabbed the small mirror from the bedside table. With the mirror close to the woman's nose, he filmed it directly under her nostrils.

No breath.

No smudges on the mirror.

"Dead," he declared again.

He stopped the filming and left the room. After another minute, he uploaded the file for the hacker to access when he came online.

His job was over. He had done what the hacker had asked of him.

He had killed a random girl. One that resembled Clara.

He had done it.

But somehow, it didn't feel very good. He hadn't thought saving his daughter's life would feel horrible.

He dropped to the living room floor and curled up in a ball. There was work to do. He needed to deal with the body. But first, he needed to deal with the overwhelming emotions of what he had just done as sobs wracked his body.

Anton was still crying on the floor like a smitten child

when glass broke in the house somewhere.

A man shouted.

That fucking man was back, and now he was breaking into his house.

Anton shouted out a growl and scrambled to his feet, fists clenched.

He'd done it once, he'd do it again. That man needed to die.

He ran for the kitchen and the knives in the block on the counter.

Chapter 36

THE BOTTOM OF THE iron was mottled with bits of flesh and burnt hair. Ansgar placed it on the counter beside the ironing board. Aaron had squirmed so much under the iron that he hadn't received much of a serious burn, but his arms were raw and a deep hue of red. The pain taught a man to answer questions. Any interrogator knew that. The KGB were experts in that field, and Ansgar had learned from a few of their retired agents in Afghanistan.

Over a dozen police cars had converged on the front of the hotel. They would investigate the airport van incident. Aaron was the suspect they were searching for, as well as his friends who left in the airport van. No one would be looking for Peter Ford.

In one minute, he would leave. The stairs would offer ample egress, and unless the area were roped off, Ansgar would walk away to find another hotel room where he would check in under another alias and get back to work.

He collected his gear and walked over to the closet where the hotel safe held the two small bombs left over from the job on Aaron's dojo. He punched in the code, opened the door, and placed the devices in a small bag.

It was risky leaving the hotel armed with a Glock and two explosive devices, but he had no choice. Leaving the gun behind was out of the question as it matched the bullets on the airport van, and he needed the explosive devices. If he encountered trouble, he would deal with it. He was not above killing a cop.

Back in front of Aaron, he slapped him awake. The pussy of a man had passed out when the iron's burn proved too much for him.

Ansgar yanked the sock out of Aaron's mouth and tossed it aside.

"You have less than a minute to live. Tell me what I need to know, and it'll be a bullet in the forehead. Refuse me, and it'll be a couple of bullets in the crotch. If, by some crazy odds, you manage to survive that, you'll be less of a man than ever before. I believe they call that a eunuch."

Aaron rolled his head toward Ansgar's voice and glared up at him with bloodshot eyes.

"Are you going to talk?" Ansgar asked.

Aaron seemed to roll his tongue around in his mouth as if he was chewing candy. His lips separated, then a gob of saliva shot up and onto Ansgar's shoulder. He barely jerked when Aaron spit on him.

"You chose your future, Aaron," he said. "It didn't have to be this way."

Ansgar raised the Glock and leveled it on Aaron's crotch.

"Any last words?" Ansgar asked.

He paused at hurried footsteps outside the door. They drew closer. Someone knocked on the door.

"Open up. Police."

The sound suppressor on the Glock was good, but he couldn't risk shooting Aaron with a cop six feet away. The only way out of the room was through the door the cop stood at. A moment of indecision hit him.

The knock came again.

"Coming," Ansgar yelled. "Just a minute."

He slipped the Glock into his waistband and retrieved the sock from earlier. With one hand on Aaron's hair, he forced the sock back into Aaron's mouth, then leaned close to Aaron's ear to whisper.

"Just one noise. If you do anything to signal the cop, I will have to kill the cop as well. You die anyway. Understood?"

Aaron nodded. Ansgar believed Aaron was resigned to his fate.

Ansgar got to his feet. The line of sight from the door wouldn't reach Aaron. He could get rid of the cop and get out of there seconds later. Everything was about timing. He knew that better than anyone.

At the door, he looked out into the hallway using the peephole.

Just one uniformed cop standing there. No one else. No tough blonde girl and none of Aaron's friends.

Ansgar flicked the lock off and opened the door with a crack.

"I'm sorry to wake you, sir, but we have an emergency —"

An arm shot out as someone touched the cop near the trapezoid area of the neck. Then the cop crumpled to the hallway floor.

Ansgar reacted by trying to slam the door shut, but something blocked him. He pushed, then peeked around the edge and saw the man who had jumped off his tenth-floor balcony.

"Alex?" he grunted.

Surprised, he paused when he saw him completely unscathed from the hundred-foot drop. How could he have done that?

Alex redoubled his efforts, and the door shot inward, knocking Ansgar off balance.

Like a charging orangutan, the young man launched onto Ansgar and jammed his hands into his flesh. He flailed his arms and shouted for the man to get off him, but then a pain bolted across his chest. That area went numb along with his arms. Breathing became a chore.

Ansgar stumbled backward as strength fled his body. He fell backward and hit the carpet hard, breathing almost nonexistent now.

Alex yanked Ansgar's feet back and straightened his body. His shoulder and arm burned like acid had been splashed across him.

What the fuck did that little shit do to me?

He lay there as Aaron's friend dragged the cop's body inside the room and closed the door.

Ansgar understood that the tables had turned.

He felt the first tinge of fear as the small man removed the ropes from Aaron's wrists and ankles.

Maybe he wouldn't survive this ordeal after all.

Chapter 37

ANTON HELD THE BUTCHER knife close to his chest, both hands wrapped around the handle. He had turned off the kitchen lights. The house was wrapped in darkness. Minor amounts of light came in through the windows. Without knowing the house like he did, a stranger would have trouble navigating his way around.

The sound of glass breaking had come from the back somewhere. In the kitchen, he stood so his field of vision ran the length of the hall and ended at the front door. He waited until whoever had broken the glass entered the corridor in search of him. He knew his rights. Someone broke into his home. He felt threatened. Using the knife to hurt the man would be acceptable. Killing him not so much.

But Anton intended to kill him. A couple of jabs to the throat and the man would succumb to his injuries rather quickly.

While he waited, fantasies flashed through his mind. Was there a way to kill the man and place him over the girl's body? The story could work.

Anton had let the girl inside the house to find safety from a man chasing her. Anton was reluctant at first, but the girl looked like his daughter. It made sense. When he set her up in the guest bedroom and left to get some sleep, someone broke in. By the time Anton reached the guest bedroom, the man had smothered the girl to death with Anton's pillow.

Without thinking rationally, Anton stabbed the man repeatedly in self-defense. He was sorry he took someone's life and would have to live with that knowledge. What jury would convict him on such a defense? DNA, fingerprints, nothing would work against him because it was his house. Of course, he had touched the pillow. At one point, he had touched everything in his house at least once.

So he waited for the man to show himself.

Then he would slice the man's throat open and call emergency services. He would be an emotional wreck, and when it was all over, he would plead for Clara's return.

And life could return to the way it was, minus the indiscretions in Aarhus. Since Damien was in jail, Anton would have to let that fun go for a while. He would wait until things settled down, then see what happened.

Sweat dripped off his chin. The knife vibrated in his grip. He waited, the house silent, a dead girl in his guest room.

The soft sound of someone moving around somewhere in the house doubled his heartbeat. The man was inside. This was the deciding moment. Without the intruder's death, explaining the dead girl was much more difficult, and the man at the door earlier seemed to be quite certain he had her.

A man like that would remain persistent. So persistent that he would break in to help the girl.

Anton could only wish.

More shuffling down the hall.

Anton pushed off the counter. He held the knife in front of him as he started out of the kitchen. He was a concerned homeowner, and someone had broken in. A telephone call to the police could wait. The immediate danger needed to be dealt with first.

The door on the left was the bathroom facing the front of the house. The small window was intact. No one was there.

Something bumped the wall, followed by a man huffing and puffing.

What the fuck is that?

Anton continued walking, each step careful, slow, the knife leading the way. The heavy breathing grew louder as he drew closer to the guest room.

Did he break into the guest room?

He placed his back against the wall and waited a moment longer, listening to the sounds coming from the guest room.

It was definitely a man. The grunting and heavy breathing was too masculine. Through the wall, Anton heard the man mumble something with the sound of agony, like a wounded animal whining in a bear trap.

Was the man injured? Did he hurt himself coming in, and that was why he hadn't forged his way through the house yet?

A police siren wailed in the distance, then cut off. They were probably still searching for the man who pepper-sprayed those two girls. They would never think to look in Anton's home. He was an upstanding citizen. He worked for the government and paid his taxes—as large as that amount was—every year. Pepper-spraying people was not something Anton's neighbors would expect.

More panting came from the room. Anton eased away from the wall, turned on his heels, and tentatively placed his hand on the doorknob.

The man on the other side of the door began talking.

"Please hurry," the man said. "Ambulance, too. She's stopped breathing."

Anton let go of the door, leaned back, and kicked it open. The man hovered over the girl on the floor, his hands on her chest. He was pumping her rib cage, trying to get her heart going. He completely ignored Anton, bringing his mouth down onto the girl's and forcing air into her. Then he was back up and pumping again.

Anton had lost the ability to blame everything on an intruder. This man had called the authorities. They were on their way. How could he cover that up?

The room tilted momentarily as madness overcame him while he watched the man perform CPR on a dead girl in his guest bedroom. A rumble began in his chest and came out of his mouth as a roar. He raised the weapon and charged the man. At the last second, the man rolled off the girl and away from Anton, his hand wrapping around Anton's wrist.

When they fell back and landed on the carpet at the foot of the bed, the man twisted Anton's wrist backward until he screamed, and his fingers opened. The knife dropped harmlessly beside them as they struggled.

The man was a strong opponent, his hands faster than Anton's. After three punches to the abdomen, Anton rolled sideways and off the man. When he got into a crouched position and turned to face the intruder, the man had the knife in his hands. His eyes seethed in rage, and his clenched teeth seemed ready to bite the head off anyone who challenged him.

The man lunged downward, stabbing fast and deep into Anton's left foot. Before any pain resonated through his body, the man pulled the knife out and stabbed Anton's right foot.

Anton screamed.

The man shoved Anton away from him so hard he stumbled a few steps, then fell into the wall and landed on shards of broken glass.

He screamed at the pain in his hands where chunks of glass embedded themselves. As the man tended to the dead woman on the floor on the other side of the bed, an intense pain flowed from the wounds in his feet. Without wanting to, he dared to look at the damage the knife had caused and almost threw up when he saw the blood oozing out of his feet just below the ankles.

Sirens were the only thing that drowned out his voice.

Flashing blue and red lights filled the house as the authorities showed up out front.

There was nothing left for him to do but accept the consequences. He had screwed up and now would pay for it.

Clara was as good as dead to him.

Anton screamed and screamed again as the intruder ran from the room to open the front door.

Maybe he could say the intruder attacked him, and then the man killed the girl.

Maybe.

But he doubted any story he came up with would work.

Other than the truth. That might work.

264

Chapter 38

DESPITE NAUSEA FROM THE searing pain in Aaron's arms, the pain between his legs had subsided some. When he saw Ansgar sprawled out on the carpet, he ran for the immobile police officer and dragged him inside the room before shutting and locking the door.

"Who's this?" he asked Alex, pointing down at the man he had just dragged inside the room. "Real cop?"

Alex nodded.

"Dangerous."

Alex shrugged. "Needed to get back inside without being shot at."

Ansgar was still on the floor, struggling to breathe properly.

"You hit the C3 nerve root?"

Alex nodded and faced Ansgar.

"Grab his bag," Aaron said. "We're leaving. Then strip

the cop." Alex turned back to Aaron, one eyebrow up in a questioning way.

"Strip the cop," Aaron repeated. "Put on the uniform, then get ready to leave. You're going to carry this man out of a fire while I help."

"A fire?" Alex whispered.

"Fire," Aaron repeated, then stared down at Ansgar. "My friend hit your C3 nerve root. It sticks out from the third vertebrae on the side of your neck. When the root was pushed into your bone, your chest, and shoulders would have gone numb. There's pain, too. Since the C3 nerve controls the diaphragm, breathing would've stopped but regained as soon as Alex let the nerve go. You should still be in distress, but you'll live. For now. We're going to carry you out of here. Then take you to a place where you will die."

Ansgar watched him from the floor, gasping breath after breath through his mouth. The nose job Sarah gave him made it doubly hard to breathe.

Aaron rolled Ansgar onto his side, yanked the gun out of the man's waistband, and slipped it into his own pants. Alex was almost dressed now. The cop's uniform was slightly big on his small frame, but Alex made it work by tucking it in where he could.

"How did you survive the fall off the balcony?" Aaron asked.

"Sheets," Alex said. "From above. Climbed down." He began buttoning up the blue shirt. "Left them hanging long enough to drop to the balcony below." He slipped his feet into the cop's shoes. "Went over the edge, gripped the sheets, and swung onto the balcony below." He stretched out his arms. "And here I am."

Aaron was shaking his head. "No fear of falling?"

"Never." Alex stopped what he was doing and stared at Aaron as if he was confused. "Never," he repeated. "Otherwise, I would fall."

"Right. Of course."

Aaron checked the wounds on his arms. The pain resonated over his ruined flesh, but nothing a little salve wouldn't help.

With an eye on Ansgar, Aaron took the bag and pulled the two explosive devices out. He scanned them to see if there were easy instructions but found nothing but a couple of switches and a small keypad with five buttons.

Alex moved in front of him as loud banging came from down the hall. It sounded like they were clearing the building.

Alex put his hand out. Aaron gave him the bombs. Alex ran his fingers over the keypads and set the timers on the devices.

"How'd you know how to do that?" Aaron asked.

"Dojo's hidden camera feed. After accessing the DVR, I watched him do it on my cell phone."

"Brilliant."

Alex placed one in the safe and closed the door. He placed the other in the hotel room's microwave.

"We have two minutes," he said.

Aaron dragged the cop to the edge of the door, ready to pull him from the room, then returned to Alex.

The Clock was breathing better now. His eyes remained cool and calm. Like he thought he still had a chance to get out of the predicament he was in.

Alex leaned down and touched several nerves in

Ansgar's neck. The man winced, but his eyes stayed open.

"What was that?" Aaron asked.

"Adding pain." Alex stood up.

"Aren't you going to knock him out?"

Alex shuffled his feet, then kicked Ansgar in the side of the head hard enough to snap the man's head sideways.

"Shit, you could've broken his neck," Aaron said.

Alex shrugged minutely. "He's out for a while."

Together, they lifted Ansgar onto Aaron's shoulders and approached the door.

They stood by the door, side by side, Ansgar on Aaron's shoulder, the cop at Alex's feet. Alex had gathered his clothes and placed them in Ansgar's bag. Once they were clear of the building, he would change back into them. He wore the bag like a backpack, up out of the way.

With twenty seconds left, Alex opened the door and dragged the cop into the hallway. Aaron exited the room behind him. Two officers were talking to people in their rooms at the other end of the hallway.

"Help," Aaron called. "There are more people in there. And a bomb—"

Both of Ansgar's devices blew in unison inside the room, and the punch from the explosion dented the wall beside him.

Alex pulled the fire alarm. It resonated throughout the hallway, drowning out the shout from one of the cops.

They ran toward them to help as Alex led the way onto the stairs in his uniform, dragging Aaron behind him. On the way down to the main floor, they took turns holding Ansgar's dead weight. Alex's uniform cleared the way for the few people they encountered on the stairs. On the third floor, Aaron had to take a break and catch his breath.

Alex grabbed Ansgar's wrist and checked the time.

"I know," Aaron said. "We'll go. But this guy's heavy."

Alex carried Ansgar's feet for the last three levels while Aaron held him under the man's shoulders.

Once they were outside, Aaron pulled Ansgar back up onto his shoulders. They kept to the outer perimeter and moved in the shadows. Emergency services were focused on the front of the building. Police and firemen crowded people at the exits and kept them in groups, moving them toward the grassy areas beyond the parking lot. A steady stream of people exited the hotel, keeping most of the authorities busy.

Alex led Aaron behind a firetruck, where he stopped.

"What now?" Aaron asked. "We need a ride."

Alex pointed at a police car two vehicles over.

"What?" Aaron asked through breaths. Ansgar seemed to be getting heavier by the second. "Steal it?"

Alex raised his hand. A set of keys dangled from it.

"I didn't just bring any cop up to the room. I needed to bring one that drove here. One that would have car keys in his pocket." Alex pointed at the cruiser. "He came here in that car."

"Brilliant."

They started around the trunk of another car, and Alex unlocked the cruiser. In the darkened area of the parking lot, they secured Ansgar in the back seat.

Alex jumped in the driver's seat and fired up the engine. That made the most sense as he wore the uniform. Aaron hopped in and slammed the door.

"Get us clear of this area."

He thought of Sarah and the times she had stolen a police car. He couldn't wait to see her again and tell her what Alex had done for him and what he had endured with Ansgar. He would be sure to include stealing the police car, the attack on the policeman, and the stolen uniform. They would laugh over drinks when this was all over.

Just Sarah and him.

Within minutes, they were out of the area and headed toward the hospital where Daniel had taken Benjamin.

Things were finally shaping up.

Chapter 39

Parkman hadn't thought about anything the entire time he tried to get Sarah breathing again. He couldn't bear the thought that Sarah had died. To comprehend it would be to accept failure. He was supposed to be in Skanderborg for Sarah. The man who took Sarah's life had walked right by him. After attacking the two girls, the man had eluded Parkman's search long enough to take Sarah and murder her.

It was Parkman's fault. All of it. There was no way he could live with that knowledge. Sarah had done incredible things for so many people, and Parkman let her die. How could he face her parents now? How could he face Aaron?

If Sarah were alive, she would kick his ass for letting her die.

The authorities arrived and banged on the door. Olafson cowered in the corner, bleeding from his wounds. Sarah was dead on the floor in front of him. Twenty minutes or more now. Loss of oxygen to the brain. He had tried everything to get her heart going again. What could they do? At least once, maybe twice, he thought he saw her chest rise as she took on air, but it was a trick of the lighting.

Reluctantly, as Clara's father screamed in pain in the corner, Parkman pushed up off the floor and walked in a daze to the front door. He flicked the lock and pulled it open.

They spoke in rapid Danish.

Parkman shook his head and pointed at the room.

"They're in there," he muttered, his body, his being, his soul, utterly defeated.

Sarah was dead, and it was his fault. Sarah was dead, and he had no idea what he would do about it or how he could move on. Numbed, he watched five men enter the house and slip by him. Two were uniformed officers.

Parkman released the doorknob, crossed the small foyer, and entered the room. Two men examined Olafson while another touched Sarah's neck. After a moment, the man left Sarah and moved to help with Olafson.

The officers separated, one moving toward Olafson, the other to stand beside Parkman.

"What happened here?" the officer asked.

Parkman pointed at Olafson. "He killed her. When I tried to revive her, he came at me with a knife. I disarmed him and stabbed his feet so he couldn't get away." Parkman looked down at Sarah's peaceful face. "Seemed like the thing to do at the time."

"Who are you? How did you come to be here?"

Parkman faced the cop. He felt tired, like he hadn't slept in a month.

"I'm a friend of hers. I was looking for her. When I

called Sarah's parents, they told me she might be at this address with Olafson." He moved slowly to look at Olafson. The man glared back at him, listening to what he told the officer. "Sarah's father texted me a picture of Anton's face. When I saw him, I knew who he was. Anton Olafson is the man who pepper-sprayed those two girls by the water earlier tonight. I'm sure they will verify my story."

The cop glanced at Olafson, then back to Parkman.

"How are you inside this man's house?"

Parkman frowned, then pointed at the room's window. "I broke that when I saw Sarah on the floor tied up."

"You broke into this man's house?"

Parkman squared his shoulders and turned to face the cop. "He murdered Sarah Roberts, and you're worried about me breaking in?" If that were true, he would spend a few years in a Danish jail because he would clobber the young cop upside the head for being an inane imbecile.

"No, sir, just trying to establish everyone's role in the events this evening."

Parkman unclenched his fist and looked back at Sarah.

"Everything that man has said is a lie," Anton shouted.

The ambulance attendants were placing gauze over his feet wounds as he winced.

"That man broke into my house. He killed that girl and attacked me. He's the only one still standing. I'm Anton Olafson, Director at the NC3. Arrest that man for murder and attempted murder at once."

The officer touched his belt where handcuffs were stored.

Parkman placed a hand on the cop's shoulder. The cop didn't attempt to remove it.

"I will go with you. I will answer questions for days. But

if you attempt to arrest me, I will break the hand that touches me." He stared bullets into the young cop's face. "I'm an American citizen, and that woman is also an American. She is important to a lot of people. I ride with her to the hospital. Once she's officially pronounced dead, we will talk. Arrest me, then, if the story supports that. But for now, I ride with her. Understand?"

The cop's hand came away from his belt. He exchanged a glance with his partner. The partner nodded.

"I'll ride with you," the cop said.

Parkman took one more look at Sarah, then trudged with heavy feet toward the open front door.

"Just keep me away from Anton. I will rip off his face and piss in his eye sockets if I am within ten feet of him."

He made it outside, took a deep breath of the night air, and started for the ambulance. Halfway across the parking lot, he pulled out his small package of toothpicks, dropped them in the grass, and stopped to stare down at them. Somehow, they looked pathetic. Lost and lonely. Slim tiny pieces of wood made to pick food from teeth. He'd used them as a toy for as long as he could remember. Something to soothe him. A vice of comfort. They offered him nothing, lying on the lawn of the man who murdered his Sarah. They had nothing to give him.

He bent to retrieve them, then fell to his knees beside the package. He covered his face with his hands and let the grief out. It came in waves. His shoulders hitched as he flipped to his side, then rolled over and stared up at the Danish night sky. Tears moved down the side of his face and collected in his ears. He blinked them away and tried to stop crying. He needed to get through the next few days and be strong for

Sarah.

Someone walked by him. Then someone else. He rolled away from them. The toothpicks were right in front of his face now. He wrapped his hands around them and held them tight, thinking of Sarah in Mexico recently. Sarah in Vegas. When she foiled the woman who wanted to use a bomb at a convention. When Sarah saved all those women in Amsterdam and Toronto.

Sarah had been there selflessly for so many over the years. Where was Vivian when Sarah needed her the most? Was Parkman Vivian's answer? Was he supposed to be here an hour earlier? If that was the case, Vivian failed Sarah miserably when she needed her the most. Sarah couldn't count on Vivian, and now everyone would know that Sarah couldn't count on Parkman.

He curled into a ball and tried to keep the wave of grief in. This wasn't the time. He was Sarah's only contact in Denmark. He could positively identify the body. He could help arrange for her to fly home to her parents.

Her parents.

What would Caleb and Amelia think of him now that he failed her?

Someone tapped his shoulder.

"Sir, they're loaded up and waiting for you."

Parkman rolled over and got to his hands and knees. He pushed off the ground and stood up. With his shirt sleeve, he wiped his face and let the officer lead him to the back of the ambulance.

"Where's Anton?" he asked.

"He left in the other ambulance."

"Where are we going?"

"It's a thirty-minute drive to Silkeborg's Regional Hospital. They will tend to Sarah there. When that's done, I'll need to take your statement."

The cop helped Parkman up into the back of the ambulance. He sat on a side bench by Sarah's head. The cop hopped up, and his partner closed the back doors. A paramedic sitting by Sarah's feet knocked on the wall that separated the back from the driver. A moment later, the emergency vehicle started away.

Parkman stared at Sarah's face. Her lovely, unblemished face. She looked so peaceful now. Like she could finally sleep and get the rest she so deserved in life. It wasn't any consolation, but rest in peace would actually mean something for Sarah Roberts.

Her chest moved.

He blinked and leaned closer.

Nothing. Sarah's chest was rigid, only moving with the vibrations of the ambulance.

Something crinkled in Parkman's hand. He looked down and saw he was holding the toothpick package.

A small, short chortle escaped his lips. From the corner of his eye, he noticed the cop glance his way.

He pulled out a toothpick and slipped the package into his back pocket. Examining the small piece of wood for a moment, he held it between his thumb and index finger. Then he popped it into his mouth.

Sarah would want her final ride in an ambulance with Parkman at her side, a toothpick in his mouth.

In life, Sarah was perfect.

In death, even more so.

He leaned back against the ambulance wall, rolled the

toothpick from side to side, and stared at his Sarah, remembering the good times.

Sarah would live on in his memory until he died.

Sarah would always live on.

He cried.

Chapter 40

Ben Wilson rolled out of bed cautiously. The pain in his lower back could flare at any time. After such a long nap and a day of eating horribly, the pain usually flared up. Any wrong move, and he would stumble around the house eating anti-inflammatories for the rest of the night. This evening would be important, and he didn't want to screw that up by moving too suddenly.

He had fallen asleep five hours ago, and now, if the clock in the corner was right, it was two in the morning. So much was happening out there. He didn't want to miss a thing. The fear of losing Ansgar when he was so close. The thought of Anton not doing what was asked of him. Clara escaping. Jessy's brother walking away unscathed. All these things kept him busy, and right now, he needed to be busy. It kept his mind off the pancreatic cancer the doctors told him would take his life one day. Their stupid mortality-rate charts were ridiculously low. Even Stage One barely made it to double digits. He had to be Stage Four by now. Ben recalled Stage Four as having a survival rate of about one percent.

Fuck cancer.

A Mars bar rested on the bedside table beside him. He idly wondered if he'd ever get sick of them. Without looking, he dropped his hand onto the table, felt around until he bumped the bar's packaging, then brought it over his face in the dark and ripped it open. Like other people who woke to steaming cups of coffee, Ben savored the taste of his Mars bar when waking. He ate slowly, rolling the nougat around his tongue and sucking the chocolate off it. He would always remember the day Mars Dark came on the market. Unlike the American version of the Mars bar, the Canadian one he bought by the case never had a trace of peanuts. His average number of bars per day was in the dozen range. Did it matter that he knew the time and date of his death? Could the chocolate bars affect his health negatively in the short time he had left to live? No way. There would be no let-up on the Mars bars or something stupid like that. No reprieve. Maybe tonight, he would eat an extra dozen just to ensure he got his fill before he died next week.

Becoming obese, the early stages of diabetes setting in, Ben had gone to the doctor with his mother before she died to discover he had exocrine pancreatic cancer. Also known as adenocarcinoma pancreatic cancer. The abdominal and lower back pain and the yellowing skin were worsening, but what did it matter? He was dead, regardless. Why do chemo? Why be prodded and poked for years? Why not sit at home and enjoy the few years he had left?

Once the chocolate bar was finished and he'd licked his

soiled fingers, he rolled out of bed slowly, waddled to the bathroom, and did his business.

Hair mussed, teeth unbrushed for days, he trudged out of the bathroom and headed for his bank of computers. Where was everybody? What was The Clock doing? Had Anton found a random girl to kill yet?

Once he logged onto his system by typing the password *fuck_cancer_twice*, he quickly checked the day of the week. The date with Jessy was coming up. After years of being bullied, beaten up at school, and misunderstood as a feminine boy who liked other boys, Ben Wilson had grown a thick skin. Then, with his whole life ahead of him, his own pancreas betrayed him, and he began a long, arduous journey of falling apart from the inside.

When people complained on Facebook that life wasn't fair, he laughed. They had no idea what he'd been through. They had no idea how much he hurt on the inside. The daily pain. The threat of death this month or next.

All he had were the few games he played and his Mars bars. Without them, he would've killed himself directly after the diagnosis.

Euphoric with the knowledge his final act was coming, he tore off the end of another Mars bar and chomped half of it before he noticed Anton Olafson had sent him a video file.

He stopped chewing, frowned, leaned closer, and clicked to open the file.

When he saw what Anton had sent him, he swallowed what was in his mouth and almost choked. Ben Wilson—PAIN—watched as Anton placed a pillow over a girl who looked like Clara Olafson and held it down until she was dead.

Ben's heart raced in his chest as he watched. He adjusted his bulk on the worn office chair and leaned closer, not wanting to miss a single second of the captivating video. The Mars bar forgotten temporarily, he studied the computer screen as Anton placed a mirror under the girl's nose.

Her eyes. It was her eyes that did it for Ben. That dead stare. Like the ceiling in the room was a captivating hypnotist. The stupid girl had fallen victim to Anton, and he had done it.

Now Clara was to be set free.

Ben paused the video. He would watch it back a dozen times, but for now, he needed to reach out to Ansgar. Hopefully, the fool was still able to take direction. After the recent debacle with Ansgar's attitude, which made him less a professional than Ben had previously thought, maybe the mercenary would make things right by doing as he was told.

Ben typed his message. Before hitting send, he looked up and debated the context of the message. Maybe Ansgar needed a small push, a little more incentive.

Ben's fingers danced over the computer keyboard. He brought up a couple of financier's accounts, linked them to bank accounts, and began a hack that took him a half hour. Once funds were placed into his holding company illegally with virtually no way for them to trace it back to him, he finished his text to Ansgar.

Remove the girl. Do it ASAP. No longer needed. Ever. The bonus has been transferred to your account. Regular fee plus generous bonus. Just do it now and confirm with a photo.

He hit the send button.

After eating the bar, he grabbed two more from the case

in the corner, sat back at his desk, and watched Anton's video repeatedly.

On camera, somewhere in Denmark, Anton said, "Sarah Roberts, I now declare you … dead."

Ben said the girl's name in his head.

Sarah Roberts.

Why did he know that name? Who was she?

He opened another screen and searched her name. Screen after screen filled with her picture and who she was. Realization settled in over him.

He set the Mars bar beside the keyboard and watched Anton's video again. He had to make sure Sarah was dead. He had to be absolutely sure. If Sarah Roberts was involved, she could foil his plans. Probably the only reason she was involved was to come after him, and he couldn't have that.

The video was convincing enough. Sarah Roberts appeared to be dead. No doubt about it. Unless Anton was in on it. Some kind of conspiracy to get to him. Someone like Sarah could do it.

Chocolate bars forgotten, he researched Sarah deeper.

When he learned that Aaron Stevens was her boyfriend and that Aaron's dojo was blown up earlier this week, the news speculated that Sarah had missed warning him.

"Aaron Stevens is with Sarah?" he mumbled to himself. "Shit." He pounded his fist into his other hand.

That's shaking a stick at a hornet's nest. The internet was full of Sarah Roberts's exploits. She even wrote a batch of books about her life's adventures.

"And Ben just had to go after her boyfriend. That's fuckin' dangerous."

Why was Sarah in Denmark? Being killed by Anton?

And wearing clothes that made her look like Clara?

"What the fuck is going on?" Ben asked out loud. "Do I smell setup?"

He had to locate the hospital Sarah would've been taken to. He needed into their computers. He needed to see when she was admitted and when she was declared dead.

If Sarah Roberts weren't dead, he would need another layer of security. Hiding behind his computers wouldn't be enough for that psychic bitch.

Ben suddenly recalled all the stories over the years of her helping the Toronto police. She was not someone to mess with.

A thought dashed into his mind. Was Aaron Stevens declared dead yet? Did they find his body in the aftermath of the dojo explosion? If not, where was he, and what was he up to?

Ben launched a search for Aaron without success. They were still combing through the wreckage of his dojo. He set an alarm in his system after sending out electronic spiders to search for Aaron's name. It was a small program he wrote himself, similar to a find-your-cell-phone application. Instead of homing in on the cell phone, his program homed in on what he typed to search for. The second someone entered Aaron's name into a computer anywhere locally, and in some cases globally, Ben would know seconds later.

Once that was done, his fingers raced over the keys as fast as he could, searching for answers on Sarah that only he could get. But with everything this extensive, it took time. Hacking into secure websites and government computers wasn't an easy task. Ben was up to the challenge, but it would take the better part of the night to discover what he needed to know.

The Mars bar in his stomach churned with the acid of nervousness and made him feel sick.

Sarah Roberts scared the shit out of him. He had to know if she was dead.

Then he would solve his other problems.

Like why Ansgar wasn't responding to his text.

The sensation that his ideas and plans were slowly unraveling came over him. He wondered if he would even make it to the Tuesday meeting with Jessy. If Sarah Roberts was alive, he doubted he would.

What Ben saw Anton Olafson do on camera to Sarah would piss her off. Then she'd come looking for him, and no amount of servers and routers would ever stop someone like Sarah.

Not when she had a voice from the other side advising her.

Nothing could stop her.

Ben ran a search to triangulate Ansgar's cell phone. It was near a hospital in Etobicoke. He frowned. What's Ansgar back there for? Hurt his nose again?

Next, he spent ten minutes getting into the hospital's computer system. He got in far enough to see the names of the people being admitted within the previous few hours. Daniel and Benjamin showed up. Clara Olafson, too.

"What the hell are they all doing there?" he whispered. "And why is Ansgar outside?"

He needed someone in his corner. But who?

He tapped his fingers on his chin until a name popped into his head.

Jessy's brother, Shawn Bryant. The youngest homicide

detective on the force. Maybe Ben could get him involved somehow and keep him involved until Tuesday.

He quickly triangulated Detective Bryant's cell phone and saw he was at the hospital.

"What the fuck? Why's he there? Was someone murdered?"

Open-mouthed, he stared at his computer.

"How long did I sleep?"

He quickly texted Ansgar to take them all out. Finish this as soon as he can. Then Ben revealed where they were. The Clock would have money. Lots of it, he typed.

Ben continued his search for Sarah Roberts and Aaron Stevens. A soft beep announced that one of Ben's spiders had caught something. He opened the link and saw that Sarah had been admitted to a hospital in Silkeborg, Denmark.

She had been brought in and declared dead on arrival.

He leaned back in his chair and clapped his hands so hard they stung.

"Shit wave on a Bingo. The wicked witch is dead."

He grabbed a Mars bar and started eating. Things were already looking up.

Now he just needed to find Aaron if he was still alive. Then have him killed so he could carry out his own personal vendetta against Homicide Detective Shawn Bryant.

Chapter 41

AARON GOT ALEX TO park a block from the hospital behind a retail store that had gone out of business. Ansgar was still unconscious in the back seat of the cruiser. Getting any closer to the hospital could draw unneeded attention their way.

"What if they're not here?" Alex asked as he got out of the cruiser.

"They're here."

Aaron exited the vehicle and walked around to stand beside Alex. He'd pulled out his personal cell phone, then held it up for Aaron to look at.

"No text from Daniel," Alex said. "We have no idea where they are."

"They're here," Aaron repeated. "We passed five cruisers near the entrance to the hospital, two unmarked. Cops are here taking statements and matching them to what their colleagues have found at the hotel by the airport. Probably not letting Daniel use his phone."

Alex leaned down and glanced in the back window of the cruiser.

"What about him?" he asked.

Aaron stepped back to join Alex. "You stay here with him. I'll go inside and see if I can find out what's going on. Make sure everyone's safe."

"If he wakes up?"

"Hurt him. Put him back under."

"Can I ask questions? Do you care?"

"Do whatever you want. Just don't kill him. We need to learn who hired him. That's where this ends."

Alex leaned against the car and crossed his arms.

"Go. We'll be fine here."

Aaron didn't wait to be told twice. He started away, but Alex shouted at him.

"Wait," Alex said, the cell phone in his hand.

Aaron turned back around. "What?"

"Ansgar's phone. Just got a text."

Without going back to Alex, Aaron asked, "What'd it say?"

"Told this shitbag to kill Clara, Daniel, Benjamin, and you if you're still alive. Said they're all in there." Alex pointed at the hospital.

"See, told you they were here."

"But how does this guy know?" Alex pointed at the phone.

Aaron shrugged. "Must be some kind of hacker. Otherwise, he works at the hospital. Doesn't matter. His killing dog is done."

"He offered Ansgar a lot of money." Alex glanced at the

pavement. "Who would want us dead so bad?"

"Don't know. You're going to have to ask him when he wakes."

Alex looked in the back seat of the cruiser at Ansgar. "I might just do that."

Aaron started backward, then turned and ran the length of the city block, jumped over a small bush, and entered the hospital parking lot. The emergency entrance was on his left. He headed that way, enjoying the cool night air on his burning forearms.

Once inside, he headed to the nurses' station. Behind a Plexiglas partition, a woman in her sixties sat at a computer station, reading glasses resting on her nose. A pink string suspended from the glasses wrapped around her neck.

"How can we help you?" she asked without looking at him.

"Burned myself."

She lowered her head to look over the upper rim of her glasses and winced when she saw Aaron's reddened forearms.

"Painful?" she asked, meeting his eyes.

"Quite."

"I'll fetch someone to get you right in."

Aaron stepped away from the counter as she spoke into a phone on her desk.

"Sir?" the nurse called.

Aaron moved back toward her.

"Your name?"

"Aaron Stevens."

"Date of birth."

He told her.

An access door opened, and a young man in a white lab coat approached Aaron. He gestured for Aaron to follow him.

The nurse looked at him over her glasses again. "When you're done with the doctor, I'll need the rest of your information."

"No problem. I've got my health card right here." He made an effort to point at his pocket as he headed toward the open door. The doctor led him to a cubicle, where he pulled the curtain half closed.

"I'm Dr. Paul Shelp," the doctor said. "How did you manage to do that?"

Aaron looked down at his forearms, suddenly very hungry. He thought about how long it had been since he'd had anything to eat and couldn't remember.

"An iron. A prank that went wrong."

"A prank?" Dr. Shelp asked, one eyebrow raised. His eyes danced over Aaron's face, studying something. He was probably trying to ascertain whether he was telling the truth. "And did this prank cause the other bruises and rope burn there." He pointed at Aaron's wrists. "It seems you're also missing a finger." The doctor stared him in the eye. "Was that another prank as well?"

Aaron stepped closer and came to stand directly in front of the doctor. "I need to know where my friends are."

To Dr. Shelp's credit, he didn't flinch when Aaron invaded his personal space. "Your friends?"

"Earlier tonight. Gunshot wound in the leg."

"Oh, them."

"Where are they?"

"Is that another prank?" Shelp asked as he grabbed something off the counter behind him. He tore a package open and squeezed a white salve out. With plastic gloves, he proceeded to rub it on the burns on Aaron's left arm. The intense cool salve made Aaron shiver.

"No prank. We were shot at."

The doctor didn't look at him this time, but Aaron saw the doubt on his face.

"What have you heard?" Aaron asked. "They're okay, aren't they?"

Dr. Shelp applied the salve to Aaron's other arm.

"Your friends came in with a fantastic story of kidnapping and murderous hitmen." The doctor stopped what he was doing and placed the empty packaging in a small receptacle. "I must admit, their story swept through the emergency department as rumor mixed with facts turned fiction."

"I assure you, it's no fiction. Where are they?"

"In custody, last I heard."

"Custody?" Aaron had to contain himself from shouting. "My friend was shot. How is that a crime?"

"According to a witness, that's not what happened." The doctor moved toward the curtain and pulled it out of the way. "And now you've reached the limit of my knowledge. To know more, you would need to go join them."

Aaron left the cubicle and eased past the doctor. "Where are they?"

Dr. Shelp pointed to his right. "Around that corner."

Aaron started away but didn't get five feet before the hospital lights blinked off. Emergency lighting kicked in. Someone gasped. A buzzer flared somewhere.

Suddenly the hospital was a commotion of people calling out to get the power back on.

What else could go wrong?

Aaron ran past three empty cubicles, turned a corner, and almost bumped into a tall cop. The emergency lighting was enough for Aaron to see Daniel standing by Benjamin's bed. Both men were handcuffed to the pole beside the bed. Large white bandages surrounded Benjamin's leg like a huge tourniquet. Clara sat in the cubicle beside them, a female cop holding her hand. Two men in suits stood at the end of Benjamin's bed.

They all turned to look at Aaron as he stumbled upon them.

"Look who's back from the dead," the man on the left said. "Care to tell us why you faked your death in the dojo explosion? These people," he waved an arm toward Daniel and Benjamin, "seem to have grand stories to tell. Yet I have a dead airport van driver and his stolen van parked outside. I'm guessing their fingerprints will be all over the van's interior. Any chance you can bring an air of sanity to all of this?"

"Outside, you'll have all the answers you need."

The cop stepped closer to Aaron. "Oh yeah? And what's outside?"

"The man who shot Benjamin. The same man who killed that driver." He pointed at Clara. "She'll recognize him. He's the man who kidnapped her."

The cop's attitude sickened Aaron as he hitched up his belt and offered his colleagues a cocky smile. "Gentlemen, it seems the mighty and powerful Aaron Stevens isn't just back from the dead; he's come bearing gifts." The cop released his waistline and shot a hand out. "Please, lead the way."

Instead of smacking the man a dozen times, Aaron led

the way with two detectives on his heels.

Chapter 42

THE AMBULANCE MADE IT to the Silkeborg Regional Hospital in less than twenty-five minutes, as the roads were clear at that hour. They wheeled Sarah inside, where a weary-looking doctor came out and checked for vital signs.

Parkman watched it all in a detached state. He would go through the motions. Identify the body. Prepare flight arrangements to have her taken home. Talk to the parents. Go through the details and have Sarah buried. Then it would be over. There would be nothing. Ever since he paired up with Sarah on the human trafficking ring working out of crypts in Europe, his life had a purpose. This girl kicked ass, and he loved her for it. The world needed more Sarahs, and somehow, the world just took the only one they had.

Parkman followed the doctor as he pushed Sarah's body down a long corridor toward the hospital morgue. One of the Danish police officers stayed close to him but gave him breathing room.

Sarah had been declared officially dead. Parkman approximated that Sarah had taken her last breath just over an hour ago. Slightly less than an hour and a half separated him from the time it would've taken to save her had he bumped into her before she entered that house. That hour and a half were gone forever, never to be taken back.

Just like Sarah Roberts. Gone forever …

Like a zombie, dazed and confused, he watched as the doctor placed the gurney with Sarah's body on it against a wall of metal drawers. In the harsh cold light of the morgue, Parkman approached Sarah's body on the gurney.

"I'm so sorry, Sarah," he whispered.

Delicately, Parkman lifted the white sheet off her face and looked at her. The years, the memories, swept over him. His legs weakened, and he stumbled back, having to grab the edge of the gurney to stay upright. How could she be gone? So young yet. So much left to do.

Maybe it was better. She had been through a lot in her short life. Pain, suffering. Maybe this was her final rest, her permanent vacation. No one could get to her here.

He placed the sheet back over her face.

At least she had Vivian now. The sisters were back together. He imagined them running around, dancing, and laughing at the joy of being together on Vivian's plane.

The one way he could accept Sarah's fate would be to be happy for her. She was with Vivian now. Everyone would miss her, but she could still be with them, watching over them like Vivian did with Sarah. Overall, it was okay and would be okay. Everything was okay. This was meant to be. He had to believe that. If he didn't believe that, the alternative was insanity.

Parkman stepped away from Sarah's body and dropped onto a chair by the door. He hung his head in his hands and wept for Sarah.

Someone shuffled along the hallway. Parkman wiped his face and glanced up.

The Danish cop from Olafson's house came into view from around the corner.

"We will need a statement from you, Mr. Parkman," the young cop said.

Parkman wiped his nose. "I'll give it when I'm through here," he said, his voice choked, sinuses clogged.

The cop sighed and stepped back. "I'll wait by the exit."

The cop's polished shoes reverberated throughout the morgue as he walked back along the corridor. After a moment's pause, a door creaked open, then closed.

He was alone with Sarah again, probably for the last time. The silence was deafening. He adjusted his pant legs, sat back, and stared up at the ceiling tiles. A million tiny holes in the tiles stared back. Beyond them, nothing.

Something rattled from across the room.

He blinked.

It rattled again.

His heart rate increased. A morgue with strange noises was bound to freak him out, but this noise was different. It sounded like someone was trying to breathe.

He lowered his head and scanned the room. He was alone with Sarah's body on the gurney. Unless one of the dead from inside the wall of drawers was making a miraculous comeback, then the noise had to have come from an air duct.

The sheet over Sarah's face caught his eye. He wouldn't

have seen it if he weren't staring at it. The sheet moved. He was sure of it.

Cautious not to be buying into some form of a delusion, Parkman got up off the chair and stepped toward her.

The sheet moved.

This time he saw it plain as day.

It rose, then settled back down directly over her face.

Could she be breathing?

If she was, then how could a doctor declare her dead?

He moved closer. The sheet moved again.

When he was halfway across the room, Sarah's hand twitched.

He refused to believe it. How could it be possible? It would be a miracle. One that he'd be willing to accept. But how?

Vivian. It had to be her. Vivian had done something to Sarah to make her only *appear* dead.

He rushed over and tore the sheet back.

Sarah blinked rapidly. Eyes open to slits, she turned to face him.

"That," she said, her voice cracking, "sucks."

Euphoria swept over him, and he almost jumped on the spot, then had to collect himself lest he fall as his legs instantly weakened.

"Sarah!" he shouted. "You're alive."

"Help me up," she moaned. "My body is too heavy. Gotta get used to it again. And why does my chest hurt so much?"

Parkman threw the sheet to the side and grabbed her hand. Convinced he was dreaming the entire thing, he helped her into a sitting position. Still dazed and confused, but now, for other reasons, he waited for Sarah to gather herself on the side of the gurney.

"Oh man," she muttered. "Does this ever suck."

"What sucks?" Parkman asked, his face a mask of elation and joy.

"Being in this body. It's so heavy." She looked around the room, then at him. "I was with my sister."

He nodded vigorously. "And?"

"We talked."

"And?"

"There's a lot to do yet."

"Good."

"She said it wasn't my time."

"Good."

"So here I am."

"Good."

"Stop it."

"What?"

"One-word answers. Pissing me off."

"Okay." He smiled.

She looked up at him, her top lip pulled back slightly.

"Oh, right. No one-word answers. Got it."

"I need out of here." She started off the stretcher. "We have to get to Toronto."

"What?"

She stopped moving and looked up at him. "Parkman, I know you thought I was dead, and now I'm not. That's good. You can be happy. I'm not, but you can be. But I need you to come back to the guy I know. Help me out of here. Get me on a plane to Toronto."

He grabbed her arm and helped her to her feet.

"Of course. I'm just so ..." his voice trailed off. "Shocked."

"Okay. Be shocked. That's fine. Just don't act like it."

"Done."

She started for the door.

"And no one-word answers."

"Right." He caught her looking back at him. "Got it," he added.

He led her down the corridor where the Danish cop had just gone.

"Sarah, we need to talk about a couple of things."

"The cop outside this door?"

Parkman shot a look at her. "You're psychic now?"

"Mostly. It's what Vivian and I talked about. Our new pact."

"Pact?"

"Parkman," Sarah said, a warning in her voice. "We're working on those one-word answers, right?"

"What did you talk about?" he asked, ignoring her last question.

"Too much to cover now. I'll fill you in on the plane."

He stopped her before exiting the corridor.

"Sarah, at least tell me this."

"Go ahead."

"How are you still alive? I saw your body. A doctor declared you officially dead."

"Vivian did it. Somehow, she took over my body and stopped my breathing so Anton could record the murder on his cell phone. I floated out of my body and watched him use a mirror under my nose to prove I was dead." She stared off at nothing. "It was the craziest thing I've ever done. I mean," she met his gaze, "it's not every day you can say you watched yourself die, right?"

"True. But that was over an hour ago."

"I know. While Vivian and I talked, she made my body breathe in intervals when no one was watching my corpse. I breathed the whole time in the ambulance. When the sheet moved, it looked like vibrations from the road."

"She's taken over your body before, hasn't she?"

"Yes, but for small intervals. It's very exhausting for her. Once I was dead, though, that was easier for her. She could do it while talking to me."

"So you were dead, then? Floating around?" He used his hands to flutter in the air. "You left your body?"

"Yes. Even went through a life review. Like when people say their life flashed before their eyes. Did the whole thing. Chatted with my sister—it was so good to see her—made a pact, and here I am. Now, let's go."

"Wait. One more thing."

Sarah leaned against the wall, touching her chest gingerly. "Damn, this hurts. You pumped my chest too hard."

"So sue me. I wanted you alive. And why are you so lethargic if you were breathing the whole time?"

"Officially, my body was dead for an hour. That's why it's not acting normal yet. Every limb has pins and needles right now. Internal organs, too. My heart is racing, forcing blood to move where ten minutes ago it was settling. I feel pretty fucked up right now, and it's pissing me off. Makes me irritable. Can we just go?"

Parkman pulled her off the wall and wrapped his arms around her.

"I'm so glad you're back." His voice cracked.

"Don't get too sappy on me," she said, her words muffled by the fabric on his shoulder as he clung to her tight. "We still have lots to do if we're going to save Aaron. And Alex is out there all alone with an assassin. I saw him asking the guy a bunch of questions. Violent stuff. They need us."

"I don't know what I'd do without you," he said. "I thought it was my fault."

"Parkman?"

"Yeah?"

"Let me go."

He opened his arms. She settled back against the wall.

"It wasn't your fault. This was all Vivian's doing. A higher purpose. I'll tell you more on the plane. You'll understand everything. I even saw the letter she wrote you. You're supposed to be here now. Not before I met Anton and entered his house, but after. That was supposed to happen. So let the rest go."

"Okay."

"Now, let's do this and get out of here."

The door opened in front of them. Two Danish cops blocked their way.

"What do we have here?" the older one asked. "The dead girl rises."

"Parkman," Sarah whispered. "Get me out of here."

"You're not going anywhere, Sarah Roberts." The cop stepped forward and clamped a hand on her arm. "You're supposed to be dead. We're about to charge someone with murder, and you're walking around the hospital morgue." He glanced at his partner and shook his head. "Someone has a lot of explaining to do."

Chapter 43

AARON LED THE POLICE officers outside the hospital and across the parking lot to the retail store where they had parked the stolen cop car. Halfway there, he wondered what they would say when they saw Alex dressed as a cop, standing by a stolen police car, wearing the uniform of an officer they had knocked out back at the hotel.

Was Ansgar enough of a catch to expose themselves to that much heat? How stupid of a move was this?

He almost turned around and headed in another direction. But when would this end? How would it end? Would one of them be charged with the murder of the airport van driver? Once they launched a full investigation, they would have the bullet casings and the trajectory of the bullets that entered the vehicle. And why shoot Benjamin? Why drive him to the hospital if they were guilty of murder? Wouldn't Clara's word absolve them of charges? What would the hotel clerk's story be? And what about the cop Alex coaxed into coming to the hotel room, where he got knocked out and stripped?

The waters were definitely muddy, and it would take considerable time to un-muddy them.

He looked down at the ground while he walked, wondering if he'd been hanging around Sarah too long. They couldn't go around knocking out cops and stealing police cars. This had gone too far. It was time for Clara to stay in police custody until this was over and for them to answer for their actions. He would explain that he felt what they did at the time was the right thing to do. They were running from a hitman. How could they know if more were coming or not? Extreme measures were taken.

"How much farther, Aaron?" the mouthpiece cop asked.

"Right behind this retail store." Aaron pointed.

"What are we going to find there?"

"Ansgar Holm, the man who murdered the airport van driver. The man who kidnapped Clara Olafson. Ansgar Holm goes by the nickname, The Clock. He's an ex-Navy Seal sniper."

"The Clock?" the cop sounded surprised. "You're saying The Clock's real name is Ansgar Holm?"

Aaron chanced a look at the men walking with him. "You know The Clock?"

"Who doesn't? Some say he's trying to duplicate what the Jackal did in the eighties."

Aaron had never heard of The Clock. Of course, he didn't run in circles where the names of assassins were routinely discussed, but he found it odd that random police officers would know that name.

The hospital didn't have metal detectors. Aaron had been

able to enter the hospital, meet Dr. Shelp, and find Daniel and Benjamin without ditching Ansgar's Glock in his waistband. So far, the cops hadn't asked him if he was armed and hadn't searched him.

If they thought for a moment that Aaron was a suspect, then it wouldn't be a stretch for them to think they were walking into a trap after traversing the hospital parking lot in the dark and effectively leaving the premises. He also had to consider that the Glock in his waistband shot the airport van driver.

That left Aaron with two choices.

Either he wasn't a suspect, or these officers—who hadn't identified themselves by name yet—were genuinely curious who Aaron had captive behind the retail store.

Or the cop was with Ansgar, and Aaron was walking into a trap. Could all the officers back in the hospital be in on some kind of conspiracy, or had he been hanging around Sarah too long?

Aaron stepped around the corner of the retail store building and pointed.

"There's the police car—"

The cruiser was gone. Alex was gone. Ansgar Holm was gone.

Broken glass was scattered on the concrete where the car had been parked.

What the fuck happened?

"Where, Aaron?" Mouthpiece asked. "Where's the cop car?"

"It was right there. I left Alex with the cruiser." He jerked his head back to look at the officers. Then spun in a circle in search of the car. Worry for Alex rose in his throat. What could've happened to him? "Ansgar was in the back seat. He couldn't have gotten out."

"Police car?" Mouthpiece asked. "Like an actual police cruiser?"

His partner had stepped back into the shadows. Aaron was sure the man had his weapon out.

"Hey, take it easy." Aaron raised his hands, chest high. "We have The Clock. We have the guy behind all this."

"Where, Aaron?" The cop moved closer. "I don't see him. And maybe you could tell us. How did you happen to come across a police car?"

"Look," Aaron said. "Listen to me." He turned left, then right. The parking lot was empty. No police car within an entire city block. "They were here."

"Aaron, turn around."

He faced the cop. "Don't do this."

"Turn around." This time the cop's words were strained. His patience had snapped.

Something clicked off the cop's belt line. Handcuffs dangled from his fingers.

"Put these on." The cop tossed them to Aaron. He caught them with ease. "Don't resist arrest," he added. "I don't want to have to use deadly force. I know how fast you are. I'm not coming close to you. So put those on yourself."

"Don't do this. I'll come peacefully."

"Aaron, we know you. We were willing to trust you. Until now."

The partner had his back to the building, covering them.

Aaron was out of options. After one cuff was on, he reached around behind his back and locked the other wrist in. Then he spun around and lifted his hands to show the cop that they were locked in place.

He turned back around to face the cop.

"What now?" Aaron asked.

Mouthpiece's cell phone dinged. He unclipped it and read the message. When he met Aaron's eyes, a renewed fire brewed in them.

"What?" Aaron asked.

The cop stepped back and lifted the phone for his partner to read. Then the partner glared at Aaron.

Mouthpiece deposited his phone in his pocket and started for Aaron.

"You guys gonna tell me what the fuck is going on?" Aaron asked, a sudden urge to turn, run, and take his chances flared in him.

Mouthpiece grabbed his arm and yanked him back toward the hospital.

"You have the right to remain silent. You have the right to retain legal counsel. Anything you say—"

"What are you arresting me for?" he asked. Did the cop at the hotel text him? Did the clerk mistakenly issue a statement that it was Aaron who shot the airport van driver?

"Aaron Stevens, you are being arrested for the murder of Len Wallace, the Park 'N Fly van driver. We have a witness."

The other cop clamped onto Aaron's other arm, and together they half dragged him across the hospital's dark parking lot.

At their cruiser, Mouthpiece pushed him against the car and patted him down.

At the small of Aaron's back, the cop's hand stopped on Ansgar's Glock.

"What's this?" He yanked it out and held it up for his

partner to see. "Odds are, this was the weapon that killed the driver. What do you say, Aaron? This the weapon?"

There was no point in debating with these men. Nothing he could say would convince them to take their cuffs off him and let him walk away. He also didn't want to lie, which would be found out later.

"Good investigating there, dickweed. That's the gun that shot the driver. I'll put that in my statement. That gun is the murder weapon. But I didn't do it."

"Of course, you didn't. You just happen to carry murder weapons around with you like the rest of us normal folk carry house keys."

They shoved Aaron into the back seat of the cruiser and slammed the door.

"Fuck you, Aaron Stevens. Fuck you."

The cops disappeared inside the hospital.

Chapter 44

AARON WAS DRIVEN TO the police station, processed, and placed in a holding cell until someone was supposed to come and take his statement.

Mistakes had been made. Bad decisions fell through. He was supposed to take care of Clara, and he screwed that up. At one point, they were safe in a hotel room, and now he had no idea where everyone was.

The mouthpiece cop, Detective Shawn Bryant, read Aaron his rights. Once that was done and he was processed, Aaron understood the cops were bringing Daniel and Clara in. Benjamin would remain at the hospital under police guard until he could be moved to the police station.

He leaned against the door and stared out into the corridor through a small square window.

What had happened to Alex? Had Ansgar gotten the better of him? Maybe Ansgar had a hidden weapon of some kind. Could Alex be dead, and they'd find his body in the coming days? If so, that was on Aaron. It was stupid to knock that cop out at the hotel and steal his uniform and his cruiser. The cop knew what Alex looked like. It would only be a matter of time before Alex would also be up on charges.

But they'd done it, and at the time, it made sense because of how dangerous Ansgar was.

So where was Ansgar? Was it all worth it?

Aaron pushed off the door and sat on the wooden bench that ran the length of the back wall of the small holding cell.

He wasn't worried about the murder charge. It was a waste of time, and the charges would be dropped within days as soon as they took Clara's statement. It would all work out. But until then, Alex was on his own. Of all the people he knew outside Sarah, if someone were alone and had to survive without support for a few days, it would be Alex. He'd make it.

Three hours later, the sun rising and filling the left side of the corridor with morning light, an officer knocked once, then opened the holding cell door. Despite the early hour and the fatigue that came along with it, Aaron shot up from the wooden bench and followed the officer without any drowsiness. He was eager to give his statement and get this over with.

An hour later, after his statement was taken by a female officer named Liane Carmen, he was led to an interview room.

"Would you like a coffee or water?" Carmen asked.

"Coffee. Black."

Carmen nodded and eased the door shut.

Ten minutes later, Officer Carmen returned with a cup of

black coffee, then slipped out the door.

The coffee was long gone, and he needed a toilet. The door opened again, and Detective Bryant entered, followed by his partner. Neither man appeared to have been given the benefit of sleep since he'd seen them last.

Bryant sat opposite Aaron's chair while his partner stayed by the door.

"Rest well?" Bryant asked.

Aaron fiddled with his empty coffee cup and spoke without looking up. "Come to release me?" he asked.

"I'm confused about something," Bryant said.

Aaron waited. He released the coffee cup and sat back in his chair, doing his best to ignore his raging bladder.

"Why are you guys involved with someone like Ansgar Holm? Why would such a high-profile assassin run around Toronto gunning for you?"

Aaron shrugged. "Wish I knew."

"Are you saying you're unaware of any provocation you initiated?"

"That's what I'm saying. Other than what's in my statement, all I know is I was supposed to get Clara from him and protect her after that. What better way to keep her safe than to have her with you lot."

"Clara mentioned Sarah Roberts was the girl who originally attacked Ansgar in the hotel room. Then Sarah flew to Denmark. Any reason why?"

"Sarah has her own reasons. I often don't learn them until after the fact."

It felt good to be forthcoming. It took a lot of energy to fight the authorities or to lie to them. Maintaining a fabricated story at this point was reckless. They had saved

Clara, and Benjamin was shot while leaving the hotel. An innocent man was killed. In their panic, they hurt a cop, stole his cruiser, and got out of there. Any jury would understand. At least, he hoped.

"We looked into Anton Olafson and where Sarah Roberts might be at the moment. You would be surprised what we found."

That got his attention. He hadn't had any updates since Sarah left for Denmark. They'd been so busy with Ansgar that he hadn't even taken a moment to try to get a message out to her.

Aaron leaned forward and placed his forearms on the table.

"Tell me. What did you find out?"

The officers exchanged a glance that appeared sour, demure.

Bryant tapped his fingers on the table.

"Something happened in a place called Skanderborg," Bryant said.

"Yeah, that's where Sarah was headed."

"Well, we're not getting a lot on what happened in Skanderborg, but we do know that Sarah and Clara's father are in the hospital in a place called Silkeborg."

His stomach dropped. "Hospital?"

"Clara's father has stab wounds. A friend of Sarah's did it and is to be formally charged within the hour."

"Sarah's friend?" Aaron asked. "You mean Parkman?"

"Yeah, that was the name."

Aaron blew air out of his mouth. This was bad. Very bad. Why attack Anton Olafson? Wasn't he a good guy? If not, why were they protecting Clara? He shook his head as if to dislodge cobwebs. Did it ever make sense when dealing with Sarah? But that was what he loved about her. The mystery, the intrigue. It all worked out in the end, though. Didn't it?

"What about Sarah?" he asked. "Why is she in the hospital?"

Bryant pushed off the table and got to his feet.

"Hey," Aaron said. "Where are you going? Tell me what happened to Sarah."

The partner opened the door and stepped out into the corridor. Bryant stopped in the doorframe.

Aaron stared at him, gaping.

"I'm sorry, Aaron. There's no good news to tell you about Sarah."

"What does that mean?" he asked, sickness and rage brewing in his stomach.

Bryant lowered his head and looked at the floor. All the mouthpiece talk from the hospital was gone. Behind the mask, the bravado, the tough smart-aleck cop, was a humble man. One with a heart and genuine feelings. Aaron saw all that in the expression on the detective's face and didn't like it because it meant what he had to say pained him.

"Is she—" Aaron couldn't say it. He couldn't ask if Sarah was dead.

"We talked to the officer at the hospital. He spoke good English."

Aaron slapped the table. "Please, Bryant, tell me what you know."

"Sarah was brought into the hospital, DOA. I'm sorry, Aaron. I really am."

Aaron slumped down on the chair hard as Bryant shut the door.

Then his world collapsed, and he slipped off the chair and curled into a ball on the cold concrete floor.

He stayed like that until the interview room door opened again two hours later.

Chapter 45

THE DANISH AUTHORITIES WERE professional and polite. They were prepared to do their jobs and let the courts figure things out. But Sarah didn't have time to hang around in Denmark to let the courts discover she was the victim. Parkman had simply protected her when she was out or lying dead, as the officers kept calling it.

"I'm not understanding what the problem is," Sarah said.

"Then explain how you came to be at Mr. Olafson's house."

They were in a small room the hospital provided. Two police officers remained with Sarah and Parkman while two others had arrived and were guarding the door. As far as Sarah had heard, they were to remain in the hospital until Sarah's test results came back. The doctors wanted to make sure she was okay to discharge. Especially after originally declaring her dead.

The young cop in front of her seemed motivated to do his job by the book. His older partner gave Sarah the impression that this was a training session.

"We already told you that," Sarah said, trying to keep the exasperation out of her voice but failing. "I am here on behalf of Anton's daughter, Clara. She's staying with my friends in Toronto when I flew here."

"Anton claims you're wearing his daughter's clothing. He has claimed information in his statement that someone has threatened to kill his daughter and that if the information of your whereabouts leaks out, his daughter will be murdered." The young cop—Sarah forgot his name—held his hands out to his side. "Do you understand how this must look to us?"

"However it looks, Anton attacked me. In fact, he killed me. When Parkman attempted to revive me back at the house in Skanderborg, Anton attacked him. Why are we still here? Tell me, why isn't Anton being arrested for murder or attempted murder?"

The young cop seemed out of questions. He referred to a pad of paper he'd made notes on, scanned something, then looked up.

"What's your name again?" Sarah asked.

"Officer Martin."

"Okay, Officer Martin. Are you aware of the high-profile case in Aarhus involving a man named Damien?"

The young cop started at the mention of Damien's name. He glanced at his partner, who pushed off the wall and stepped closer to Sarah. She felt Parkman's eyes on her.

"What do you know of Damien?" the older cop asked.

"Suicide. While in custody." She watched their reactions.

"It happened just over two hours ago. Virtually impossible for me to know that, having been dead and all."

"Who told you?" Martin said.

Ignoring him, she pushed on. "Damien ran a little underage ring in Aarhus. An embarrassment to the people of Denmark. Correct?"

She suddenly felt ravenous. When was the last time she'd eaten? She licked her lips. Her mouth was dry, too. Before leaving and finding their way to the airport, she would have to eat a cow. Maybe two. When her stomach growled in hunger, she wondered if they had heard it. No one seemed to take note. They were too engrossed in what she had to say.

"Anton Olafson was one of Damien's top clients. And I can prove it."

The older cop stepped back again and crossed his arms.

"Really now? And how can you back up such a claim?"

She frowned and looked at Officer Martin. "Is he always like this? Or is the stupid act just for show?"

"Excuse me?" the older cop said, louder now.

"I said I can prove it. That is how I back up the claim. By fucking proving it. How else?"

"Please forgive my English," the cop said, sarcasm coating every word. "What I mean is, how are you to go about proving that? By what means will you provide us with proof?"

"Pictures. Kept on Anton's computer. Since erased. I can get them. I know where they are."

As soon as she said that, she knew it was a mistake.

"How would you know where they are? Or are you trying to establish a motive for Anton wanting to kill you?"

"They are on a computer in Toronto."

"Of course they are, Miss Roberts." The older cop threw up his hands. "And you think we're just going to let you leave here to fly home and get us this evidence?"

"Yes, that's exactly what I'm thinking. Unless you have charges against us, you will let us leave, or our one phone call will be to our embassy." She turned to Parkman. "Unless there's a pizza delivery place close by. I'll call the embassy. You order ten large pizzas. I'm famished."

Parkman nodded and blinked. "I'll get the food."

The older cop paced back and forth. He did this several times, then stopped.

"Why you are in Denmark in the first place is a mystery. What has happened since your arrival is a mystery to me. Your story doesn't make sense. What Anton did doesn't make sense. But I can tell you he's not a murderer. Not Anton Olafson, the director of the NC3. I also fail to understand how he would be involved with the man who killed himself in his holding cell tonight." The cop turned to face Sarah. "You must understand, this all looks like some kind of smear campaign against Mr. Olafson."

"I can see how it would, but there is one bit of proof left that will prove he is a murderer."

"What, Miss Roberts?"

"His cell phone. He recorded the entire act."

The cop put his hands on his hips, his head slightly tilted to the side. "And why would he do that?"

"You'll have to ask him."

Officer Martin got up from his chair and stood beside the old cop. After a nod between them, without a word, they stepped from the room.

"Not sure how that went," Parkman said. "You seemed to

keep your cool, though."

"Just hungry. And worried for Alex and Aaron. I don't like what I saw happening in Toronto."

"What did you see?"

The door opened, and the Danish cops were back.

"Okay, let's go. We've talked to the doctor. Other than a little bruising, you're fine to leave. Both of you."

"Where are we going?" Parkman asked.

"To the police station to write a full statement. We'll decide what charges, if any, will be filed after that."

"And what about the proof Sarah mentioned?"

"We'll get to that. We'll stop at Olafson's on the way to the police station. His house is still roped off as a murder scene. I want to see what's on his cell phone myself. Maybe he did record the murder." The cop shrugged. "Maybe he didn't. But it'll go a long way to us trusting you if he did."

They started out of the room and through the hospital's main corridor toward the parking lot.

"Never thought you'd get a chance to tour your own murder scene, eh?" Parkman whispered to her.

"Already toured it when I was dead," Sarah said, a half-smile on her lips.

"Does the video exist?" he asked, low enough for only her to hear.

They stepped out the front doors and turned toward the police cars parked twenty feet away.

"Absolutely." She held her stomach. "Once they see it, it won't be long before we're free to leave."

"How do you know?"

"Some information comes to me like déjà vu now. Like I've seen it before, and then it begins to happen. I can even see hours or days ahead. But only certain things. The visions are attached to emotions as well. It's still very weird. I'll tell you more on the plane."

"Are we going to be on a plane soon?" he asked.

"Yes, but there are a few more hoops to jump through first. One we won't like much."

"Which one?"

The older cop opened the back door for Sarah. Before getting in, she turned to Parkman.

"All of them," she said, then dropped into the car.

Chapter 46

PAIN HAD DONE IT. He considered himself the best man who walked the earth. He had located Aaron Stevens on the hospital computer and found the grid to turn their power off temporarily. A glitch in their software allowed him access, but it came back on five minutes later and locked him out.

Texting Detective Bryant was brilliant. Before he ruined Bryant's life, he might as well perform like a monkey for Ben. Aaron would be held on suspicion of murder and possibly charged unless a lot of evidence was discovered in his favor.

Sarah Roberts was dead, and Anton was in the same hospital in Silkeborg being treated for something. Probably a self-inflicted injury to have the authorities believe he was defending himself from Sarah.

Ben couldn't be sure about all the details, but it looked like everything was playing out nicely.

There was one more play in his book, one more layer of security he wanted to create just in case Sarah Roberts wasn't really dead. According to several reports he'd read on her, she had escaped death dozens of times and helped the police in several criminal cases. She had enemies all over the world, and recently a drug cartel in Mexico had been destroyed when they went up against her.

So how could one man, Anton Olafson, kill Sarah with a pillow? It didn't make sense. Ben had watched the video but refused to believe his eyes. In a few days, it wouldn't matter. On Tuesday, he would meet with Jessy, bring her back to his house, and murder her. Then he would call her brother, Detective Shawn Bryant, and have him respond to the murder where he was the actual target.

At that point, Sarah would be a footnote. Nothing of concern whatsoever. The dead Sarah was no concern at all right now, but he needed this extra layer of security if she wasn't dead and he couldn't source that information.

It took him the better part of seven hours to hack into the required government website, add Sarah's name to it with a photo reference and a brief bio, then remove all traces of having been there.

When he was done, he brushed the half a dozen Mars bar wrappers off his desk, opened another, and ate it slowly, despite the toothache that was starting. He'd be dead before the sun set on Tuesday. How bad could a toothache get in that short time?

He bit into the chocolate bar, used the sore tooth to chew, and leaned back in his chair, feeling accomplished.

"Do your worst," he said to his tooth. "I've done what I came to do, and no one can stop the denouement now."

Upon the last swallow, he set his fingers on the dirty keyboard and brought up his email program. After attaching several pictures of Anton Olafson and his indiscretions with underage boys to the email, he addressed it to the Skanderborg Police and hit send.

Anton Olafson would burn in hell for what he did to defenseless boys. Just like Ben's torturers when he was a small defenseless boy. They would all pay for what they did. First, take something from them they love, then destroy their lives. Clara from Anton, then send pictures to the police. Jessica from Shawn, then have Shawn up on murder charges.

"Brilliant," Ben said without pausing as he typed. "Fucking brilliant."

Chapter 47

AARON WAS NUMB FROM the news about Sarah. It had been at least two hours since they opened the door. A female officer stepped in and asked if he needed a washroom or a coffee.

His head in a cloud, Aaron took the washroom option. When he was finished, the officer escorted him back to the interview room, where a large black coffee sat on the table.

"How long am I supposed to be here?" Aaron asked.

"Not sure," she said. "I'll get Bryant to come to see you."

Aaron nodded, not interested in a fight with her. He just wanted out. He wanted to go see Sarah's parents. Stay with them. Deal with the funeral.

The door closed, startling him. He had zoned out, not even noticing the officer leave.

How could Sarah be dead? They were just together a few short days ago at the hotel. It seemed impossible. He paced the floor, thinking up scenarios to make it all disappear. The information was false. The hospital read the name wrong. Someone was hiding the fact that Sarah was still alive. The information couldn't be true. It just couldn't be. He had to believe she was alive, or he'd go insane. The grief would be too much to bear. The heartache. To lose Sarah, his dojo, and his freedom all in less than one week was too much to handle.

Until he saw a body, Sarah was alive and well in his mind. That's what he would go by. She was alive and well. Aware it was a coping mechanism, he'd rather think that way than the alternative.

The door opened behind him. He stopped pacing and faced Detective Bryant and his partner.

They eased inside the room and shut the door.

"Good news first?" Bryant said. "Or bad news?"

"I need good news first."

"The hospital in Denmark called back."

"And?"

"They claim there was a mistake in taking a reading of some sort. After some medical jargon, it turns out that Sarah Roberts isn't dead after all."

Aaron accordioned at the waist, dropped to the floor, and lifted his arms over his head to grasp his hair. On his knees, he moaned and bowed twice as if he was praying, taking large breaths in and out.

"I knew it. I fucking knew it." He hopped to his feet and shook his arms as if ridding them of the grief that had encompassed him moments before. "That girl can't be killed. Okay," he took in a deep breath, then exhaled it. "What else?"

"She's in police custody at the moment," Bryant went on.

"Not sure why or what charges they're preparing, but she isn't free to go yet and may not be for a while."

"Doesn't matter." Aaron waved a dismissive hand. "She'll get out of it whatever it is."

Bryant hitched up his belt and hooked his thumbs in his pant line. His partner wiped his nose and leaned against the door, staring at the ground.

"What?" Aaron asked.

"The bad news," Bryant said.

"I thought the part about Sarah being in custody was the bad news."

Bryant shook his head slowly, his eyes never leaving Aaron.

"Then what?" Aaron said. "Go ahead."

"We talked to the clerk at the hotel. He claims he saw you and your entourage leave the hotel with Clara. His statement, along with the staff who were working earlier in the day, claim there was an altercation in a room on the tenth floor."

"Room 1034," his partner added.

"Right. 1034."

"Ansgar's room," Aaron said. "Where he had Clara tied up."

"Well, according to witness accounts, it's shaping up to look like you guys barged in, beat a man named Peter Ford, and then kidnapped Clara from her room across the hallway. There's no mention of Ansgar Holm or The Clock anywhere. So far, there's been no evidence of the assassin even being in Toronto. We also have a witness who claimed you or your friend has a keycard for a vacant room—"

"1134," the partner said.

"Right, 1134. That room is fucked up, and the bedsheets are tied to the balcony. Anything on that?"

Aaron stepped forward and immediately regretted it. The partner pushed off the door and stared him down. Bryant's hands slipped out of his belt line.

"Aaron, you're not cuffed out of sympathy for the burns on your arms. That can change. We're trying to get to the bottom of this mess. Until we do, you're staying put. In here."

"That's the bad news?"

"No. The bad news is they are preparing charges against you that include the theft of the police car, assaulting a peace officer, and murder in the second degree, to name a few. The bad news is you may need to get used to the inside of one of these rooms. By the end of the day, the charges will be officially filed, and you'll have an arraignment by the morning. But don't count on bail. You're a flight risk. Your passport is probably full of stamps from all the traveling you've been doing to the States and Mexico."

"And what does Clara Olafson say about all this? She knows we saved her. She was tied up in that room with Peter Ford. She knows I didn't shoot the van driver. Huh? Tell me. What's her statement say?"

"She hasn't given one. Still at the hospital. Not sure it'll matter at this point. Not when several witnesses are coming forward and video coverage in the hotel lobby showing you leave with her, then running back in with a short, wiry-looking guy. Then leaving again through a side stairwell with Peter Ford over your shoulder and the wiry guy in the police uniform that was stolen from an officer who was knocked out by room 1034. Was it you who set those bombs off, too?

Come on, Aaron, tell us everything. Clear the conscious, clean the soul."

"Fuck you, Bryant. Looks like I need a lawyer. Stay out of my face from now on. Talk to my lawyer. I've nothing to say to you. You've set your mind to what happened, and you're preparing the evidence to fit that dialogue. So fuck you and your horse. You and your partner need to leave. This conversation is now illegal as I've asked for a lawyer, and you're still standing there with a thumb up your ass." The last words came out in a shout, his pent-up emotions coming unhinged. "Get out of here!" he yelled.

The partner opened the door and slipped out. Bryant backed up, an arrogant smile on his lips. Before the door closed, he stuck his head back in.

"You'll burn for this, Aaron. You're going down, little boy."

The door closed and locked.

Aaron let out a breath and dropped back to the floor, curling up in the corner and trying to calm his breathing.

It would all work out in the end.

At least, that's what he told himself repeatedly for the next several hours.

Chapter 48

Once in Skanderborg, the Danish police located Anton's cell phone in his house and were able to watch the video he took as he held the pillow over Sarah's face. The video made it abundantly clear what had happened. Sarah told Officer Martin to watch closely as Anton moved away from the camera to grab the little mirror of how her chest moved. She was taking on air even then.

They left Sarah and Parkman inside Anton's guest room while the Danish police privately conferred. While they were talking in the living room, Sarah slipped into Clara's bedroom and rifled through her dresser drawers. Once she found what she was looking for, she returned to stand with Parkman.

"What was that for?" Parkman whispered.

"You'll see." Sarah smiled.

A superior officer was called in before they drove

Parkman and Sarah to the new larger police station being built, where the officers were to record their statements. Three large pizzas were brought in.

Officer Martin sat behind his desk, drinking what looked like a cup of tea.

"Sarah?" he said as she finished the last piece of pizza. "Can you and Parkman remain in the area for further questioning if needed?"

"How long?" Sarah asked.

"A week at the max," Officer Martin said.

Sarah shook her head and swallowed. She wiped her mouth.

"Can't do it. I'm needed in Toronto."

"I could detain you until charges are laid against Anton."

"You could try," Sarah said. She pointed a finger at him. "But we both know that wouldn't fly."

"How do you figure?"

"You have video proof a high-ranking Danish official, Anton Olafson, tried to kill me. My friend Parkman stepped in and saved my life. It was touch and go there for an hour. Danish doctors thought I was dead. They wheeled me down to the morgue. When I call my embassy, you don't think this blows up in your face, and I'm on the next plane out of here?"

As she spoke, Martin's face reddened with embarrassment. Or was it anger? She couldn't tell right away.

"You're right, Sarah. You're free to go. But I may be in touch."

"Call anytime." She headed for the door. "Tak for the pizza."

"Velkommen. Oh, and leave my office door open."

She stepped out into the main office of the police station and closed Martin's door. Parkman was across the room, waiting for her by the front doors. He got up from the chair he sat in and headed toward her.

"We good?" he asked.

"We're good." She started for the door. "Get me on a plane. Alex and Aaron need me in Toronto before Tuesday."

"Why Tuesday?"

"Not sure yet."

"Right."

When they stepped out into the sunlight, Sarah caught Martin's eye. He stood near the door to his office, hands on his hips, watching them leave.

"Parkman, we must be on a plane and off European soil as soon as possible."

"Why? What's happening?"

"Don't exactly know. Just a feeling."

They headed toward an idling taxi by the visitor parking area.

"This new arrangement with Vivian difficult to navigate?" he asked.

"Something like that. Yet there are things I know without a doubt."

"Like what?"

She stopped beside the cab and faced him. "I can see that we are flying back to Toronto together, but we don't want to enter the airport together. Weird, eh?"

He frowned. "Why can't we be in the airport together?"

She shrugged indifferently. "I have no idea. Just don't enter the security checkpoint and customs with me, or we'll both be in trouble. Serious trouble."

"Okay. When do I go through?"

"Don't know. I'll get to that."

They hopped inside the taxi.

"Take us to the nearest airport," Sarah said.

"That's in Billund. About an hour's drive."

"Then go. We need out of here yesterday."

The taxi pulled away from the police station as more details came together for Sarah.

Her pact with Vivian was working, but as with any new arrangement, it would take time to develop.

But time was in short supply.

Chapter 49

THE TAXI PULLED UP in front of the Billund airport after the driver had talked at length about Legoland and how the owner of Legoland had invested and built the airport so it was easier for him to come and go. He said it started in 1961 when the son of the owner of Legoland built an eight-hundred-meter-long runway and a small hangar. By 1964, the airport began handling public traffic and continued to expand until today. Over two and a half million passengers from around the world use the Billund airport yearly.

"Legoland even has a LEGO version of the airport that you can build," the driver added, seemingly so happy to have imparted this knowledge to American tourists.

Parkman paid the driver the huge fee for the one-hour ride, and they got out. Sarah led Parkman inside, where she found a coffee and pastry shop. Once they had their coffees, she sat at a small circular table and closed her eyes momentarily. A chair scuffed the floor as Parkman pulled one out to sit across from her.

"You okay, Sarah?" Parkman asked.

She opened her eyes. "Yeah. Just trying to see more of what's about to happen."

"What's about to happen?" he asked.

"Don't know. That's why I'm trying to see more."

"Right. Okay."

They sat quietly for another couple of minutes, eating and drinking.

"When you're done with your coffee," Sarah said as she gestured at his half-full cup, "go buy a ticket to Amsterdam or Copenhagen or wherever. Then see if you can get a ticket from there directly to Toronto. When you're done, come back here and tell me the flight times and numbers. Then I'll go buy the same."

"We can't do it together?"

She shook her head.

"Why not? We're clear of the mess in Skanderborg. Let's just buy our tickets and fly to Toronto."

Sarah reached across the table to clasp his hand.

"Parkman, the trouble was never in Skanderborg. Sure we needed to go there, but the trouble is in Toronto. Aaron and Alex are in the thick of it. Oh, and Benjamin got shot."

"Benjamin got shot?" Parkman jerked back. "Why is he always the one who gets shot? Is he okay?"

"A leg wound. He's still in the hospital."

"Do you know all this because of your new arrangement with Vivian?"

"Something like that. I have to explain it from the beginning."

"Is that why you know details about them but not us?"

She nodded. "If we separate, we make it out of this airport. Both of us. If we don't separate, we don't make it out. I'm just able to see a single detail. Only the end scenes show up in my visions from my sister."

Parkman pushed his chair back. "Going to get my ticket now, then." He walked away without another word.

Ten minutes later, he was back with his ticket.

"I fly in one hour."

Sarah read his ticket and flight times then memorized the flight numbers.

"Got it. Now head through security, and I'll see you on the plane. Going to buy my ticket now." She hugged him briefly. "Remember, I'll see you on the plane. But until we're in the air, you don't know me. And don't wait for me."

"Got it. Just be there. I can't leave without you."

"I'll be there. But Parkman, you have to promise me something."

"Not sure I'm going to like this."

"Whatever happens, whatever you see, get on that plane. Do not stay here. You have to fly out today. Even if that means leaving me behind. Promise me."

"I can't promise something like that—"

"Parkman, you have to. Promise me."

She stared into his eyes, returning his gaze, unwilling to speak again until he gave in.

Without further delay, he said, "I promise."

Sarah gently touched his arm, then walked away. She bought a ticket in her name at the KLM ticket window and produced her ID. Then she bought a ticket for Clara Olafson and used the ID she had found in Clara's dresser. The ticket agent printed both tickets and pointed at the security area where Sarah was to go, as the plane would be boarding in thirty minutes.

Once Clara's ticket was safely stowed, she strode toward security. Something was going to happen, but what exactly was still a mystery. The new pact with Vivian gave Sarah access to Vivian's *psychic* eyes, and it gave Vivian access to her *earthly* eyes. Vivian got to live through Sarah as if she was implanted into her consciousness. The opposite was true for Sarah now. She could live in Vivian's awareness which allowed her to use Vivian's psychic ability at will. That's how she knew about the evidence being on Anton's cell phone. She knew about Benjamin's bullet wound and what was happening to Aaron and Alex. She also knew what was coming on Tuesday and needed to find a way to stop it. A lot of what was coming and what she could do to stop it was easy to glean from Vivian as she was as close to Sarah now as if she was in her body. It took dying to have Vivian enter her consciousness in a similar way Sarah's soul was thrust back into her body.

The one thing Vivian warned Sarah about was that Sarah would never be allowed to view future events that affected her personally. Whatever was about to happen at the airport affected her and her alone, hence her obstructed view of the events.

There was one consolation, though. Like déjà vu, Sarah could see something coming and how she would feel about it, but not the actual event. Otherwise, she would be walking toward airport security blind.

It had nothing to do with Officer Martin back in Skanderborg. In fact, at that very moment, Martin was opening an email from a man in Toronto that Sarah needed to see on Tuesday. In that email, Officer Martin would view pictures of Anton Olafson in compromising positions. Once the youth in the pictures were identified, they would match with the case files from a recently deceased suicide victim named Damien. Anton Olafson would have a new list of charges added to his attempted murder charge. He would end up dying in prison at the hands of a fellow inmate in a shiv attack two years after he was convicted and placed in a maximum security prison.

She saw all that coming but couldn't see what would happen in the next five minutes.

In line at airport security, her stomach spun with nerves. What she was about to do was a simple thing, really. Just walk through security and leave the country. Her passport was up to date. She wasn't wanted on any outstanding warrants. She'd only been in Denmark a few days. She was murdered, endured a near-death experience, woke up from death, and here she was about to leave Denmark. Simple really.

An old Shakespeare line from Hamlet flashed through her mind about Denmark and something being rotten. Another thought slipped into her mind. Not knowing the future drove her nuts, yet every single person around her didn't know the future. She ought to be more grateful for what she was given when it was provided.

Thanks, Vivian, for that thought. You're a real sport. Appreciate it.

As she stepped up to the metal detector, she spied Parkman on the other side, holding another coffee cup, waiting for her to walk through.

A commotion to her left caught her attention. Four airport security members were jogging toward her position.

Here we go. This has to be about me.

She walked through the metal detector. The woman monitoring it waved her by. She started toward Parkman, a funny feeling in her stomach that she wouldn't make it to him.

Heavy footfalls drew closer. More members of airport security came up from her right, and still two others from her left. She slowed, stopped, and turned around to address them when she was ten feet from Parkman.

"Sarah Roberts?" one of the officers said.

Sarah nodded. "That's me."

"I'm going to need you to come with us."

"I have a plane to catch. What could this be about?"

"Ma'am, you won't make your flight. Please, come with us."

"I'm not going anywhere until you tell me what this is all about."

The officer shot a glance at a few of his colleagues for support, but they all just kept staring at Sarah. They were being cautious. Too cautious.

Vivian, what the hell is this?

"Sarah Roberts, you're on a no-fly list. I can't permit you to fly. You're going to have to come with us."

Adrenaline pumped through her. She took an extra deep breath as her heart beat in its cage made of sore bones.

"A no-fly list?" she asked, looking as bewildered as she felt. "How's that? What list?"

"The list is issued by your American government. It says it right here. You're suspected of sympathizing with terrorists. You're to be detained, Miss Roberts."

"Fuck that," she said.

She turned and ran toward the two officers on her left, bowled by them before they could grab her, and headed for the exit that led outside.

When she shouldered into the door, an alarm went off somewhere in the building.

A quick glance over her shoulder gave her stomach something else to feel sick about.

Her pursuers had grown in number, and a few of them had weapons in their hands now.

They were ten feet behind her.

Sarah dropped low, turned, and ran past a maintenance van parked by the door.

Something tripped her. She stumbled to the ground beside the van. A man's arm lodged around her throat. His hand clamped over her mouth.

At the second the exit door burst open, and airport security officers spilled out, the man wheeled Sarah under the maintenance van and out of view of the pursuing authorities.

Chapter 50

Ben Wilson was convinced the universe was working in his favor. How could he lose when everything worked out? Even when things went wrong, he was winning.

"Amazing, really," he murmured as he studied the computer screen.

Sarah Roberts was alive.

She was revived at the hospital and left the city of Skanderborg. When he'd logged onto the closest airport and sent his spiders searching, her name came up at the Billund airport. She had bought a ticket to come to Toronto via Amsterdam.

But that's where she was stopped.

If he hadn't taken precautions earlier and placed her name on the no-fly list, she would have arrived before Tuesday morning.

It had taken him seven hours to add Sarah's photo, name,

and a brief bio of her terrorist sympathies to get her grounded at any airport she wanted to use. Sarah Roberts was done, and she could do nothing to get to Toronto on time.

Absolutely nothing.

It was late. Anton was done for. Ansgar was off the map somewhere. Aaron was going down for murder. Everyone was tagged and bagged. His job was complete. Now he needed sleep.

One more evening of mayhem tomorrow, and then fate would arrive on Tuesday. He looked forward to that day. No more back pain. No more pancreatic cancer. No more people talking shit about him. Just the lives of assholes either ended or ruined.

He turned off his computer screens, got up from his desk, and thought about one more Mars bar, but declined it as he wasn't feeling too good and waddled to the bathroom.

Ten minutes later, staring at the ceiling in bed, he thought about Jessy. Maybe he would fuck her one more time before he killed her. Really mess with Shawn's head when they autopsied the body later. Everyone would think it was a rape and murder thing, but Jessy wouldn't mind. She hated herself. One compliment here, one nice word there, and her clothes would come off, thinking they were getting back together.

He snapped his fingers in the dark. That was it. He would beg for her back. They could make a go of it. She would do it for sure. No issues whatsoever. They would have sex; then he would strangle the life from her worthless emo existence.

Once Shawn arrived, he would carry her lifeless body outside toward him, the toy gun in his hand. When he tossed her body aside, the toy gun would come up and aim at

Shawn, and the detective would kill him and have to live with that for the rest of his life.

He would be doing Ben a favor because there was no way he could kill himself, and he wouldn't let the cancer kill him over the next few months.

Ben Wilson would not wither away and die like his mother had.

He had more dignity than that.

And more brains.

Chapter 51

A SMALL CROWD STOOD by and watched at least a dozen security personnel chase Sarah. To see Sarah run like that, pursued by so many airport security on some trumped-up claim that she was on the no-fly list, was preposterous.

And there was nothing he could do.

Except make his way to the plane.

He had promised Sarah he would. There had to be a solid reason for her making him promise he would get on the plane no matter what happened. Whether it was something she knew or was quite positive about, Parkman had no choice but to get on that plane.

It pained him to think he was leaving her behind. What would Aaron say when he landed in Toronto without her?

When Aaron found out Sarah had died and Vivian had written Parkman a letter telling him to go to Skanderborg, what then? He was just happy no one knew he had been drinking the night of the Burning of the Witch.

Shoulders slumped, he started along the wide corridor toward his gate just as the announcement came over the speakers above that boarding was commencing for his flight.

Two more officers raced by him in an airport vehicle. He turned to watch them, knowing they were after Sarah and feeling absolutely useless as he could do nothing to help her. Stepping in now would only get him detained as well.

He slowed by his gate. A line had formed. They were boarding the front half of the plane, and at least forty people waited to have their passports scanned and ID checked. He waited on the side for fifteen minutes until the final boarding call was announced, and the line was down to a few people.

After glancing over his shoulder, he pulled out his passport and opened it to the page with his picture.

The Danish girl in front of him wore a horrid perfume. When the line moved forward, Parkman stayed back. He turned sideways and breathed deeply. It wasn't that the girl had bathed in the stuff. It was just the smell wasn't to his liking.

After a maddening few minutes, he made it to the KLM attendants, got his passport checked, and was waved through to the access tunnel.

Parkman turned around and stared back at the interior of the airport before entering the tunnel.

No Sarah. The waiting area was empty.

He had to leave her behind.

He'd promised.

Head dipped, shoulders slumped, Parkman started down the ramp to enter the plane that would take him out of Denmark.

Chapter 52

The hand covering Sarah's mouth was large and firm. He moved below her and whispered in her ear.

"Friendly. Stay quiet."

Her nod was a short burst, suppressed by the hand holding her head back against the man's chest.

The officer who had talked to her inside the terminal was talking to someone at the back of the van, describing Sarah, asking if they saw which way she went. Another worker moved closer.

"Yeah, I saw a girl," the maintenance worker said. "She ran that way."

"That way?" the officer asked, incredulity in his voice.

The man holding Sarah lightened the pressure on her mouth. She took a deep, quiet breath in through her nose and lifted her head enough to stare at the feet of the people talking. With her forehead an inch from the van's chassis, she surmised it had been parked there for a while as no heat resonated off it.

"You mean to tell us she ran toward the runways?"

"Ahh, yup," the man said. "But she turned and headed that way after."

"Toward the parking lot?" the officer asked.

"Yeah, that girl ran fast."

The officer stepped away. "All units," he said, the sound of the radio's feedback answering him. "The female suspect appears to have gone toward the parking lot. All units report to the parking lot and stop all vehicles leaving. I want the exits cordoned off."

The feet scuffled away from around the van leaving the legs of two men as they continued to unload boxes onto a small skid.

The man below her released her mouth.

"Wait," he whispered. "Don't move."

They waited, her palms sweaty, her back soaked as all her body weight pressed down on the man below her. His abdomen was hard, like a bodybuilder fresh from the gym. They had slid under the vehicle on one of those square pieces of wood on wheels that mechanics used to get under cars.

The word *creeper* popped into her head. The board was called a creeper so mechanics could *creep* under vehicles.

Vivian, useless facts are great, but getting me out of this mess would be more useful.

Two words flitted through her mind like the echo over a canyon.

I am.

Someone slapped the side of the van twice.

"Go." The short word burst from the man's mouth under

her. The creeper slid sideways, and the Danish sun blinded her momentarily.

Hands latched onto her and dragged her to her feet. She blinked and tried to see who it was but didn't fight them. The man on the creeper had said they were friends. It was either them or airport security.

She was shoved into the back of the van, her eyes acclimating instantly. The bodybuilder who had dragged her under the van jumped up with her shaking the van with his weight, and the man outside slammed the van's back doors closed.

The man outside smacked the back door twice.

"Sarah?" a man said behind her, his voice familiar.

Sarah turned to look into the eyes of Darwin Kostas.

"It seems I received a strange letter from your sister about a week ago," Darwin said, his grin wide and warm. "Thought I'd do what she asked." He shrugged. "It's worked for you all these years."

Tears welled up in her eyes. "Oh, Darwin, it's so good to see you."

"You too, Sarah, but there's no time. You need to leave." He held out his hand. A passport protruded from his fingers. "Clara Olafson's passport. I received it via special delivery this morning from Toronto."

"What?" Sarah said, staring down at the Danish passport. After a moment, she took it from him. "How?"

"Aaron sent it to me. Must be part of his letter from Vivian."

"But how?"

"He said you'd ask. Told me to tell you to remember when he took Clara to her hotel room and got clothes for you before you flew here."

"I remember."

"He snatched her passport, and after you went to the airport that night to fly to Denmark, he Fedex'd it to a mailbox I rented here in Billund. According to Vivian, he was supposed to protect the Danish girl and mail you her passport. My letter told me to be by door A3 here at the airport and give it to you when you come running out with the authorities on your ass." He shrugged again. "So here we are."

"But how could Vivian have seen such detail all those years ago?"

The same as you often do now, Sarah.

She tilted her head as she listened to her sister.

"Vivian talking?" Darwin asked.

Sarah looked down at the passport in her hand. "Sometimes this shit still surprises me."

"Me too, man, me too."

She raised her head and stared into his eyes. "It's so good to see you, but it appears I have to leave again."

"I know. Bruno here will see that you get to the plane on time."

The bodybuilder nodded once. The man had to be seven feet tall and as thick as a tree.

"He'll stand out too much," Sarah said.

"He's also the only way through a pack of security guards if you're stopped again. Don't worry about Bruno. He'll take the heat. He wants to. There's a huge bonus in it if he gets arrested."

"Bonus," Bruno whispered.

Darwin grabbed a bag beside him and held it out to

Sarah.

"Take this. Put it on. It'll help you appear more Danish."

Sarah rifled through the bag and pulled out a top and new jeans. Bruno turned away when she started to change. Darwin didn't have to ask her to remove the clothes the security officers saw her in. They were the clothes she'd died in. It was good to be rid of them.

Once she was changed, she placed a large hat on her head and smiled for Darwin.

"All good?" she asked.

"Almost."

He pulled a small, amber-colored bottle out of the bag and sprayed copious amounts of disgusting perfume on her neck.

"What's that?"

"To complete the package."

"It'll bring attention to me," she gasped, trying not to breathe herself in.

"You'll be fine. Now go. And Bruno, take care of my girl here."

Bruno grunted and grabbed the handle of the van's door.

Sarah didn't know if the grunt was derisive or in agreement.

"Bruno?" Darwin said.

Bruno turned back to look at Darwin.

"I'm serious. Watch over her with your life."

"Understood, Boss," Bruno said, his voice as solid as his biceps. In that one word, Sarah felt the man's commitment as much as heard it.

Darwin slapped the inner wall of the van once.

They waited. He took her hand, clutched it tight, then let

it go.

"Stay safe, and we'll see you soon, Sarah. I love you like a sister, only more."

"You know I love you, too, Darwin." She planted a kiss on his cheek and moved back to crouch beside Bruno.

Someone slapped the van's outer wall twice.

The coast was clear.

Bruno slammed the door open and hopped out. He raised a hand to help Sarah out and then walked her to the door she had exited from earlier when being chased. The door was propped open, the alarm from earlier silenced.

Back inside the terminal, Bruno ushered her along the wide corridor, blocked her from the view of the security agents checking people at the metal detectors, and walked her toward her gate. With her clothes different, the large hat, and the new smell, Sarah walked through the Billund airport with a seven-foot tall bodybuilder as if he were her boyfriend.

She didn't see Parkman anywhere at her gate and felt the first pangs of fear. What had he done? Where was he? Could he have gone against his promise to her and chased after the officers?

Bruno leaned down to her ear.

"I leave now. Stay here. In line. I watch from over there. When you board, when the plane leaves, then I leave. Otherwise, your life is in my hands, and I won't let go. Understood?"

Sarah looked up into the steely determined eyes of a man built for the Greek Olympics of old and an honor-bound system most men wouldn't understand today.

"Understood," was all she said to him, a warmth spreading over her.

That was all he wanted to hear. A one-word answer. The corner of his lips lifted in a half-smile. Then he moved to the left and disappeared behind her.

If a brawl erupted around her on any given day, she wanted that kind of man in her corner.

The line edged forward. She looked over her shoulder to watch Bruno retreat to a small coffee kiosk.

That was when she saw Parkman sauntering toward her.

With the brim of her large hat pulled down, she faced forward and waited. Parkman stepped in behind her, just as he should.

Good man. Kept his promise.

Sometimes it's better to not have the whole story and just follow your word and do what's right anyway. Isn't that the definition of honor? Doing what's right when no one is looking?

The line edged forward. At the small kiosk, the flight attendant took Clara's passport, checked the photo, glanced at Sarah, then swiped the passport and handed it back to her. Sarah produced the ticket she had bought in Clara's name with the boarding pass, and the woman waved her through.

Sarah walked the ramp and entered the plane. Once seated, her stomach mixed with acid to the point where she held a hand over it. Despite how much she'd been through, this high-tension shit still got to her. Reminded her she was human. Which was the reason it didn't bother her that she wasn't jaded and probably never would be.

Minutes later, Parkman shambled down the aisle toward her. She lowered her head so the hat would cover her face. Not until they took off would she speak to him. They could have been seen together at the airport before buying their tickets.

He sat across the aisle from her in the same row.

The captain's voice emitted from the speakers. They were ready to leave. The doors closed moments later, and the plane taxied out to the runway.

She thought of Bruno watching from the airport window. Of Darwin in the van waiting for his mercenary to return, sad that Bruno didn't earn a bonus. Maybe one day Sarah would contact Darwin and get Bruno shipped over to her on loan. She could find a way to offer him a financial bonus for busting some heads.

The plane thrust forward as it prepared to take to the air. Danish soil dropped below the plane as it left the ground, and she was safe, gone from the airport security, away from the Danish authorities.

Now all she had to do was get to Toronto and deal with the one man behind everything before he died. Homicide Detective Shawn Bryant had some explaining to do as well.

She lifted the brim of the hat and faced Parkman. His arms were crossed over his chest, his head back, eyes closed.

"Excuse me, sir," she said.

Parkman opened his eyes and looked at her. Realization dawned on his face, and his eyes widened.

Sarah held a finger to her lips. "Shhhhh."

"What the? How the hell?"

"Come sit beside me. The window seat is empty. We've got a lot to talk about."

Chapter 53

BEN WILSON SPENT THE last day of his life preparing for death. He didn't fear death. If anything, it would be an end to the pain, to the suffering. Since there was nothing after death, he would become nothing, which was okay with Ben. Nothing was better than the something he had now.

The sun shone through the windows of his mother's house. He walked across the room and looked down at the street. He had never been happy living in downtown Toronto. To be on such a busy street with so many people coming and going at all hours of the night and day. The relative quiet after midnight was the primary reason he worked through the night and slept during the day.

But not today. This Tuesday was special. Today Detective Bryant would experience karma like never before.

Ben turned back to his computer. He had not heard from Ansgar all weekend, and as of this Tuesday morning, none of his spiders could track Ansgar's whereabouts or the whereabouts of any of his aliases. Nor could he triangulate the man's cell phone.

Aaron Stevens had been formally charged with murder, and his friends were charged as accomplices. They were being detained until some kind of court meeting tomorrow. Anton Olafson was under arrest at the hospital in Denmark, where he was still healing from wounds sustained at his house in Skanderborg, which Ben's spiders couldn't find anything else on.

None of that mattered to him anymore. Anton Olafson was a bad man. This was his comeuppance for what he had done to all those boys over the years. None of it would've come to light if Anton hadn't shut down Ben's hacking job months ago when Ben had gotten into the Danish Land Registry. They'd caught him because Ben had carelessly published data retrieved from the Land Registry site on a forum and entered into a debate on Danish laws. He had no idea the Danes were as good as they were at tracking IP addresses.

When they found his, they yanked the post off the forum and shut him down. The Danish Data Protection Agency worked closely with Anton Olafson, the Director of the NC3, to sever Ben's access. Going after Anton had been a side gambit. Something to have fun with.

Because Ben enjoyed playing God. If he could, then why not? Judgment Day. Since there was no God, he might as well act like one.

When Ben discovered Anton had a daughter, he hacked into her system easily and began talking to her through Plenty of Fish. Knowing her interests and needs, her wants and desires, it wasn't long before Clara was drawn to him. Ben told her he was a rich sports store owner in Toronto. Of course, he would send her a plane ticket. Round trip, all expenses paid, to Toronto, Canada, and the rest was history. Clara had fallen for him.

Ben had had his doubts about Anton fulfilling the murder task. Would he actually murder a random girl? Could he go through with it?

Once Ben saw what Anton was doing to those boys, Ben had no choice but to go after their pimp, Damien. He emailed evidence from Anton's computer and got Damien arrested in Aarhus.

Then to play with Anton. It was so simple, it was laughable. Death was the ultimate consequence, and Ben's death wasn't only coming, it would be of his own doing. Then there would be nothing. No Judgment Day, no reincarnation, no nothing. If God were real, there'd be no suffering. If he truly loved us, why place us on Earth to feel pain, to suffer?

So Ben became the pain and created LEGACY: PAIN PACT. He was the Passive Aggressive internet Nomad who wanted Performance, Action, and a Commitment Transaction out of people.

Ben had loved acronyms ever since he learned that Iron Man's Jarvis was named in honor of the former butler named Edwin Jarvis. The name actually stood for Just A Rather Very Intelligent System.

On the wall of his master bedroom office, a sign read F.A.I.L., First Attempt In Learning. Ben had learned enough and failed as many times. Only death was left, and he was ready.

He had set his computers to wipe their hard drives clean. They were loaded with information that would incriminate him after his death. He didn't want that. The public would spew sympathy on Detective Bryant if any of it came out.

What he had ready for his game, LEGACY: PAIN PACT, had been uploaded and would launch tomorrow when it did not receive a prompt from his computers. Since they would be defunct soon, that prompt would not come, thereby launching the game onto the internet. Once the authorities discovered where its host was, they would shut it down, but Ben would've won for the time being. By then, his game would be seen by hundreds, if not thousands. He could only hope it would go viral.

After his last lunch of three Mars bars, his stomach churned, and he thought he might vomit them back up. Maybe Jessica would come in time for him to vomit on her. Could be something the stupid emo was into.

He snorted a laugh. "Shit wave," he whispered.

At three on the dot, Jessica knocked on the door downstairs. The hard drives were almost done wiping. Close to another hour to go. He'd wanted them to finish so he could use a sledgehammer to break them into pieces before he left for the vegan café.

But they would still be here when he returned.

She knocked again.

"Persistent little bitch, eh."

He checked the main computer and saw it had fifty-three minutes left. The abort key flashed in the center of the screen.

"Fuck that," he muttered.

He activated the screen saver with one button and left the room. Downstairs, he adjusted his new shirt—not new, just never worn—sprayed cologne on his neck, set the bottle on the kitchen counter, then entered the main foyer and opened the door.

Why didn't she just use her house key like before?

Jessica couldn't have looked more pathetic than she did at that moment. Her hair was still black but shinier somehow. The boots were still rugged-looking and black. But the nail polish was red this time.

"Less goth?" he asked, studying her nails.

"Never goth," she smiled with her tiny mouth. Then blinked rapidly twice. "Hate goth. Not me."

Something about her was different. She seemed edgy, maybe even a little nervous.

"You okay?" he asked. "You don't look so good."

"It's this."

Jessy twisted around and leaned forward to reveal a large white bandage taped to the back of her shoulder.

"Tattoo?" he asked.

She twisted back to face him. "Yup."

"Of what?"

"A three-headed dragon."

He recoiled as if slapped. "A three-headed dragon? What the hell for?" Pain flashed in her eyes briefly. He tried to calm his reaction. "I'm sorry, what I mean is, how is that tattoo significant to you?"

These fucking emos and their gentle egos.

"The dragon itself represents my inner fire."

"Oh, yeah," he blurted out. "I can see that. Inner fire. Yup."

She actually thought his sarcasm was a genuine comment. She continued without missing a beat.

"Each head of the dragon represents my three dimensions."

He stepped back and leaned against the wall dramatically. "Wow," he gasped. "What dimensions? Pray tell."

Jessy giggled and dipped her face, appearing shy now.

Are you fucking kidding me? How do people like this even function in society? Like pay rent and shit.

"I'm honorable to a fault. I'm funny, and I'm loving. One dragon makes you laugh, one will stand by you, and the other will always love you."

He stared at her. He waited. She looked down at the welcome mat below her feet. What was she waiting for? Validation? He couldn't give it to her. He couldn't add to her fucked-up-ness.

"Oh hey, Jessy, that's something," he managed to get out. "That's, um, wow, can't wait to see the dragon."

Her head shot up. "Really? Thanks." She backed up and started down the four steps to the sidewalk.

"Hey, where are you going?" he asked.

She turned back, a frown creasing her tiny forehead.

The dragon's forehead.

"I thought we were going to the vegan café for my birthday?"

"Oh, right. Yes, we are. Just give me a sec."

He slammed the door shut. Then clenched his fists and stomped his feet five times.

"Ohhh, that girl drives me mad."

He yanked open the hallway closet and retrieved the nickel-plated magnum from its case. A toy. Not even loaded with water. Completely empty. And not something a cop would know from five feet away.

He didn't need the gun until they were back in the house, and he'd killed Jessy. Vegan café first. Back to the house after. Kill Jessy, destroy computers, then call Detective Bryant over.

Two hours left to live.

He slipped the gun into the back of his pants and covered it with his shirt. Why not carry it for the last two hours anyway? Carrying it made him feel closer to the end.

And who knew? What if someone robbed the café, shot the place up, and killed Jessy, and homicide were called in?

He could be dead meat where the vegans hang out.

He let a laugh escape his lips.

"Hilarious."

When he opened the front door, Jessy was still standing there, looking as lonely as ever on the sidewalk.

"You sure you're okay?" he asked again as he closed the door behind him.

She nodded and covered her mouth at the soft giggle that escaped her lips.

Oh my fuck, one hour with this bimbo bowler from Buffalo, and anyone would kill themselves.

He went to lock the front door, then frowned and turned back around to face her.

"Hey, you still have my house key? You wanna lock the door?"

She shook her head, mussing up her hair. "Left it at home this time." She shrugged, but not just any shrug. This one had her shoulders pounding her ears. "Next time."

Then she hopped to the right and walked away.

Holy shit wave, I'm gonna kill her before we get one city

block.

He locked the door and started after her.

"Jessy, wait up."

364

Chapter 54

SARAH ROBERTS WATCHED AS **Ben** Wilson dropped down the front steps of his house and followed Jessica Bryant along the sidewalk until he caught up to her. Jessica was playing her part wonderfully. If anyone had any doubts, they would have been allayed by now.

The bandage on her shoulder covered the wire the Toronto police had installed so they could hear everything Ben said to her. The tattoo idea was Jessica's, so she could hide any demeanor changes or nervousness under the guise of the new tattoo's irritation.

Ben was a mean, patronizing son of a bitch. His time was coming.

Detective Bryant sat beside her in the police cruiser, holding the house key to Ben Wilson's home. Once they had approached Jessica yesterday and told her what Ben had been up to and discussed their plan, Jessica handed over Ben's house key. No one knew what Ben had in store for Jessica, but they didn't feel he would harm her in public. Her brother had instructed her not to enter Ben's house under any circumstances.

After hours of coaching, no one had mentioned the house key. What if Ben asked for it back? What if Ben wondered where it had gone? Yet Jessica handled that question with ease when he asked.

Maybe when this was over, she should get a three-headed dragon tattoo after all because if anyone warranted it, Jessica Bryant did.

Detective Bryant pushed the button on the microphone in his hand.

"Clear." He set the mic down.

"You coming in?" he asked.

"Wouldn't miss it for the world," Sarah said.

They jumped out of the unmarked cruiser. Parkman and Aaron hopped out of the other unmarked cruiser parked behind theirs.

Once Clara had made her statement and Sarah offered hers, the police had no choice but to release Aaron. Sarah had asked for a favor, though. Don't do anything electronically yet. As far as the police were concerned—and their computer system—Aaron Stevens was still being held on a second-degree murder charge. Once Sarah and Parkman met with Detective Bryant, everyone was on board.

Ben Wilson wouldn't know what hit him. He probably thought Sarah was still in Denmark. Parkman wasn't a threat, and Aaron was in jail. In Ben's world, there was just Jessica and Shawn to deal with. Exactly how Sarah wanted it to be.

Aaron had protested that they weren't doing enough to

find Alex and Ansgar. Where could they be after almost four days? Could Alex be dead? Could Ansgar have fled the country? Sarah had assured him that Alex was not dead and that they would see him soon.

The group heading up to Ben's house included seven police officers, Parkman and Aaron. Bryant used the key on the front door and entered the building. He placed the search warrant he'd received that morning on a side table and ran for the upstairs, where Jessica told them the computers were kept. A room she had never been allowed to enter.

Sarah stayed on his heels, no sense of danger coming to her. Ben didn't have the house alarmed or booby-trapped in any way.

Bryant hit the top of the stairs, looked both ways and turned to the right. Sarah followed him into the master bedroom.

The place was a mess. Mars bar wrappers littered the floor and desk. Coke cans had been flung aside and piled up in two different corners. She even caught sight of a cockroach running under an empty bag of potato chips.

"This guy doesn't believe in hygiene," she muttered, holding a hand to her nose. "Shit, what's that reek?"

"Body odor," Bryant said.

Sarah moved to the desk with all the computers and hit the space bar on the only keyboard. All five screens lit up.

Bryant's radio pierced the silence. "They're entering the café now."

He brought it to his mouth. "Roger that."

A small window popped up in the middle of the largest screen, asking for a password.

"Do you know what it is?" Bryant asked.

"Not sure," Sarah said as Parkman and Aaron entered the room. "Give me a sec." Sarah closed her eyes and listened for Vivian.

"What's that smell?" Aaron asked.

"Please," Sarah said.

"Right. Sorry."

She focused on Vivian and asked her for help.

A moment later, her fingers tingled. She opened her eyes, leaned over the desk, and placed her fingers on the keyboard.

They typed on their own:

Fuck_cancer_twice

She hit enter.

The screen opened to a countdown.

"Thanks, Vivian," Sarah whispered.

In twenty-three minutes, the hard drives would be wiped clean.

"Have you got someone who can stop this?" Sarah asked.

Bryant watched the screen, mystified. "How the hell did you do that?"

"I didn't. My sister did it. Now, a hacker? Someone good with computers?" She smacked his arm to wake him up. "Come on, Bryant. We have to save what's on these systems."

She snapped her fingers twice. He jerked and looked her way.

"Of course." He tilted his head and yelled, "Officer Crystal Lewis. You're needed up here."

The bedroom door moved a foot as a uniformed officer stepped inside the room. Evidently, she was waiting outside the door to be called in.

"Turn that off," Bryant ordered. "Save what you can."

Officer Lewis strode past Sarah, dropped her hands to the keyboard, and the little window with the timer on it disappeared.

"Done," she said.

Her hands typed fast, searching the computer's hard drives for names, people, and places.

"It's all here, sir." The screen changed. "The video from Anton Olafson in Denmark. The record of all of Ben's communication with Anton and Ansgar Holm. Everything's here, sir."

"Perfect. Pack it all up. I need everything off this computer logged in as evidence." He faced Sarah. She watched his eyes move to Parkman and Aaron. "We got him, guys. It's over."

Sarah jolted, then frowned. She turned her head slightly upward, then to the side, listening for something.

"We have a problem," she said.

"What?" Bryant asked.

"Yeah, what?" Aaron echoed.

"Ansgar. He's close. And Ben. There might be trouble at the café."

Detective Bryant snatched the radio off his belt and pressed the button.

"All units, report in your positions."

A series of radio bursts followed.

"What's Jessica's 10-20?"

"In the café with the suspect, over."

"Any problems?"

"Not yet, sir."

"You anticipating any?"

"No, sir. It's just …"

Shawn walked to the bedroom window. Sarah followed him.

"Two men walked into the café immediately after the suspect. One of my guys thinks the two men were following the suspect. I've checked, but they're not any of our guys."

"Okay, all units are clear to apprehend the suspect. Take him now. Do you hear me? Arrest Ben Wilson. Get him away from my sister. Go!"

Chapter 55

BEN SAT ACROSS FROM Jessy and stared at her messed-up face. The way she scrunched her mouth when she talked. The way she giggled and then covered her mouth. The new tattoo would probably look like shit. And who applied that makeup to her eyes? He couldn't figure that shit out. Emos all dressed the same while trying to be different. They all wore their pain on the outside so everyone could see just how fucked up they were. How was she supposed to get a job, get married, have kids and maybe even be a part of some kind of women's club one day looking like that?

Unless none of that was on her agenda. But seriously, you don't have to be cookie-cutter normal, but you can't change your appearance too far, either. People will be people, and they will judge others—harshly.

He realized that was exactly what he was doing to her at that very moment. But what did it matter? He wasn't interviewing her for a job.

He had ordered a hemp tofu salad of some kind. Only the coleslaw was recognizable. After two bites, he was done. It was a tasteless mush of goo draped over bits of lettuce. He wondered how people could eat such shit.

Jessy had ordered some kind of burrito with samosa bites and a soup that the waiter told them had butternut squash, potato, spinach, mushrooms, and garlic in it. The thing smelled like it came from the bottom of an outhouse. Looked like it, too. Yet Jessy eagerly slurped it up but had to go slow due to how hot it was.

He slid his plate aside. "Not hungry," he said. "But don't worry, I'm paying." He offered her a quick smile, then dropped it. "It's your birthday, right? Lunch is on me."

She glanced at the salad on his plate, shrugged, then dove back into her soup. Ben placed his legs wide and leaned back in the uncomfortable chair to get as far away from her slurping as possible.

I would have never guessed my last day on earth would be spent eating chunky bullshit at a vegan café.

The restaurant was small, with only enough seating for twenty to thirty people. Two long-haired hippies left over from the sixties sat at a small table by the exit door near the back. Another couple seated by the front windows was dressed like they had just stepped out of an eighties Duran Duran video.

His eyes wandered to the table by the front door after two men came in and sat down. The one guy was quite large. His back faced Ben. He wore a coat that was too warm for this weather and a baseball cap. The large man kept his head down as if he was eating, but he had no food yet. In the chair opposite the large man, a small, thin man, maybe in his twenties, surveyed the café as if looking for something. The small man's eyes alighted on Ben, then shot away as he glanced down at the table.

That was odd.

The man's eyes were ablaze. Like he was angry or knew Ben and hated him. Ben had never seen the guy in his life, yet there was an odd sense of recognition in that brief second their eyes locked.

Ben stared longer, watching the two men at the table by the door.

"You okay?" Jessy asked.

Ben snapped his head toward her. "Of course. Why do you ask?"

"You were staring at the door." She lowered her mouth to the soup-filled spoon hovering over her bowl. "You looked concerned."

"It's nothing. Just thought I knew that guy at the door—"

They were getting up from their table when Ben looked back at them. Even though the big man hadn't turned around yet, something was familiar about him now. His build, his height. The name of a man similar to him was on the tip of his tongue, but he couldn't place it.

Jessy touched his arm. Ben flinched and jerked sideways to glare at her.

"What?" he asked, his tone sharp, clipped.

"It's my birthday lunch," she said, her voice lowering in volume with each word. Her face appeared sad now, demure. "Please, spend it with me."

"I am, aren't I? Just thought I recognized—" Movement outside the restaurant caught his eye.

Armed men in tactical gear were approaching the restaurant from across the street. Traffic had stopped outside.

What the fuck is that?

Chairs scuffed the floor near the back. The hippies were up and running out the door beside their table, their food forgotten.

The Duran Duran couple had stopped eating. They, too, watched the armed men form a perimeter outside the restaurant.

Ben's head spun until he placed a hand on the table to steady himself. The action outside couldn't be for him. Something else was in play. It had to be. His computers were almost wiped clean. Nothing could be traced back to him. No one knew who he was.

Jessy hadn't noticed what was happening outside as her back was to the window.

The two men stood by their table near the front door, glaring at him. The big guy looked horrible. His nose was swollen, both eyes were purple, and his lips were cut with dried blood caked in each corner. The large man raised his hands and tried to clench them into fists, but it was obvious he couldn't. At least three fingers on each hand were mangled without any form of bandage or splint evident. How the man wasn't writhing in pain was beyond Ben.

Beside him, Jessy twisted in her chair to glance outside.

The name flashed in his mind. Ben recognized the big man. They'd never met in person, but Ben knew what he looked like as he examined all the faces of the men he hired.

Ansgar Holm.

The private military contractor he'd hired to take out Aaron Stevens and Clara Olafson. The man who disappeared days ago after displaying a disgusting attitude.

"Ben Wilson," Ansgar said his name. "Or should I call you Pain?"

When Ansgar spoke, most of his teeth were broken or missing. The image of a hockey player flashed into his mind.

What the hell happened to make you so fucking ugly?

Ben shot a look outside. More cops were coming. Jessica pushed her chair out to get up. Ben lurched across the table and clamped onto Jessica's forearm, then yanked her over to him knocking his shitty coleslaw plate to the floor. With his other hand, he snatched the nickel-plated magnum from his waistband and aimed it at Jessy's forehead.

"Stay back," Ben shouted.

Embarrassingly, his voice cracked. The gun shook in his hand. Jessy moaned but, to her credit, didn't shout out. Her hair dangled into the remainder of her soup bowl in front of her.

"He's got a gun," Jessica said.

"Damn right," Ben added.

"Get me out of here," she whispered.

Ben adjusted his bulk to be more comfortable in the seat as pain shot up from his lower back. This was not the time to deal with the cancer.

"I thought you said he was weak?" the small man said. "That this guy hid behind his computer and talked all that shit."

"I did," Ansgar mumbled. "He is. A regular keyboard Nazi."

"That gun doesn't look weak. If he kills the girl, I kill you."

"Fuck you," Ansgar roared. "He's mine."

Ben couldn't take it anymore. What were these two talking about? He glanced out the café's windows. It looked like the authorities had the place surrounded. Cars had moved in to form a wall. Armed officers were planted behind them, only their heads and arms visible, guns pointed at the café.

He gripped Jessy's arm tighter and turned back to Ansgar.

"What are you doing here?" Ben asked.

"I've come for you. That last text didn't sound like a good deal to me."

"Which one?" Ben asked, already knowing exactly what he had typed to Ansgar.

Ansgar had pissed him off, pushed him too far. He'd told Ansgar that he would reveal to the world who the man was. All his aliases would come out, and exactly what hotel he stayed in at any given time. Ansgar had fucked with the wrong hacker. Ben had also typed that he would detail Ansgar's jobs that he'd been hired to do so the authorities could match them up to actual crimes. Ansgar would rue the day he agreed to work for PAIN.

"You upset me," Ben said, any strength in his voice diminished. "I just pushed back."

"I upset you?" Ansgar moved one step closer. "I upset you?" he repeated. "And you threaten to ruin me?" He moved closer again.

"Stay back," Ben said. "I'll kill her."

"I've met stupid before," Ansgar said. "But you beat stupid at a professional level."

"What?" Ben's throat spasmed when he spoke.

"You think I care about that girl's life?" Ansgar asked, his tongue slipping through the nubs of teeth. "The fact that you're pointing the gun at her makes you the dumbest idiot on the planet."

Ben scanned the windows. If it was possible, even more cops had pulled up out front. Jessy kept her head down on the table.

Ansgar moved again.

Ben swung the gun toward Ansgar. He let go of Jessy's arm and placed two hands on the magnum.

"Stay back," he blurted out, trying to be assertive.

"Game's up, Mr. Pain." Ansgar smiled. The grin was horrid with all his injuries. Even a smile like that would hurt because of the damage to his lips and face. "We're both caught. Drop the gun."

Jessy edged away from the table. He debated letting her go. This was falling apart too fast. How could he get to Detective Bryant now? How could he make him pay? He didn't even have a real gun. Ansgar was going to kill him before he had a chance to do anything. And now his arms were starting to ache from holding the gun up too long.

"That's right," Ansgar said softly. "Let the gun fall."

Ben forced the weapon back up. Then an idea hit him. The cops out front weren't here for him. They were after Ansgar. They must have tracked the hitman to the café. Had to be. How would they have gotten mobilized out front that fast if they were after Ben? They must've followed Ansgar, and now they were ready to take him. Ben just happened to get in their way.

"You've fucked up my plan," Ben said.

"You fucked mine."

Ansgar took another step, even though the gun was aimed at his chest now.

A door banged to Ben's left. Jessica was clear of the building.

The little guy behind Ansgar touched something on the side of the big man's neck. Ansgar tried to shake him off. He spun and drove a gnarled fist toward the little guy.

The fist was knocked wide like a paper airplane flying by. The small guy released Ansgar's neck, dropped to the floor, and spun his legs in a wide circle.

Ansgar's feet were swept into the air. His body seemed to float horizontally for the briefest of moments like a magician had levitated him, then Ansgar dropped like a block of concrete. The cheap floor of the café actually vibrated. The second he hit the floor, the small guy lunged atop him. From Ben's vantage point, the small guy's arms floated over Ansgar's face, then stopped.

He looked directly at Ben. Slowly, the small man got off Ansgar and backed away from him. Ben lowered the gun until his wrist rested on his thigh, the toy gun still aimed in the small man's general direction.

"He's asleep," the small man said. "Just us now."

"Who are you?" Ben asked.

"Nobody."

Ben raised the gun. "A name," he shouted.

"Alex."

The small man moved back farther until he was beside the table he'd sat at earlier. Alex was within reach of the front door.

"Stop moving," Ben screamed. "It's maddening. I'm trying to think."

Ben blinked. Before he could threaten Alex again, the small man dropped and disappeared out the door.

"Shit wave," Ben hollered to the empty café.

All that remained inside the café was a sleeping Ansgar and Ben with a toy gun.

And a bevy of police and tactical units outside.

Ben turned his attention to the café's front window and watched as dozens of men in uniform stared back at him.

Then he saw someone he recognized. His tormenter from all those years in grade school and high school. The one man this day was supposed to end with had made his appearance. What were the odds?

Detective Bryant stood across the street, binoculars in his hand. He raised them and looked Ben's way.

The people beside Detective Bryant made Ben blink twice to clear his eyes. It was impossible. There's just no way it could be true.

Aaron Stevens stood to Bryant's left, wearing a Kevlar vest. To Bryant's right, Sarah Roberts also wore Kevlar.

The small man who'd just felled Ansgar was being fitted with a vest as everyone appeared to be drilling questions at him.

Had nothing worked over the past week? Were all his efforts to make people pay for their actions fruitless?

How could Sarah Roberts be here? It was virtually impossible. He had hacked into the government website and placed her on the no-fly list. She was detained in Denmark. Someone was playing a trick on him.

He scrambled up from the chair despite the pain in his lower back. His heart raced in his overweight, unhealthy body.

"I could use a Mars bar right now," he shouted. "But I'm pretty sure you stupid vegans won't have that."

Behind the counter of the café, he frantically searched for a weapon. Something he could use against Ansgar if he woke up. Shoving cups and lids out of the way, his hand bumped into an employee's purse. The zipper stuck, but he got it open. A quick search revealed no pepper spray and no gun.

The employees?

They must've run out through a door in the back.

He marveled at how funny the brain worked when under duress. Normally, back in his office, he'd cover all the bases, make sure he knew every facet, every detail of what he was doing.

But as soon as he saw the cops outside and then Ansgar, he lost track of what was happening around him. He barely noticed Jessy scampering out the door. He had no idea where his waitress or the other employees went.

He ransacked the underside of the counter in search of a real gun, but the people of Toronto rarely carried guns to work. Maybe the boss kept one in case they were robbed?

"Who would rob a vegan place?" he asked himself.

"Ben Wilson," someone shouted on a loudspeaker outside. "Come out with your hands up. It's over."

"Fuck you guys."

Ben kept looking for a weapon.

Chapter 56

As promised, Detective Bryant gave Sarah, Parkman, and Aaron a vest. Since Sarah was the one who had brought them the information needed to put all the pieces together, Bryant had wanted her on point through the entire event. Not to mention, he was counting on his sister getting away from Ben unharmed.

What Sarah hadn't accounted for was the buildup of police cars before they had arrested Ben. That was an easy way to spook the man into doing something careless.

As they arrived, Bryant spoke on the radio with the officer in charge at the café. Officer Scott Awalt secured the area and even extracted several people from the café. Based on his assessment, two people were still inside, plus Jessica and Ben.

Officer Awalt handed Bryant a pair of binoculars so he could see inside the café better. When he was done, Bryant handed them to Sarah.

She scanned the inside.

"Anything we need to know?" Bryant asked.

"Yes. Ben will not shoot Jessica. Of that, I'm sure. I've been told she will be out here with us very soon. The two men standing a few feet from the front door are Ansgar and Alex. Alex is with us."

"What the hell?" Aaron muttered behind her. "How is Alex in there?"

Sarah lowered the binoculars, then handed them over to Bryant.

"Look at the small man. Blond. He's one of ours. He's in there attempting to defuse the situation."

Bryant used the binoculars. "Any way you can get him out here?"

"I'm thinking he'll be out here soon enough."

"Wait," Bryant snapped. "Wilson just turned the gun on Ansgar. He released Jessica." Bryant appeared to be jamming the binoculars deep into his face. "Jessica has dropped out of sight. I think she's running for the back door—"

"There she is," Sarah blurted.

Jessica ran bent over into the arms of a tactical officer crouched five feet from the door and was escorted away from the building. From where Sarah stood, she saw Ansgar and Alex standing close to the front door, Ben still in his chair.

"They're fighting," Bryant shouted. "Shit. Ansgar's down. Wow, that Alex can sure move."

Sarah saw a flurry of activity through the café's windows.

"All units hold," Officer Awalt spoke into a radio on the other side of Bryant.

Alex popped back up into view and edged back toward the door. A moment later, as if Ben had let him go, Alex bolted out the front door.

Ben Wilson was alone in the café with Ansgar out of sight.

When Alex approached them, Bryant yanked out a vest from the trunk of his cruiser and dropped it over Alex's head.

"How did you come to be in there?" Bryant asked.

It was the same question on everyone's mind.

Alex leaned over and moved past Bryant without answering. He hugged Sarah, then faced Aaron.

"When I saw you coming toward me at the hospital that night, I panicked. Ansgar had woken up. He was kicking the back window. It broke before you got halfway across the parking lot. Glass everywhere. He was unmanageable. You had two cops with you. I thought," he shrugged, "if we were going to be arrested, it would be better if it was just you. I would talk to Ansgar, learn what he knew, then help solve everything and get you out later. I thought both of us locked up wasn't a good idea."

Aaron tapped Alex on the shoulder. It was the only time Sarah ever saw anyone touch Alex.

"You did good, Alex. But how did you get here? Right now? At this café?"

"Through several painful techniques you've taught me, I learned everything from Ansgar. He's in bad shape. He had done a background check on Ben Wilson as he always likes to know his clients. A private firm in the UK does this for him. A large fee, and they hunt people. As it turns out, Ansgar knew Ben's address." Alex shrugged like it was no big deal. "Ansgar wanted to talk to Ben. I thought, hey, bring them together, see what happens." Sarah moved closer. Bryant seemed to be listening, but he brought the binoculars back up to his eyes and stared at the café. "We waited for Ben and followed him this morning. I had no idea you guys were here, too."

Aaron hugged him. "You did good, little man. Real good."

Alex appeared forlorn. It was like he knew he'd done well, but it was a sad and lonely few days without communication with the special people in his life. Even though they were reunited, Sarah felt he needed to purge more.

"Ben's behind the counter doing something," Bryant said. He removed the binoculars from his face. Two red circular rings framed his eyes. "Give me the loudspeaker."

Officer Awalt handed it to him.

Everyone turned to the windows as Detective Bryant brought the loudspeaker to his mouth.

"Ben Wilson," his voice boomer. "Come out with your hands up. It's over."

Chapter 57

Ben headed for the kitchen in the back of the small café and found a butcher knife resting on a chopping block. He hefted it up and examined both sides. Could he use a knife on someone? If Ansgar woke, would he be able to take the knife from him with his fingers mangled up as they were?

Ben leaned against a metal counter cluttered with some kind of vegan burgers to collect his breath. What did he want to do? What was his goal? Nothing had worked. Nothing whatsoever. But how was that possible? How could he have been thwarted so masterfully?

Sarah Roberts.

Her name kept coming up. She would've known what Ansgar was up to. She would've been able to warn everyone. She flew to Denmark to be Anton's victim, so no one had to die. But how could she fake what he watched on the video Anton sent him? Unless it was edited. That had to be it. The video was doctored. Everyone was in it against him. As always, just like when he was in grade school, they were all out to get him.

He yearned to be at his computer at that moment. The damage he could do to these people. He would plot and destroy their lives one by one for what they did to him.

The loudspeaker outside called for him to leave the building voluntarily. They warned that they would be coming in soon.

The phone rang. They wanted to talk to him.

He had no plan, backup plan, or option out of this.

But that was what he wanted in the first place. No way out. He was dying of pancreatic cancer and wanted his school tormentor to pull the trigger. Make him live by taking the life of another human being for the rest of his life.

"Thwarted again," Ben whispered.

He pounded his fist into his other hand as he glanced around the kitchen. Plastic utensils and party favors cluttered a table at the rear wall. It looked like someone had booked a party for later.

"No party today, folks. Today someone dies at your little shit vegan café."

He spied a thick roll of moving tape, and an idea from a movie he saw once struck him. The plan would work. It was brilliant.

He set the butcher knife on the metal counter with the vegan burgers, ran over and pulled two small strips of tape off the roll, and affixed the nickel-plated magnum to the back of his neck. In a mirror in the employee washroom, when standing straight on, he couldn't see the gun. Later, with his hands above his head as he surrendered, a hundred guns aimed at him, they wouldn't expect Ben to yank a gun out from between his shoulder blades and aim it at the cops.

"Fuck it. If I'm going out this way, I might as well have it rain bullets."

Confident the gun was taped well enough with the handle in the best position to grab with his right hand, he stepped from the washroom and walked over to the metal table to grab the butcher knife.

The knife was gone.

"What the …?"

His body was breaking down. At least, that's what it felt like. After years of sitting, eating chocolate bars, and drinking Cokes, knowing he was dying anyway hadn't helped his respiratory system. He couldn't breathe right. His heart seemed to skip a beat as it raced in his chest.

Where could the knife have gone? The police had not stormed the building. It had to be Ansgar. But where was he? Ben put the counter to his back to ensure he was alone in the kitchen. Was he trapped here? Was his final plan to be shot down in a hail of bullets also thwarted?

"Nothing's going to stop me now," he said as he clenched his hands and took a couple of deep breaths.

He grabbed two small steak knives off the counter beside him and then let a short laugh escape his lips.

Steak knives in a vegan establishment. In another life, he would hack their computer systems and show the world how idiotic vegans really were.

He briefly wiped his palms as the small knives slipped in the moisture from his hands. The phone rang again. The loudspeaker announced he was out of time.

Ben stepped from the kitchen.

He didn't get one foot through the doorway before Ansgar smashed into his bulk and knocked the two steak knives out of his hands. Ben hit the side of the counter hard. The edge dug in above his hip, shooting pain through his abdomen. He grunted and dropped to the tile floor.

Something clunked into his exposed arm. He screamed and tried desperately to inch away from his attacker. Whatever had hit his arm jerked out and away, freeing him.

The butcher knife!

Ansgar stood over him, blood dripping from the knife, a wild madness in his eyes.

"Because of you." Ansgar hacked at Ben, made contact, then ripped the blade out again. Ben screamed. "Because of you, I'm all fucked up. I was a good sniper. An even better merc. A little boy with a computer bested me."

Ansgar raised his hands to show his fingers. The blade was painted in blood. Some had squirted along Ansgar's hand, too. But the pain hadn't come yet. Just a mild tingle telling him something wasn't quite right.

Ansgar's smile was lopsided.

"I know. Pretty, ain't I?" Ansgar clutched the butcher knife with his palm curled around the handle. His fingers barely curled at all as they probably couldn't bend in their current state.

Ben screamed, breathed rapidly like he'd dropped after running a hundred-meter dash, then moaned as the pain started in.

Ansgar laughed, the butcher knife poised, ready to strike Ben. Ben kicked his feet out in a last-ditch attempt to stop the attack. He connected with Ansgar's ankle, which slipped on blood smeared on the floor. Ansgar's knee buckled smacked the drawer beside him, and down he went.

Ben was already spinning sideways as Ansgar fell. He plucked one of the dropped steak knives off the floor, twisted back, and brought the knife down into Ansgar's lower back at the same time the butcher knife entered Ben's thigh.

This time they yelled together.

Their combined voices drowned out the loudspeaker as Detective Bryant said something about entering the café.

Ben had to get up. He needed to leave. He needed his denouement. There was no way he would be thwarted again.

The pain came in waves. Blinded by it momentarily, he pushed off the floor and found that only one arm still worked. The other had a gash in it. Tendons were severed, and ligaments, too.

Ansgar writhed on the floor beside him, trying to reach around and pull the knife out of his back, but his broken fingers wouldn't cooperate.

Ben got into a sitting position leaning against the counter. Blood pooled around him like he sat in a circle of spilled ketchup. How much time did he have left?

Time? The Clock?

"Time's up for The Clock," he said.

The other steak knife was two feet from him. He leaned over, slipped in the blood, and sprawled out on the floor. He was able to reach the knife now. Back up on his buttocks, more blood oozing out of his wounds, Ben inched toward Ansgar. The man had been able to clutch the knife in his back but could not pull it free.

"Here, take this, Sniper."

Ben brought the second knife down and forced it into Ansgar's abdominal flesh. The man went rigid under Ben's hand. He lifted the knife out as blood squirted up and stabbed Ansgar again in a different spot. Ben did this seven times before loss of blood and exhaustion stopped him.

Ansgar vibrated under his hand. Ben blinked and stared down at Ansgar's face. His eyes blinked erratically as his body went into a seizure.

The threat of Ansgar was over. Ben pushed off the man's back, but his legs wouldn't support him. On his buttocks, he slid sideways until he was leaning against the counter by the cashier's till. Only five feet separated him from the table where he had had lunch with his ex-girlfriend only ten minutes ago.

"That escalated quickly," he mumbled.

Someone was at the side door. Boots pounded down on the café's floor. They were coming in. The pain would stop very soon. He thought of his mother and her pain in the end. He asked himself how much pain was coming in his future had he stayed alive? It wasn't such a raw deal for the minute or two he had left.

"Ben Wilson," a man shouted. "Hands on your head."

Ben raised his good hand over his head and wrapped his fingers on the butt of the toy gun taped to the back of his neck.

Like they were fresh out of a video game, men in battle gear surrounded him. He thought he recognized Detective Bryant in the middle.

"On the floor," came the command again. "Lie down."

Ben waited for two more breaths. He wanted as many weapons trained on him as possible. When the dozen or so men formed a semi-circle around him, and he felt it was the right time to die, he yanked the gun off his neck. The tape ripped like he tore off a bandage, but it was nothing to the mounting pain in his limbs where the butcher knife had done its work.

Over his head, the gun came up. Men shouted something. One final warning. He aimed the weapon at them and closed his eyes.

When the bullets came, he felt a thousand small punches. Like he had laid out on the grass in a hail storm as he'd done as a child.

Then his hand snapped back violently.

Someone had taken the gun.

The hail stopped.

He felt himself slipping down, the floor lubricated with his crimson soul. Boots pounded around him. A chaotic orchestra of noises assaulted him as he tried to blink the blood away. The light faded, noises swam in and out, pain throbbed, and he knew his heart beat its last few measly rhythms.

Someone touched his throat.

"I feel a pulse," a woman said.

Someone else leaned close. He could feel their presence.

Ben used up the last of his strength to open his eyes one final time.

Detective Bryant bent over Ben's face holding the toy gun.

"Why?" Bryant asked, shaking the gun. He looked at it, then back to Ben. "Jessica cared about you. I liked you. Sarah told me why you did this. The teasing was harmless. It's what guys do to each other."

Ben gasped. Liquid spit out of his mouth.

"I remember you, Ben," Bryant said. "For what it's

worth, I'm sorry. But you should've called me out. I would've done right by you. I'm a good man now, Ben." The noise around them drowned Bryant out. Then his voice came back in. "You didn't have to do this, but we saved your computers. We stopped the shutdown. We got everything, Ben."

Ben's eyes widened as he gasped his last breath. That meant his game wouldn't launch because the computers would send the signal that they were still up and running. No one would know how to launch LEGACY: PAIN PACT after that.

He tried to say, *thwarted again*, but his body wouldn't respond or take another breath.

Then he floated away, and all his pain ceased.

Chapter 58

"DID YOU KNOW IT was a toy gun?" Bryant asked.

Sarah stared out through the window of the Starbucks on Yonge Street. Without taking her eyes off a distant minivan, she brought the cup to her mouth and sipped the dark roast. They had chosen this Starbucks for its location just off Highway 401. Aaron was scouting out new locations for another dojo. The insurance money was coming through soon, and he needed a new location. Benjamin would heal and wanted back. His physio was performing katas in the dojo. Daniel had two youth classes he wanted to continue, and Alex was teaching black belts an advanced form of some kind of gymnastic Shotokan karate.

It would be good for everyone to get back to work. Especially Aaron. The wounds on his forearms were healing well. Other than mild skin damage, nothing was hurt too badly. He wasn't upset when he heard a detailed explanation of what Alex had done to Ansgar while Alex extracted information from the hardened Navy Seal.

Sarah let a smile crease her lips when she thought of Alex. What an amazing fighter. And he did that entire disappearing act for Aaron. To work on Ansgar where no one could interrupt him. To figure a way out of the mess they seemed to be sinking into. He had complained that Aaron and Sarah always had all the fun. Alex wanted a small piece of the renegade life and got what he asked for.

She drank more of her coffee.

"Sarah?" Bryant prodded.

She faced him. "Sorry?"

"I asked if you knew about the toy gun."

Sarah glanced at Aaron, then back to Bryant. "Would it have mattered? What Ansgar did to him … there was no coming back from that."

Bryant clapped his hands. "I guess that's it then."

"Guess so."

She was willing to be professional with Bryant. There was no particular beef with him. Just that, at the core, he was the bully who pushed Ben Wilson to do what he did to so many people. Ben had been prepared to kill Bryant's sister to get back at him. Sometimes the consequences for people's actions are far greater than expected and often unfair. But sometimes, people don't realize just how much they hurt others.

Sarah might not have a personal beef with the man, but she also had no love for him. Had he changed since high school? Was he different? Did he say those things to Ben as Ben died just to get the final jab in?

Sarah would never know. That was the thing with

Vivian's new pact. If Sarah *needed* to know something, Vivian offered it freely. But if she didn't *need* to know, information was withheld. Sarah couldn't be given anything she wanted at any time. Otherwise, she would be all-knowing, and no one could play God on earth—even though hundreds of thousands of people tried that every single day.

Bryant pushed his chair back. "I'll leave you two alone then."

Sarah returned her gaze to the minivan across the street. Yonge Street was busy. It was a Saturday in Toronto, and they were just north of the 401. People went about their business oblivious to what Aaron and Sarah had to discuss. Once Bryant left, she would break the news that she had to leave yet again.

"Sarah?" Bryant turned back when he was a few feet away. "I got that no-fly list shit taken care of. Your name has been removed."

She smiled up at him. "Thanks."

"Found everything we needed on Ben's computer. I personally called the authorities in Denmark to let them know there was a mistake. Told the Americans, too, as you hold an American passport. Thought they'd want to ensure it was out of their system."

"Good."

"You know, it's funny." He chortled.

"What is?"

She offered him a deadpan face. A week ago, she was dead. Days before that, she thought Aaron was dead. It had been a rough week dealing with Vivian. Overall, she just wanted a night alone with Aaron. No more statements. No more police interviews. And no more questions about how she knew what she knew about Ben Wilson. Telling them about Vivian didn't fly with most of the cops she dealt with. To his credit, Bryant listened because he got a call from a retired Toronto Detective named Waller, someone Sarah worked with years ago in Toronto when a group called the Rapturites were after her.

Bryant moved a few steps closer to the table. "The Danes were flummoxed as to how you got away from them. They scoured the airport for days after. Watched the camera footage. Did everything short of bringing the military in. Asked me how you did it." He shrugged. "I didn't know, so I couldn't tell them." He stepped closer to the small table. "How did you do it?"

"Does it matter now?" she asked.

Bryant didn't like that answer. "There is one more thing I have to ask, though."

"Go ahead."

"We all know about your abilities. How you know stuff." He brought his hands to his temples and shook them. "Something in there tells you things about people, places, and the future."

"You're moving toward a question. I can feel it."

He placed his hands back at his sides. "You told us who Ben was, where he lived. His plans for my sister. We wired her and sent her in. Everything was exactly like you said. Since you've never met the man before, I'd call that psychic."

Sarah stared at him, her face expressionless.

"Since you're psychic, I have to ask. Did you know beforehand that Ben Wilson and Ansgar Holm would die in that vegan café?"

Sarah didn't flinch. She waited for two breaths, then lied. "No."

Bryant waited for three breaths, his eyes not leaving hers. This was a contest of wills she would not lose.

He blinked.

"It's just," Bryant said, "knowing beforehand would make you somewhat complicit in their deaths. We could've stopped Ben before he entered that café. We could've been told his weapon was a toy. If you knew any of that, then withholding the information caused him to die."

He would've been dead inside six months, anyway.

"Understood," was all she said, thinking of Darwin's man Bruno in Billund.

"Hey," Aaron interrupted. "Is that really fair? Sarah doesn't know everything. Only what her sister tells her."

"That's fine. That's what I told my superiors."

This was a lesson in what to tell the authorities and what to hold back. Or what to outright lie about. Sometimes it was for the greater good.

Ben's pain was over. He was in a better place now, back with his mother. Ansgar was gone and wouldn't be available for hire anymore. There were a lot of people in the world who were going to be left alone now that Ansgar and Ben were gone.

Bryant glanced at Aaron and then walked away.

"Bryant," Sarah called after him.

He stopped at the door and looked back.

"I used Clara's passport to get out of Denmark. Wore her clothes. Just walked by airport security and got on the plane."

Sarah lifted her cup and sipped from her coffee to signal that she was done talking.

Bryant hesitated at the door, nodded, then stepped outside. He passed the window in front of her, placing sunglasses on his face, then disappeared where the window stopped.

She would see him again very shortly. Once she was done in Kelowna, she had to come back to Toronto. Something was stirring on the horizon, but she couldn't see the details yet. She only hoped he wasn't such a prick the next time.

"Were you being hard on him on purpose?" Aaron asked.

Sarah turned to face Aaron. "Do I need to go easy on him? He's a decent cop. Case solved. His sister's life was spared. He'll go his way. We'll go ours."

"Fair enough. But why so serious? You okay?"

She reached across the table and touched his hand. "I just want this time with you. We're both alive. We're still young. Let's go to our hotel room and enjoy our time together before I have to leave."

"You're leaving?"

"Tomorrow."

He frowned. "Why so soon?"

"Problems in Kelowna."

"Kelowna? Again?"

She nodded and drank the rest of her coffee.

"Aaron, find a spot for a dojo. Start renovations. Stay busy. Get your men teaching classes again. Do it soon. When I'm done in Kelowna, I'll come right back here. I have business here in Toronto."

"What business?"

"No idea yet. Shit, Vivian isn't even telling me why I'm going to Kelowna yet."

"What?" He leaned back. "Then what? I mean, why?"

"It's this new communication thing. Hard to get used to at first."

"Then how do you know you're even going?"

"What time is it?"

Aaron pulled out his phone and checked. "Just before five."

"I need the exact minute."

"It's 4:57 p.m."

"In two minutes, we'll both know why Kelowna."

Aaron slipped his phone away. "Okay. Then where do we have dinner tonight?"

"I need meat. How about a steak at The Keg?"

"You're on. There's a great Keg on Jarvis. We'll drop down Mount Pleasant. It'll be faster than taking Yonge Street south at this hour."

"When we leave, you lead the way."

Aaron finished his coffee, got up from the table, and tossed their cups in the trash. When he came back, he sat beside her and checked the time.

"4:59 p.m."

The door opened, and Parkman stepped inside the Starbucks. He scanned the café until he spotted them, then headed their way.

"Hey, guys." He pulled out a chair and plopped down, a toothpick dangling from his mouth.

"Hey," Aaron said.

"Hey," Sarah added.

They waited. They stared at him.

"What?" Parkman said.

"You just show up and sit down?" Sarah asked. "Nothing

to tell me?"

"I called Bryant. He said he was meeting you guys here at four o'clock."

"That meeting just ended. Go on," Sarah prodded.

"I got a call from an RCMP officer in Kelowna."

"Yes."

Aaron touched her hand. She flipped it over, and they clasped hands.

"They need your help."

"With what?"

"Wouldn't tell me over the phone. But did say that when you were there last, you antagonized one of their cops—"

"As I should have."

Parkman nodded. "I know. I was there. But he was killed horribly."

"Wasn't my fault."

"No, Sarah. It wasn't." Parkman looked from her to Aaron, then back to her. "You okay?"

"Yeah, just need a break. Been through a lot lately."

"Of course. If anyone understands that, it's me."

"You're right. I'm sorry."

He waved her off. "No need to apologize. Look, the cop just said it would be a good chance for you to come back to Kelowna and help them. Do something good for them as they are still trying to make a better name for themselves in that city. Their image was damaged." He held up a hand. "Not your fault. Just, this would go a long way to fixing things."

"You up to coming?" she asked.

"Already bought us two tickets out of Toronto's airport tomorrow afternoon."

"Will I ever get used to that?" Aaron asked.

Sarah turned to him. "Used to what?"

"You just knowing shit. I mean, that's basically what you just told me. To a tee."

She raised his hand and kissed it. "I only know what Vivian shares with me."

"It's changed, though, hasn't it?"

"Oh yeah," Parkman blurted out.

They looked at him. He smiled, then rolled his toothpick.

Sarah twisted farther in her seat to face Aaron. "Over dinner, I'll tell you everything that happened when I died. And I'll try to explain the pact Vivian and I made."

"It's a doozy," Parkman added.

When Sarah looked at him, he offered her a blank look, then flipped the toothpick to the other side of his mouth.

"What?" Parkman exclaimed. "Just saying."

"You know." Sarah lowered her head and shook it back and forth. "I really love you guys. I'm happy I'm alive and not dead."

"That's good," Aaron said.

"So I can kick your asses."

Sarah smacked him. Aaron grabbed her wrists, dragged her closer, and kissed her forehead.

"Take it easy, little Sarah," Aaron said. "Or I'll have to take you to your room and spank you."

She wiggled out of his grasp and put a finger in her face, waving it back and forth.

"Don't threaten me with pleasure."

They laughed until Parkman's cell phone rang. He answered it his usual way.

"Parkman." A pause. "What? Again?" Another pause. His jaw tightened. "I'll tell her." He hung up.

"That was the cop I've been telling you about. There's been another bombing. Two people dead. Downtown Kelowna on Harvey Street. Their hands are tied. They have no idea what the hell is going on. My contact has resorted to begging you now."

"We'll go. We'll be there tomorrow."

"I told him earlier."

Aaron's hand gripped Sarah's tighter.

"I don't want to lose you," he whispered.

"You won't, baby. You won't."

Afterword

DEAR READER,

I have nothing against vegan cafés. That should go on record right away. It was simply a plot point. Nothing more. I don't frequent them. I eat meat, but I'm a firm believer in live and let live.

As some may know, I lived in Skanderborg for three months back in 2011 and have often returned to visit this wonderful city. I attended the Burning of the Witch ceremony during the Midsummer event in June 2011. I'd never seen anything like it before and added it to this story for several reasons. I've walked Anton Olafson's street, passed by the Skanderborg Rowing Club, and had coffee at the library just like Parkman did. I've been to Silkeborg (not the hospital, though) and taken the fifteen-minute train ride to Aarhus several times, where I've walked the shopping streets. Just as

Anton did that day, he was hunting a random girl to kill; I've tasted whiskey for free in the store called Salling and had cappuccino by the canal in Aarhus. That's one of the many wonderful advantages of spending years touring Europe. These scenes are specific to actual places and events as I write these scenes. Hey, they're always saying, "Write what you know," so I do. Watch for pictures of these locations on Facebook.

Denmark is a wonderful country. I'll be heading there again this Christmas (2016) and will be spending considerable time there in the future.

Back in the 1990s, I spent a lot of time researching spirituality, the other side, and near-death experiences (NDE), which led to philosophy and the study of several religions. I spent time in a Pentecostal Church and listened as they spoke in tongues. I attended a Mormon Church with a lovely Mormon family. I even spent a weekend at their home and benefitted from headaches as they didn't serve coffee, which has caffeine, an addictive substance.

In my personal search for meaning in the 1990s, I stumbled upon spirituality and chose that as what I would assign my beliefs to. Nothing man-made, no organized religion, just a belief in a higher power and the ability to be nice to people, do good things, and make someone smile because, in the end, they're all struggling like the rest of us.

Spirituality led me to investigate NDEs. What is on the other side? Where do we go when we leave our muscle and bone encasement?

In 1998 I read an earth-shattering book called *Life After Life* by Raymond Moody. Originally written in 1975, this book was a study of the NDE phenomenon. Moody interviewed and studied one hundred people who had been declared clinically dead but were revived at a later time. These people were from all walks of life (no pun intended), from different parts of the country, and had no way to collaborate their stories. Yet they all spoke of a similar experience. One of a tunnel, a light, and a life review. Some saw dead relatives who had passed before them.

What amazed me was that no one saw Hell or anything resembling Hell. Even suicides were saved.

I read Raymond's other book, *Reflections on Life After Life*, and continued my thirst for knowledge with Betty Eadie's book, *Embraced by the Light*. In Betty's book, she had gone for routine surgery, began hemorrhaging, and died on the table—she was dead for over four hours before waking up without brain damage or any other side effects. In fact, she's still alive today.

The longest recorded NDE is just over three days when a man was hit by a car and died. Three days later, on the autopsy table, as the blade made the first incision, his eyes popped open, and he asked why he was being cut in such a fashion. Medical texts confirm this case.

Having said all that, I didn't feel it was much of a stretch to have Sarah dead for just over an hour—not to mention the bits of oxygen Vivian helped Sarah's body take on while she was dead.

In some North American hospitals, such as in British Columbia, Canada, people who die are often left in their beds for up to an hour to allow the spirit time to leave the corpse. Once transferred to the funeral home, the body is left to rest for three more days to confirm that the person is, in fact, deceased.

I'll close on this topic with these parting thoughts. I don't write this Afterword to change your beliefs. I'm merely expressing mine. I accept and have no issue with whether people believe in a higher power or not. It doesn't really matter in the end because we all go home. There has been too much study in this field to be wholly debunked. I've spent years researching this material, as evidenced in my novels like *The Redeemed*, Sarah Roberts book eleven.

Remember, a belief is simply an opinion—one you're not willing to negotiate. An atheist can become a believer. A believer can lose faith. But at that moment, the one where they are fervently devout, try—just try—to change their minds. My point is, don't try to change anyone's mind. Believe what you want. Embrace it for yourself, and then live and let live. And don't hurt anybody because of your beliefs. Or blow people up. That's not a religious belief. That's an ideology. Or a sickness.

Moving on …

Sarah's debacle at the airport in Billund was close to home for me. Going through security checkpoints, and being pulled aside to have documents checked, have been something I've gone through several times in the past as I travel a lot.

In Amsterdam, I was pulled by customs and held for half an hour once. During that trip, while I was in Greece, my passport expired. I renewed it at the Canadian embassy in Athens in March of that year. My passport was up to date, and I was ready to travel again. But I didn't keep my old passport. The one that had the entry stamps and visas in it. So when I got to the Amsterdam Schiphol Airport almost seven months later on my way to North America—which means I was leaving the Schengen Area—I was detained as my new passport had no entry stamps.

As a Canadian, you're only allowed ninety days without a visa in the Schengen Area. Since my passport had no entry stamps, they couldn't tell when I entered the Schengen Area. The issue date on my passport was March, when it was renewed, meaning I had to have been in Europe in February as I would have had to submit my documents to have my passport renewed in the first place. That put me in the area for over six months, well past the ninety days.

I had nothing on me to back up my claim that I was allowed to stay. No visas. No entry stamps. Nothing. They were highly suspicious of me and told me I would be written up, fined, and have a possible entry ban for as long as one year.

Sure, it was completely my fault, and that would suck as my family was in our house in Greece waiting for my return in the coming weeks.

So what did I do?

I talked to them. Attempted to smooth things out. Explained that I was allowed to stay. Showed them old plane tickets that I had stored in my phone for when I had entered the Schengen Area and when I'd left. Yes, I had overstayed, but I'd only stayed three months (ninety days) in Greece, then flew to Denmark during the summer. This was all true, and I had the plane tickets to prove it.

I had once talked to a Danish immigration officer in Aarhus, and he told me that ninety days was the rule for the entire Schengen Area, but if you spent ninety days in one country and want to spend ninety more days in Denmark, they wouldn't mind. It's not official, but they wouldn't mind.

When I was in Italy and overstayed my ninety days by three months back in 2013, I talked to immigration in a city called Citta De Castello, and they also said a few months wouldn't be a problem.

In the end, for whatever reason, the two customs officers I was dealing with in Amsterdam called their supervisor, and a decision was made.

I would receive a stern verbal warning and would not be written up. There would be no fine or entry ban as I moved around and stayed in several countries. This isn't an official law, but it has been allowed from time to time. So don't think I was getting preferential treatment. Others who were pulled with me were also given warnings. Although one unfortunate soul had overstayed a year and was getting in a lot more trouble.

So when Sarah's standing in the security area and dealing with customs, my stomach churns for her because it's happened to me.

That's just one story of many that I've got after dealing with authorities in various situations. I'll add more in upcoming Afterwords as they apply to situations in my books.

Ben Wilson's love of acronyms is actually my love. I often live by them. S.I.S.T., Students Invested Stocks Traded, was the one I came up with in high school when a few friends joined me on the Toronto Stock Exchange. We bought shares in Sun Ice, a company that was the official sponsor of the 1988 Winter Olympics in Calgary, Alberta. Being new at the game, we lost money, but dealing with brokers and buying and selling shares in grade eleven was a fantastic experience.

Several readers' names were used with permission. Below I've added the names and want to thank each and every one of them for their involvement. I have so much fun adding names and can't wait to add more in the next batch of books coming.

A special thanks goes out to Lisa Brown, Glenn Miller, Karen Miller (no relation to Glenn), Pam Prall, Paul Shelp, Liane Carmen, and Crystal Lewis.

I think that about sums up The Pact. Hope you enjoyed this adventure in Sarah's life. I look forward to hearing your thoughts when you comment on my Facebook wall and on Amazon when you leave reviews.

By October, *The Terror*, book 18, should be available. Sarah heads to Kelowna to root out a homegrown terrorist who seems to kill randomly. Then in late fall, *The Chase*, book 19, will come out. What a crazy ride that one will be as the Toronto mafia hunt Sarah. They've got a bone to pick with a friend of hers named Darwin Kostas.

If you haven't already, check out *The Immortal Gene*, the Jake Wood Series book one. (Insert shameless plug here) Book two, *The Immortal Target*, is available as well. I'd recommend reading *The Immortal Gene* first, though.

Lastly, I've been given written permission by Nicole Arbour Management to add this link to her video, Dear Vegans. I thought it was funny (she is a comedian, after all), and I hope you do, too. Ultimately, her message is simple and in line with mine: don't make it a religion. Do what's best for you. Live and let live. A special thank you goes out to Nicole Arbour and team. Keep up the great work coming out of Toronto!

And finally, don't blame the editor or the beta readers.

All mistakes are mine.

Signing off for now. Warmest regards to you and your family, and stay safe out there. Take care of yourself and each other.

And keep reading.

Sending my love …

Jonas Saul

About Jonas Saul

Jonas Saul is the bestselling author of the Sarah Roberts Series—more than two million sold!—and has written and published over sixty thrillers. After acquiring an agent, he signed several deals in Los Angeles, with MadRiver Pictures optioning his Sarah Roberts Series— over forty books!—(currently in development).

Jonas has often outranked Stephen King and Dean

Koontz on Amazon over the past decade. He's regularly invited to be a guest speaker, teacher, or workshop presenter at international writing conferences and film festivals worldwide. He hosts an annual writer's retreat in Greece, where he currently lives. He focuses his teaching on how to get tension and emotion in every scene, on every page, how he made it as a creator/writer, the path to success in this business, and the pitfalls to avoid. He also hosts a reading retreat in Greece with guest authors, yoga retreats, and hiking retreats. Visit the Imagine Greece Retreats website at www.imaginegreeceretreats.com, or email him directly to discuss an opportunity to join one of the retreats at jonas@imaginegreeceretreats.com.

Jonas is also a professional freelance editor. He works for several publishers and does private editing for clients, with many testimonials on his website at www.imaginepress.org, which details each author's response to Jonas's editing skills. Email Jonas directly for an editing quote at editor@imaginepress.org.

To book Jonas for a speaking engagement at a writer's conference/festival, to have him on your jury at a film festival, or even to say hello, email Jonas directly at jonassaul@icloud.com.

For updates on releases, hit the "Follow" button on Amazon or Bookbub, and join Jonas on Facebook, where he's most active.

Contact Jonas Saul

Linktree: Find me here

Email: jonassaul@icloud.com

9 781998 047406